Headway

Battling Demons, Volume 4

Kris Morris

Published by Kris Morris, 2016.

HEADWAY

First edition. October 31, 2016.

Written by Kris Morris.

Also by Kris Morris

Battling Demons

Battling Demons

Fractured

Fragile

Headway

Insights

A Cornwall Christmas

This is an unauthorised work of fiction. All royalties paid to the author will be donated to TheHorseCourse, a children's charity in Dorset, England. Thank you for supporting the work they do with abused and neglected children!

Thank you to my dear husband for believing in me, my sons for inspiration, and my friends Carole, Abby, Janet, and Anneke for ceaseless encouragement and for tolerating my insecurities.

Special thanks to my dear friend Abby Bukofzer and my son Karl for assisting with editing. And to my talented husband, Tim, for designing my book covers.

Chapter 1

When one thinks of Cornwall, the ridiculously narrow lanes, and the tall hedges lining them, often come to mind. The hedges served as field boundaries at one time, erected as long ago as Neolithic times to prevent the despoliation of land by travellers attempting to pick their way through the mud and ruts.

And many of the lanes are hundreds of years old. Generations of people moving from hamlet to hamlet and farmers driving livestock and crops to market, stirred up the road surfaces. This allowed the frequent rains to erode them so they now sat some five to ten feet lower than when they were originally constructed, leaving the tops of the hedges towering above the cars that now passed between them.

The occasional rogue branch ticked against the side of the van as the Ellingham family wound their way past the field gates towards the farm.

Louisa, with Jeremy following behind, pulled off on to a passing place to allow a tractor to inch its way by. She peered at her husband in the rear-view mirror and exchanged glances with Ruth. "You okay?" she asked him.

Her voice jarred him from his brown study. He tugged at his ear and cleared his throat. "I'm fine. I was just ... thinking."

He ducked his head to see out the windscreen ahead of him as they turned off the tarmac and on to the long gravel driveway. The fresh coat of white paint and the new roof gave the house a tidy appearance that he hadn't seen since his childhood days here.

"Well, this is an improvement," he said as Louisa shifted the gearbox into park and stepped from the van.

She came around to the sliding door and released the restraints on her husband's wheelchair before lowering the ramp. "Not just an improvement—it looks lovely! Don't you think, Martin?"

He rolled himself on to the driveway and looked around. "Mm. The roof certainly looks more sound."

Seeing Jeremy approaching from where he had parked a few yards away, James began to kick his feet, expressing his displeasure at being confined to his car seat in a parked vehicle. His mother came around to free him and then returned to raise the ramp and close the sliding door before following her husband to the back porch.

Al greeted them at the kitchen door. "Looks like yer makin' good progress, Doc. When do you get all the—the whatsits off yer arm and legs?"

Martin squirmed and hissed out a breath. "The fixators will come off when the fractures have healed and they're no longer necessary. Obviously."

Louisa's hand settled on his shoulder. "It's hard to know how long, Al. Months yet, though."

"Sure ... sure, that makes sense." The young man crammed his hands into his pockets and pulled up his shoulders. "You wanna take a look around?"

"We'd love to," Louisa said, hoisting James higher on her hip.

Martin followed after his aunt as she and Al led them into the dining room. Louisa and Jeremy brought up the rear.

"Oh, Ruth! This is beautiful! I never would have thought this old house could have so much charm! And look at Joan's old table. It's just lovely." Her eyes scanned around the room. "You and Al have such vision! Don't you think Martin?" she asked, waiting expectantly for her husband to follow through with an appropriately flattering remark.

"Mm, yes."

A warning glance was delivered and he added, "Very nice."

"It's Al's vision. I'm here as a pecuniary necessity, really," Ruth said, giving her assistant a crooked smile.

Al scratched at his chin. "Yeah, that and to tell me when I'm bein' totally daft."

Martin's hand caressed the refinished old maple dining table. What had once been a scuffed, utilitarian bit of furniture, serving as a place to store crates of freshly harvested vegetables or to keep boxes of newly hatched chicks up out of the way of draughts, was now a thing to look at. The table top shone, reflecting the glow of the lights burning overhead.

Louisa was correct in saying it was lovely. Martin couldn't deny that. Even Margaret Ellingham could enter this house now without fear of dirtying herself.

But it wasn't the house he remembered from his childhood anymore. That house was chock full of a lifetime assortment of trinkets. Rocks collected here and there, mementos of special occasions, books from every decade of the last century and beyond. It was a home where a small boy could delight in an entire summer of exploration. Where the focus was on the people inside the walls of the house, not the furniture and decorations that needed to be protected from the filthy hands and feet of children. In short, it was a house filled with Auntie Joan, and all signs of her seemed to have been wiped clean or painted over now.

He remembered the day he had walked in on Joan and the vagabond painter his former receptionist had hired to paint the windows of the surgery. He squeezed his eyes shut and gave his head a small shake, trying to dislodge the image of the young man living out his Oedipal fantasies with his pensioner aunt on the kitchen table.

He had collided with the sofa table as he fled the house, post-haste. He rubbed, absently, at the wound to his thigh as he thought of the large bruise the corner of the table top had left on his leg. Not all happy memories, it seemed.

"Martin? Martin, shall we go and take a look at the old clock?" Ruth asked, bringing him back to the present.

"Mm, yes. I'd like to see it."

"It's in the front entryway. Jeremy, why don't you join us. You might find this interesting as well."

Martin brought his wheelchair to a stop in front of the old timepiece. "Where had Joan been keeping this? I don't remember seeing this one before," Martin said as he turned the latch to open the door on the front of the clock case.

"It's not Joan's. It's mine actually. It was in your grandfather's house when he died. It's one of the items he chose to leave to me, God only knows why. A not-so-subtle reminder that I'd better heed my biological clock lest I find myself a spinster at the age of eighty-one, perhaps."

"Quite likely."

Ruth gave her nephew a blank stare. "I prefer to think of myself as a confirmed bachelor girl, Martin."

He gave her a grunt before peering up into the clock case. "This is a Robert Williams clock ... probably dates from the early eighteen hundreds. Very, very valuable, Ruth. I really don't think you want me mucking about with it ... the way my hand is right now. I could direct you to someone competent to do the job, though." He looked up, wide-eyed, at the time piece.

"I don't want someone *competent* to do the job, I want *you* to do the job, Martin."

He turned a defiant glare to her. "I *am* competent, thank you very much! I'm just a bit ... ungainly at the moment," he grumbled, turning back to tinker with the pendulum.

"Jeremy, try to reason with my nephew. You can see as well as I can that he's itching to get his hands on that thing. I need to go check on the others." She moved off towards the stairs, calling back over her shoulder. “He’s wilful though; so be persistent!”

Martin threw his head back. “Ohhh, pfft!”

Jeremy crossed his arms over his chest and gave his patient a grin. “So, you repair clocks?”

“Yes. My grandfather introduced me to the hobby.”

The aide pulled a chair over and sat down, peering in at the clockworks. “Why clock repair?”

“Horology.”

“What’s that?”

“It’s called horology. The art of making and repairing timepieces. My grandfather spent some time in America, working with a cardiovascular surgeon by the name of Robert Gross. He was born blind in one eye, so to help improve his depth perception, his father gave him progressively smaller clocks to take apart and put back together. The man’s colleagues worked alongside him for years before discovering he was visually impaired.

“I was already fascinated by my grandfather’s pocket watch—the way all the parts support one another. If one part quits working or malfunctions the entire system breaks down. When he told me the story about his American friend, it made me all the keener.”

Martin studied the internal organs of the patient in front of him. “He gave me a broken pocket watch one day, along with a tool kit and a book on horology. We sat in my father’s study, and he told me to diagnose the problem. He was quite pleased when I was successful.”

Jeremy noticed the glimmer of a smile on the phlegmatic man’s face. “You have a close-knit family, then?”

Martin turned quickly. “What makes you say that?”

“It just sounds like an extraordinary moment ... between you and your grandfather.”

Martin averted his gaze, swallowing hard. “It was.”

"So, that's what got you interested in clock repair?"

"Yes. It's about as close as you can get to being a surgeon without having a live patient in front of you." Martin toyed with the chain inside the clock and it began to chime.

"Hey, did you get it fixed?" Jeremy asked, crouching down next to him, peering up into the workings.

"No. I just got the gears to advance enough to activate the chiming mechanism. It really needs a complete overhaul and a jolly good cleaning."

The aide stood up, yawned, and stretched his arms. "Well, I think you should fix it. I think you'd make your grandfather very proud if you did."

Martin averted his eyes and mumbled. "I don't know about that."

"Should we go and track down the others?"

"Erm, yes." Martin gave the clock a backward glance as he moved off.

Chapter 2

Martin and Jeremy found themselves alone downstairs. Footsteps could be heard overhead and James's occasional squeals echoed through the stairway.

"Go on up and take a look around, Jeremy. I'll be fine on my own," Martin said as he made his way towards the kitchen.

"Nah, interior decorating's not really my thing. I just kinda wanted to see where you spent your summers."

Martin sat looking at him for a moment before averting his eyes and focusing his attention on the changes made to his boyhood holiday home.

"They've knocked out a wall over here and opened the kitchen up into where a storage room used to be," he said, surveying the space with an analytical eye. "Seems logical. Mm."

Rolling his chair over to the window he gazed off towards the old barn, remembering the scenarios he used to conjure up in his youthful mind. The building became the stage for many of his fantasies. The cave where he would hunt down and slay snarling dragons. Or the castle he would defend, the big heavy barn doors squeaking in protest as he slammed them shut against the enemy onslaught. The ladder to the hayloft becoming a prop as he scaled Mt. Everest.

His aide's voice interrupted his reminiscing. "How many summers did you spend here?"

Martin wheeled his chair away from the window and towards the original kitchen area. "I first came when I was six. I spent every summer holiday here for seven years."

"That must have seemed pretty exotic to a city boy."

"Not really. This seemed more like home than London did. A safe haven from the—" Martin hesitated, then cleared his throat and wagged a finger towards the doorway. "Maybe you should go see about what the others have gotten up to."

Jeremy stepped over to the bottom of the stairs and listened for a moment. "Sounds like Al's talking about the work that still needs to be done." He moved back to the kitchen and wandered about, examining the photos that had been framed and were now adorning the walls. "Is this you here?" he asked, a smile spreading across his face.

Martin wheeled over and peered up. "Yes, that's me. I don't remember that picture, though." He looked to be about six or seven years of age. He was sitting in a fluffy pile of straw, clad in denim bib and brace overalls.

"Why do you say this farm was your safe haven?" Jeremy asked as he scanned the other pictures in the room.

"That's none of your business," Martin replied sharply.

He rolled himself through the dining room and back towards the front entryway, opening the case door on the old clock and examining everything carefully. His aide was right. It would make his grandfather proud to see his grandson put the old timepiece to rights. But it would pose a real challenge given his current limitations. However, he thought he could do the work as the strength and dexterity came back in his hand.

"Will you need to come out here to work on it, or can you take the parts home with you?" Jeremy asked as he approached from behind.

Startled, Martin spun around. "Ah ... Jeremy. Do you think you could help me get the clock taken apart and out to the van?"

"If you tell me what to do. Sure, I can help."

"Take the hood off the top first—the cover over the movement. Take hold of the sides and it should slide forward."

Jeremy pulled on the cover, lifting it off and setting it on the floor.

"Good. Now you need to remove the time weight—that right hand weight. Just lift it off the hook it's on."

The aide raised the object up, and it slipped from its hanger.

"Very good." Martin's critical gaze followed him as he walked over and placed the weight next to the hood of the time piece.

"What's next?" Jeremy asked.

"We need another pair of hands. Go upstairs and get Al."

Jeremy gave him a grin. "You're not going to go running off if I leave you here by yourself, are you?"

"That joke is getting worn a bit thin, don't you think?"

"Sorry, Martin. I'll be right back." The young man's eyes darted away before he moved towards the stairs, taking the steps two at a time.

He returned a minute later with Ruth's assistant. "What d'ya need, Doc?" the young man asked.

"We need another pair of hands when we remove the clockworks. When you take out the pendulum and the chime weight, the top of the clock can tip forward. So, Al, you need to hang on to that entire mechanism behind the dial while Jeremy lifts the parts out of the case base. We don't want the movement falling on to the floor." Martin tipped his head back, watching his crew carefully to make sure no damage was being done to the valuable object.

"Jeremy, just lift up on the pendulum arm slightly and tip it back a bit. It should drop off."

Once the pendulum and chime weight were lying to the side, Martin instructed Al to remove the screws that secured the movement to the top, and Jeremy lifted the mechanism up and away from the case.

"Al, help him with the chains. Make sure they don't scratch the case or get caught on anything as he lowers it down."

The young Large set the works on the floor and brushed the dirt from his hands. "Well, that was easy enough. I'll fetch a box, and we can pack it up in the van. You wanna come with me, Jeremy ... see the old barn?"

The aide turned to his patient. "Do you mind?"

"No, no. Go ahead. I'll be fine here."

Martin stared down at the parts, wondering if he was going to regret taking on a project such as this.

"Al, get a blanket to wrap it up in, too!" Martin yelled as the young men disappeared into the kitchen.

He wheeled his chair over to the living area and picked up a photo album that was lying on the coffee table. The hinges on the back door creaked, and moments later he noticed a movement out of the corner of his eye. His receptionist was watching him from the doorway.

"Mm ... Morwenna," he said, giving the album a toss on to the table.

"Hi, Doc. It's been a while, eh?"

"Yes. Yes, it has." He nodded vigorously enough to ease his self-consciousness as the young woman eyed him.

She walked into the living room and sat down on the sofa. "Kinda weird not seein' you all the time. A little boring, really."

"Yes. I'm sorry about that."

"Oh, it's okay. I've been keepin' busy. Working at the fudge shop. Helping Al out here at the farm, too." She sighed and then tapped her fingertips together as her eyes scanned the room. "Miss bein' at the surgery, though."

"Mm, yes."

Morwenna toyed with the brightly coloured beads on her bracelet, and Martin's fingers drummed against the armrest of his wheelchair before his social awkwardness replaced the uncomfortable silence in the room.

"I was just looking at those old pictures," he said, jabbing a finger at the just-discarded album.

"Ah."

He cleared his throat. "The—the yard looks nice. Ruth said you've been—"

Morwenna jumped to her feet and wrapped her arms around him. "Oh, Doc! I'm so sorry!" She stepped back, looking him up and down, noting the fading but still visible scars on his face, the fixators on his legs, and his damaged arm, visible inside the sling.

She turned her head away, and Martin squirmed in his chair as her shoulders began to tremble.

Oh, gawd. Please don't cry. "Bloody hell," he muttered. "Ohhh, don't do that, Morwenna," he groaned.

She spun around, and wrapping her arms around him again, she buried her face in his shoulder.

He raised his arm reluctantly, patting her on the back. "Okay, okay. That's enough."

Backing up, she wiped the tears from her cheeks with her palms. She sniffled loudly and Martin pulled his handkerchief from his back pocket, handing it to her.

"I'm sorry I didn't come to see ya, Doc. I *knew* I'd get all worked up like this. And I know you don't like it. So, I just stayed away. But I really did wanna come and see you. I was just afraid—"

"It's okay, Morwenna."

"No. No, it's not. I should'a come anyways. I was kinda scared to see you. Al told me how bad you'd been hurt and all. I was just scared that maybe—"

"Morwenna, I really didn't feel up to visitors. It's fine."

She forced a smile through her sniffles. "I can come and keep you company now, though. If you want, that is. I could even bake you something. Not like bread, cause I'm no good at bakin' bread. But like a treat—biscuits—maybe a cake—even a pie."

She prattled on nervously. "I haven't ever actually *made* a pie before, but how hard could it be, right? I mean, all ya gotta do is mix a little flour and water together and roll it out—put it in a plate. Fill it up with some sliced apples or something, throw it in the cooker, and there you have it. But then you don't really like that kinda thing so that'd be silly. Maybe I could—"

Martin reached for her wrist, cocking his head as he mentally recorded her heart rate. "Have you been taking amphetamines again?"

She pulled her hand away. "Course not! I threw 'em all out soon as I knew what they were." She plopped back on to the sofa. "Seriously ... I could come over to your aunt's and keep you company."

Martin stared at his lap as his fingers began to tap away again. "I'm at physical therapy at least half the day and I sleep a lot, so there's no need. Mm."

He cleared his throat and looked up at her. "I'll be opening the surgery back up in a few weeks. Just half days, but I'll need you back then. We can go over the details when the time gets closer."

"Great! That'd be great." She got to her feet and stood in front of him, her hands wedged under her arms.

Footsteps could be heard descending the stairs, and Martin breathed out a sigh of relief.

"It's too bad you can't see what they've done up there, Martin. It's just so charming!"

Martin turned at the sound of his wife's voice.

"It's lovely ... what they've done to this place. Joan would be so pleased if she could see this."

"Mm, yes. Are we done here, then?" Martin asked, anxious to extricate himself from the uncomfortable gaze of his receptionist.

Louisa cocked her head at him and glanced at Morwenna, noticing her red-rimmed and puffy eyes. "Yes, Martin. I think we *are* done here." Then turning, she added, "I'm sorry, Morwenna."

Martin looked at her, one eyebrow raised as she shot him an angry glance. "Problem?" he asked.

"Oh, *Mar-tin.*" Her ponytail whipped to the side before she stomped off towards the kitchen.

Jeremy stayed and had dinner at Ruth's cottage that evening, and then helped Martin with his medications before saying goodnight. The internal workings of the clock, which had been disassembled at the farm, had been carried in by Al and Jeremy and now lay, carefully packaged in a box, in the corner of the bedroom.

Even Martin couldn't miss that Louisa was angry with him about something. She had been politely conversational with Jeremy, but had answered all of *his* questions with a frosty *yes, no,* or *Oh Martin, I don't know!* What he had done this time to raise her ire, he couldn't fathom.

He transferred himself to his bed and rolled on to his side to wait anxiously for his wife. He knew he would be made to understand the error of his ways when she came in to join him. He closed his eyes and took several deep breaths to ease the tightness in his chest.

When he opened his eyes again sunlight had filled the room, and she was staring back at him. He sighed, his heart heavy. It seemed no matter how hard he tried to be the husband she wanted him to be, he managed to bollocks things up, often not knowing what it was he did wrong or failed to do correctly.

"Good morning," she said, pulling the blankets up around her neck.

"Good morning. Sorry, I fell asleep before you came to bed last night." He struggled to turn on to his side to face her.

"Yes, you did."

He opened and closed his mouth several times before the words were released. "Louisa, did I do something wrong?"

Her lips drew into a thin line, and he was almost certain he felt a cool waft of air flow from her mouth when she opened it. "Martin, what did you do to upset Morwenna yesterday?"

He shook his head. "I didn't do anything. She just got upset."

"Martin Ellingham, people don't just *get* upset. You must have said *something* ... done something."

"I didn't *do* anything!" he squeaked. "I was just sitting in the living room when she came in and got all ... emotional. Maybe it was hormones. I don't know! Why does everything always have to be my fault, Louisa?"

"Well, what exactly was said Martin? And don't you dare blame this on that poor girl's hormones again."

He rubbed the heel of his hand against his forehead and squeezed his eyes shut, trying to remember what exactly had transpired the day before. "I believe I asked her how she was and told her the yard looked nice. She looked me up and down and then burst into tears, saying she was sorry she didn't come visit me. That's it."

"Oh."

He sat himself up on the bed. "*Oh?* Is that all you have to say—*oh?* An entire evening of the silent treatment when I did nothing wrong and you say, oh! I was wracking my brain trying to figure out what I'd done to upset you!

"Louisa, I know I've earned my reputation for being an insensitive git, but will you ever be able to give me the benefit of the doubt and not just assume the worst of me? Why do you even want to be married to someone you have so little confidence in ... think so little of?"

Louisa lay quietly. She had slipped back into her old habits and in a big way.

"Martin, I'm sorry. I owe you an apology. I shouldn't have assumed you had done something to upset Morwenna, and even if I had, I should have talked it over with you straight away rather than lying in bed all night thinking the worst of you. I hope you weren't too worried about why I was angry."

Martin's brows drew together in a vee and he huffed out a breath. "Of course, I was worried, Louisa." He turned his head towards the windows. "I worry every time you're cross with me."

"Oh, Martin." She reached up and brushed her hand across his sleep-tousled head. "So, what did you do when she started to cry?"

Martin eyed her warily. "She had her arms around me so I just ... Well, I didn't know *what* to do, so I patted her on the back. I didn't know how to deal with her, Louisa! It was *awful*! Her crying like that! And I was trapped in my chair! It was awful."

"Oh, Martin. And then I just added to it." She leaned forward and pressed her forehead to his. "Learning to be a better wife is just as difficult for me as learning to be a better husband is for you."

He ran the backs of his fingers down the bridge of her nose. "Two steps forward, one step back."

"Hmm?"

"Two steps forward, one step back. Like the frog trying to climb out of the well. For every two steps he takes up the side of the well, he slides back one step."

Martin gave her a small smile. "He does make it. It's just an arduous climb. And it takes time."

Louisa leaned forward again and let a kiss linger on his lips. "Then I guess we'll just need to be patient with one another until we get out of the well.

Chapter 3

Martin had given Jeremy Sunday morning off. Not only because he was feeling uncomfortable about every one of the aide's days being interrupted by the morning and evening duties in the Ellingham household, but because it would also give him an opportunity to try managing the morning routine on his own.

He was able to get himself in and out of the shower fairly easily, but getting the faucet turned on and then off again posed a greater challenge. Leaning in any direction stressed his still-recovering abdominal muscles and rib cage, sending pain through his torso as he reached for the tap. But he had managed. And he had proven to himself that he was up to the task.

"How's it coming?" Louisa asked as she stuck her head in the bathroom doorway.

"I'm almost done, but I can't reach down far enough to get this bloody hardware dry!" Martin said, exasperated that his freshly showered self was now perspiring heavily as a result of his efforts to reach his lower legs.

Louisa ruffled her fingers through his damp hair before smoothing it back down and placing a kiss on the top of his head. "I have an idea. Just wait," she said as she hurried off.

She reappeared a minute later. "Why don't you try this?"

"That's your hair dryer," he said, waggling a finger at it and eyeing the device suspiciously.

"I know what a hair dryer is, Martin."

He shook his head at her. "That blows hot air."

"I know what it is, and I'm aware of what it does."

Kneeling down beside the chair, she held the appliance out to him. "Try it. This button adjusts the speed, and this one adjusts the temperature."

"How do you turn this contraption on?"

"You've never used a hair dryer before?" She gave his short-cropped hair a gentle tug with her fingertips. "No, I s'pose you haven't. You must feel like Alice in Wonderland at times."

Martin snapped his head around to look at her. "Alice who?"

"You know ... the story about the girl who falls into a rabbit hole and ends up in a strange world of talking animals and other things she's never experienced before."

He gave her a blank stare, and she leaned down to kiss his cheek. "The girl—Alice—she keeps changing size. At one point, she's a mile high in fact."

Martin screwed up his face. "Rubbish."

"It's a classic, Martin. There's a baby that turns into a pig, a trial where the King of Hearts is the— Oh, that's a playing card by the way. They're used to play games ... like Bridge, Rummy, Canas—"

"*Yes*, I'm familiar with playing cards. But ... my fixators."

Louisa went to plug the hair dryer into the wall as she continued her summarisation of the story. "Oh, and they play croquet. Only the mallets are flamingos, and the balls are hedgehogs."

"Sounds ghastly."

She tapped the hairdryer against her hand. "You should read it sometime. It's considered to be one of the best examples of the literary nonsense genre."

"Sounds about right."

"I could download the movie version if you like. You could watch it with the sound off," she suggested as she averted her gaze, attempting to stifle the snicker that was trying to escape.

"Louisa! The hairdryer ... please!"

"Sorry, Martin. This is what one would call good-natured teasing by the way." She caressed his cheek before letting her palm glide down over his chest, suggestively.

"Oh, for goodness' sake!" Exasperated by his wife's puerility, Martin picked up his towel from the edge of the tub and leaned forward again, trying to reach the water droplets on his fixators.

Louisa turned the hair dryer on and began to blow a stream of hot air at his legs.

"No, no, no, no, no! That's hot!" he said, grabbing the device from her hands.

"It's not *that* hot, Martin. I mean it's not hot enough to burn you or anything ... is it?"

He tipped his head, eyeing her with a scowl as he explained through clenched teeth. "Metals—are thermal conductors. The metal pins—go into my bones. How do you suppose it would feel—if you heated them up? Not comfortable, I can assure you."

The thought brought a sudden, more serious tone to Louisa's side of the conversation. "No matter what the temperature might be, that metal doesn't look *comfortable*," she said, giving a demonstrative shudder. "Here, you adjust the temperature."

He slid the button to the side, and the device blew out cooler air. "Mm, seems okay."

The hairdryer turned out to be quite effective in getting the metal dry. Now all he had to do was to get dressed.

Having already laid his clothes out on the bed, he sat, planning his strategy before forging ahead. He could pull his left leg up much higher than his right, so he pulled his right trouser leg on first. It took him more than a half dozen tries before he was able to get his foot started through the hole. But once he had managed that step, pulling the fabric over the hardware went surprisingly smoothly.

Step two required that he backtrack a bit. He had pulled the right trouser leg up too far and couldn't quite get his left leg lifted high enough to reach the opening in the garment. After pulling the right leg back out a bit, he was able to get the left leg threaded through the other side.

He rolled his chair over to the assist pole once he had worked the garment up past his knees. Hanging on to the waistband with his right hand, he pulled himself out of his chair with his left. He now stood with one hand on the pole and the other trying to keep his trousers from falling back down around his ankles.

He tried to work the clothing up using his injured right arm, but he lacked the strength in his grip to do so. "Louisa! *Louisa!*"

"What is it, Martin?" she asked as she hurried back into the room.

"I need to let go of the pole so I can get my pants pulled up. I don't want to lose my balance and fall. Stand next to me and put your hand on my arm if I start to tip."

She shook her head. "Oh, I don't know Martin. This sounds risky."

He huffed. "My strength is fine; it's just a proprioception issue. If I feel your hand on my arm it'll give me perspective, and I can get myself balanced again. We do this exercise all the time in physiotherapy." He gave her an encouraging nod.

"Well, all right. But be careful."

Martin pulled the garment up the rest of the way, and with the trousers safely on, he sent his wife back to the kitchen to finish preparing breakfast. He sat back down in his chair to work his vest and then his shirt over his arms and torso. He had been buttoning his shirts himself for the last week, a challenging and often frustrating exercise. But he was finding it to be good therapy, and it was getting progressively easier with time.

Louisa looked up from the cooker when she heard her husband enter the kitchen. "Well, look at you! Very well done, Martin!"

"Yes. Could you help me with the shoes and socks?"

She looked down at the items laying in her husband's lap. "Oh, Martin. You won't be able to get your shoes on those swollen feet."

"I want to try. I can start walking tomorrow, and I can't very well be doing that in my socks."

She looked at him dubiously. "I s'pose we can give it a go."

Once the socks were on, she opened up a shoe as much as possible and tried to get it on his foot. It was obvious to both of them that the dress shoes he normally wore with his suits would never work.

"You might just have to keep wearing your slippers for a while, I'm afraid," she said patting his foot and looking up at him sympathetically.

Martin was adamant. "No. If I'm going to start walking, I want to have shoes. I need something with more stability than my slippers have."

"I tell you what, let's have our breakfast, then make a trip to Truro," Louisa said before getting to her feet. "And you better have a lie-down before we go. You look exhausted."

Louisa called Carole Parsons while Martin was napping. Carole gave her the name of a store that carried orthopaedic shoes.

"If Martin feels up to it, why don't you join us for dinner later," she suggested.

"Oh, Carole. That sounds wonderful. But we have Jeremy coming at seven to help Martin get settled for the night."

"We can certainly eat an early dinner if that would help on your end. I wouldn't imagine it'll take too long to get his shoes. And Martin could have a rest in the guest bedroom if he wants.

But I don't want a repeat of the last disaster, so let Martin make the decision."

"I'll discuss it with him, and we'll see how he's feeling when we're finished shopping."

By the time Martin woke and Louisa had packed the nappy bag, it was almost eleven. And it was approaching noon when they arrived in Truro.

"We could stop and get something to eat at that little place downtown. You know, where we went after our session with Dr. Newell a while back. You seemed to approve of their menu."

Martin shook his head. "I'm not really hungry. Maybe we should just get the shoes and go home."

"You've been ravenous all the time for the last several weeks, Martin. What do you mean you're not hungry?"

"It *means*, Louisa, that I have no desire to eat!"

She pressed her lips together as she glanced at him in the mirror, and then pulled the van into an empty office parking place. "Are you feeling all right?"

"I'm fine. Let's just go get the damn shoes."

She reached back to feel his forehead. "What are you *doing*?" he asked, batting her hand away.

"I'm checking you for fever, Martin. You're not acting right."

"Well, tell me how you think I *should* be acting, and I'll do my best to humour you."

"Martin, did you take your medication this morning? Did you get your morphine?"

He hesitated and Louisa's features tightened. "*Did* you take your morphine?"

"Yes. I ... took it."

She looked at him askance. "*Martin*. What are you not telling me?"

He screwed up his face. “Do you have to look at me like that? It makes me feel like I’m a bloody twelve-year-old.”

She sighed and her face softened. “Sorry. Force of habit, I guess. But you need to be honest with me.”

“I’m always honest with you, Louisa. But I may have cut the dosage back a bit.” He fidgeted in his chair, knowing he was going to get an earful.

“Martin Ellingham, you are impossible! Why in the world did you do that? You’re in pain now ... *aren’t* you!”

“Louisa, keep your voice down; you’ll wake James,” he said as he brushed his fingers across his son’s cheek.

She narrowed her eyes at him and he threw his head back. “I don’t have therapy today so it seemed like a good time to see if I could get by with a little less medication.”

“Well, obviously, you can’t. Do you have more with you?”

“Of course, I do,” he mumbled. “I don’t like the way I feel when I’m on it though, Louisa—the sluggish feeling. I’d like to be able to get by without it by the time I’m back to seeing patients. Can you understand that?”

Her husband’s profound intellect was such an important part of his make-up, and to have it dulled probably added to the sense of vulnerability that she knew he was experiencing.

“You *need* to take it. I do understand what you’re saying, but you still need to take it.” Louisa reached into the nappy bag and pulled out a bottle of water. “Here you go. Now take it,” she said as she pressed it into his hand.

He sat for a few moments with his jaw clenched and his eyes closed. Then he reached into the pocket of his trousers to pull out the bottle of pills.

“I’m sorry, Martin.” Louisa watched as her disconsolate husband swallowed the medication and handed the water bottle back to her.

“Okay, let’s go and get those shoes. Maybe by the time we’re done with our shopping you’ll be more comfortable ... feel like eating something," she said as she gave him an encouraging smile and a pat on his knee.

The sales clerk proved to be very helpful, and they left the store quickly with a pair of trainers as well as a pair of casual shoes that were not only comfortable, but didn't look like something someone's diabetic grandfather would wear.

Louisa turned to her husband after they were back in the van. "Are you feeling any better?"

He scowled back at her. "It's hard to tell. I wonder sometimes if the medications really help with the pain or if they just make me too stupid to notice it."

"Martin, stupid is something *you* will never be," she said as she turned the key in the ignition. "Erm, we have an invitation from the Parsons to stop by ... if you feel up to it. Carole mentioned that you could have a lie-down in the guest bedroom if you're tired."

Martin saw a visit to the Parsons as an opportunity to talk with Chris about his transition back to seeing patients, and he pushed his fatigue aside. "No, I think that would be fine. I am hungry now, though. Could we get some lunch first?"

"That sounds wonderful. I'll call Carole and let her know to be expecting us. Are you okay with having dinner at the Parsons' later?"

"Yes, that'd be fine ... if you want to." He leaned his head back and closed his eyes.

Chapter 4

Carole was always the consummate hostess and greeted them warmly when they arrived at the Parsons' home. Louisa watched with mild amusement as her husband obligingly tolerated her hugs, kisses, and positive critique of his new attire. She stepped in to relieve his misery, however, when she noticed a pink flush begin to work its way up his neck.

"Carole, it's wonderful to see you again."

Good grief, you'd think we hadn't seen each other in years, Martin thought as he watched them embrace.

"And little James, I think you've grown since I saw you last!"

It's only been a week; she couldn't possibly see a change. Although he liked his friend's wife, Martin quite often found her perplexing, much as he did his own wife.

"Well, come on in. Make yourselves at home. I'll go and chase up that husband of mine."

"It's okay, I can find him," Martin said before wheeling himself through the living room and down the hall to his friend's study.

"Mart! How are you doing?" Chris asked, looking up from the papers on the desk in front of him.

He took in a short breath and hesitated a moment. "I'm ... okay."

"Just okay considering your present physical condition, or just okay for some other reason?"

Rolling himself into the room, Martin jabbed a finger at the array of papers. "Taking your work home with you these days?"

"Nope. And you didn't answer my question. What's up, mate?"

Martin brushed imaginary lint from his trousers. "It can just be awkward ... with Louisa. I can't help but feel inadequate."

"You're at a tough point in your recovery, Mart. You feel well enough to want to get back to your usual activities, but physically you aren't able to yet."

Chris waited for some sort of reaction but was rewarded with his friend's silence. "Look, you *still* have a job to do. You need to get yourself back on your feet. Focus on that." He shot a rubber band at him. "Try to be patient. And be a little selfish for once in your life."

Martin toyed with the rubber band then peered up at him. "You didn't answer *my* question." He gave a nod to the papers.

"Ah. Just some ideas I'd like you to look over. We need to establish some protocols before you return to work. Take this home with you. Then let me know your thoughts." He handed Martin a file. "We'll get together in another week or so and compare notes. My chief concern is that we handle things in a manner that limits your exposure to pathogens as much as possible. *You'll* probably be looking at this from a more practical standpoint—what will or won't work with your practice situation.

"I want to get these decisions made so we can allow plenty of time to train Jeremy and your receptionist. Do you think you'll feel up to handling the training?"

Martin was a goal oriented person. Goals gave him a sense of control and direction in his life, and Chris had just handed him a gift. "Yes. Yes, of course. I can go through this with Jeremy tomorrow. I'll try to get started with some training sessions next week."

While the men were deep in conversation in Chris's office, Carole and Louisa chatted in the kitchen.

"How's life with the patient been? Tough at times I would imagine." Carole put the last of the vegetables into the stew she was preparing, and slid two loaves of bread into the cooker.

With James gnawing on a piece of Melba toast, Louisa bounced him on her lap. "We've had our tense moments, but ... Well, I'm responsible for some of that I'm afraid. Martin's trying. He's *really* trying, and he gets overwhelmed. I think he feels like he has no control over his life at the moment."

She leaned over to set James down on the floor with several of his toys. "I think I've been adding to his stress lately. I don't mean to, but I've been falling back into some old habits that contributed to our problems a few months ago ... old ways of thinking."

Carole eyed her suspiciously. "You haven't had thoughts of leaving, I hope. Oh, Louisa, you two have come through so much together!"

"No! I've worked through that. It's this tendency I have to always think the worst of him. I walked in on the end of a conversation he'd been having with his receptionist yesterday, and I noticed she'd been crying. I automatically assumed Martin had said or done something to upset her. I gave him the silent treatment the rest of the day. I'd intended to talk to him about it last night, but he fell asleep before I got James down for the night."

Carole came over with two cups. "Tea?"

"Yes, please." Louisa picked through the basket of tea bags in the middle of the table. "I talked to him about it this morning and found out he had done absolutely nothing wrong. His receptionist hadn't seen him since the accident and was upset by his injuries."

Carole poured hot water into the two cups and slid the pitcher of milk and bowl of sugar across the table. "She must be quite fond of Martin."

"Don't tell *him*, but I think there's some truth to that. Thing is, I immediately placed the blame on Martin." She stirred sugar into her cup and tapped the spoon against the rim. "But in my defence, he does have a pretty well established pattern of behaviour. So, it was pretty natural for my mind to go the direction it did."

"Hmm, maybe."

"What? You don't agree?"

"To some extent. But you're his wife, not his mother. I would imagine having spent the last—what has it been, fifteen years of your life—playing mother and disciplinarian to classrooms full of children, your natural tendency would be to have your mind go in the direction it did. Maybe that had more to do with how you reacted than Martin's typical behavioural patterns did."

Louisa drummed her fingers on the table. "Are you saying I treated him like a child? Carole, I'm just trying to—to—I don't know. It's embarrassing when he says the things he does to people. Why does he have to upset people all the time? Why can't he show that sweet, gentle side that I get to see?"

Carole gave the stew another stir before joining Louisa at the table. "I'm curious ... why is it so important to you that everyone else sees Martin the way you do?"

"Hmm, I guess I never thought about it. Maybe I just don't want to have to make apologies for him."

"Has he asked you to do that? I can't imagine that goes over well with Martin."

"No. Quite the opposite. It annoys him when I do it," she said, tracing her finger around the handle of her cup.

Carole picked up her spoon and stirred milk into her tea. It clinked against the cup as she tapped off the drips. "Louisa, how many years has Martin been the GP in that village? Four—five years now? If the villagers can accept him for who he is, why can't you?"

"They *don't* accept him, Carole. They call him tosser all the time. Laugh at him. Teachers at the school make snide remarks about him, make a big deal about it whenever he comes to a school activity. And I know they don't understand at all why I married him."

Carole got up and went to the cupboard, returning with a package of chocolate digestives. "I think we need a little self-indulgence for a conversation like this," she said as she placed the biscuits on the table. "Louisa, why does it matter so much to you what these people think of him? Have they tried to get to know him? Those same people are probably all too happy to benefit from his medical skills. But then they talk that way about him behind his back?

"I can understand why you might wish other people could know him the way you do, but why do you think it's *his* responsibility to make that happen? That's asking an awful lot of a guy with his history. He has good reason to not trust people, you know.

"He's trying and that's all you can ask of him. Don't expect social interaction to ever be something enjoyable for him. He may be able to learn to go through the motions ... learn the pleasantries that most people pull out at the appropriate time. But you know as well as I do that he's always going to be painfully awkward in social situations."

"I do understand that, Carole." Louisa gazed off momentarily before absently stirring another spoonful of sugar into her tea. "I guess it's like my father all over again when Martin does things that anger people."

"What do you mean by that?"

She fixed her gaze on her son, playing on the floor. "My dad has a bit of a history with trouble ... and the law. He likes to gamble. He stole money from the village. Money that was supposed to go to the lifeboat fund. He thought he had a sure winner and he could pay the money back, but... Anyway, he's in prison now for something else he did."

She peered up at her friend. "He was in on a plan to break into a warehouse with explosives—a robbery. They didn't get away with it. It's a long story, but Martin ended up throwing the bag of explosives over the cliff." A small smile spread across her face. "The bag landed on the rocks where a pair of choughs were nesting. Shame about that, but it was an accident."

"That does sound a bit like Martin," Carole said.

Louisa worked a biscuit loose from the package. "I s'pose I feel guilty for the things my father's done. Martin's a brilliant doctor, and he's helped so many of the villagers. But none of that counts because he's always making people angry."

"What do you mean, none of that *counts*? You aren't expecting that his skills as a medic will serve to ... I don't know, atone in some way for what your father did, are you?"

Louisa knitted her brows and sat quietly for a moment. "I don't think I consciously had that expectation. But maybe he *could* smooth things over a bit with the villagers. Maybe they'd forget abou—"

"Louisa! I'm sorry, girl. But your father's in prison for good reason. The poor choices he's made in his life are not your fault. And most certainly not your husband's. Martin's never done anything dishonourable in his life, as far as I'm aware. Yes, he's gruff, blunt, and clueless when it comes to understanding people. But he's a good man. To expect him to make up for your father's wrongdoings is terribly unfair. That's your *father's* lookout."

Carole stood up and began clearing the dishes from the table. "Did you ever think that maybe Martin could benefit from having you as his ally? He certainly never had a mother or father that he could count on to back him up. And it sounds like he could use a bit of help in that village."

She returned to the table and took a seat. "Louisa, love that big grump of yours for all the wonderful qualities that you know are there. And be thankful that he finds you to be so very special that—that *you* are the one person he's allowed into that secret world of his. That he's such a different man with you and James."

Louisa stared across at her. "Wow. I feel like I've had a proper dressing-down now."

"Sorry. I didn't mean it that way. Well, maybe I did just a little. Chris and I have known your husband for a long time. When we first started dating, Martin made me really uncomfortable. He seemed like such an oddball. But Chris thought the world of him, and I thought the world of Chris, so I tried to keep my opinions to myself. And lo and behold, I started to really like that guy of yours. So, sorry for the rant. The mother in me came out, I'm afraid."

"No, no. It's probably something I needed to hear." James crawled over and grabbed on to Louisa's jeans, pulling himself to a standing position and giving her a triumphant smile.

Chapter 5

With the stew simmering on the hob and the bread now baking in the cooker, Carole suggested that they take their tea and join their husbands who had already made their way to the family room. James squealed when he saw his father, kicking his feet and struggling to free himself from his mother's arms.

Louisa set the boy down on the floor, and he scrambled towards Martin. Chasing after him, she scooped him up moments before he reached his destination. He screamed in protest and reached his arms out to his father.

"Martin, do you mind?"

"No, that's fine." He waved his hand, gesturing for his wife to put the boy in his lap.

"Do you want to go see your daddy?" she said.

She held the child's plastic giraffe, squeaking it several times as she danced it through the air in front of his face. Martin winced at the noise, and James made *his* feelings known as well by screwing up his face.

Louisa knelt down next to them, and Martin took the toy from his wife's hand, passing it silently to his son.

"Martin, Louisa's told me a little about the health aide you have helping you out," Carole said as she sat down on the sofa next to her husband. "It sounds like it's a great match ... the two of you."

"Yes. It's working out well. He's bright and has acquired a great deal of knowledge since nursing school."

James reached a slobbery hand up and patted it against his father's cheek, and Martin wiped the trail of spittle from his face. "Jeremy's writing a paper addressing the deficiencies in our home health care system, Chris.

"He's had me review what he's written so far. It's thoroughly researched, and he raises some very legitimate questions about how we prioritise patient needs. You'll find it quite informative, I think."

Chris leaned back on the sofa and crossed an ankle over his knee. "I'm anxious to meet this kid, Mart. If I make a trip over your way next week, maybe the three of us could have lunch together. I know I'd feel better about turning you loose in your surgery if I laid eyes on your future assistant first."

"I think that could be arranged. I'll talk with Jeremy about it and get back to you."

Martin looked down at his small son and his face softened. The monotony of adult conversation had lulled James to sleep. He pulled him closer into his embrace, and the boy nuzzled his face into his chest.

"That *is* a lovely sight, Martin. You with a son," Carole said. "Never in my wildest dreams would I have seen it coming." She turned to Louisa. "How are things going with the new childminder?"

Louisa got up and pulled a chair over next to her husband's wheelchair before taking a seat. "Oh, Poppy. She's wonderful. She's very reliable and takes her job seriously. And best of all, James likes her. Maybe even Martin." She cast a furtive glance in her husband's direction.

"Mm, yes. She seems to be quite adequate," he said as he stroked the back of the baby's hand with his finger. "There's something going on between her and Jeremy, though. I hope it doesn't cause problems."

Louisa cocked her head at him. "What do you mean, going on?"

"Well, surely you've noticed, Louisa. He stares at her—she stares at him. He smiles—she blushes and bats her eyes. She's forever bringing him food or tea." He grimaced. "And they have to stand there *ogling* each other before she let's go of whatever it is she has in her hands."

Louisa tipped her head down and eyed him questioningly.

"What?"

She shook her head and exchanged bewildered glances with Carole. "I'm just surprised you would notice these things."

Martin's cheeks warmed. "I, er ... Well, I—I see the same ridiculous faces when I watch the television in the afternoon."

"What on earth are you watching, Martin?" Louisa asked.

"Some miserable excuse for entertainment. I think it's called Coronation Street." He sneered. "I see the same ridiculous expressions and body language on that show, and they invariably end up in—in—" He began to squirm as his wife and friends stared back at him. "Oh, come on. Don't make me explain this to you!"

Louisa struggled to contain an amused grin. "Dr. Newell has Martin watching the television with the sound off everyday ... to help him recognise facial expressions."

"I think Barrett's on to something, Mart. The exercise has proved quite effective in your case anyway," Chris said as he gave his friend a smirk.

"Mm. Yes," Martin mumbled.

A few moments of awkward silence elapsed before Chris slapped his hands down on his knees. "So, Mart ... how is it to be back in the village? Lots of visitors? Or has Louisa been able to stem the flow of curiosity-seekers?"

"A couple have managed to slip through the cracks, but it's been tolerable. I want Jeremy to go to the surgery with me this week, so I can start reviewing the patient files. I'll have to face the music then. The villagers seem to have a sixth sense when it comes to ferreting out gossip, so there'll be no avoiding them once I leave my confines."

James Henry sneezed, startling himself awake momentarily. His father jostled him in his arm, and he soon fell back to sleep.

"Martin, they're just concerned is all," Louisa said.

"No, they're not. They're just collecting information to share on Caroline Bosman's ghastly call-in show," he grumbled, grimacing at the thought of his physical woes being discussed on live radio.

"They've probably been playing Chinese whispers for the last seven weeks. It wouldn't surprise me if I've been reported dead several times over already." He glanced over at his wife, and she shifted her gaze to her feet.

"Oh, please tell me I haven't been the topic of conversation on Caroline's show."

Louisa fidgeted, trying to avoid eye contact with him. "There may have been ... a bit. But they don't mean any harm."

He threw his head back. "Bloody—" James began to stir as his father's voice crescendoed, and Martin waited for him to settle before he began to speak again. "This is none of their business!" he said with a hushed stridency. "What's been said, Louisa?"

"Martin, maybe this is something we should discuss later."

"Don't worry about us. If Martin wants to know, go ahead and tell him. You've got me curious now," Carole said as she leaned her elbows on her knees.

Twisting her wedding band back and forth, Louisa said warily, "There may have been some speculating. But that's been straightened out now," she quickly added.

Martin's jaw clenched. "Speculating ... about what?"

"About the cause of the accident. Some people said—or may have said—well, there may have been some mention of alcohol being involved. But that's all been set right now, so there's no need to get upset about it."

"What! But I don't even drink for Chrissake!" he squeaked.

Chris rubbed a hand over his balding head. “Well, it’s good to know *this*,” he said, straightening himself in his chair. “We can be prepared for the questions that’ll no doubt be raised by the Commissioning Group. I’ll get an official copy of the police report to add to your file, Mart. There were no doubts left after the investigation, so try not to worry about this.”

The problems that harmless village gossip could cause hit home for Louisa when she realised the potential effect that this could have had on her husband’s career, if not for the irrefutable evidence found in the accident investigation. “Martin, I’m sorry,” she said as she laid her hand on his arm.

Carole broke the tension in the room. “Well, dinner’s about ready. Louisa, would you mind helping me get it on the table?”

The visit at the Parsons had been a welcome diversion from the usual daily schedule for both Martin and Louisa, but by the time they returned to Portwenn, Martin was exhausted.

Jeremy arrived shortly before seven that evening, administering his patient’s medications and helping him to get ready for bed.

“I’m finished, Mrs. Ellingham,” he said as he came through the kitchen. “Unless there’s something else you’d like me to do, I’ll be off. Martin’s pretty worn out tonight, so I skipped the massage. I’ll do it in the morning.” He lifted his coat off the rack and slipped it on.

“Thank you, Jeremy. I’m sure we can manage if anything else needs to be done.”

She waited until the aide had closed the door behind him before going upstairs to get herself ready for bed. She stopped in James’s room and stood by his cot, watching him as he slept before leaning over to place a light kiss on his forehead.

“Martin, are you awake?” she asked softly, after crawling into bed a short time later.

“Hmm?”

She stroked her fingers up and down his arm, and then placed her palm against his cheek. "I just want to say I'm sorry for how I've been with you, thinking the worst of you and expecting so much of you."

His eyes opened slowly, his brow furrowing as he stared back at her. "I'm sorry?"

"I haven't been fair to you. Carole and I were talking today. Well, Carole did most of the talking. Anyway, we were talking, and Carole asked me why I feel a need to make apologies for you. And why I feel a need to have everyone else see you the way that I see you.

"She really made me think about why I treat you the way I do, and it almost makes me sick to have to admit this to myself, Martin, but I think I expect you to make up for my father's mistakes ... in a way. I tell myself that I want the rest of the village to see all your wonderful qualities so that they'll like you. That you'll be happier because of it. But that's not true. All you want is for James and me to love you ... like you the way you are."

Martin rubbed his tired eyes, trying to wake himself up. "I don't follow, I'm afraid."

She leaned over and pressed her cheek to his. "I think ... I think to some extent, I've been pushing you to change so that the people around here would like you—for me. That maybe if they liked you, that might make up for some of the things my father's done. The whole thing with the lifeboat fund money and his breaking into the warehouse scheme. Although, you did put a stop to that."

Martin wrinkled up his face. "I don't think I exactly endeared myself to them when I blew up their precious nesting choughs."

"Well, yeah. But you didn't steal from them. I think I've kinda hoped they'd forget about my father's taking that money if you were that brilliant and wonderful, dedicated doctor that you are, but without the rough edges. *That's* what I mean when I say that I haven't been fair to you."

Martin struggled to get himself sat up in the bed. He stared back at her. "Louisa, is *that* why you married me? You thought you could make me into the village's idea of the perfect GP and they'd put away their pitchforks?"

"Oh, Martin. No! I married you because I love you very, very much, and I want to spend my life with you. All those things that I said in that letter, about why you deserve me ... *those* are the reasons I married you. As for my father—he'll have to atone for his own bloody mistakes."

She pushed him back on to the bed and laid her head on his chest, listening to the steady rhythm of his heart. Inhaling deeply, she breathed out a sigh. "This is very, very nice."

"Yes." He stroked his palm across her shoulders before allowing her curves to lead it languidly down her back and across her bum. It travelled slowly northward, working its way under her nightdress to seek out her other feminine places.

Louisa brought her knees under her and leaned over to nuzzle kisses behind his ear, allowing his hand to roam freely.

"Louisa," he said as his fingertips stroked lightly across her breasts.

"Hmm?"

"I feel I should point out that blowing up a warehouse with the intent to steal the contents is a *crime*. Blowing up nesting rare birds ... *that's* a mistake."

"Martin, be quiet. You're spoiling the moment."

"Mm."

She reached back and turned out the light.

Chapter 6

"So how did you do going it alone yesterday?" Jeremy asked as he massaged the oedema out of Martin's limbs the following morning.

"It was slow. But I didn't have to spend the day in my boxer shorts. It was difficult getting my trousers pulled up." Martin grimaced as a jolt of nerve pain shot up his thigh.

"You managed in the end, though?" The aide straightened up and reached for a vial of heparin and a syringe.

"I had Louisa stand next to me in case I lost my balance, but I didn't have any problems."

"Good. That bodes well for the big test drive on dry land. I'll help you with your shower today ... give you a little break," the young man said as he took hold of his patient's healthy arm and pulled him to a sitting position.

Jeremy was drying the last beads of water from Martin's lower fixators when Louisa stuck her head in the bathroom door a short time later.

She flashed her husband one of her special smiles before her gaze shifted to the aide. "Could I have just a moment with my husband before I need to dash off, Jeremy?"

"Certainly. I'll go straighten up a bit in the bedroom," he said, getting to his feet.

Louisa stepped aside to allow him past, and then pulled the door shut behind her as she joined her husband in the bathroom.

He looked at her with cautious curiosity, cocking his head. "There a problem?"

"No problem, Martin. I just haven't had any time alone with you this morning." She sat down on the edge of the tub, next to her husband's wheelchair. "I wanted to give you a proper goodbye without embarrassing you in front of Jeremy."

"I see."

She leaned over the side of the wheelchair and pressed her lips to his, allowing them to linger just long enough to bring a flush to his face.

Smiling, she brushed her fingers over a rosy-coloured ear. "You'll be careful today, won't you? Ed said that you'll be prone to falls for a while."

He reached for a towel from the side of the tub and began to rub at the moisture still clinging to the fixators on his arm. "I'll have Kieran and Max there, Louisa. They know how to handle things."

"Well, I'll be thinking of you today ... thinking about last night."

"Ah." Martin ducked his head and glanced over at the door.

"Don't worry, I locked it," she said.

His eyes flitted again to the barrier between them and the aide on the other side before settling again on his wife. "It's a thin door."

"Then I better watch myself, hadn't I?" She stood up and looked in the mirror, taking a moment to brush her hair back into place before leaning over to give him a final kiss goodbye. "I'll see you after school then?"

"*Yes* ... after school," Martin said, his eyes glistening as the corners of his mouth nudged up.

"He's all yours, Jeremy," Louisa said as she hurried through the bedroom and down the hall.

She made a brief stop in the kitchen to say goodbye to James and to let Poppy know that she was going to be staying at the school through the lunch hour. She had an interview scheduled with a potential replacement for Stu McKenzie's friend.

There had been a formal meeting with the liaison to discuss the teacher's difficulties in his position, but there didn't seem to be any progress being made in regard to the man's refusal to recognise his own shortcomings. In the end, Louisa had made the decision to dismiss him, something she had never had to do before in her years as head teacher.

It was a typically crisp early November morning, and the grey sky held a heaviness that predicted rain. Louisa trudged down the hill on Dolphin Street before continuing on past the Platt.

"Oh, Louisa!" a shrill voice called out behind her.

She spun around to see Sally Tishell trotting in her direction. Groaning internally, she continued on towards the school.

"Louisa, if I could just have a quick word."

"What is it, Mrs. Tishell?" A gust of wind raced down the hill, blowing Louisa's coat open. She gathered it around her and buttoned it up tightly as a shiver ran through her.

Sally hurried to keep pace, finally taking hold of Louisa's coat sleeve to bring her to a stop.

Louisa turned impatiently to face her. "Yes?"

"Louisa, I would just like to say ... if either you or Dr. Ellingham should *ever* be in need of any assistance, I would be more than happy to offer my services. This must be a very difficult time for you both," the woman said, oozing sycophantic sympathy.

"Thank you, Mrs. Tishell, but my husband and I are doing just fine." Louisa tried to mask the disquietude that the woman evoked in her with a chilly tone and an icy stare.

"And how *is* our good doctor, may I ask?"

"Mrs. Tishell, I'm running late as it is. I have to go." She shook free of her grasp and turned to continue up the hill, leaving the chemist standing with shoulders sagging.

A promising start to the day, Louisa muttered, rounding the gate at the school. She turned back and watched as the chemist headed back in the direction of her shop.

She didn't know how to feel about the rather odd woman. *She has to be lonely. Confined to that little shop all day ... no husband at home. And she's a bright woman, so I can understand her attraction to Martin.*

But it was terribly unsettling to see the way she still looked at Martin. Or perhaps it was just her own anxious imagination.

Louisa shook off her unease and continued on into the school. She had far too much on her plate at the moment to let Sally Tishell occupy her thoughts any longer.

Martin had his own anxieties to deal with that morning. He sat in his wheelchair, trying to push back his concerns about the next big phase in his recovery. He felt the same trepidation he experienced the day he first stepped on to his fractured legs.

The pain that would come with stressing his limbs further didn't worry him. That he had become inured to. It was the fear of falling that was weighing heavily on him. Here at the physiotherapy centre he had his therapists standing by to assure that he stayed upright. But once he was back home again, especially once he began to venture out on to the streets of the village, would there be someone to help him get to his feet again if he fell? His greatest fear, however, was the thought of the ridicule he may have to endure.

"Martin? Are you ready to give it a try?" Kieran asked, the hand he had placed on his patient's shoulder finally getting his attention.

Martin licked his dry lips and tried to loosen the tightness in his throat with a forced swallow. "Yes. Let's just do it."

"Okay, see if you can stand up. Then hang on to the walker. Just wait for a few minutes and get used to the feel of the new set-up before you try to take a step," Max instructed.

Martin was still not allowed to bear weight on his injured arm, so a lot of time and effort had gone into strengthening the muscles in his legs. He could now shift his centre of balance forward and raise himself out of the chair.

He got to his feet and grasped on to the walker with his left hand. The device had been equipped with a platform on which he was to rest his fractured forearm, allowing his elbow to take the weight that the arm would ordinarily carry. The brace that the orthotist had fitted him with would help to support his weakened shoulder.

Max stood on one side of him and Kieran on the other. Jeremy stood back, arms crossed in front of him.

"All right, Dr. Ellingham. Whenever you're ready, step off with that left leg first," Kieran said.

Martin felt the muscles contract in his thigh as he swung his leg out in front of him. His foot landed heavily on the floor.

"Good, good! Now move the walker forward and then bring up the other leg." The young man gave him a smile. "Excellent!"

He was ambulating again, but Martin feared he looked very much like his son as he toddled around the coffee table. He tried to push those thoughts aside and focus on the task at hand—getting from one side of the room to the other.

Although his therapists seemed very happy with his progress that morning, Martin felt his confidence wavering. He found it difficult to gauge where the floor was in relation to his foot as he set it down, and he had a tendency to drag the toes of his right foot as he pulled that leg forward.

The therapists were on alert for any adverse physical effects that the new stressors could be placing on their patient. But Jeremy, watching from the side-lines, had begun to notice the fatigue and uncertainty that was beginning to register on his face.

Having traversed the length of the room and back, Kieran and Max helped Martin to drop back into his wheelchair.

Jeremy stepped forward and pulled Kieran aside. “I think he needs a break. I’m going to take him to lunch. You can work with him some more when we get back.”

The therapist’s brow wrinkled. “That wasn’t our plan for the d—”

“Your plan can be changed. I know my patient, and he needs a break,” the aide said with finality.

Kieran looked back at Martin as he sat in the wheelchair, his eyes closed. “Yeah, sure. Whatever you think.”

Jeremy put his hand on his patient’s shoulder. “Martin, I’m starving. Let’s go and get something to eat. We’ll get back at it after lunch. What do you say?”

Martin nodded his head as he rubbed a palm across his eyes.

After returning from lunch, another hour was spent practicing navigating corners, moving the walker in an efficient manner, and negotiating uneven surfaces. By the end of the session, some of Martin’s confidence had returned.

It was late afternoon before they arrived back in Portwenn. Louisa had just returned home from the school and was playing on the floor in the living room with James. “We’re in here!” she called out when she heard the door to the kitchen open.

“Hi, Louisa. How’s your day been?” Jeremy asked, walking over to tousle James’s hair.

“Fine. How did it go for you?” She got up and walked to her husband’s side, bending over to give him a kiss.

Martin breathed out a long sigh and gave her an anaemic nod of his head.

Jeremy glanced from his patient to Louisa. “He made excellent progress. Although, I’m not sure it feels that way. Eh, Martin?”

“I’ll be in the lavatory,” he said before moving down the hall.

The aide gave her a feeble smile. "I'll help him get cleaned up then come back later to take care of his medication."

Louisa worried her wedding band. "Is he okay?"

"He's just exhausted. I think things look insurmountable at the moment. We'll let him have a warm shower, I'll massage those painful limbs, and then he can have a lie-down. He'll feel more positive after a rest."

Once Martin was in bed and had fallen off to sleep, Jeremy went to the kitchen to collect his coat. Poppy was just getting ready to leave for the day as well, so he accompanied her down the hill.

Conversation was limited to such innocuous topics as the weather and the high rental prices in the village until they reached the Platt where they would go their separate ways.

Jeremy shifted his backpack up on his shoulder and then shoved his hands into his pockets, attempting to discreetly dry the sweat from his palms. "Erm, I was wondering, Poppy ... would you want to have a drink at the pub tonight ... after I finish up at the Ellingham's?" he asked.

Poppy pulled up her shoulders and gave him a timid grin. "Yeah, I'd like that. What time?"

"I should be finished by half seven. Can I stop by and pick you up when I'm done?"

"Okay. I'll be ready."

The two parted company, Jeremy heading for the car park and Poppy turning to head up Church Hill. She glanced back at him over her shoulder, watching as he moved away, then started towards home, a contented smile on her face.

Louisa put James Henry down that night and hurried to tuck into bed next to her husband. There was a chill in the air and she nestled into his warm mass.

"You seem unusually quiet tonight. Everything go okay at therapy?" she asked as she stroked her fingers lightly across his chest.

He kept his eyes focused on the ceiling as he shook his head. "It was a hard day. I'm just tired. How was your day? Did the interview go well?"

"It *did* go well. He's young, but I think he'll make a very fine teacher. I would have preferred someone with more experience, but beggars can't be choosers, hmm?"

"Mm."

Louisa raised up, putting her cheek against his. "It *will* get easier. It *will* be okay."

He squeezed his eyes shut against the emotions that were threatening to surface. "I know," he answered hoarsely.

Reaching back, she turned out the light. Martin rolled over to face her, wrapping his arm tightly around her waist and pulling her in close. "I don't like being the object of ridicule, Louisa," he confessed in the security of the darkness. "There's very little that hurts more than being the object of ridicule."

Louisa put her hands on his cheeks and kissed him. Then, resting her forehead against his, she held him while his body trembled as he shed silent tears.

Chapter 7

Martin's physiotherapy sessions in Wadebridge meant that he and Jeremy had a daily ten-mile commute together. This provided them with two short blocks of uninterrupted time in which to discuss the rapidly approaching day when patients would once again be limping, coughing, moaning, and whinging in the door to see the doctor.

"Jeremy, do you think you could help me get up to the surgery when we get back to Portwenn?" Martin asked as they were leaving the centre on Thursday. "I'd like to make some notes in the patient files for you."

"Sure, that shouldn't be a problem. I'd like to see your set-up."

"You may be disappointed. It's very small. But it *is* efficient."

"That's what I was expecting, actually. Can't imagine *your* surgery being anything less than efficient."

Martin pulled in his chin, not knowing whether to take his aide's comment as a compliment or sarcasm.

He cleared his throat before flipping through the small pad of notes that he had begun to carry with him. "I also thought I could colour code the files ... alert you to which patients have conditions that need to be monitored, and maybe flag those who are chronic whingers.

"I also have a couple who are blatantly hypochondriacal and a number of them who are constantly trying to wangle a contraindicated prescription out of me.

"Be careful that you don't make assumptions based on what you hear from me. But it might prove helpful if you have a bit of background information on the more predictable patients," Martin said as he pored over his notes.

"Sounds logical." Jeremy turned and gave him a roguish grin.

Martin lowered the notepad to his lap and glowered back at him. "Are you mocking me?"

Jeremy returned his hostile reaction with one of bewilderment. "No, of course not. I like you ... respect you."

The aide took in a deep breath and worked his hands around the steering wheel. "I'm sorry, Martin. I overstepped my bounds. I guess I felt a bit of a friendship developing and ... well, I'm sorry. That was unprofessional of me, and it won't happen again."

Martin sat silently before turning his gaze to the scenery as it passed by. His stomach began to churn as he replayed the exchange of words in his head. He could comprehend neither the intent of his aide's comments nor the sensations that were swirling around in him.

His fingers began to drum on the armrests of his wheelchair and his ragged breaths attracted Jeremy's attention.

The aide pulled off on to a passing place and parked the van.

"Martin, are you all right?" he asked, watching his patient with growing concern as the tapping stopped and he gripped the armrest.

He raised a trembling palm to his aide. "Just—give me a minute," he said, grabbing again for the armrest as he tried to quiet his hands. He closed his eyes and forced himself to think about Louisa, to imagine being curled up next to her in bed. He focused on her warmth and softness, the security he felt when her arms were around him. His muscles began to relax, and he drew in a deep breath, holding it until the tightness in his chest began to ease.

"I'm sorry. As you know, I have panic attacks sometimes. It was just a panic attack."

"Was it what I said?" Jeremy asked tentatively.

Martin shook his head. "I couldn't understand what ... what..." He glanced over at him and huffed out a breath. "I have difficulty understanding emotions. Your emotions and my own in this case."

"Is there a neurobiological basis for it?"

"No!" Martin snapped. Then he shook his head. "I'm not sure—I don't think so—I'm not sure. I'm fine now, though, so we can go."

Jeremy reached back into his bag and pulled out a bottle of water, handing it to him before backing the van out on to the road.

Nothing more was said of the incident, but Martin couldn't quit thinking about it. He couldn't make heads or tails of the conversation; nor could he understand his reaction to it. It was something to take up with Dr. Newell, he decided.

They stopped back at Ruth's cottage so that Martin could shower and change. Then he rang Ruth to let her know that they would be doing some work at the surgery.

Jeremy insisted that they drive up Roscarrock Hill, despite his patient's best efforts to persuade him to walk the distance from Ruth's to the surgery.

Martin swallowed back the lump in his throat when they entered the kitchen. It had now been almost eight weeks since he left home on that fateful day. It would be good to get moved back in again—very good.

But first he needed to be less dependent on the wheelchair and, at the very least, be able to get up and down more than the one step his therapists had limited him to in physiotherapy. Goals to work towards.

Martin had been pushing himself to reach those goals within the next couple of weeks so that they could relinquish Ruth's cottage back to her and he could resume his medical practice.

They couldn't move back to the surgery until he was able to scale the stairs. And he couldn't very well ask Ruth to tolerate patients traipsing in and out of her temporary quarters.

Martin led his aide under the staircase and past the consulting room.

"This is the reception room and that's Morwenna's desk. I thought we could limit patient access to the rest of the house if you use the desk that's just inside the lounge. I'll show you where that is," Martin said as he walked laboriously past the front door and ducked through the doorway.

"It's just around here." He turned the corner into the living quarters.

"We'll set up a partition, temporarily ... keep the simpler patients from wandering off where they're not supposed to be."

Jeremy blinked back his astonishment at his patient's heavy-handed comment about his fellow villagers.

"I don't want this to be any more intrusive for James and Louisa than is absolutely necessary," Martin continued. "Morwenna will provide you with the patient files as necessary. If you have need of anything, just let her know. She's very efficient and is well acquainted with how the practice operates."

Jeremy raised his eyebrows and nodded. "Looks like it should be a very workable situation."

Moving his walker forward, Martin headed back through the reception room and into the consulting room.

"Ah. This is where you work your miracles," Jeremy said as he looked around Martin's well maintained, and orderly domain.

"Mm. I don't know about that," he mumbled. "Like I said, it's small but efficient. I'll want you to help me go through and inventory all my medications and supplies. Then we'll get an order in to Mrs. Tishell if needs be."

Jeremy headed back through to the reception room. He wasn't a small man, but he didn't need to stoop to get through the doorways in the building either. He would be most aptly described as sturdily built. His charmingly unruly head of light brown hair and his clear blue eyes made him look much younger than the twenty-seven years of age that he actually was.

They spent the next two hours going through files. Martin would make the necessary notes in each of them, and then Jeremy would look them over. If he had any questions, Martin would add a clarification to the notes.

The aide kept an eye on his patient, noticing the ever-increasing signs of fatigue. He had hoped that Martin would sense his own need to take a break and call a halt to their work session of his own accord, but he was either too engrossed in what he was doing, or he had chosen to ignore his growing weariness.

Jeremy finally intervened. "Okay, Martin. You've done enough for today. Let's get you home so you can rest a bit."

Martin looked up with bleary eyes. "I'm fine. We'll be finished with this drawer inside of an hour."

"Nope. We're done. We can work on this again tomorrow; it's not going anywhere." Jeremy put the last of the patient notes back in the file cabinet, marking where they left off, and then rolled the drawer shut with emphasis. "Come on, let's go see if we can find you something to eat, eh?"

Martin furrowed his brow and pursed his lips. "Yes."

"You know, Martin, I've agreed to be your assistant mainly because I think that, given your personality, you'll make a speedier recovery if you keep reasonably busy. *Reasonably* being the operative word here.

"But first and foremost, my responsibility lies in keeping you as healthy as possible and moving down the road to recovery. You *will* be my boss in regard to your patients, but I must insist that I call the shots when determining what's in your best interests. If you can't agree to that then this will *not* be a workable situation."

Martin stared back at the young man, his eyes narrowing. He wasn't accustomed to taking orders, and resentment began to smoulder beneath a composed surface.

No further words were exchanged until they pulled up in front of Ruth's cottage and Martin opened his mouth to speak. "I can agree to your conditions. But I expect you to be discreet around my patients. My health is *none* of their business."

"Good, I'm glad we could come to an understanding. Thank you, Martin."

"Mm, yes," he replied, pulling in his chin.

Louisa had started preparing dinner by the time patient and aide entered the empty kitchen, and the aroma emanating from the cooker served to whet Martin's appetite.

He went to the refrigerator and removed two of his shakes, dropping them into the bag that was attached to the front of his walker. "Jeremy, can I get you anything? Some orange or apple juice?" he asked.

"No, thanks. I'll just get myself some water," the aide said before taking a glass from a shelf and filling it at the tap.

Martin made his way back to the table, dropping heavily into a chair.

Jeremy took a seat across from him. "Erm, Martin. There's something I'd like to discuss with you."

"Oh?"

The young man took in a deep breath "I've, er ... I've gotten to know Poppy fairly well. We've chatted on occasion here at your house, and we've gone out together a couple of times this week."

Martin stared across the table at his aide, knowing where the conversation was headed. But he was not in a hurry to make it easy on the young man. If he was seriously interested in Poppy, then he would be willing to endure a bit of angst for her. And Martin had his qualms about this budding relationship. Poppy was shy and sensitive, and he didn't want to see her hurt, especially under his watch.

"So anyway, I just wanted to discuss it with you ... since we *are* both under your employ."

"Discuss what with me?" Martin asked, forcing his aide to be more direct with his question.

Jeremy scratched at his head. "Seeing Poppy ... going out with her! Is it all right with you?"

Tipping his head back, Martin peered down at him with an air of authority. "Mrs. Ellingham and I have grown quite fond of Poppy, as has James. I expect you to conduct yourself appropriately with her. And your relationship will *not* be allowed to affect your job performance. Is that understood?"

The aide swallowed the nervous lump in his throat. "Yes sir."

"Good. Then if this is something Poppy would like to pursue, you have my blessing."

"Thank you, Dr. Ellingham. Well, I have dinner plans so I'll just ..." the aide said gesturing towards the door.

"Mm, yes." Martin hesitated. "Erm, Jeremy."

He whirled around. "Yeah?"

"Mrs. Ellingham and I feel the same about you as we do about Poppy. Don't disappoint us."

The doctor's tone may have been gruff, but his words eased the tension that Jeremy had been feeling since the incident in the van earlier in the day.

Martin was reading the most recent issue of the *BMJ* when Louisa entered the kitchen a short time later with James in tow.

"Well, hello! I didn't hear you come in. How was your day?" She leaned over and placed a kiss on his cheek.

"Fine, and you?"

"Good. It helps to have a full *and* fully functional teaching staff again. How did therapy go?" she asked, slipping James into his high chair.

"It was fine."

Louisa narrowed her eyes at him. "Martin, is that all I'm going to get tonight ... fine?"

He shook his head. "Sorry, my mind's on a conversation I just had with Jeremy."

"Oh, what about?" She pulled open the door of the cooker and peered in.

"He wanted my permission to see Poppy."

"Oh!" Louisa came around the table and wrapped her arms around him. "How 'bout that; you were right about those two," she said, nuzzling her nose into his neck. "And it's so sweet that he asked you, Martin. What did you tell him? I hope you didn't say some—"

She caught herself before the words came out, but they both knew that she had once again thought the worst of him. She stepped back and gave the tea towel in her hand a gentle toss on to the table.

Their eyes locked and Martin took hold of her hand, pulling her to him. He kissed her gently. "It's all right; it's just a habit. You want to try again?"

Louisa blinked back tears as she gave him a small smile. "What did you tell him?"

"Just that he'd better behave himself with her."

"Very good, Martin," she said, placing another kiss on his cheek.

"I did also tell him that I wouldn't allow their relationship to affect his job performance. You might want to have the same discussion with Poppy."

"Hmm, you're probably right. I'll talk with her in the morning."

Louisa got up early enough the next day to allow time to have a discussion with the childminder before she had to leave for the school. She was just finishing her cup of coffee when Poppy came through the door.

"Good morning," Louisa said as she rinsed her cup and put it in the dishwasher. "How are you?"

"I'm good, Mrs. Ellingham. Hello, James." She leaned over and kissed the baby's head.

"Care for a cuppa, Poppy?"

"Erm, sure." An uneasiness began to build in her as she sensed this was not going to start out like a typical morning. She watched nervously as her employer set a teacup in front of her and filled it with hot water and then dug around in the basket of teabags until she found what she was looking for.

"Milk?" Louisa asked, setting the bottle on the table.

"Yes, please." Poppy fidgeted in her chair. "Is there something wrong, Mrs. Ellingham? Did I do something wrong?"

"Oh, of course not, Poppy! I just wanted to have a word with you before I left for work. Dr. Ellingham happened to mention that he'd had a conversation with Jeremy yesterday and—"

"Oh, yeah. He told me about that," a nervous Poppy interjected. "I'm glad that you're okay with us goin' out."

"Yes, well... we are, but I do want to clarify something. Your job performance must not suffer in any way because of your relationship with Jeremy. I don't want you to be distracted from your childcare duties."

The girl shook her head vigorously. "Oh, I won't let that happen."

"Good. Well then ... I hope Jeremy will conduct himself in a gentlemanly manner."

Poppy dipped her head, smiling self-consciously. "I think Dr. Ellingham made that very clear to him. It's really very sweet

... what he said. You know ... about how you an' him have grown fond of me ... and Jeremy, too."

Louisa cocked her head at her and hesitated a moment. "Yes, it most certainly is." A knowing smile crept across her face as she headed down the hall to say goodbye to her husband before leaving for school.

She glanced at her watch. *Ohhh, how can I always be running late? I even got up early today!* she thought.

She came through the bedroom and walked up behind him as he stood in front of the bathroom sink brushing his teeth.

Her arms snaked around his waist and she laced her fingers together over his stomach. "Do you have any idea how good this feels ... to hug you while you're standing up?"

"Mm." He shook his head, moving the toothbrush around as he waited for the timer to shut the apparatus off.

"It feels absolutely wonderful." She tightened her grip.

"Louisa!" he choked out, toothpaste spattering. "That hurts!"

He doubled himself over to defend his tender abdomen and to wash away the toothpaste that was now dribbling down his chin.

"Martin, I'm sorry! Are you all right?" She moved quickly to caress his belly with her palm.

"I'm fine," he said, waving a dismissive hand in the air.

Louisa tipped her head down and peered up at him as he tried to discreetly blink away the tears. She put her hand on his cheek. "I'm sorry. I forgot. I'm really sorry."

"I'm fine now; don't worry about it."

"Hmm. Well, I wanted to say goodbye before I leave. Will I see you at lunch?"

"Mm, no. I, er ... I spoke with Dr. Newell last night. I'm going over to see him today. Jeremy's going to drive me to Truro after physiotherapy." He busied himself with getting his shaving supplies out of the cabinet, avoiding eye contact with her.

"That's good ... that you called him ... if you felt the need to see him," Louisa said, eyeing him uncertainly. "Just be careful on the drive ... okay?"

"I'm not the one driving." He turned slowly to face her before sitting back on the edge of the vanity. His eyes softened as he looked at her, and he pulled her closer. "I'll miss you today."

"I'll miss you, too. And I'm sorry for hugging you too hard."

"It's all right. Maybe you could—could make it up to me later."

Chapter 8

Martin watched out his window as they crossed the River Camel bridge, his thoughts turning to the night of the accident. Most of what he could remember of the horrendous experience was murky and fading from his memory.

But there were certain aspects of that night that were as vivid as if they had happened only yesterday. The sounds as the rescue team peeled the vehicle away from his body, an agony he never before could have appreciated. The fear of leaving his wife and son as the lorry raced towards him. And the overwhelming sense of helplessness. He closed his eyes and imagined Louisa's arms around him.

The Royal Cornwall medical campus was abuzz with activity when they arrived, and Martin felt conspicuously on display as he worked his way, laboriously, towards his therapist's office building. Jeremy waited with him until Dr. Newell came out to the reception room and then excused himself to meet up with former co-workers for lunch.

"Martin, well done!" the therapist said. "I certainly wasn't expecting to see you standing on your own two feet today. Come on back."

Dr. Newell led the way down the hall, stopping periodically to wait for his patient.

"Sorry, I'm still ... working on it," Martin said as he struggled to pull his now tired legs forward.

Pulling the door closed behind them, the psychiatrist helped him into a chair.

"Well, Martin, you mentioned on the phone that you'd experienced a couple of panic attacks," he said after taking a seat behind his desk. He flipped through the pages in a file before looking back up, giving him a penetrating stare.

Martin's gaze flitted towards the window.

"How have you been sleeping? You look pretty tired," the man said.

"I do sleep; I just wake up frequently."

"Is that a pain issue?"

"To some extent." He brushed at his trousers with the backs of his fingers as a breath hissed from his nose.

"I'm not sure what that means," Dr. Newell said, tipping his head to the side. "Are you saying there's more to it than that?"

"The pain wakes me up, but then I can't stop thinking about things." His fingernails clicked against the wood armrest of his chair. "I worry about ... different things."

"I would expect worry to be a very natural response to what you have facing you. I'm sure most patients who've experienced this sort of physical trauma have similar concerns."

"Why do you say that? I would think you, of all people, would know better than to make such a broad generalisation. No two patients are the same."

The psychiatrist tipped back and watched him for a few moments before answering. "I said other patients probably share *similar* concerns, Martin. Worries about how much improvement they'll ultimately see in their physical condition, if there'll be problems down the road, how long it'll be before they can get back to work, surgeries yet to—"

"Yes, I get the picture! But not all worries are related to the physical injuries, are they?"

"No. There could be financial concerns. The stresses that come with the many medical appointments and surgical procedures that may lie ahead. Tensions between a husband and wife ... family members. The—"

"Oh, for God's sake! Those are all manageable concerns. What about finding yourself lying on the pavement somewhere? And no one will help you to your feet because they think you're a miserable git!

"Or the ridicule? People in that village seem to find endless amusement in my blood issue. I can only imagine the hilarity when they see me trying to get up and down those hills using a—a damn *walker!*" Martin sputtered. He took in a deep breath and turned towards the window.

The psychiatrist rolled his chair forward and jotted a few lines of notes into his patient's file and then tapped his biro against his lips. "What do you mean by manageable concerns?"

"I wouldn't think the concept would be so difficult to grasp. I'm working on getting the practice set up so that I can go back to seeing patients. I'm putting my all into the physical therapy. I know what to expect with the upcoming procedures."

"And the concerns about going out in the village ... what makes those *un*-manageable?"

"In the five years I've been in Portwenn, I haven't been able to do anything to stem the flow of clever quips about my blood issue. I very much doubt I'll be able to do anything about the heckling *now*."

He furrowed his brow and huffed. "I've only given them additional—*fodder* for their punch lines. And why would they help me up when presented with an opportunity to—to—whip out their mobile phones and get a picture instead?"

He wiped the sweat from his brow with an unsteady hand. "Mark my words. Given the chance, *someone* will snap a picture of me! Face down in a pile of—*detritus* on the slipway! And you can bet they'll have it circulating through that—that—*village of—of ignorants!* Plaster it across the front page of that local—*g-gossip rag* they call a newspaper! They'll be queueing-up at the checkout counters before the ink is even dry!!"

Martin squeezed his eyes shut and flopped back into his chair. "I'm sorry. I think I'm feeling a bit tense."

"There's no need to apologise, Martin. We're in this room to work through these issues, and the best way to do that is to get things out in the open." The doctor came around and perched on the desktop. "How are you coming on your homework assignments … watching the telly every day, are you?" Martin wrinkled up his nose. "Yes. It's godawful, you know."

"Well, I appreciate your humouring me on this one. How's it going?"

"I think it's been helpful. I've been noticing facial expressions more lately." He shifted some weight from his right leg. "I actually find it interesting to some extent. It's a bit like watching a patient when trying to make a diagnosis. Watching their gait when they walk, how they carry themselves, how they sit in a chair."

Dr. Newell smiled and nodded his head. "I know that I learn a great deal about people just by watching them."

Martin's legs had begun to pound, and he shifted again in his chair.

"Do you need to put your feet up?"

A jolt shot through his left shin, and Martin stifled a groan. "I'm sorry. I think I—should."

The psychiatrist dragged a coffee table over, positioning it in front of him and lifting his legs on to it before wedging pillows under them.

Martin sighed. "Thank you."

Dr. Newell sat down on top of his desk. "I'd like to get to the issue that prompted your phone call to me last night. Why don't you tell me about these panic attacks?"

"The first occurred the day you stopped by my aunt's house. I told Louisa that I wanted to start seeing patients. She … didn't take it well. I experienced the usual symptoms of a panic attack—breathlessness, sweating, nausea. I actually vomited."

He paused, rubbing his palm against his thigh. "The second attack occurred yesterday. I was in the van with my aide, and he made a comment. Something about how he wouldn't expect my surgery to be anything but efficient. I wasn't sure if I should take it as a compliment or if he was ridiculing me.

"Then I was explaining my plans for organising the patient files. He said *sounds logical.* Something I know I tend to say. He gave me a look … a grin. I knew he was imitating me. It made me angry. I asked him if he was mocking me. He got an expression of—of—"

Martin rubbed at his forehead and deepened his scowl. "I don't know. He seemed to be upset that I would think that of him. He assured me he wasn't mocking me … that he liked me … respected me."

Dr. Newell leaned his forearms on to his thighs. "Did that make you feel better about the conversation then?"

Shaking his head, Martin snapped back at him. "Of course not! It confused me! I tried to identify the emotions, but I couldn't. So, I tried to think about what I was feeling physically, but I couldn't suss that out either.

"It felt like I was going to—to explode. I wanted to just release all the pressure that I was feeling inside … start hurling insults at him to relieve it. But he looked so afraid that he'd upset me.

"Everything seemed to be all …" He pressed the heel of his hand to his forehead. "He said he thought a friendship was developing between us and—"

Martin licked his lips and took in a deep breath. "I didn't trust him. Why did he have to say that?"

"Say what, Martin?" Dr. Newell asked as he leaned his forearms on his thighs.

"Why did he have to say he liked me … respected me? I didn't know what to do with that and panic took over."

The therapist got down from the desk. “Martin, I’m going to get a glass of water. Would you like one?”

He nodded his head silently.

“While I’m gone, I want you to think about what you might have been feeling yesterday. See if you can put a name to your emotions.”

The door closed behind the psychiatrist, and Martin closed his eyes, sighing heavily. *Why is he asking me to do this? I just told him that I didn’t understand the emotions!*

He replayed the incident in his head, trying first to remember the physical sensations that he had experienced. Then he tried to put a name to the emotions that he was feeling. Things became muddled again, the emotions all seeming to merge into one single reaction ... panic.

It was a reaction Martin now recalled experiencing before, when he was young. He thought about incidents long forgotten, swept under the rug. And that feeling of panic began to break apart into separate components—emotions.

By the time Dr. Newell returned to the room, Martin was beginning to understand what had happened to him the day before.

The therapist handed him a glass of water and then slid back on to the corner of his desk. “Well, were you able to sift through that emotional mish-mash you experienced yesterday?”

“I got a bit side-tracked. It reminded me of experiences in my childhood ... things that happened at boarding school.” He wiped his sweaty palms on his trousers.

“Go ahead. I’d like to hear about it, if you’re willing to discuss it.” Pulling his arms behind him, the psychiatrist leaned back on his hands.

Martin closed his eyes briefly, as he tried to collect his thoughts. “I, er ... had a very difficult time making friends. It wasn’t that I didn’t want friends. I suppose you could say I was shy. And I got off to a bad start at school. I was younger than the other boys, still six when I arrived at St. Benedict's. And I've told you about the bed-wetting issue. So, I was seen as being different right from the start.

"Shortly before half term, a new boy arrived at the school and we became friends. Life was a lot easier ... for a short time. But my friend pretty quickly became aligned with the rest of the boys after he found himself being subjected to the same treatment as I was—because of his association with me.

"It was bad enough when he just quit talking to me. I didn't understand what I'd done wrong. But the other boys talked him into stealing a five pound note from the maths teacher's desk drawer and put it under my mattress.

"When we came into class the next day, the teacher asked if anyone knew anything about the missing money. My friend pointed the finger at me. He said he saw me put it under my mattress. I, of course, knew nothing of it and tried to defend my innocence, which in the end earned me several more whacks with the cane for, as the headmaster put it, being a barefaced liar. I got an even better walloping from my father when I went home for half term a week later."

Dr. Newell got down from his perch on the desk and pulled a chair up by his patient. "Did you ask your roommate about it ... why he did it?"

Martin shook his head. "I couldn't bring myself to talk to him. He laughed along with the other boys about it, and I felt embarrassed ... humiliated really." He looked off towards the window before speaking again. "I felt alone ... abandoned. It was an impossible situation at that boarding school."

"Tell me about your other friendships during your years at the school."

Martin gave a derisive snort. "The same kind of thing happened two more times. I learned pretty quickly to be wary of any outward expressions of congeniality."

Dr. Newell cocked his head at him. "So ... no friendships at all at boarding school?"

"There were a couple of boys who I considered friends, but they both ended up moving away. It didn't really matter, I never trusted them anyway."

"Think about those early friendships, Martin. Then think about your conversation with your aide yesterday."

"Yes. I think I figured things out while you were out of the room." Martin stared at him, blinking back tears. "I don't trust people. I don't trust people enough to form friendships."

"Ah, but that's not entirely true, is it? Chris Parsons seems to be quite a good friend. What is it about Chris that allows you to trust him?"

"I've known him for a very long time—since medical school. He's never once done anything to betray my trust. Just the opposite in fact. He's put up with a lot from me, and I've certainly put our friendship to the test. He's never wavered, and he's been there for me when I've needed help.

"He knows things about me that no one else does. A few things that even Louisa doesn't know. He's always respected my privacy. What I share with him stays between the two of us. I suspect his wife's privy to some of it, but I trust her as well."

Dr. Newell tapped his fingertips together. "I'm curious, Martin. What do you mean when you say there are things that Chris knows about but Louisa is unaware of?"

"Things that have just never come up in conversations with her. Things she's never asked about and I don't think to tell her about."

"I see. So, it's not secrets that you've been keeping from her for some reason?"

"Of course not!"

"Good." The psychiatrist got up and took a seat behind his desk, making a few more notes in his file. "Now that you've had some time to reflect on yesterday's panic attack, can you tell me about the emotions you were feeling?"

"Mm, yes. I think I've come to realise that when something frightens me I tend to respond by getting angry. I got angry with Jeremy yesterday, but I couldn't understand why. I think, though, that maybe I was afraid he *was* mocking me. That I'd let my guard down, and now he was having a laugh at my expense.

"Being the object of ridicule is—" He squeezed on to the arm of the chair as he checked his emotions.

"Take your time, Martin."

"When I couldn't understand whether he was complimenting me or being sarcastic, it was confusing. Then when I thought he was mocking me, I thought—I thought I was being made the object of ridicule. That hurts ... physically hurts. I experience chest pain and my breathing accelerates, my heart starts to pound. It all came at me too fast. So, I got angry with him."

"And when he told you that he likes you and respects you? Did you feel anything then?"

"I'm not sure. He caught me off guard. I suppose good ... for a moment. Then I was worried ... afraid I'd mucked it up." He rubbed the heel of his hand roughly against his forehead. "But I don't know if I want to go there anyway."

"Why do you say that?"

"Didn't we just cover this? My attempts at friendship haven't gone swimmingly in the past, have they?"

"In your childhood, no they didn't. But as an adult, you've been able to build a friendship with Chris Parsons."

Martin pulled in his chin and stared at the floor for a few moments before responding. "Yes."

"Martin, I think you experienced something analogous to an oxidation-reduction reaction, except that instead of mixing different chemical species, you were mixing emotional species,"

Dr. Newell said as he toyed with a paperclip. "You went from several *negative* emotional species to a more *positive* emotional species, then back again to a negative species in the span of what … less than half a minute? And this all occurred inside a closed chamber, so to speak."

The paper clip tapped against the desktop as the therapist furrowed his brow. "What I mean by that is that you're just learning to recognise these different emotions, and you were just not quite prepared to handle the rapid swings coupled with the intensity of the opposing emotions. The end result was like mixing hydrogen and oxygen. You had a violent reaction. Does that make sense to you?"

"Yes. Yes, I think it does."

"Now, panic attack number one. This isn't the first time that you've had a reaction such as this to your wife's anger." The therapist glanced at his watch. "*Ach*, I have another patient coming in about fifteen minutes. I tell you what, let's plan to resume our Friday sessions at four o'clock next week. Will there be someone to drive you over here?"

"Yes, I think that I should be able to make something work," Martin said as he struggled to his feet.

"All right. Between now and then, I'd like for you to think about the emotions that you've experienced when your wife's anger has triggered these attacks. Make a list of the emotions for me and we'll discuss it next week. How's that other list I asked you for coming along? The list of emotions you felt when you were bullied or unfairly punished."

"I'm working on it. You mentioned that it could be in narrative form, so I've been trying to recall particular instances and write about them."

Dr. Newell got up and stretched his arms up over his head. "Well, focus on the unfair punishments. I'd really like to explore that next week as well."

He put his hand on Martin's arm. "And try to remember that people mature. Yes, there will always be those people who just never seem to grow up, but the majority of people *do* mature and develop morally as well. You're not on your own anymore either, Martin. It might be time to give friendship another go."

Chapter 9

Martin had been exceptionally quiet on the drive back to Portwenn, and Jeremy looked over at him, worriedly. The silence in the van grew more and more oppressive as the miles of barren moorland passed them by.

Jeremy was struggling to control his predilection towards verbosity, a trait of his that was well-acknowledged by his peers. He began to unconsciously tap his fingers on the steering wheel, blowing out a deep breath of air.

At the same time, his passenger wanted to break the awkward silence with a plea for leniency after his peculiar behaviour the day before.

Martin opened his mouth several times, wanting to apologise but found he lacked the emotional fortitude to allow the words to flow from his tongue. And so, the painful silence continued until it was fractured by the aide's voice, announcing a needed petrol stop in Wadebridge.

Martin pulled his wallet from his back pocket and handed Jeremy two fifty pound notes before the aide got out to fill up the tank. When he returned to the van, he handed the change back to his patient. "Is there something bothering you? Is it something I said or did?" he asked.

Martin looked up quickly. "No, of course not."

Silence returned to the van, neither of the men speaking for several uncomfortably long moments, before the doctor asked, "Erm, what did you mean when you asked about my—my challenges having a neurobiological basis?"

The aide winced and breathed out a heavy breath. "I'm sorry I asked about that, Martin. I know it's none of my business."

His fingers tapped against the steering wheel. "I—I guess I was wondering if maybe it was Autism Spectrum Disorder."

Martin's eyes snapped as his brow lowered. "Oh, for goodness' sake, Jeremy!"

The aide rubbed a hand over the back of his neck, his shoulders slumping. "Sorry."

Hesitating, Martin took a leap of faith, trusting in Dr. Newell's understanding of human relationships. "I, er ... spoke with my psychiatrist about our conversation yesterday ... what you said about feeling a friendship developing between us."

The aide turned and stared at him, unblinking.

Self-conscious under the young man's gaze, Martin wagged a finger towards the road. "Why don't you go ahead and drive," he said.

Once Jeremy had pulled out of the parking place and his attention was focused in front of him, Martin continued. "I'd appreciate your discretion with respect to what I'm going to share with you."

"Whatever you have to say will be held in the strictest confidence." Jeremy gave him a sharp nod.

Martin feigned interest in the scenery that passed by his window. "I had a difficult childhood. It may have had a negative impact on certain aspects of brain development.

"I thought all my life that the things that were done were deserved. My father had a temper and ... one could say his disciplinary methods were severe."

The aide noted the tension in his patient's jaws and wondered for a moment if it might be wise to save the conversation for later. He went over a quick plan of action in his head in case things went awry. "What sort of disciplinary methods?"

Martin stomach began an anxious churning, and he took another great leap of faith. "Whacks with his belt, sometimes a table tennis bat. Whatever happened to be within reach.

Sometimes the back of his hand." He shrugged his shoulders. "Constant criticism ... belittling."

Jeremy squeezed on to the steering wheel. The last part was something that he, too, was familiar with. "Did your mum get upset ... when your dad would beat you or belittle you? Or was she afraid of him?"

Martin swallowed hard. He couldn't begin to imagine his mother being the least bit concerned for his welfare. "My mother never wanted a child. No, it didn't bother her. I think she actually got some kind of perverse pleasure out of it."

Jeremy blew out a breath. "Wow. My dad's a royal arse ... always has been, but Mum always defended me."

Patient and aide looked at one another, finally making eye contact, and Martin felt a connection with the young man. He massaged the area around the laceration in his thigh, and then asked, "Did your father abuse your mother, Jeremy?"

The young man's hands tightened again on the steering wheel. "He still does. I've tried to get her to leave him, but she's devoted to the guy. He dotes on her most of the time. But then he gets a little too much alcohol in his system, and he gets aggressive. He doesn't drink very often, but when he does..." he shook his head... "he *really* drinks."

They rode in silence for several miles before the aide asked, "Your mum ... she's not a warm person I take it?"

Martin almost smiled at the irony of the question. "She didn't want me touching her."

"So, do you see them often?"

Wincing at the memory of his mother's last visit, Martin said, "She was here a few months ago, supposedly to notify me, two weeks after the fact, that my father had died. It was difficult to see her touching James ... being aware of the harm she can do. I wouldn't have had her, but Louisa invited her in.

"I'd not told Louisa about my parents, just that we'd had a falling out a few years ago. She's aware of things now, but there's still a lot she doesn't know about my past … my upbringing. She knows enough to understand how my childhood affected me … caused problems that I'm now trying to work through. She would have left me if I didn't deal with all of this. But she doesn't need to know everything. If things come up, I'll tell her about them. Otherwise … she knows enough."

The aide raised his head as the pieces began to fall into place. "Ah, the sessions with Dr. Newell."

"Mm, hmm." Martin grimaced as he shifted himself to face the aide. "Our conversation yesterday—I'd like to explain. I have a difficult time with emotions. It's hard for me to understand them, and I tend to get angry when things get … emotional.

"When you said you … well, that you—you liked me, I felt … positive. But friendships haven't worked out well for me, so when you mentioned a friendship developing, it triggered too many emotions … and the panic attack." His gaze shifted back to the scenery. "I just wanted you to know."

Jeremy kept his eyes on the road ahead, but a smile crept across his face. "Thanks Martin. I'm glad you told me."

It was mid-afternoon when they arrived back at Ruth's cottage. Martin made himself a sandwich and had a lie-down before he and Jeremy drove to the surgery to work on patient notes. By the time they returned, Poppy had left for the day and Louisa had arrived home.

She sat working on scheduling at the kitchen table while James sat on the floor, filling and emptying a cooking pot with wooden blocks.

"Well, hello you two," she said, as they came in the door. "How did the trip to Truro go?"

"It was … fine," Martin said, exchanging knowing glances with his aide.

James reeled around at the sound of his father's voice and scrambled over. He clutched on to his trousers and pulled himself up before Jeremy scooped him into his arms, pre-empting any unfortunate fixator mishaps. James wriggled to free himself, reaching out to grab on to Martin's shirt.

"Just a minute, James," Martin said, his tone soft but firm. He moved to the table and dropped heavily into a chair.

"This kid is, without a doubt, a daddy's boy," Jeremy said as he lowered the baby on to his father's lap.

Louisa smiled as her husband's face relaxed, and his chest swelled.

Martin leaned over to place a kiss on the boy's head, lingering to breathe in the sweet smell. Looking up, he became uncomfortably aware of the eyes watching him. Clearing his throat, he handed James his plastic giraffe.

"Jeremy, would you like to join us for supper tonight?" Louisa asked as she began to pull her papers into a pile.

"I appreciate the invitation, but I already have plans."

Martin raised his eyebrows at him. "Poppy?" he asked.

"Yes, we're going to Bert's for dinner."

Louisa stirred the soup that was bubbling on the hob before reaching for the loaf of bread she had picked up at the bakery. "Well, I'm afraid we can't compete with that."

Martin looked up at his wife. "Your cooking is much better than anything I've ever eaten at Bert's, Louisa."

"Thank you, Martin. But I was referring to the company, not the menu," she said. "And, if I recall correctly, Bert makes a delicious soup that you seem to thoroughly enjoy."

Louisa walked behind him, tickling his neck with a fingertip and whispering into his ear. "I enjoy it as well." Her sub rosa comment sent a flush of colour across his cheeks.

"Oh? Maybe I'll give it a try," the aide said, shoving his hands into his pockets.

Martin ducked his head. "Mm, it's not on the menu."

Louisa took a few steps back and leaned over to place a kiss on the top of her husband's head. "It's a shame it's not, isn't it?"

Martin glanced over at Jeremy then back at his wife. "Perhaps it's just as well."

Jeremy, looking somewhat confused by the direction the conversation had taken, made a move towards the door. "I'll be back at seven to help you get ready for bed, Martin."

"Don't worry about it Jeremy, you've had a long day. I'll manage just fine for one night."

"What about your heparin injection?"

"I can manage it. We'll see you in the morning," Martin said, returning his attention to his son and the plastic giraffe.

Louisa came down the stairs that evening, having just gotten the baby down for the night. Martin had his feet up on the sofa and a medical journal in his hands. She leaned over him from behind, placing her palms on his cheeks and tipping his head back so that she could kiss him. "I missed you today."

He relaxed, letting her cradle his head in her hands, and closing his eyes, he let her presence wash over him.

Louisa watched his face as the ever-present stern expression dissolved into one that could be best described as contented. She leaned over again and buried her face in his neck, drizzling kisses along one side, then the other, before lingering at the hollow of his throat. He released an almost inaudibly soft moan, which was translated into a subtle vibration against his wife's lips.

"Martin," she said softly. "I believe there are still amends to be made ... hmm?"

"Yes," he croaked as the journal slipped from his hands and on to the floor.

"How 'bout I go get ready for bed and come back down to take care of that matter."

He swallowed hard. "Mm, yes."

Louisa stood up, letting her fingertips toy with his ears briefly before she moved towards the stairs.

Martin was waiting for her when she came into the bedroom a short time later. He turned back the covers and moved over on the bed. "I don't think you're appropriately dressed for amends-making, Louisa."

She smiled at his hint of playfulness and slipped her nightdress ever-so-slowly over her head, allowing her husband's eyes to wander.

His gaze was fixed on her as she climbed up next to him. There was a chill in the night air, and her place in the bed, which he had intentionally warmed for her, seemed to wrap her in his love. She stretched out against him, and he pulled her in even closer.

"Oh, Louisa," he moaned in the throaty velvet voice that never failed to kindle a desire in her.

She pressed her lips to his, passionately.

Pushing himself against her, he nudged her gently on to her back. His lips were drawn south, and he placed a lingering kiss on each breast. Moving carefully, yet somewhat awkwardly, he stretched out on top of her.

"Martin," she whispered. "Do you think this is a good idea? I don't want you to hurt yourself."

"Shh, shh, shh, shh, shh. I'm here now," he said, his voice soft and seductive. "I may as well crack on, don't you think?"

She smiled up at him. "Yes, Martin. You go right ahead and ... crack on."

As they lay next to each other a short time later, Louisa brushed her fingers through her husband's damp hair. "That was ..." she sighed, "just absolutely beautiful, Martin. Thank you."

"Mm, you're welcome. It *was* a good idea after all."

"Yes, Martin. It was." She reached up and placed a tender kiss on his lips.

Chapter 10

Friday brought with it another session at the physiotherapy centre in Wadebridge as well as a cold rain and driving wind. Despite Mother Nature's efforts to dampen his spirits, Martin found himself feeling more positive about the progress he was making.

He had seen noticeable improvement in both the strength and the stability in his legs. He now used the walker mainly to help him with the lingering balance issues. His right leg still wanted to drag at times as he brought it forward, causing him to stumble.

There had been slow but steady progress with the dexterity and sensitivity in his hand as well. He needed to be cautious; it was easy for an injury to occur to his right hand without his being aware of it. By the time he felt the heat from a hot pot handle, he had often sustained a burn. For this reason, he was continually being shooed away from the cooker by his wife.

Their afternoon duties at the surgery completed, they returned to Ruth's cottage. Martin sat at the kitchen table as Jeremy set the box containing the internal workings of Ruth's clock on the old sheet covering the table top.

He stared at the assortment of parts, wondering if he'd gotten himself in too deep with this particular project. He sighed, remembering what the village's former constable, Mark Mylow's *old mum* had said. *Start as you mean to go on.*

He grasped the movement and laid it down gently. So far, so good. Opening the tool kit he had received from his grandfather, he removed a small screwdriver.

"Mind if I watch?" Jeremy asked.

He gave the young man a scrutinising look. "Why?" No one had ever taken an interest in his rather unconventional pastime before, and the aide's apparent curiosity made him leery.

"I'm just wondering how the thing works. But if I'm going to be a distraction, I can take off."

Martin gave a shrug of his shoulders, and the aide pulled up a chair.

Lifting the cover from the mechanism, Martin began to examine the dozens of tiny wheels, rods, bearings and cogs inside, looking for any that might be missing or any obviously broken parts that would keep the clock from operating properly. Assuring himself that all pieces were present and accounted for, the surgeon began the task of removing the individual constituents, laying them out in an organised manner on the trays he had placed in front of him.

"I've heard taking a clock apart can be dangerous," Jeremy said. "That clock repairers have lost fingers when doing it." He picked up a tiny cog and looked it over before returning it to its former place.

Martin kept his eyes focused on the work in front of him. "Yes, that's true. It's not usually the clock repairers who lose fingers, though. They know enough to release any tension in the mainspring before working on the movement. It's the idiots who think they can save money by doing the job themselves that end up short a digit or two."

Jeremy peered up at him. "I suppose people don't realise there's a potential danger, though."

"Maybe."

"So, how does one of these work anyway?"

Reaching behind him, Martin picked up the book Chris had given him, the motion sending a sharp pain through his rib cage. He grimaced.

"You okay?" the aide asked.

"Yeah, I'm fine." He opened the book up to an exploded view of the internal workings of the specific movement he was repairing. "Come over here, Jeremy."

The aide went around the table to look over Martin's shoulder as he explained the mechanics of the action, pointing out the parts in the diagram.

"This clock uses chains and weights to swing the pendulum. When the bob at the bottom of the pendulum arm swings to the left as you look at it, the top of the arm swings to the right. That causes the drive gear to transfer rotation to the rest of the gears, eventually turning the escapement gear. That's the little mechanism that allows the gear to advance, one tooth at a time."

Martin picked up a small metal piece and handed it to his aide. "Without that little bit there, the weights would drop to the floor. One turn of this large gear, the drive gear, becomes sixty turns of the escapement gear. And this set of gears here insures that the minute hand rotates at twelve times the rate of the hour hand."

The corners of the aide's mouth nudged up in response to his patient's obvious passion for his hobby. "What is it that you find enjoyable about repairing clocks?"

Martin sorted through his tool kit looking for a smaller screwdriver. "Working with the small pieces is challenging. It requires focus. The diagnostic aspect is enjoyable. I suppose it's also the way the components are interdependent, much as they are in the human body, or any other higher organism for that matter."

"A bit like a Rube Goldberg invention, eh?"

Martin furrowed his brow at the young man. "In that there's a chain reaction of events you mean?"

"Right." Jeremy picked up the reference book and thumbed through it.

"I guess you could look at it that way, although Rube Goldberg deliberately over-engineered his machines to make a very simple task complicated. A *complete* waste of time, in my opinion. Whereas clocks take a rather complicated concept—time—and make it understandable to even the most witless human beings," Martin explained as he held up a tiny gear in front of him, inspecting the small teeth adorning its perimeter.

"See right here? There's a small bur on this tooth that will have to be filed smooth." He held the piece up so that the sunlight, now filtering through the lace curtains covering the kitchen window, would backlight the minute flaw.

"That little bitty thing would cause a problem?"

"Yes, definitely. Any imperfection will be magnified exponentially as the slight drag that it causes is transferred to each gear down the line."

Jeremy looked at Martin now with a bit of awe in his eyes. "Do surgeons have to be this precise?"

"Yes, if they're competent. Fortunately for the patients of the surgeons performing hack jobs, the human body is more forgiving than a timepiece is. Our bodies can repair much of the damage done to them. A good outcome after vascular surgery, however, is particularly demanding of precision."

Martin gave the tooth on the gear a final swipe with the file before wiping it clean with a soft white cloth.

Jeremy continued to observe, trying to refrain from asking too many questions and to control his loquaciousness. The pair sat in silence for several minutes as Martin worked.

"Was your grandfather a perfectionist as well?" Jeremy asked, unable to tolerate the verbal vacuum in the room any longer.

Martin laid the gear he'd been working on down. "Yes, I would say he demanded a great deal of himself ... others as well. He told me once that the expectations of life depend on diligence. That the clockmaker who would perfect his work must first sharpen his tools. I learned some years later that what I thought to be sage advice from my very wise grandfather was actually a quote by Confucius, redrafted to have a more profound impact on a seven-year-old boy enamoured with clocks. It *was* effective; I've remembered it all my life."

He hesitated before quietly saying, "He died that day."

Jeremy glanced up quickly, not sure if he had heard him correctly.

"Excuse me, I need to use the lavatory," Martin said, turning himself away from his aide, but not before Jeremy saw the moisture gathering in his eyes.

Louisa and James came in the door a short time later with a bag of vegetables and a newspaper-wrapped fish in the basket underneath the child's pushchair seat.

"Hello, Jeremy."

"Hi, Louisa ... James," the aide said laying the clock repair book on the table.

"Well, a certain someone will be pleased ... monkfish for dinner tonight. It seems like it's been a rare commodity at the market lately." Louisa craned her neck to look into the living room. "Where *is* Martin?"

"He went to use the lavatory, but it might be a good idea if you checked on him. He seemed a bit ... emotional when he left the kitchen."

"Oh, dear. What's happened?" Louisa asked, hurriedly shoving the groceries into the refrigerator.

"Nothing really happened. We were just talking and the subject turned to his grandfather. Martin seemed upset by it."

"Hmm, I see." Louisa lifted James from his seat before settling him into the high chair with a teething biscuit and a Sippy cup of water.

"Jeremy, would you mind watching this one for a bit? I'll just go and..." she said as she gestured towards the hallway.

"No ... that's just fine, you go ahead. Let me know if you need anything."

The door was closed as Louisa approached the bedroom. She slipped in quietly. Martin was lying on his side facing away from her, not sprawled out as he usually did for an afternoon lie-down. She crawled up next to him, spooning against his back and wrapping her arm around his chest.

He turned his head, glancing back at her, and she kissed the back of his neck. "Wanna talk about it?"

"Louisa..." he groaned.

"Okay. Then maybe you can tell me what I can do to help."

"You're doing it."

She moved closer and tightened her grasp.

They lay in silence for several minutes before Martin spoke. "I had a conversation with Jeremy the other day ... in the van on the way back from Wadebridge. It resulted in a panic attack."

"What triggered it do you think?"

He reached for her hand. "I spoke with Dr. Newell about it yesterday. I was confused."

"And what words of wisdom did he have?"

She shifted to the side as Martin turned on to his back. Laying his palm across his forehead, he said, "He thinks the attack was caused by having conflicting emotions thrown at me too quickly. I couldn't keep up and it was overwhelming."

"I see. What was it that Jeremy said to upset you?" Louisa propped herself up on an elbow and peered intently at him.

He rolled his eyes. "He said that he liked and respected me ... that he felt a friendship developing."

Louisa gave her husband a soft smile and brushed her hand across the top of his head. "Well, that's really not news to *me*."

"What? You knew he felt that way?"

"I can tell that he admires you, looks up to you. Kind of like a big brother almost."

"Well, you could have *warned* me, Louisa!"

"Warned you?"

"*Yes*. I wasn't prepared for it."

"Martin, I think it's sweet ... cute."

"*Cute?*" He curled up his lip. "Jeremy may have confused me, but I have no idea what to do with ... *cute*."

Louisa traced her fingertip around his face before placing a kiss on his lips. "Sorry, Martin. I *do* think it's nice that he sees you the way he does, though. It's a compliment."

"Hmph, we'll see about that."

"And just what is *that* supposed to mean?"

"Mm, nothing."

"Mar-tin."

He looked up at her. Her no-nonsense expression a clear indication that she would not tolerate his evasiveness. He huffed. "I'm saying that he may not be prepared for how difficult I can be."

Louisa's lips drew into a straight line. "You mean you think he just doesn't know any better than to like you? Kind of like Chris following you around like a stupid dog?"

"I'm sorry I said that. Chris is a good friend. I shouldn't have said what I did."

"Did you ever consider that maybe Chris sees through that hard shell of yours to the very fine man you—"

Martin shook his head. "Louisa, I'm just saying that Jeremy doesn't know me that well. When we start working together, he'll find out how difficult I can be."

Louisa sat up and moved back on the bed. "Martin, you are a very introverted person. I'm more extroverted—I like to socialise.

"But something that I've noticed with you and Chris is just how close you really are. I know *you* don't see your relationship that way, but you understand each other. Chris seems to get why you react to things the way you do. And since your accident, he seems to understand what you need to get well. In a way, he understands you better than I do."

Martin screwed up his face and focused his eyes on the cracks in the ceiling. "That's disturbing."

Louisa slapped a hand down on his arm. "Martin, that's a really *wonderful* thing! I have more friends than you have, but I don't have any relationships that are as intimate as what you and Chris have.

"As Joan would say, we are what we are, and *you* don't need a lot of friends. You just need a few really good friends, and I think Jeremy *will* be a good friend for you. He sees the honest and well-meaning man you are and doesn't seem to be bothered by your slightly—abrasive surface."

She leaned over and kissed his nose. "You know, maybe Chris *is* like the dogs that always seem to follow you around. They want to be around you because they sense the kindness in you that's so well hidden from most people."

She tipped her head down. "Do you feel better about it now?"

Martin hesitated, the furrow between his brows deepening. "About ... what?"

"About what was bothering you ... that Jeremy would change his mind about wanting to be your friend."

"*That's* not what was bothering me."

Louisa huffed out a breath and shook her head.

He blinked his eyes at her. *"What?"*

"Martin ... I thought you were worried that Jeremy might not want to be your friend once he gets to know you. *What* ... was the discussion we just had all about?"

"I believe you were saying that you have more friends than I do, and that's okay with you." He looked at her out of the corner of his eye. "Did I miss something?"

"But what about Jeremy changing his mind about being your friend?"

"That's *not* what was bothering me, Louisa. I only brought up my appointment with Dr. Newell because I don't want you to think I'm slipping back into old habits."

Louisa closed her eyes and took a moment to think through the conversation that had just occurred. Her shoulders sagged. "I'm sorry Martin. I jumped to a conclusion. I assumed there to be a problem where there wasn't one. Now ... care to talk about what *is* bothering you?"

He cupped her cheek in his hand. "Louisa, I appreciate your concern, but no, I don't want to talk about it. It's not bothering me anymore. By the time you finished talking, I didn't even remember it." He raised up and kissed her. "So, thank you."

Chapter 11

The front door opened and Ruth's voice rang out through the house early on Saturday. "Good morning!"

"In the kitchen, Ruth!" Louisa called back. She knelt down and pulled three plates from one of the lower kitchen cupboards. "Martin, should I put bowls on the table for fruit?"

"Yes. I'll cut up a melon," he replied as he beat a bowl of eggs, preparing them to be scrambled. He stopped periodically to shake the cramp from his arm and to massage his hand and fingers.

Louisa eyed her husband apprehensively. "Maybe I should finish that up for you."

"I'm fine Louisa," he snipped back.

Ruth entered the room, diverting Louisa's attention away from the breakfast preparations for the moment. "Hello, Ruth," she said as she walked over to embrace her.

The elderly woman stood, arms at her sides, awkwardly abiding the unrestrained affections before pulling a chair out from the table and taking a seat. "The waves are really hammering away at the cliffs today. I don't know how you two stand the winter gales, living over there by the water. I felt like woodpeckers were hammering at my head all night."

"Well, it shouldn't be much longer before you can move back in here," Martin said as he rinsed the whisk before adding it to the load already in the dishwasher. "I'm making good progress on the stair climbing machine at therapy, so by the end of next week we should be able to get things back to normal."

Ruth watched her nephew sceptically. "Are you sure you're not pushing things too hard? It's only been two months since your accident you know."

Martin glanced over his shoulder at her, his scowl deepening. "I'm very aware of when my accident occurred, Ruth. And it's been ten weeks, not two months."

"I stand corrected. I'd just hate to see you set yourself back."

"I have no intention of doing any such thing."

Ruth held her hands up in front of her in capitulation. "Fine, I won't say another word."

Louisa looked anxiously at her husband. The tension he was feeling was obvious in his tightly set jaw and pursed lips. She took three juice glasses from the cupboard and put them on the table, stopping to give him a reassuring caress on his back before returning for the cups.

There was a period of tense silence before the tea kettle began to hiss its readiness. Louisa breathed a soft sigh of relief as she lifted it from its base and brought it to the table. "Would you like a cuppa, Ruth?" she asked.

"Yes, I do believe I would. Thank you," she said as she dropped a teabag into her cup.

Louisa jerked her head towards Martin and gave the old woman a sharp shake of her head.

After giving her a bemused stare, Ruth redirected her attention to her nephew. "You know Martin, there's absolutely no reason the villagers can't continue to make the short trek to Wadebridge a while longer," she said, peering up at him. "Perhaps you should take the opportunity to do some writing."

"I thought you weren't going to say another word." He grabbed the chef's knife from the drawer, squeezing the handle tightly as he closed his eyes and inhaled deeply.

Reaching for a melon, he placed it on the cutting board in front of him. His movements became more forceful as he began to take out his frustration with his aunt's apparent negativity on the hapless cucurbit. He lifted the knife up, and stabbing it into the cantaloupe, began to make his midline incision.

"Martin, do you want tea or coffee this morning?" Louisa asked as she refilled the kettle and plugged it into the socket.

"I don't care! Just make me whatev—" The grip in his weakened hand gave out, causing the knife to slip and slice into his left index finger. "Oh ... shit!"

"Martin! Watch your language in front of Ja—" Louisa's admonishment was brought up short when her fiery eyes snapped in her husband's direction. Blood was running freely down his hand and into a puddle on the cutting board.

She grabbed the tea towel from the oven door and wrapped it around the wounded appendage. "Ruth, we need you over here."

Picking up on the minor drama unfolding in the room, James began to fuss in his high chair.

"Louisa, I'm fine. Just get me some disinfectant and a plaster!" Martin snapped, his vexation growing exponentially with each new pair of eyes that focused on him.

"Let me see it," Ruth said as she took hold of his hand and removed the tea towel. "This is going to need more than a plaster, Martin." She held it up in front of his face. "See."

"Oh, gawd," he groaned as his stomach began to churn and the light began to dim.

Louisa grabbed the nearest chair and set it behind him, pushing him into it.

"I can take care of it, but you need to tell me what to do," Ruth said as she inspected the wound more carefully.

He glanced up at the clock and pulled his hand away from the elderly woman. "It's almost nine. Jeremy will be here in a few minutes; he can take care of it."

Louisa picked James up and returned to her husband's side. "That's bleeding *a lot* Martin. I think I should take you over to Wadebridge."

He shook his head vigorously, "Jeremy will be here before we could even make it past Trelights."

"Yes, but I think you're going to need stitches in that." She set the baby on the floor with his toys and retrieved another towel from the drawer.

"It looks much worse than it is. The heparin I'm getting is preventing it from clotting."

Louisa lifted her husband's hand from his lap and began to remove the bloodied towel, but Martin stopped her, waggling a finger. "No, no, no, no, no. Leave that one on there. Just wrap the clean one around it," he barked.

His gaze met hers and his face softened. "It'll bleed more if it's disturbed. Just wrap the other one around it," he said softly. Nodding towards the counter, he added, "I'm sorry about the melon."

Louisa tucked the second towel in around the first. Then she walked over and washed off the knife before slicing off the blood-spattered area of the melon, throwing it in the bin. "It's fine, Martin." After washing the cutting board and the countertop, she proceeded to prepare the remainder of the fruit for their breakfast.

Martin looked on in abject horror. "What do you think you're doing?"

"I'm getting our breakfast ready."

"But that's all biological waste now! We can't eat tha—"

"Martin. *Be—quiet.* There is absolutely *nothing* wrong with this part of the melon! No one's going to force you to eat it if you don't want to!" She turned to him, her face red with anger. "But *I* want melon with my breakfast! So—*shush*," she said, emphasising her final words with a jab of the knife.

Jeremy arrived a few minutes later, and he and Martin went into the bathroom to clean up the inadvertent incision.

"Well, you're getting my day off to an interesting start," the aide said as he unwound the outer towel. "You're not testing my abilities before you turn me loose on your patients, are you?"

Martin glanced up at him, studying his face for any expression that might explain the intent of his remark. Jeremy gave him a wry smile, revealing the tongue-in-cheek nature of his question.

"It was *idiotic* is what it was," Martin moaned. "I let myself get distracted."

The aide began to slowly peel off the last layer of towelling that had been soaking up the blood, and he set it by the sink.

Martin kept his eyes averted as Jeremy rinsed the wound.

"Hmm, let me apply some pressure to this and see if we can get the bleeding stopped. What do you think, Martin ... stitch it or not?" The aide looked up to see his patient's head turned, his face pale, and beads of perspiration sitting on his forehead. "Are you okay?"

"Just ... cover it up. And get rid of those bloody towels!" he snapped.

Jeremy looked at him askance.

Louisa stuck her head in the door. "Can I get you anything?"

"Yes, could you take these." The aide handed the towels past his patient and Martin closed his eyes and drew in a slow breath.

Louisa leaned over and kissed his head, following it up with a caress of her hand across his cheek. "Hanging in there?"

"Yes, but take those away ... now!"

"Sorry. Let me know if you need anything," she said before she left the room.

"Well, how do you want me to handle this ... stitches?" Jeremy asked again.

"Just do what you think is best." Martin looked up at the young man, sighing heavily as they made eye contact. "I have a bit of a problem with blood."

The aide narrowed his eyes. "What do you mean? You're a doctor. And you were a surgeon."

"I'm aware of that, Jeremy. The blood sensitivity's why I'm a GP now. I couldn't handle surgery anymore."

Jeremy leaned over and pulled a box of gauze pads from his bag and unwrapped several of them, laying them on top of the cut on his patient's finger.

"Why did you opt for a surgical career if you're affected this way?" he asked as he put a folded-up towel on his lap. He laid Martin's hand on top of it and applied pressure to the wound.

"It developed twelve years after I became a surgeon. It came out of nowhere, and I just couldn't operate anymore. So, I'm … here."

"I'm sorry, Martin. I've read some of your papers and have heard people talk about your surgical skills."

Martin opened his mouth to speak, but the words refused to come. He waved a dismissive hand through the air. "I'm a GP now, and that brings its own rewards."

"How do you handle it as a GP? You still have to deal with blood." Jeremy added another gauze pad to the wound and pressed against it.

"I … vomit, then get on with my work. It's humiliating though, and it's been the source of a lot of jokes since I came here. I thought I had it under control for a while, but it came back. I'm not sure why."

The aide kept up the pressure on his patient's finger for another ten minutes before looking under the gauze. He shook his head. "I think we're going to have to stitch this. Sorry."

"Mm, it's okay." Martin rubbed his eyes, the stressful morning beginning to wear on him.

"Well, I guess we should go up to the surgery to do this properly. It's kind of ironic that the first patient I'll see will be my boss, eh?" he said, giving Martin a roguish smile.

Martin looked back at him, his gaze unwavering. "I'm sorry I wasn't upfront with you about my blood issue, Jeremy. I'll understand if you change your mind about the job as my assistant."

The aide reached into his bag for a bandage roll and wrapped it around his patient's finger and hand. "You can't get rid of me that easily, Martin. If anything, I respect you more now than I did fifteen minutes ago. I'm afraid you're stuck with me."

The two men made their trip to the surgery and returned to Ruth's cottage an hour later, three stitches now in the patient's finger.

"Jeremy, we've turned breakfast into brunch. Would you like to join us?" Louisa asked as she set a platter of bangers on the table next to the bowl of scrambled eggs.

"Yes, I would. I'm so hungry I could eat a horse."

"Well, we're not serving horse, but you're welcome to what's on the table. Have a seat." She set a bowl of chopped banana and a piece of Melba toast on the highchair tray. "Ruth, would you watch James for a minute?"

"I believe I can manage," the elderly woman said as she took a seat next to the baby.

"Martin ... a word please?" A tight-lipped Louisa tipped her head in the direction of the hall before hurrying off. Martin followed after, finding her sitting on the bed in his room. He ducked through the doorway, suddenly feeling like a prisoner being led to the gallows.

"Louisa, I'm sorry. I shouldn't have been trying to use that knife when I was distracted ... upset by Ruth's words. I'll be more careful in future," he said, dropping on to the bed next to her.

He steeled himself for the expected castigation to come, but was taken aback when his wife burst into tears and threw her arms around him.

"Oh, Martin! When I saw you bleeding like that it brought back this flood of horrible memories and—and this awful feeling of fear and absolute helplessness. I could smell all the same smells, I could hear your moans and—and—oh, *Martin!*"

Oh, God, he groaned internally. He could think of nothing that he could say to calm his wife. He held her as she sobbed into his shoulder.

"I could see you, Martin. This image of what you looked like that night in the trauma centre. Your blue lips and your pale face. The absolute terror in your eyes. The bones. And—and ... *the blood!*" Another great round of sobs ensued.

He held her tighter. "I'm sorry, Louisa. I'm very sorry you saw all that." He kept his arms wrapped around her until she quit trembling and then pulled his handkerchief from his back pocket and wiped her tears.

"Martin, I don't want you to feel sorry. Please, don't feel sorry. I'm better now; I just needed to hold you."

He took her face in his hand and tipped her head back, brushing a kiss across her lips. "Maybe you should come with me when I see Dr. Newell on Friday. It might help to talk with him about this."

"Hmm, maybe." She brushed at the tear stains she had left behind on her husband's shirt. "Martin, I'm sorry I got so angry about the melon. I was trying to keep it together in front of Ruth and I guess the ... I guess the melon served as cover maybe."

"Oh, good. You're *not* going to eat the melon then?"

She patted a hand on his chest. "Come on, Martin. The others are probably wondering what's happened to us." Holding on to his good arm, she helped him to his feet. "I'm starving. *And* ... I quite fancy a bit of melon," she added as she walked off ahead of him.

"Louisa? Louisa!" Martin sighed.

Chapter 12

When Martin and Louisa joined the others at the table, Jeremy and Ruth were already tucking into their breakfast. And James Henry had finished his chopped banana and Melba toast.

"Sorry to keep you all waiting." Louisa pulled out a chair and took a seat.

"Oh, there's no need to apologise," Ruth said. "Your son was getting hungry, and Jeremy and I decided it would be impolite to leave him to dine alone."

Peering up at her nephew's wife, the elderly woman took note of her red rimmed and puffy eyes before dropping a spoonful of scrambled eggs into the toddler's bowl.

She set it down in front of him, and the little boy eyed it warily. He was accustomed to hard-boiled eggs. This appeared to be an entirely new substance. One which he now began to investigate with the eyes and mind of a proper scientist.

First, he observed, taking note of the lumpy consistency and the colour of the substance. Then he looked to his great-aunt, questioning the safety of actually ingesting it.

"Well, go ahead," the elderly woman said. "You want to grow up to be big and strong like your father, don't you, James Henry?"

He gave her a wonky grin before returning his attention to his breakfast. Having completed the first two steps in the scientific process, he now arrived at a hypothesis. Given the similarities between the said substance and the aforementioned chopped banana, as well as outcomes of prior experiments on substances provided by Aunt Ruth, the matter left in his bowl this morning was likely to be palatable and almost certainly harmless.

Moving on to step four. He carried out his experiments, first testing the tactile qualities of the lumps. Martin screwed up his face as his son watched a fistful of eggs ooze through his fingers.

The child then tested the viscous properties, placing a lump on his high chair tray before pressing down on it with his palm. He also took note that the lumps seemed to lack the adhesive quality of his morning banana when subjected to the same degree of applied pressure.

The final and most dangerous step in his experimental process was the tentative taste test. Licking the substance from the back of his hand, he immediately spit it out again, waiting to account for all variables before coming to his conclusion. The new substance was indeed safe to eat.

"Did Aunt Ruth give you some scrambled eggs, James? That's yummy, isn't it!" Louisa singsonged.

"How's the finger, Martin?" Jeremy asked.

"It's fine. Still numb, but ... it's fine," he said, ducking his head. "Mm."

Louisa spooned some now lukewarm eggs on to her plate before passing the bowl to her husband. "So, did we miss any interesting bits of village gossip while we were out of the room?" she asked.

Martin shot her a disapproving look. This was a quality in his wife that he found to be less than attractive. It smacked of the village ways that he so loathed.

"Not gossip, per se," Ruth said. "I did mention to Jeremy that I'd heard there had been quite a set-to at the pub last night. A local, lives over near St. Kew I understand, got into it with an out-of-town fisherman. Naturally, sides had to be taken by every other man in the establishment.

Martin looked up, an abrupt interest in the discussion taking hold. "Who was the local?"

Louisa and Ruth glanced over at him, surprised that he would insert himself into such a conversation.

"I haven't the foggiest idea," the elderly woman said. "But my source did tell me PC Penhale was nearly beside himself when he was given the opportunity to use both his Taser and his handcuffs at the scene of the crime."

"What! Why wasn't I called? Whoever was Tasered should have been medically evaluated!"

Ruth tipped her head down at him. "Need I remind you, Martin, that you are not a practising physician at the moment?"

Louisa noticed a subtle slumping of her husband's shoulders as he poked at his eggs. She reached under the table and caressed his knee. "Well, it turned out all right in the end, then?" she asked.

Ruth dabbed at her mouth with her napkin. "I would assume so. Some of the local men managed to subdue the rabble rousers. And if it makes you feel any better, Martin, Joe Penhale had forgotten to charge his Taser."

Martin threw his head back. *"Idiot,"* he muttered.

Jeremy sat, a smile growing on his face. "I'm really beginning to look forward to my new job. It sounds like quite a stimulating work environment."

Martin screwed up his face at him and mumbled unintelligibly.

The ring of a mobile could be heard and Martin reached into his pocket. "Ellingham!" he barked. "Ah. Yes, Chris."

He glanced around at the faces staring at him, and struggled to get to his feet. "Just a minute, Chris."

Ruth watched as her nephew walked laboriously from the room and out of earshot and then she turned to Louisa. "How do *you* feel about Martin's return to work? Do you think he's rushing things?"

Louisa set her teacup down. "I think that Martin *needs* to be back at work. How it will affect him physically remains to be seen, but I do know that he needs it to stay healthy mentally."

Ruth leaned towards her, lowering her voice. "Yes, but there are other things he could do that wouldn't be as physically taxing. The medical community would be delighted to have him publish another paper."

"Ruth, I'm anxious about it, too. But Jeremy will keep a close eye on him and will do all that he can to keep Martin's exposure to whatever bugs may be making the rounds to a minimum. Hmm, Jeremy?" she said, giving the aide a nod of her head.

"Yes, I will. Martin's been going through the files with me this week so that I'll have some familiarity with the patients before the practice opens again. And I agree with Louisa; Martin needs this."

Ruth shook her head. "I don't think he's ready. I just have a bad feeling about this."

It suddenly occurred to Louisa that Martin was Ruth's closest living relative. If anything should happen to him she would probably feel quite alone in the world.

"Ruth, you have Martin, but you also have James and me," she said. "I think between the three of us, we can make sure that nothing happens to him. Besides, we have Jeremy's help too, hmm?"

"I suppose you're right," Ruth said forcing a smile to her face.

Martin re-entered the kitchen, and the conversation was brought to an end.

"Jeremy, do you have plans for dinner this evening?" Martin asked as he dropped into the chair next to his wife.

"Not at the moment. What did you have in mind?"

He turned to Louisa. "That was Chris Parsons on the phone. He was wondering if Jeremy and I might be able to come over to Truro to have dinner with him tonight. There are some issues that need to be discussed before the surgery reopens. You and James are invited as well. Carole thought the three of you could go do something together while we're talking things over."

Louisa sighed and Martin noticed how tired she looked. "If it's too much, we don't need to go."

"No, no. I just have a lot to get done this weekend. But I do enjoy spending time with Chris and Carole. So, let's go."

"Maybe you should have a lie-down this afternoon," Martin suggested as he pulled his mobile from his pocket.

"We'll see. I have to get some laundry done, and I need to prepare for conferences in a couple of weeks." She got up from the table and began to clear the dishes.

"Let me do the laundry. Bring it down and put it by the washer. I can handle it."

Metal utensils clinked against ceramic as she picked up her husband's plate, kissing his cheek before straightening back up. "I think your day has been eventful enough already. You don't need to add to it with the surprises that James leaves in the laundry basket."

"I'm used to James's surprises. Please ... I want to help."

Louisa gave him a steely gaze. "You'll stop if it's too much, right?"

"Yes." He looked at his aide. "So, are you available?"

"Yeah. It'd be good to get some of this stuff hammered out. And I'd like to meet Dr. Parsons."

"Good, I'll call him back, then."

Arrangements were made for Jeremy to meet Chris and Martin in Truro at five o'clock, and then the aide left the Ellingham's for the day.

Louisa laid James down for his nap shortly after one o'clock. Martin was folding laundry at the kitchen table when his wife came into the kitchen.

"Well, he's out like a light. Should we go and do the same?" she said as she wrapped her arms around him from behind.

"I'm almost done here. You can get a head start if you like," he said as he folded a miniature pair of jeans and added them to the pile in front of him.

"All right, but don't be too long. And thank you for doing that," she said softly as she nuzzled her nose behind his ear.

Louisa was snoring lightly by the time Martin finished his laundry task. He kicked off his shoes and pulled his left leg up on to the bed, following it with his more troublesome right leg. He still needed to take hold of the fixators on that leg, using the added strength of his arms to get it hoisted on to the bed, but each week he could see improvement.

He slipped under the blankets and moved over next to her, before quickly drifting off to sleep.

They were awakened an hour later by the happy chortles of their son. Martin wrapped his arms around his wife and buried his face in her hair, inhaling deeply.

"I should go and get James. He's probably getting hungry," she said, tipping her head back to look at him.

He tightened his grip on her and rolled himself on to his back, pulling her on top of him.

"Be careful, Martin! We don't want to have to explain any more injuries to Chris, do we?" She pressed her lips to his, stroking them lightly with the tip of her tongue before trailing kisses across his cheek to the warm smooth skin behind his ear.

"I'm fine. And this feels very nice," he said, swallowing back the emotions that were tightening his throat. He caressed her shoulders and allowed his hand to wander down to the small of her back, working its way under her jumper.

Louisa took in a small gasp as her husband's warm palm pressed against her. "Martin, do you know how much I wanted this from you ... when things were so rocky between us?"

The movement of his hand stopped abruptly, and she pushed back to look at him. There was confusion in his eyes as he blinked them slowly.

"What?" she asked.

"I, er ... didn't know you wanted that. I knew that you weren't happy with me a lot of the time and sometimes you looked at me like..."

She tipped her head down and peered up at him. "Like what, Martin?"

He shook his head and began to push her away.

"I need to use the lavatory," he said as he tried to roll off the bed.

She grabbed hold of him and pushed him back down, causing him to wince as his shoulder joint shifted uncomfortably. He squirmed out from under her hands to a more antalgic position.

"Sorry, that hurt, didn't it?"

"Mm."

"Martin, I won't let you out of this bed until you complete that last thought. I looked at you ... how?"

He closed his eyes and blew out a slow breath. Then licking his lips, he said, "My mother. I thought that you were having regrets, and I was just trying not to—to make things worse. I just assumed that..."

"Assumed...?"

Martin rubbed his palm over his face. "Louisa, I—I saw that same expression on my mother's face throughout my life ... every time she looked at me. It wasn't an expression that meant she wanted affection from me. Quite the opposite."

"I think I understand," Louisa said softly. "It's too bad we couldn't talk about this before now, though. Why didn't you tell me?"

His brows pulled down as he stared off at the ceiling. "I'm not sure."

"It doesn't mean I don't want you if I have a moment of anger with you. You know that, don't you?" she said, brushing his cheek with her fingertips.

"I *understand* that now. But ... physically, I still react the same way. I don't seem to be able to control it."

Taking his hands in hers, Louisa kissed one, then the other, placing extra kisses on his freshly wounded finger. "Just as you will never be like your father, Martin, I will never *ever* be like your mother. I will always love you no matter how much you frustrate me. And I will always want you ... desire you physically. I enjoy it very much, and it reassures me ... lets me know you still want me."

"Mm, I see. I'm sorry then ... that I didn't reassure you before." He gave her a small smile. "From now on, I'll try to reassure you on a regular basis."

The baby's sweet chortles were rapidly devolving into cries of frustration and Louisa looked with resignation at her husband. "Well, I'm sorry to say that you'll have to reassure me later." She kissed him and slipped from the bed.

Chapter 13

Carole picked Louisa and James up at the restaurant where their husbands were meeting before they went off to look through the shops on Lemon Street.

Chris wasn't as particular as Martin about his dietary habits, but he had worked hard over the last couple of years to shed some weight. So, they met Jeremy at what was touted as the best sushi bar in Cornwall. Although, given that Cornwall wasn't a hotbed of cultural diversity and the restaurant was the *only* sushi bar in the county, the accolade earned it more snickers than punters.

Jeremy approached the table, and Martin gestured towards him, inadvertently revealing his freshly wounded digit. "Chris, this is Jeremy Portman, my—"

"What on earth did you do to your finger?" Chris interjected, latching on to his hand.

Martin pulled it away and shook his head. "Just a minor mishap in the kitchen. Jeremy put in a couple of stitches." He gave a nod towards his aide. "This is Jeremy Portman, Chris. Jeremy, this is Chris Parsons, the head of our CCG." He hesitated, fidgeting with his napkin and ducking his head. He gave Chris a glance out of the corner of his eye before mumbling, "And he's my friend."

Tugging at his ear, he cleared his throat as Chris and Jeremy exchanged knowing smiles before picking up their menus.

"So, Mart ... have you and Jeremy worked all the potential bugs out of this dicey plan of yours?"

"What d'you mean, *dicey?* I've thought this through, organised my patient files with *very* clear and detailed notes, Jeremy and I have been at the surgery every day for the last— "

"Martin! I was joking, mate."

"Ah." Martin poked at a piece of sashimi with his chopsticks and peered up at him, his cheeks nudging up.

Chris rested his elbows on the table. "Well, do you think you're going to be ready for the masses to descend on you?"

"I think Jeremy's as well informed of the ins and outs of the surgery as he possibly could be."

"Martin's outlined everything clearly, and we agree that safeguarding his health is of primary importance," Jeremy said.

"I'm sure there are issues that will come up as we move along, but both of us feel reasonably well prepared," Martin said, reaching for the bowl of prawn crackers in the middle of the table.

Chris leaned back in his chair. "Sounds like you have things well covered. But I think it'll be vitally important to lay down some ground rules for the villagers in advance. You mentioned the last time we were together that there's a radio station in Portwenn."

"Yesss?" Martin eyed him warily.

"I did some checking, and I understand that woman's phone-in show airs Tuesday and Thursday mornings."

"No, no, no, no, no. Don't ask me to do *that!*"

Chris stared at him with his arms crossed, and Martin's chin dropped to his chest. "Is it *really* necessary?"

Chris picked up a piece of shrimp and dipped it into a bowl of eel sauce. "It's not only necessary, Martin, I'm going to insist on it."

"Oh gawd," he groaned. "Caroline Bosman has to be one of the most annoying women in that entire village."

"Oh, come on. It won't be that bad. And it'd be the ideal medium to get the word spread about the surgery opening back up. It would also be an opportunity for you to answer any questions people may have."

"Oh, they'll have questions! None of them will have a *bloody* thing to do with the operation of their local surgery, though, I can guarantee you that much!"

"Martin, try not to get yourself worked up over this. It would give the villagers a chance to get all those prying questions answered ahead of time, so you won't have to be fielding them when they're sitting on the exam couch in your consulting room. And Jeremy could go with you ... deal with those more intrusive questions."

The aide sat, stock-still. "I—I—I'm not really very good in front of large groups."

Chris looked over at him imperiously. "Firstly, you won't *be* in front of a large group. Secondly, Dr. Ellingham will need you there," he said with finality. He slapped his hand down on the table. "So, that's that sorted."

Martin and Jeremy exchanged funereal glances before returning to their meal in silence.

When the waiter brought the cheques, Chris and Jeremy reached for their wallets. Martin held up a hand. "I've got it this time. I owe you both."

Jeremy gave him a bewildered look, and Martin held up his bandaged finger. He looked over at Chris and opened his mouth to speak, but the words refused to flow.

"I know mate," Chris said patting him on the shoulder.

All was quiet at the Parsons' home when they arrived. Louisa, James, and Carole had not yet returned. Chris directed his guests into the family room.

"This is a beautiful home, Dr. Parsons ... and a beautiful location," Jeremy said. The wood at the back of the lot was still visible in the darkening sky, and he was familiar with the neighbourhood. The yards were immaculately kept, and most had been professionally landscaped. Very different from his boss's tidy but rather Spartan home.

"Who's the musician?" he asked, noting the grand piano in the corner of the room and the two guitars parked on stands nearby.

"Well, the real musician in the family is my wife. She's a pianist. She's also a private music teacher. My son and I just play around with the guitars."

"I play, too. Do you mind?" Jeremy asked pointing to the instruments.

"No, not at all. I'd like to hear what you can do," Chris said as he settled himself into a chair.

Martin lumbered over to the wall of windows on the southeast side of the room and gazed out at the full moon rising behind the trees. The soft sound of the guitar chords took him back to his medical school days when Chris would wind down in the evenings strumming Beatles tunes.

"Mart ... Martin!"

Martin whipped his head around. "Mm, sorry?"

"I was showing Jeremy an arrangement that I'd found of Bizet's *Pearl Fishers Duet*. It's written for two guitars and piano. Why don't you come and give it a try with us?"

He looked back at his friend with a mix of disbelief and sheer embarrassment on his face. He turned to face the window.

"Oh, come on, Martin. I've really been wanting to try this out, but Dan won't play anything that predates John, George and Paul."

"Chris, I haven't played in twenty years."

"It's a simple arrangement, and you could just play the melody notes if you want. I'd just like to get an idea of what the piece sounds like."

He glanced towards the door; Louisa could be arriving soon.

"Come on, Mart. It'd be the perfect therapy for that hand of yours. And if you don't think you can work with the right one, just play the left-hand chords for now."

"I can't," he said, holding up his bandaged finger.

Chris walked briskly to his friend's side. "That reminds me; I need to see what kind of a job this guy does with a needle and thread," he said, giving Jeremy a nod.

He relinquished his finger with a roll of his eyes. "It's fine, Chris," he said as the gauze was peeled away.

"Hmm, very nicely done, Jeremy. Neat, not too tight, and if we leave the bandage off for a bit," he said, raising an eyebrow at his friend, "I don't see any reason that it should interfere with you getting those keys under your fingers, mate."

Taking another glance towards the door, Martin screwed up his face before reluctantly taking a seat on the bench.

"Just try out a C major scale first ... see how it feels," Chris said. "You'll want to start on that white key to the left of the two black keys there."

"Don't be a smart-arse." Martin batted his hand away and glowered up at him.

"Sorry. You did mention it'd been twenty years. I tell you what, we'll go chase up something to drink ... give you some time to warm up." He jerked his head in the direction of the kitchen, and Jeremy followed him out of the room.

Martin closed his eyes and tried to block out the churning sensation in his stomach. Then he placed his right hand on the keyboard and forced his reluctant fingers up and down the keys. The contracted muscles stretched painfully across the back of his hand. He grimaced and hissed out a breath before trying again.

"Martin's a really fine musician, but he hasn't played since medical school," Chris explained, handing Jeremy a bottle of beer before pulling one out of the refrigerator for himself.

"Why not? Just no time left in his schedule?"

Chris hesitated, smiling when he picked up on the single line of notes, recognisable as the melody to Rachmaninoff's 18th variation. "Ah, I love this one." He pulled a glass from the cupboard and filled it with water.

Shaking his head, he returned his attention to his friend's aide. "I'm not sure why Martin quit. Quite frankly, I'm shocked that I got him this far tonight."

Chris and Jeremy stood listening a bit longer before returning to the family room. Martin stopped playing when he saw the pair emerge from the kitchen, and he began to get up from the bench.

"Oh, no you don't, Mart. You said you'd try this Bizet thing with us, so stay right there." Chris spread the sheets of paper out on the rack in front of him before pulling two music stands out and setting a chair in front of each of them.

Martin's shoulders sagged. "Chris, I really don't feel like—"

"Okay, here we go. Three, four... "Chris said before starting the first measure.

A stream of air hissed from Martin's nose and he shot his friend a dark look before putting his fingers to the keys.

The trio fumbled through the first two lines before Martin dropped out, "No. No, this isn't going to work. You two take it on your own."

"What's wrong, Martin? You were doing just fine ... better than we were," Chris said.

Martin rubbed his eyes and placed his fingers back into position. The second time through, the parts began to blend together.

"Let's take it from the start again. Then we can pick it apart a bit more," Chris suggested.

Martin, ever-so-slowly, began to forget about his surroundings, pain, and limitations, and his focus turned to the music. "You're coming in on the front end of beat three in bar forty-four, Jeremy. And, Chris … watch in bar twenty-three. You're clipping that dotted minim short."

Chris peered up at him from behind his music. What he had found to be his friend's overly-censorious and annoying habit twenty years before was now music to his ears. He fought back a smile and returned his attention to the notes in front of him.

"Oh, that's lovely!" Louisa said as they entered the house from the garage a few minutes later. She moved towards the entry to the family room with James in her arms.

Grabbing on to her sleeve, Carole held her back, walking quietly over and peeking around the corner. She clapped a hand over her mouth and turned, wide-eyed.

"Well, miracles never cease! Chris got Martin on the piano! How do you suppose he managed that?" she whispered.

Louisa cocked her head at her. "What are you talking about?" she whispered back.

Carole realised too late that this was perhaps information Martin had never shared. She gave a jerk of her head and walked back to the other end of the room.

"You didn't know that Martin played the piano?"

"No!" Louisa whispered stridently.

"He used to play all the time but then just quit suddenly … refused whenever we'd ask. He never said what the problem was, but I think it had something to do with that bi— "Carole cleared her throat softly. "I think it had something to do with Edith."

"*Montgomery*?" Louisa hissed. Next to Margaret Ellingham, there was probably no woman she disliked more. Martin never discussed her, but she knew that her husband had been in a romantic relationship with her during medical school. And she had witnessed Joan's animus towards her when they ran into one another at the Royal Cornwall. Joan had taken her to an antenatal check-up, and as luck would have it, Edith happened to be her obstetrician.

The woman had appeared, seemingly out of nowhere, and was trying to ignite a flame in Martin again when Louisa returned from London to tell him she was pregnant. Edith's presence contributed greatly to her and Martin's difficulties during that time. Thankfully, she had since gone back to London to practise medicine.

Louisa would have liked to listen longer, but James Henry let out a squeal, putting a stop to the music.

Martin pushed himself up from the piano bench and reached quickly for his walker. By the time Carole and Louisa entered the room he was, what he determined to be, a safe distance away from the instrument.

"Well, hello. How was the big meeting?" Louisa asked, trying to sound nonchalant.

"It was productive," Chris said as he set his guitar back on the stand.

Martin cleared his throat and glanced nervously at his watch. "We should be going, don't you think. It'll be after eight by the time we get home."

"Yes, I suppose we should," Louisa replied. "I think James has worn himself out today."

Chris insisted on bandaging Martin's finger again before they left, so it was almost half eight when Louisa pulled up in front of Ruth's to drop her husband off before going to park the van up on Silvershell Road. Martin was tending to his fixator pins when she and the baby returned.

"I'll just go and put James to bed. Be down in a tick," she said as she stuck her head in the bathroom door.

"Mm, yes." Martin was feeling a mix of apprehension and guilt as he waited for his wife. He busied himself with his evening injection of heparin.

Louisa mentioned nothing about music when she returned, and Martin hoped she was still unaware of his covert ability.

They read quietly on the sofa together, Martin with his journal and Louisa with her latest novel. His hand stroked her head as it rested in his lap, just above the wound to his thigh.

She looked up from her book occasionally to see his gaze fixed on her. His eyes flitted back to his journal when he noticed her looking at him.

Ah, my Martin, she thought. There were moments when she wished her husband would lose his awkwardness around her, but she couldn't say that she didn't find it rather endearing.

The gentle but firm caresses across her head continued a while longer before they stopped and his thumb brushed slowly across her jawline.

She kept her focus on the page in front of her, but the words faded as his fingers began to toy with the top button on her blouse. With the dexterity of a surgeon, he slipped it through the buttonhole before working his way, one at a time, down to the lower hem.

Pretending to not take any notice of what he was doing, she reached up and, wetting her finger on her tongue, flipped to the next page in her book. She could feel his eyes on her, and she took in a long, deep breath, letting it out slowly.

Martin was engrossed, watching as her chest rose and fell with each breath. He pulled his hand away momentarily, allowing it to graze lightly against her blouse, pulling the lace trimmed edge to the side where it slipped down on to the sofa.

Louisa glanced up. His eyes had returned to the journal in his hand, but he stared blankly at the page as he again began to trace his way across his wife's skin, slowly nudging the other side of her blouse out of his way.

His gaze settled on her again as he ran his sturdy fingers along the outline of her bra. He stopped at her cleavage, and she heard him take in a long, slow breath. His desire deepened, and Louisa felt him pressing firmly against the side of her head. She heard a rustle of paper as he dispensed with his journal, laying it down on the table next to him before returning his attention fully to her.

Looking up from her book, she gave him one of her smiles that were meant only for him. Taking his hands in hers, she held them to her face. "I think we should move this activity on, don't you?"

"Mm. I do," he replied hoarsely, the words catching in his throat.

Martin seemed to move from tentative and tender caresses as they lay together on the sofa, to a pure and unbridled passion when they reached the bedroom, his lovemaking conducted with such reckless abandon that Louisa was left with no doubt whatsoever that he found her physically desirable.

"Did you find that reassuring?" he asked as they lay curled up in bed a short time later.

"Yes, Martin. That was very ... reassuring. Thank you."

"You're welcome," he said as he brushed her now tousled hair from her face. "Are you sleepy now?"

She moved in closer to his warm body. "Ahhh, yes ... I am." Reaching over, she turned out the light.

They lay quietly for some moments with Martin stroking his fingers lightly up and down her arm. Louisa finally broke the silence. "Why didn't you ever tell me that you play the piano?"

His movements stopped. "You never asked."

"Martin, why would that question have ever entered my mind? That's the kind of thing I would just expect you to share with me ... without my having to ask."

She waited for a reply but got none. "Why did you stop playing?"

Louisa listened to the seconds tick away on the clock in the hallway before he finally spoke.

"I only learned because it was compulsory at school. Everyone had to play a musical instrument, and I chose the piano. If I had chosen another instrument I would have been required to participate in band or orchestra, neither of which held any appeal. And I thought it would be another aid in developing my dexterity. It also fine tunes proprioceptive skills. It seemed like the logical choice, and it turned out that I was fairly good at it."

She lightly stroked his ear. "Well, that explains why you started, but you still haven't told me why you stopped. Did you enjoy it?"

Martin rolled on to his back and rubbed his palm across his forehead. "I enjoyed it at one time, but then ... I suppose I got busy with medical school ... didn't have the time anymore."

"But Carole said that you still played in medical school. There must have been more to it than that."

"I really don't know, Louisa. Does it even matter?"

"I don't know, Martin. It might. I think it'd be good to talk about it ... don't you?"

"Why is this so bloody important to you? I got busy; can we just leave it at that?" he said hotly.

Louisa tried to push her own hurt aside for the time being. "All right. I don't want to spoil what's been a wonderful evening. But ... well, I just think it'd be good to talk about it ... so I don't worry and it's not a secret that comes between us. I'd like to know that you trust me with your feelings again."

She leaned over and kissed him goodnight.

"Louisa."

"Hmm?"

"I *do* love you."

"Yes, Martin. You made that perfectly clear to me tonight. And I love you, too."

Chapter 14

Monday morning's physiotherapy session brought with it what was now becoming tedium to Martin. When he first started therapy, it seemed like an auspicious beginning to a much-anticipated end of the nightmare that he and Louisa had been living. But he seemed to be getting more impatient as time went by, and his therapists had taken notice.

"Martin, I had a discussion with Mr. Christianson after you left on Friday," Kieran said. "He'd like us to start getting you used to using crutches while you're here, but he wants to get you fitted with a different brace for that shoulder before we start working with you."

The therapist reached for his pot of cocoa butter, slathering it over his palms before beginning to massage the aches and pains, left by the day's session, from his patient's limbs.

"He mentioned that he has you scheduled for a check-up tomorrow. He'll set something up with an orthotist for you as well."

Martin sighed. Just thinking about the gruelling day ahead was tiring. Tests, examinations, and now an orthotic fitting, in addition to his usual physiotherapy. The upside of all the poking and prodding would be a literal step in the right direction. He would certainly not mind being rid of the walker.

"Can you have me on crutches in two we—ahwrr!" Martin grimaced and pulled away as the therapist ran his hands over his injured forearm. "Geesh, be careful!"

Kieran pulled his hands back quickly and looked at his patient with a furrowed brow. "What's up with the arm, Martin? There a problem?"

He shook his head and wiped his palm across his face. "It's just nerve pain. It's fine now."

The therapist eyed him suspiciously as he wiped the cocoa butter from his hands with a small towel. "Did you have a fall ... or a blow to that arm over the weekend?"

Martin could feel the heat rising in his face, not so much a result of the embarrassment he was feeling, although that was playing a role in the reddening of his cheeks, but rather a result of his frantic attempt to come up with a plausible explanation for his current misery. He was not going to discuss his rather enthusiastic response to his wife's feminine allure, some thirty-six hours prior, with someone barely past the age of consent.

"I overdid it a bit this weekend is all. I'll be fine in a couple of days," he said more tersely than he'd intended. "Are we done here?" he asked as he sat himself up on the table and swung his legs over the side.

Kieran stepped out of the way. "Apparently so. Be sure you mention the arm pain to Mr. Christianson when you see him tomorrow. All right?"

Martin glanced up at the young man. "Mm."

The trip back to Portwenn was a quiet one, both patient and aide lost in their own thoughts. Martin's eyes tracked a lorry as it travelled down a dirt lane, approaching the highway from the left, dust swirling up into the air in cyclonic fashion. His muscles tensed as they neared the intersection and the vehicle didn't appear to be slowing.

"Jeremy, watch out!" he barked, spasms causing a crushing pain in his chest as a rush of adrenaline coursed through him.

The aide slammed on the brakes and the van skidded to a stop. The lorry shot across the road in front of them before continuing on down the lane.

Martin's hands trembled as he watched the rear end of the vehicle rush away from them, still towing a load of road dust behind it.

“Arse!” Jeremy yelled impotently at the driver as he continued on his way, probably oblivious of the disaster that had just been averted.

“Sorry, I didn’t even see the guy,” the aide said as he glanced over at his patient. Martin had his palm held to his face and the metal fixator on his right arm clicked rapidly against the fixator in his thigh.

Jeremy said nothing but made a left turn off the tarmac pavement on to a small dirt road. Martin didn’t seem to notice the deviation from their normal route home until the aide stopped the van next to a small pub.

“I need to use the lavatory,” Jeremy said before stepping out on to the gravel parking area. “I’ll be right back.”

Martin sat in the van, his eyes closed as he tried to slow his breathing and regain his composure. Jeremy returned a short time later with a shot glass in his hand.

After a few moments of rustling in his bag in the back seat, he pulled the passenger side door open and pressed a small tablet into his patient’s hand. “Doctors orders. I just spoke with Mr. Christianson. He wants you to take this ... it’s midazolam,” the young man said. He held out the glass of amber coloured liquid.

“I can’t drink this, Jeremy! Good God! Midazolam, morphine, and alcohol? Are you trying to kill me?”

The aide gave him a crooked grin. “It’s apple juice, mate. I think the incidence of adverse drug interactions is pretty low.”

Martin pulled in his chin. “Mm.” He took the glass and, with fine tremors still rippling through him, he swallowed down the medication.

“That’s likely to make you sleepy, so let’s get you home for a lie-down, eh?” The young man took the glass and ran it into the pub before getting back behind the wheel.

Martin slept for more than two hours that afternoon. He woke with a ravenous appetite but only a murky recollection of the trip home from therapy earlier in the day.

Jeremy said nothing about the near collision with the lorry and neither did Martin. When Louisa got home late that afternoon the aide sat down with them for a cup of tea.

"And how was your day?" she asked as she leaned over to kiss her husband before taking a seat next to him.

"Erm, it was fine … I guess." He thought for a moment, struggling to remember the morning's events.

Louisa pulled the tea bag from her cup and added a bit of milk. "What did you do at therapy? Anything different?"

He again sat, trying to remember what he'd been doing just hours before. "Mm, I'm not sure, something about using crutches … maybe."

"Louisa, Martin's not remembering very much because I gave him some midazolam on the way back to Portwenn."

He turned to his patient who sat staring at him with a bemused expression on his face. "There was a small incident. We quite nearly collided with a lorry on the highway. I was concerned about the reaction you had, so I stopped at a pub and called Ed Christianson."

Martin quickly averted his eyes, staring into his teacup for a few moments before pushing himself to his feet. "Excuse me," he said before heading down the hall.

Louisa began to get up to follow after him, but Jeremy gave her a shake of his head and she sat back down.

"Just give him a minute, then go talk to him," he said as he scooped two more spoonfuls of sugar into his cup.

"What happened, Jeremy?"

"Some idiot … blew right past the stop sign and cut across the road in front of us. If Martin hadn't yelled at me to stop, the moron would have ploughed right into us.

"He was shaking so bad afterwards that I thought he was going to have a complete melt-down. Mr. Christianson recommended the midazolam."

Louisa sighed. "Oh, Martin."

Jeremy got up and dug around in his bag, retrieving a package of chocolate digestives. "Good for whatever ails you," he said, holding the package out at arm's length.

She gave him a feeble smile and took one of the biscuits from the package. "They always seem to make *me* feel better."

"Martin definitely needs to talk this over with his psychiatrist the next time he sees him," the young man said as he fingered the handle of his teacup. "Dr. Newell may decide to take a wait and see approach, but he'll likely have some tips for him, too, as to how to deal with something like this in future."

He brushed the crumbs from his hands and pushed himself away from the table. "Would you like me to stay a bit longer ... until you've had a chance to talk with Martin?"

"No. No, I'll be fine now, Jeremy." Louisa got up from her chair and moved towards the hallway. "Thank you so much for all that you've done for Martin. And especially for being his friend."

Jeremy hesitated and then cocked his head. "No need to thank me. I consider both a privilege." He reached for his jacket and flipped it over his arm. "Call me if you need me. I'll be in the village until later this evening," he said, pulling the door shut behind him.

"Martin, may I come in?" Louisa asked as she stuck her head in the bedroom doorway a few moments later.

He was silent but gestured to her. She sat down and embraced him.

"Louisa, I don't know if I can do this," he said.

She pulled back, shaking her head. "What do you mean by ... *this*?"

He leaned over, resting his head in his hands. "Trying to get this mess in my head all sorted. At least I felt some sense of control before. I knew how to keep everything in order.

"Now I'm supposed to try to remember things that I'd worked hard to forget, to behave in a way that feels ... just wrong. I'm supposed to let down my defences and suddenly trust people. Open up my—my *heart* to you about things that I've worked for years to keep hidden.

"Not to mention trying to get back on my feet! And not just literally speaking! Trying to get a practice up and running again. Being a better *husband* ... and a *father*! I never would have thought those two things to even be in the realm of possibility a few years ago! I don't think I can do this, Louisa!"

"Martin, I don't think things are as bad as they seem at the moment. You've had a stressful and tiring day," she said, caressing his thigh.

He rubbed his fingers roughly through his hair. "I'm sorry. Maybe you should go ... leave me be for a while."

She pulled in a deep breath as she tried to muster her own confidence. "Okay. James and I'll go to the green grocers. Maybe pick up a fish ... hmm?" she said as she brushed her fingers across his cheek.

He sat silent before reaching for his walker and heading towards the bathroom.

Louisa set off with James, tipping her head forward into the wind and pulling the collar of her coat up protectively around her neck.

"Well, hello there. Out to pick up your dinner?" a very recognisable voice said as she stood in the checkout queue at the market.

"Oh, Ruth! Yes, I'm going to fix a nice dinner for Martin tonight." She gave the old woman a smile. "Or at least try to. He's not had the best day." She looked around for a private spot to talk before turning to the elderly woman. "Do you have time for a cuppa ... a chat?"

"Shall we go buy the child a cupcake?" Ruth asked, giving her head a nod in the baby's direction.

"Just don't tell Martin. He'll surely blame it on the sugar if James should have one of his restless nights."

They walked down to the coffee shop on Fore Street and found a table in a quiet corner.

"All right, let's hear it," Ruth said as they sat waiting for their order to arrive.

"I don't know how to help Martin. He's terribly discouraged, Ruth. He's overwhelmed by everything right now, and he doesn't think he can do all that he's being asked to do."

"Well, I told him I thought he was going back to work too early."

Louisa gave the woman a scowl. "I don't think that's the problem, Ruth. He's pushing me away again. I found out the other night that he plays the piano. He'd never told me that. I tried to get him to talk about why he quit, and he shut me out again."

The conversation came to a momentary halt when the waitress brought their tea and James's cupcake to the table. Louisa waited until the young woman was out of earshot before continuing. "I think he feels like he's lost control. And I think that frightens him ... adds to the stress he's already under because of his injuries."

"Rightly so. He feels as if he's lost control because he *has* lost control. Over the course of his life, he'd figured out a way to keep all those monsters from his past at bay. But now they've been released, and this time he's having to get control of them all at once. He can't deal with them one at a time as he did before."

Ruth took a sip from her cup before setting it back down and cocking her head at her nephew's wife. "I told Martin that he could change but that he'd have to work hard at it. I do believe he *can* change, but none of us knew that he would have this accident to deal with as well. He needs your encouragement, Louisa, but don't push him."

Louisa pulled her sleeve back to check her watch. "Oh dear, we'd better get going if I'm going to make Martin's carbohydrate curfew." She gave Ruth a tepid smile. "You're welcome to join us."

"Oh, thank you dear. But Al and Morwenna are coming to my house for dinner. Al has it in his head that we need to have an open house at the farm. Let the villagers see what we have to offer, I suppose. He thinks he has a marketing strategy, so I'll just play along."

Ruth headed back up Roscarrock Hill, and Louisa and James trudged back to Dolphin Street, the wind at their backs this time.

Chapter 15

Louisa had taken Tuesday off to accompany her husband to his doctor's appointment. This had the added benefit of allowing them to lie in bed just a bit longer than weekdays normally allowed.

It was one of those rare days when she woke before Martin. His slow, rhythmic breaths brushed her cheek, bringing a smile to her face. She propped herself up on her elbow and watched him.

The scars on his face were just barely visible now, and the weight that he had put on since the accident had softened the angles of his face. The hollows in his cheeks had filled in, giving him more of the boyish appearance she had been so charmed by when they first met.

His arm lay across his side, and she ran her finger lightly along the fixator that held the bones in place as they healed. The swelling was down significantly, and the bruising was almost completely gone. Despite his obvious discouragement the day before, Martin had come far, both physically and mentally ... emotionally.

Maybe he's been focusing too much on what's still ahead of him, she thought. *Maybe I've been too focused on the future as well. Not giving him the encouragement he needs to get through each day. But in all fairness, it'd be easier to squeeze blood from a stone than to get Martin to admit to needing anything from me.*

Louisa stroked her hand over his forearm, and he woke with a start, pulling his arm back.

"Sorry, I didn't mean to disturb you," she said as she nuzzled her nose into his neck. "Did you sleep well?"

"I slept ... fine. Thank you." He rolled on to his back and rubbed a broad palm over his face.

Louisa sat back against the headboard and pulled gently at his vest, patting her hand on her thigh. "Can you come lie over here for a while?"

He rolled towards her, resting his head in her lap and draping his injured arm over her legs.

"That's better." She smoothed her palm over the top of his head, trying to tame a rogue tuft of hair that was standing on end. "You were feeling pretty overwhelmed yesterday, weren't you?"

"Oh, let's just forget about yesterday," he groaned.

"We don't have to talk about it if you don't want to, but I do want you to know that I'm here for you in whatever way you need me to be. Even if it's to be quiet and leave you alone."

He shook his head. "I'm sorry if I hurt your feelings. That really wasn't my intent. I was ... I embarrassed myself when I couldn't remember anything, and then everything else just ..." He rolled off his wife's lap and pushed himself up before swinging his legs over the side of the bed.

"Do you think you've been letting yourself think too much about the future instead of focusing on what you need to do today?" Louisa got up on her knees and wrapped her arms around his chest, resting her chin on his shoulder. "Maybe that's why you were feeling so overwhelmed."

He blew a hiss of air through his nose. "I *have* to think about the future so that I know what I need to get done *today*, Louisa. I think I need to prioritise though and..." He glanced at her over his shoulder. "I was wondering if you might have time to help me with a couple of things."

Louisa jumped down off the bed. "I'd make time. Whatever you need, Martin."

His face contorted at the very thought. "Chris is insisting that I go on that awful phone-in show Caroline does. He wants

Jeremy and me to discuss the protocols we'll be using to determine which patients will be seen by me and which will get sent over to Wadebridge. Do you think you could help us prepare for the kind of questions that are likely to be asked?"

She knitted her brow and began to worry her lip. "Maybe it would be better if you just talked to Caroline ... didn't *take* questions."

Martin sat rubbing his thumb into the palm of the opposite hand, a mannerism that Louisa knew to be a sure sign of stress. "Chris thinks that I *should* open it up for questions ... get them answered now rather than to have to deal with them in the surgery."

"Oh, dear. This could be interesting, hmm?" Louisa said as she tapped her fingertips together.

"I'd be happy if that's all it was ... interesting."

"I'm afraid that most of the villagers don't share the same set of boundaries that you and I do. You could get some questions that might seem a bit ... intrusive."

"Of course, they'll be intrusive! It *is* Portwenn! And you certainly can't say that my previous appearances on Caroline's show have been exactly brilliant! I'm bound to make a fool of myself!"

He flopped back on the bed. "Oh, gawd. I've embarrassed myself every time I've been on that moronic show. This time I'll embarrass you as well."

Louisa lay down next to him, lightly stroking his chest. "Martin, I don't want you to worry about embarrassing *me*. If you go on Radio Portwenn and swear a blue streak, I'll still be proud of you. The only thing that I'm concerned with is that the villagers understand, in no uncertain terms, that they *must* follow the rules that you and Jeremy lay out for them or they don't get in to see you. You handle their questions however you see fit. I'll support you no matter what comes out of that mouth of yours."

Her gaze settled on his, and the tension in his face eased into the faraway look of a lovesick teenager. She leaned over and kissed him gently. "Erm, you said there were a *couple* of things you'd like my help with. What's the second thing?"

"Ah, yes." He blinked his eyes and tried to tune out the physical sensations that had begun to stir in him. "Would you be free to go out for dinner with me tonight?"

Louisa's eyes sparkled as her lips spread into a smile. "Are you asking me out ... on a date?"

"Yes ... I am," he said softly as a blush spread up his neck and across his cheeks. "If—if—if you're free tonight, that is. I should tell you though that my rather atypical attire is apt to attract attention."

"Well, everyone's going to have to adjust to seeing you out of your suit at some point, hmm?"

His brows snapped down. "I was referring to the fixators, Louisa."

"I see." She watched him for a moment and then leaned over, pressing her lips to his.

He pulled back a bit, his eyes crossing slightly as he tried to bring her proximate image into focus. "I'm serious, Louisa; people will be gawping."

He sighed involuntarily as his wife reached under his vest and caressed his chest. "Well, I *have* been fairly warned. I think I'm willing to take my chances. But right now, I think we better get up and get going or you're going to be late for therapy," she said, tapping her finger on the end of his nose.

"Mm, yes."

The morning progressed quickly. When Martin was finished with his therapy session in Wadebridge, they continued on to Truro, stopping for lunch before they had to be at the hospital for the scheduled CT scans, x-rays and lab work. They were then sent upstairs to meet with Mr. Christianson in his office.

"Martin, good to see you. You as well, Louisa." Ed gestured for them to take a seat. "Well, you're looking good," he said as he scrutinised his patient. "You have a bit more meat on those bones."

Louisa gave Martin a smile and patted him on the knee.

The surgeon opened up the thick file of medical records in front of him and then brought up an image on the computer monitor on his desk, turning it around so that Martin and Louisa could see what he was studying so intently.

"This is the CT of your husband's lungs, Louisa. They're all completely clear this time around. Not a real surprise, but it's always a relief to see a clean pulmonary image in someone with Martin's recent medical history." He leaned back in his chair and folded his hands behind his head. "No coughing or chest pain, Martin?"

"Not really. I've been feeling a bit of chest pain, but just from the trauma and thoracotomy."

Ed scribbled some notes into his file before bringing up a second image. "The left tibial fracture is showing quite a bit more hard callous formation this time around," he said, squinting his eyes at the screen.

"And here's the right one ... also looks good. Actually, better than I expected. You must be feeding him well, Louisa."

Martin reached over and surreptitiously squeezed his wife's hand.

"That left leg will need a bit more time than the right one of course, but things are moving in the proper direction. I'm very pleased, Martin. If it weren't for that bloody arm of yours we'd have you on crutches by now ... getting around a bit more easily."

"What *about* the arm?" Martin asked, pulling his hand away from his wife's. "Is there a problem?"

Ed leaned forward, placing his elbows on his desk and interlocking his fingers. "Sorry, I didn't mean to worry you. As we had expected, the arm is taking longer to heal."

Turning to Louisa, the surgeon explained, "There's a layer of tissue on the outside of our bones that contains nutrient rich cells that are needed in fracture repair. Your husband had a lot of damage to that layer of tissue. It was scraped away by the trauma during the accident as well as our repeated debridements of the non-viable tissue. New periosteal tissue had to form before the bone could be replaced, hence the delay in the healing in that arm. It's coming along though."

Ed brought up the CT scan of Martin's fractured radius and ulna and pointed out the noticeable increase in hard callous since the last scan was taken.

"I think we're to a point where we can let you graduate to crutches. I have concerns about that shoulder. But we can get you fitted with a brace that'll give you enough support to bear the weight that you'll be putting on it. You'll have to use the underarm crutches, of course. The forearm crutches would put way too much stress on your forearm."

"How long then ... before I can get rid of the walker?" Martin asked. His fingers tapped a frenetic rhythm on the armrest of his chair.

"I'll stay in touch with your physiotherapists, but if all goes well with therapy ... two weeks?" Ed cocked his head at his patient. "Why, haven't you formed an attachment to your companion over there yet?" he asked, nodding his head towards the mobility device sitting near the desk.

Martin curled his lip at the apparatus and mumbled unintelligibly.

Ed gave his patient an understanding smile. "You two didn't hit it off then I take it."

"It's a necessary evil," Martin answered, keeping his eyes glued to the floor.

Ed rolled his chair back and stood up to walk around the desk. "When I do give you the go ahead to transition to the crutches, Martin, I fully expect that you'll use good judgement on those hills over there in Portwenn. Put as much weight on those bones as is tolerable ... speed up the healing process ... but don't try to go somewhere if you aren't sure you can handle it safely. You don't want to take a tumble and end up back here in hospital.

"Yes."

Martin began to get up from his chair, but Ed wagged a finger at him. "Just hang on, Martin. Louisa, could you give us a minute please?"

She looked hesitantly at her husband before getting up and heading towards the door. Then she turned, giving him an uneasy smile. "I'll be right outside if you need me."

Ed waited for the door to close before turning back to his patient. "I wanted to give you an opportunity to address any more private concerns that you might have, Martin. Any problems you'd like to discuss between the two of us?"

He pulled in his chin. "I'm not sure what you're getting at, Ed. What did you have in mind?"

The surgeon went back around his desk and dropped into his chair. "I checked in with your physiotherapists before you arrived, just to get an up-to-date assessment of how you were progressing. There was some mention of pain in that arm," he said, giving a nod towards the aforementioned limb. "You didn't bring it up in front of your wife, so I thought you might prefer to discuss it between the two of us.

Martin squirmed uncomfortably. "No, I—I just overdid it this weekend. Just some residual nerve pain."

Ed gave him a penetrating stare. "Tell me about the pain. How severe is it? Is it a stabbing pain, burning pain, an ache ... is it constant or only triggered by movement?"

"Again ... it's just residual nerve pain. Possibly a bit of trouble with vibrational allodynia. The lymphatic massage in therapy yesterday ... well, it caused pain."

"Has the onset been sudden?" the surgeon persisted.

"*As—I—said*—it's just residual nerve pain. It's been sensitive since the accident, but I overdid it this weekend. I aggravated the nerves is all. It'll be fine. I just need to take it a bit easier and let things calm down," Martin said. "Nothing to worry about."

Ed tapped his biro on his desk impatiently. "Well, if you don't mind, I'd like to know what it was you were doing that inflamed those nerves to that degree."

"I *do* mind! That's none of your bloody business!"

"Okay, okay. I think I get the picture. Well, I didn't see anything on the CT images that could be cause for concern, so take it easy and let me know if you don't see definite improvement in the next couple of days. We can try cortisone injections if needs be. Don't make yourself suffer with this. Ice that arm before you go to bed tonight. See if that seems to help. And you better stick with a different position when you're *overdoing* it. You were probably putting too much weight on that..."

"Yes, all right! You don't need to spell it out for me!"

Martin got to his feet and Ed stood up to accompany him to the door. "I hear you're going on the radio on Thursday."

Martin whirled his head around. "Thursday? Who told you that?"

"Parsons. He was probably going to call you tonight." Ed pulled the door open.

"Oh, that's just lovely. That only gives me two bloody days to prepare for the onslaught of inane questions."

The surgeon patted his shoulder. "Well, good luck with it. And let me know if the pain doesn't improve within the next couple of days."

"Your appointment went well, don't you think?" Louisa said as they headed out of Truro.

"Yes. Yes, I do." Martin cleared his throat. "I, er ... thought maybe we could go to The Mote for dinner tonight. It's close to Ruth's, and there's not much of a hill between the cottage and the restaurant. I should be able to navigate it fairly easily."

"That sounds wonderful. I'm really looking forward to this, Martin. Dinner out and a romantic walk on top of it ... what more could a girl ask for?"

Martin could see the excitement in his wife's eyes, and he felt a sudden nervousness about disappointing her. He could count on one hand the number of actual dates they'd had, and he'd mucked up every one of them. And the cards were stacked against him for a better outcome this time around.

Chapter 16

Poppy had agreed to stay late Tuesday evening to watch James while his parents went out. The boy sat in his highchair where, in the tradition of the great Cornish abstract painters of the famous St. Ives School, he was happily smearing what was left of his dinner into a Pollock-esque painting.

The childminder ran a wet washcloth over his face, removing the residue of peas and carrots before erasing the masterpiece from the highchair tray.

"We're going to head out now, Poppy," Louisa said as she appeared in the kitchen doorway. "Be sure and call if you have any problems. We'll be right over here at The Mote."

"I will Mrs. Ellingham. Have a good time."

Martin came through from the hall and followed his wife across the kitchen, stopping to place the backs of his fingers against his son's forehead before brushing them across his cheek. "Be good for Poppy, James."

"We'll be home in time to put him to bed." Louisa placed a kiss on the top of her son's head before getting the door for her husband.

Martin stepped carefully over the threshold and out into the crisp autumn air. He pulled his recalcitrant right leg forward as he descended the ramp leading away from the back entryway, mindful to not let his toes drag as he did so.

"I've been wondering ... do you think we should ask Poppy to call us by our first names?" Louisa asked as she slowed her pace when she noticed him beginning to lag behind. "We practically insisted that Jeremy be less formal with us."

"Mm, yes," Martin said, unthinking. He tried to focus his attention on the precarious cobblestones under his feet as he navigated his way down the hill to Middle Street.

Louisa continued, "I'd just hate to have her think that we feel any differently about her than we do Jeremy. You know?"

He again tried to tune her out, determined to avoid any falls that could result in pain and embarrassment. But her voice hummed in his ears like the drone of a pesky fly.

"I want her to know that we don't see her job as any less important than the work Jeremy does for us. I can't imagine what the last months would have been like without her. She's been a—"

"*Louisa!* For goodness' sake, will you please be quiet?" Martin came to a stop and took in a deep breath. "It's fine, Louisa. Whatever you think; it's fine with me."

She folded her arms across her chest. "You weren't even listening, were you?"

Martin grimaced as his gaze darted up and down the path. "Louisa, I—" He glanced around again. "I don't want to end up on the ground. I'm trying to concentrate on staying upright. The last thing I want right now is for Joe Penhale to be hauling me back to my feet."

Her arms unfurled and she gave him a sympathetic smile. "Sorry. Can I help in any way—besides being quiet?"

"No."

By the time they reached the bottom of the hill, Louisa was becoming concerned by her husband's heavy breathing as well as his flushed, tense, and sweaty face. "How 'bout we sit for a bit before we go eat. Enjoy the sunset, maybe?"

"Mm, I don't know if that's a good idea. You might get a chill," he said. Air rushed in and out of his lungs as he critically eyed her fashionable but impractically lightweight jacket.

"You'll need to keep me warm then, won't you." She took a seat on the bench outside The Mote and patted her hand beside her. "Come on."

Martin hesitated before dropping down heavily next to her, grunting with the impact of the abrupt landing. He reached his good arm around her shoulders and tightened his grip to steady his fatigued and trembling muscles.

"This is nice," she said as she nestled in against him. She stroked her palm over his injured arm, and he pulled in a sharp breath, yanking it away.

"What's the matter, Martin?"

He hesitated and then groaned softly as his chin dropped to his chest. "Our ... activity the other night has caused a bit of a problem. But it's—"

"You mean *sex?* Your ... *reassuring* me the other night has caused a problem? Is this what you and Ed were talking about?"

"*Louisa*, keep your voice down. Please." His eyes darted around, taking note of the gaggle of teenage girls coming down Fore Street.

Her voice dropped to a murmur. "Did our *activity* hurt you, Martin?"

"*No!* Of course not," he hissed. "It's just caused a bit of discomfort." He straightened himself and donned his oratorical voice. "Vibrational allodynia— it's perhaps best defined as a painful response to a non-painful stimulus. Likely caused by a change in the dorsal horn of the spinal cord that gives non-noxious sensory informa—"

"Yes, yes, yes. I get the picture." Louisa sighed. "Well, we better be more careful in future then, hmm?"

Martin looked down at her, and his chest filled reflexively with air. "You're very beautiful, Louisa."

"Thank you, Martin." She wiggled in closer.

Despite the chill in the air, the setting sun cast a pink hue over the shops and houses around the Platt, creating an illusion of warmth. The fishing boats were just beginning to come into the harbour, and the raucous herring gulls, excited by the prospect of an easy meal, mewed and guffawed at one another like a platoon of army drill sergeants trying to instil discipline into their new recruits.

Feeling a shiver ripple through his wife's body, Martin tightened his grip on her. "Are you getting cold? Maybe we should go inside now."

"I *was* getting cold, but you're nice and toasty. And this is just absolutely wonderful. This date was a very good idea." She reached up and kissed his cheek.

His eyes sparkled in the light that was being reflected off the water, and Louisa couldn't resist placing a more intimate kiss on his lips. "This is very romantic. Thank you."

She smiled as she watched him pull his chin in self-consciously before muttering an awkward, "You're welcome."

Several diners had entered the restaurant since they had been sitting together, and Martin suggested again that they should perhaps go inside—get a table before the evening rush began. Louisa reluctantly acquiesced, helping him to his feet.

The waitress, a young woman who looked vaguely familiar to Martin, led them to a table along a wall of windows opposite the door. He grumbled under his breath as every pair of eyes in the establishment followed him across the room.

"I'm really glad that you're going to be okay ... erm, Dr. Ellingham," the waitress said, giving him a shy, coquettish grin as she handed them their menus.

"Mm, yes." Martin peered at the girl, struggling to put a name to her face.

"I'll be back in a few minutes to take your order," she said before scurrying off to tend to other patrons.

Louisa leaned over and spoke softly into his ear. "Melanie Gibson."

"What's that?"

"The waitress. It looked like you were trying to sort out who she was. It's Melanie Gibson, Alan's daughter."

"Ah," he said, tipping his head back. He refocused his eyes on his menu, pausing from his perusal now and then to cast furtive glances around him.

Louisa noticed her husband's lip curl slightly, and she followed his gaze across the room. Jimmy and Jen Millinger, Martin's erstwhile receptionist's aunt and uncle, were sitting on the opposite side of the room. Jimmy made no attempt to be discreet as he eyed Martin up and down.

"So ... what looks good to you tonight?" she asked.

He returned his attention to the menu. "Erm ... I think I'll have the sea bass. Yes ... I'm going to have the sea bass," he said with finality as he nodded and forced a small smile.

She laid her menu down. "I thought I'd get the linguine."

Their waitress approached, carrying a tray with two glasses and a pitcher of water. She blushed noticeably as she set Martin's glass down in front of him, an involuntary response that Louisa did not fail to notice.

"Are you ready to order?" she asked as she turned to Louisa.

"Yes, I'd like the linguine. And if I could get a small side salad with balsamic vinaigrette as well, please." She smiled up at the girl and handed her the menu.

Martin kept his eyes focused on his lap as he placed his order. Then, fixing his gaze on his wife, he slid his menu across the table towards the waitress.

"Would either of you like a glass of wine with your meal?" she asked.

"Just water for me," Martin said before clearing his throat nervously.

Louisa smiled up at her. "For me too, Melanie."

Glancing over her shoulder as the waitress hurried away, she turned to her husband. "What was *that* all about?"

"I'm sorry?"

"You know ... all the... "She circled her hand in the air before giving a jab with her thumb in the girl's direction.

"Mm. Ah..." Martin fidgeted with the silverware in front of him.

He mentally ran through his options. He could tell his wife about the unwanted attentions of the juvenile femme fatale, or he could revert to his fail-safe and plead doctor-patient confidentiality. Although the second option couldn't really be considered legitimate given the fact that, aside from the first unscheduled emergency visit to his surgery, Melanie Gibson's follow-up visits couldn't be classified as medical in nature.

He lifted his hand to tug at the tie that usually encircled his neck before reaching instead for his ear. "She, ah ... She—she came into the surgery one day with a dislocated shoulder. I reduced it for her and she became—" he grimaced "—*besotted* with me." Poking at his knife, he sent it spinning slowly in one direction and then the other.

"Oh, that's sweet, Martin." Louisa smiled at him as she reached for her glass of water.

He gave the fork a more forceful jab, sending it clattering to the floor. "It wasn't *sweet*, Louisa! It was awful!" he hissed out in a conspiratorial manner.

He leaned over the table. "She came by wanting to go for a walk! And she showed up in my consulting room another time, convinced there was something wrong with her because she couldn't concentrate at school. There she stood, next to my desk, while she fiddled around with the buttons on her jumper! Like a—a—a *pubescent* Mrs. Tishell!

"There most certainly *was* something wrong with her!" He leaned forward. "I found her in my bed one night!" He cleared his throat again. "And she baked me a cake."

Louisa giggled and gave him an impish grin. "You do realise, Martin ... in Portwenn, if a girl bakes you a cake and you accep—" She stopped abruptly when her husband's fiery eyes snapped up at her.

"It wasn't funny." He picked up his napkin and shook it out vigorously before slapping it down on his lap. "It's the kind of thing that can cost a doctor his licence ... or worse."

The smile on her face faded as she realised the veracity of her husband's words. "I'm sorry. That hadn't occurred to me."

She looked across the table at him as he studied his hands, slowly rubbing his palms together. "Excuse me, I need the lavatory," she said, slipping her handbag from the back of the chair.

Martin watched his wife as she disappeared down the hallway leading to the toilets and breathed out a heavy sigh. "Bugger!" he muttered under his breath. *I mucked it up again.*

Their meals were on the table when she returned. Martin had managed to accept them without making actual eye contact with the waitress.

Louisa took a detour on her way back to her seat and leaned over her husband. Taking his face in her hands, she branded his cheek with a pink lipstick kiss.

He pulled back. "Louisa! People are watching!"

"Sorry. It must be that fetching atypical attire."

"Mm, yes. Well, your dinner's getting cold."

She gave him one of her smiles that made him feel as though he mattered and returned to her chair.

They ate in silence for some time, Martin keeping his gaze focused on his plate. Louisa finally punctuated the awkward air space between them. "What do you and Jeremy have planned for Caroline's show on Thursday?"

Martin looked up. "We thought it would be best to start by having Jeremy lay out the ground rules first, then go over what the patients can expect when they see me. My limitations and the fixators ... that sort of thing. Then I guess I'll have to answer questions." His lip curled into a sneer.

"May I make a suggestion?"

He sat up straighter in his chair. "Certainly."

"You might conclude with a recap of the ground rules ... just to remind them. But then tell them how they can be of help to you. I've found that when I talk with parents it works best to start by discussing their child's strengths, then getting the student's challenges out of the way before finishing up with how the parents can help their child ... set some goals to work towards."

"We'll bear that in mind when we make up our outline tomorrow."

She gave her husband a wary glance. "And Martin, try not to have your hopes set too high that this will go smoothly."

"I am fully prepared for us to to go down like the Bismarck in the Denmark Straits, Louisa. The villagers seem to have an unerring knack for detecting my weak spots. They'll be launching salvos of rumours, misinformation, inappropriate questions and, *no doubt*, calling in to suggest folk remedies that'll ... put the lead back in my pencil!" he sputtered. He stabbed his fork into a chunk of fish, his jaws clenching. "And Caroline is their saboteur en chef ... their inside man."

Louisa reached across the table and quieted his fidgeting hand. "I think it'll be fine. Maybe just try to contain and control rather than trying to win the war," she said with a hesitant nod.

He looked up and met her gaze. His stern expression softened as her smile shifted his thoughts to something less anxiety provoking.

He was jarred from his daze by the voice of their waitress who had arrived to take their puds orders.

"None for me, thank you," he said.

"Me either." Louisa wiped her mouth with her napkin and then reached over to dab at an imaginary smudge on her husband's cheek. "I think we'll have our afters at home."

Martin's face warmed at his wife's remark as another surge of hormones began to stir in him. "The cheque, please," he said brusquely.

Melanie pulled a slip of paper from her apron pocket and laid it on the table before hurrying away.

Pulling out his wallet, he laid down three ten pound notes. "Are you ready?" he asked, looking over at his wife with just a hint of a smile.

"I am."

He got to his feet and Louisa walked over, wrapping an arm around his waist and giving him a chaste kiss on the cheek. "Thank you, Martin. I enjoyed this very much."

Mark Bridge, the proprietor, saw them heading towards the door, and he loped across the room. "Hi, Doc. Appreciate your comin' in tonight. Didn't wanna interrupt your dinner earlier, but ... well, it's good to see you up and about again."

"Mm. Yes."

Louisa gave the tall, lanky, red-head a grin. "Thank you, Mark. It was delicious."

Martin and Louisa could feel many pairs of eyes on them as they worked their way across the restaurant, and several more people came over to extend their well-wishes. But for the most part, they were left alone as they moved along, and both of them breathed a sigh of relief when they slipped out into the relative seclusion of the dark night.

A cold breeze had come up and it sent shivers through Louisa. When her teeth began to chatter, Martin stopped and shook his coat off his right shoulder before pulling his left arm back through the sleeve. "Here, put this on. You're cold."

She hesitated. "Then you'll be cold."

"No, I won't. I'm hot, actually. Besides, the coat makes it harder to move. Go ahead, Louisa. Put it on before you get too chilled."

She slipped her arms into the over-sized garment, now warmed by the heat generated by her husband's efforts. She breathed in deeply as his scent hit her nose. "Martin, could you stop for just a minute?"

He turned and gave her a quizzical look. Wrapping her arms around his neck, she pulled his head down and placed an unambiguous kiss on his lips. "Okay, we can go home now."

Poppy left shortly after her employers arrived home. She had plans to meet friends for quiz night down at the pub, and judging from her apparent anxiousness to get out the door, Martin and Louisa surmised that Jeremy was one of them.

Louisa glanced at her watch. "Well, James, it's now officially past your bedtime. Can you say goodnight to your daddy?"

Martin held out his left hand and Louisa settled the boy into the crook of his arm. James latched on to his ears and pulled his head forward. A well understood signal between the Ellingham men to touch foreheads.

Taking his father by surprise, James placed a very juicy, but well-aimed, kiss on his mouth, mimicking the endearments the younger Ellingham had so often seen demonstrated by his mother.

The boy nuzzled his face into his father's neck and laid his head on his shoulder, giving Martin an opportunity to clear away the baby drool that had been deposited on his cheek and chin. He glanced over at his wife, watching the display of affection between the two loves in her life, and despite his best efforts to conceal it, Louisa noticed the dewiness in her husband's eyes.

"I'll just take him on up then, shall I?" she said as she lifted the sleepy child from her husband's arm, wiping the last bit of moisture from his cheek.

Martin was on the sofa when she came back downstairs. He tossed his journal on to the coffee table when he heard her approaching footsteps and waited for her to join him.

"Sound asleep." She breathed out a heavy sigh as she plopped down next to him, leaning back so that she could nestle her head against his shoulder. "Can I get you anything before I get too relaxed here?"

"No, I'm fine." He cleared his throat. "Louisa ... I'm sorry about getting upset at dinner and—"

"No, Martin!" She sat up quickly and turned to face him before beginning a rapid-fire confession. "*I'm* sorry. There was nothing amusing about what happened with Melanie Gibson, and I'm sorry if I made you feel like the object of ridicule.

"And I know it's not the first time that I've done that. I mean, Mark Mylow's sister, not supporting you when Bert played that prank on you with the ketchup, making you look like an ogre and an idiot at Sports Day. I hope you know that I have the utmost respect for you. And I *can* be selfish and childish at times and—and—"

Noticing her husband's look of wide-eyed bewilderment, she stopped to take a breath. "Sorry, I got a bit carried away. I just want you to know that I'm aware I haven't been the ally I should have been for you since you came here. My allegiance *is* to you Martin and—" Tipping her head to the side, she peered up at his bemused expression. "What?" she asked.

He opened his mouth as if to speak and then shook his head.

"What, Martin?"

"It's not my fault, then? The reason you ran off to the lavatory tonight."

"Nooo, Martin! I ran off to the lavatory because I knew you were right. I felt terrible about making light of a painful experience in your life. I mean, you opened up to me about that and I made fun."

"You're sure it's not my fault?"

Louisa took his face in her hands and gave him a penetrating stare. "It is *not—your—fault*."

He released the breath he'd been holding in. "Oh. Good."

Pulling her feet out from under her, she curled up against him, his subtle scent once again making her weak in the knees. She inhaled deeply as she wrapped her arms around his chest.

"Martin."

"Hmm?" he said as he sat with his eyes closed.

"I think I'm ready for afters now."

Chapter 17

"No answer." Louisa dropped her phone back into her handbag. "I wonder what's keeping Poppy this morning? She's never been late before." She fidgeted nervously with her watch.

"Perhaps she's had a bit of trouble with her hair," Martin said dryly, giving a nod to his wife's late arrival to their wedding.

Louisa shot him a warning glance as she reached for the bottle of milk. "I have to be to work early today, and she promised she'd be here before I needed to leave. I have a mum and dad that are coming in before school starts this morning, and I can't be late!"

There was a loud buzz as Martin's mobile began to vibrate against the wood table top. "Ellingham," he grumbled as he pressed the device to his ear.

Louisa sat on the opposite side of the breakfast table, eating cornflakes and pretending to be absorbed in the morning newspaper while she listened in on her husband's end of the conversation.

"Yes, Chris."

An immediate edginess could be heard in his voice.

"I'm aware of that. Ed told me when I saw him yesterday."

Louisa peered up at him, worrying her lip.

"Well, why didn't you tell me about it on Monday then!" Martin snapped his fingers, pointing to the pad of paper and the biro sitting on the kitchen counter. Louisa handed them across the table before picking up her dishes and taking them to the sink.

"What do you mean *she* has a format she wants followed?" he growled into the phone.

James, having had his fill of dry cereal and apple juice, began to struggle to extricate himself from his high chair. Louisa lifted him up and set him down on the floor before leaning over to deposit a collection of toys next to him.

Hearing a forceful huff of air, she glanced over at her husband. He sat with his head tipped to the side, his brow furrowed, and his fingertips pressed to the bridge of his nose. This was a mannerism that had developed since the accident, usually indicative of a combination of fatigue, pain and a heavy dose of frustration.

"Oh, gawwd," he moaned. "Is that really necessary?"

She picked up her husband's coffee cup and refilled it with espresso. She had a feeling he was going to need it.

"Yes ... three o'clock." He threw his head back. "Yes, Chris. We'll be there!"

Martin slapped his mobile down on the table. His jaws clenched as he steeled himself for his wife's inevitable questions.

"What was that about?" Louisa asked as she gathered her things together to take to the school.

"Your friend, *Caroline*." He wrinkled up his nose and curled his lip into a sneer. "That woman has some serious control issues."

Louisa tipped her head down, peering up at him with raised eyebrows.

"Why are you looking at me like that?" he asked guilelessly.

She came around the table and placed a kiss on his forehead. "I guess she *can* be a bit controlling. So, is there a problem?"

"Ohhh, no problem. She just wants to meet with Jeremy and me this afternoon so she can go over the questions she plans to ask tomorrow."

"Well, maybe that's good. It might make discussing these things easier."

"Yes, I'm sure that's *just* what she's thinking." He slid his breakfast dishes forward with a clatter, attracting James Henry's attention. The boy scrambled over to investigate.

"She's going to milk this for any potential entertainment value, Louisa! She actually told Chris that she wants her listeners to ...*feel my pain*!"

"Oh, dear." Louisa scooped up her son and sat down next to her husband. "Well, maybe it's for the best that you're meeting with her today. It'll give you a chance to make your position clear to her."

"I really don't think Caroline gives a sod about my position, Louisa." He pulled up his arm and glanced at his watch. "You *do* know that you're late, don't you?"

"Oh, bugger!" She set James back down on the floor, grabbed her bag, and after hastily placing a kiss on her husband's cheek, she dashed out the door.

Noticing that his mother was gone, James turned, giving his father a lopsided grin.

Martin looked down at him, and realising he'd been left alone with the child, he called out, ineffectually, to his wife. "Louisa! *Louisa!*"

Surveying his fractured arm and legs he pursed his lips as air hissed from his nose. "Well, this is a jolly good cock-up, isn't it, James?"

He picked up his mobile and dialled his wife's number.

"Wonderful," he grumbled when it went immediately to voicemail. *Where's Poppy for God's sake?*

The baby, sensing his father's angst, grabbed on to his trousers and pulled himself to a standing position.

Jeremy won't be here for another hour, Martin thought as he picked up his mobile again and rang up Ruth's number. *"Eh!"* The phone went to voicemail.

James's short legs began to wobble and his father placed a hand on his back to steady him. When the child began to whine and pull at his sleeve, he reached down and positioned the boy's bum in the crook of his arm. He lifted him to his lap with a groan, the movement pulling at his abdominal muscles and tender ribs.

"I can't believe what your mother's done! Going off and leaving us like this!" he grumbled. "Well, James, we'll just have to make the best of it. What should we do? Watch a video?"

James looked on with rapt attention as his father opened up his laptop and drove the mouse around on the table.

"They're removing a fish hook from this man's eye by performing a vitrectomy. Given the propensity the villagers seem to have for this sort of injury, it's only a matter of time before I'll need to deal with one of these myself. If you should decide to become a doctor, James, you'll need to stay abreast of the latest surgical advancements."

The baby giggled at his father and blew a string of drippy bubbles through his lips.

As Martin became engrossed in his video, James grew bored and restless. He slapped at his father's cheek, trying to get his attention.

Martin looked down at his small son. He sighed and then typed *children's books* into the search box at the top of the screen. He clicked on the first result, and a page with a list of the best loved children's stories of all time appeared.

Martin skipped over *Where The Wild Things Are*. "That looks like it could give you nightmares, James—best not. *Huckleberry Finn* ... an excellent example of American literature, but I don't think you're quite ready for that one. Maybe in a few years."

The toddler reached a slobbery hand out, leaving a trail of drool down the laptop screen. "Ewww!" Martin pulled his handkerchief from his back pocket and wiped away the worst of the smears. "You mustn't touch that, James."

He turned his attention back to the list. "*Alice In Wonderland*—if it reads anything like your mother's interpretation, that one would most certainly give you nightmares.

"Here's one about a stuffed rabbit. Your mother seems to think you enjoy those Peter Rabbit stories. Shall we see if we can find this one about the Velveteen Rabbit?"

James bounced on his father's thigh causing him to grimace and reposition the boy.

He hit the search button and a digital library version of the story popped up. "All right, James, you have to sit quietly and listen if you want me to read to you, hmm."

The baby leaned back against his father's chest.

Martin cleared his throat. "There once was a Velveteen Rabbit, and in the beginning, he was really splendid. He was fat and bunchy as a rabbit should be."

James's gaze flitted from the laptop screen to his father's face and back to the screen again.

"For a long time he lived in the toy cupboard on the nursery floor, and no one thought very much about him. He was naturally shy, and being only made of velveteen, some of the more expensive toys quite snubbed him."

The baby watched his father's lips move as his smooth voice read on.

"Between them all, the poor little Rabbit was made to feel himself very insignificant and commonplace, and the only person who was kind to him at all was the Skin Horse. The Skin Horse had lived longer in the nursery than any of the others. He was wise, for he had seen a long succession of mechanical toys arrive to boast and swagger, and by-and-by break their mainsprings and pass away, and he knew that they were only toys and would never turn into anything else.

"What is real? asked the Rabbit one day.

"Real isn't how you are made, said the Skin Horse. *It's a thing that happens to you. When a child loves you for a long, long time, not just to play with, but REALLY loves you, then you become Real.*

"Does it hurt? asked the Rabbit.

"Sometimes, said the Skin Horse, for he was always truthful. *When you are Real you don't mind being hurt.*

"Does it happen all at once, he asked, *or bit by bit?*

"It doesn't happen all at once, said the Skin Horse. *You become. It takes a long time. That's why it doesn't happen often to people who break easily, or have sharp edges, or have to be carefully kept."*

Martin gazed down at his little boy who seemed to be engaged with the tale.

"Once you are Real, you can't be ugly, except to people who don't understand.

"One evening when the Boy was going to bed, he couldn't find the china dog that always slept with him. The nanny was in a hurry, so she simply looked about her, and seeing that the toy cupboard door stood open, she made a swoop. *Here* she said. *Take your old Bunny! He'll do to sleep with you!"*

James looked down at his father's arm wrapped around him protectively and grasped on to his thumb.

"That night, and for many nights after, the Velveteen Rabbit slept in the Boy's bed. At first he found it rather uncomfortable, for the the Boy hugged him very tight, and sometimes he rolled over on him, and sometimes he pushed him so far under the pillow that the Rabbit could scarcely breathe. But very soon he grew to like it. And when the Boy dropped off to sleep, the Rabbit would snuggle down close under his little warm chin and dream, with the boy's hands clasped close round him all night long."

Feeling a tug on his thumb, Martin looked down at his son's chubby hand wrapped firmly around his. He gave the boy a small smile, then continued on.

"Spring came, and they had long days in the garden, for wherever the Boy went the Rabbit went, too. And once, when the Boy was called away suddenly to go out to tea, the Rabbit was left out on the lawn until long after dusk, and the nanny had to come and look for him with the candle because the Boy couldn't go to sleep unless he was there. He was wet through with the dew and quite earthy from diving into the burrows the Boy had made for him in the flower bed. The nanny grumbled as she rubbed him off with a corner of her apron.

"You must have your old Bunny! she said. *Fancy all that fuss for a toy.*

"Give me my Bunny! he said. *You mustn't say that. He isn't a toy. He's REAL!*

"When the little Rabbit heard that he was happy, for he knew that what the Skin Horse had said was true at last. He was Real. The Boy himself had said it.

"That night he was almost too happy to sleep, and so much love stirred in his heart that it almost burst."

Martin tipped his head down and brushed his lips lightly against his son's soft head.

"Near the house where they lived there was a wood, and the Boy liked to go there after tea to play. He took the Velveteen Rabbit with him and before he wandered off to pick flowers he always made the Rabbit a little nest among the bracken. One evening, while the Rabbit was lying there alone, he saw two strange beings creep out of the tall grass near him.

"They were rabbits like himself, but quite furry and brand-new, and their seams didn't show at all and they changed their shape when they moved.

"Why don't you get up and play with us? one of them asked.

"I don't feel like it, said the Rabbit.

"I don't believe you can! he said.

"I can! said the little Rabbit. *I just don't want to!*

"He hasn't got any hind legs! called out another rabbit.

"I have! I'm sitting on them!

"Then stretch them out and show me, like this! said the wild rabbit. And he began to whirl round and dance.

"I don't like dancing, he said.

"But all the while he was longing to dance, for a funny new tickly feeling ran through him, and he felt he would give anything in the world to be able to jump about like these rabbits did.

"The strange rabbit stopped dancing and came quite close. He wrinkled his nose suddenly and jumped backward.

"He doesn't smell right! he exclaimed. *He isn't a rabbit at all! He isn't real!*

"I ***am*** *Real! The Boy said so!* And he nearly began to cry."

Martin stopped reading and, pulling in a deep breath, he closed his eyes. James peered up at him and began to grizzle, protesting the unexpected intermission in the story. Martin reached for his coffee cup, took a sip, and then began to read again.

"Weeks passed, and the Boy loved the little Rabbit so hard that he loved all his whiskers off, and the pink lining to his ears turned grey. He scarcely looked like a rabbit anymore, except to the Boy. To him he was always beautiful and that was—"

His words catching in his throat, Martin brushed the backs of his fingers across his own Boy's cheek.

"To him he was always beautiful, and that was all that the little Rabbit cared about. He didn't mind how he looked to other people, because to the Boy he was Real, and when you are Real shabbiness doesn't matter.

"And then one day, the Boy became ill. His face grew very flushed and his little body was so hot that it burned the Rabbit when he held him close. Strange people came and went in the nursery. The Velveteen Rabbit lay hidden from sight under the bedclothes and he never stirred, for he was afraid that if they found him someone might take him away, and he knew that the Boy needed him.

"He snuggled down patiently and looked forward to the time when the Boy should be well again. All sorts of delightful things he planned and while the Boy lay half asleep he crept up close to the pillow and whispered them in his ear. And presently, the Boy got better.

"The Boy was going to the seaside tomorrow. *Hurrah!* thought the little Rabbit. *Tomorrow* ***we*** *shall go to the seaside!*

"The trip was planned. Now all that remained was to carry out the doctor's order to disinfect the Boy's room and to burn all the books and toys that the Boy had played with in his bed.

"Just then the nanny caught sight of the Rabbit tangled in the bedclothes. *How about his old Bunny?* she asked.

"That? said the doctor. *Why it's a mass of scarlet fever germs! Burn it at once! Get him a new one.*

"And so the little Rabbit was put into a sack with the rubbish and carried out to the end of the garden. That was a fine place to make a bonfire, only the gardener was too busy just then to attend to it. But next morning he promised, he would come early and burn the whole lot.

"The sack of rubbish had been left untied, and so by wriggling a bit the little Rabbit was able to get his head through the opening and look out. He was shivering a bit, for his coat had worn so thin and threadbare from hugging that it was no longer any protection to him.

"Of what use was it to be loved and lose one's beauty and become Real if it all ended like this? And a tear, a real tear, trickled down his shabby velvet nose and fell to the ground.

"And then a strange thing happened. For where the tear had fallen a flower grew out of the ground. It was so beautiful that the little Rabbit forgot to cry, and just lay there watching it.

And presently the blossom opened, and out of it there stepped a fairy.

"She came close to the little Rabbit and gathered him up in her arms and kissed him on his velveteen nose that was all damp from crying.

"Little Rabbit, she said, *don't you know who I am? I am the nursery magic Fairy. I take care of all the playthings that the children have loved. When they are old and worn out and the children don't need them any more, then I come and take them away with me and turn them into Real.*

"Wasn't I Real before? asked the Rabbit.

"You were Real to the Boy, the Fairy said, *because he loved you. Now you shall be Real to everyone.*

"She kissed the little Rabbit and put him down on the grass. *Run and play, little Rabbit!*

"But the little Rabbit sat quite still, for he suddenly remembered he had no hind legs and he didn't want the wild rabbits to see. He might have sat there a long time, too shy to move, if just then something hadn't tickled his nose, and before he thought what he was doing he lifted his hind toe to scratch it.

"And he found that he actually had hind legs! And he had brown fur, soft and shiny, his ears twitched by themselves, and his whiskers were so long that they brushed the grass. He gave one leap and the joy of using those hind legs was so great that he went springing about the turf on them.

"He was a Real Rabbit at last, at home with the other rabbits.

"I guess that's the end of the story, James." Martin turned his gaze downward to *his* Boy, now sleeping soundly, his small hand still firmly grasping his father's thumb.

Chapter 18

When Louisa arrived at the school, Mr. and Mrs. Bollard were already waiting for her in her office. She had felt confident and well prepared to address the impact that Irene Bollard's alcohol consumption was having on their children, but her race down Dolphin Street and back up Fore Street had left her out of breath. And she was embarrassed by her own tardiness, which had an immediate discomposing effect.

"I'm so sorry Mr. and Mrs. Bollard. It's been one of those mornings, I'm afraid," Louisa said as she hung her coat over the hook on the wall and situated herself in the chair behind her desk.

She attempted a composed smile, but her lips twitched nervously, and she feared it may have come off as more of a grimace.

"Well, let me start by saying that you have two lovely daughters. Such sweet girls and so well-mannered; you should be very proud of them." Louisa looked directly at the parents, trying to project an appearance of professionalism and aplomb as she attempted to discreetly straighten her wind-blown hair.

Irene smiled back at her while Glen sat stone-faced and unflinching, looking at Louisa as if daring her to broach the thorny subject of his wife's drinking.

Louisa averted her eyes from the man's threatening gaze and opened the file in front of her. "I asked you to come in today so that we can discuss the concerns that have been raised about the girls' academic performance this year. And, I hope, to come up with some strategies to assist them in the classroom and with their homework."

She handed two copies of the Bollard children's latest performance reviews across the desk, one to Mrs. Bollard, the other to her husband.

"As you can see, we've seen a thirty percent overall drop in Gracie's scores this term, and a fifty percent drop in Emma's. This was brought to my attention by the girls' teachers, Miss Hayes and Miss Woodley, as well our school counsellor, Mr. Rhodes."

Irene glanced nervously at her husband but remained silent. Louisa tapped her fingers lightly against the desktop, hesitating slightly before continuing.

"Mrs. Bollard, the girls have mentioned in their conversations with Mr. Rhodes that they're quite worried about your health. Children need to feel secure to thrive and reach their full potential. My concern is that this worry could be contributing to Grace and Emma's difficulties here at school."

Louisa had been trying to not allow the anger that she could see building in Mr. Bollard's face to cow her, but he erupted suddenly, leaning across the desk to aim a string of vitriolic words at her.

"Stay out of this! It isn't none of yer affair, you meddlin' woman!"

Louisa rolled back in her chair slightly to put some distance between her and the face in front of her. The man gave her a dismissive sneer and spat out, "You think yer so high and mighty ... tellin' us how to bring up our girls! You need to keep yer nose outta our business and tend ta yer own! Maybe you need ta take a dose of yer own medicine ... *Mrs. Ellingham.* You aren't exactly livin' in wedded bliss with that tosser husband of yer's, are ya now?"

Glen rose from his chair and grabbed hold of his wife's wrist. "Irene, git up! We're leavin'!" He yanked his wife to her feet and then turned to storm down the hall.

Irene looked apologetically at Louisa. "I'm sorry. I know you're just tryin' to help.

Louisa folded her hands on the desk in front of her to steady them as they shook from a mix of anger and fear.

"Mrs. Bollard, my husband my be gruff, but he does truly care about his patients. If you were to want his help, he would move heaven and earth to provide you with what you need to get well. Please ... let me know if I can be of assistance to you in any way."

"Thank you all the same, Mrs. Ellingham, but my husband wouldn't take kindly to that." The woman turned and hurried off.

Pippa Woodley was in the outer office and appeared in Louisa's doorway as soon as the Bollards had gone.

"That Glen Bollard is a mean bugger. Don't envy that poor woman her husband. Makes your Dr. Ellingham seem like a pussycat! Leastwise, I've never *seen* him lay an unkind hand on you ... or the baby."

Louisa considered Pippa to be a friend, but the tone she used whenever she spoke about Martin always made her bristle. It was as if she was silently laughing at him. "Oh, Pippa, of course not! Martin would never treat either of us that way. In fact, he's very gentle with—"

The image of James sleeping contentedly in his father's arms sent a surge of adrenaline through her. *I left Martin alone with James!*

She snatched her mobile from her handbag and rang his phone, but he didn't pick up.

Grabbing her coat from the hook, she moved towards the door. "I can't believe I've done this Pippa, but I ran out of the house this morning and left Martin alone with the baby. Can you hold down the fort for a while?"

"Sure. Just go," Pippa said as she pushed her friend towards the hallway.

"I'll explain when I get back!" Louisa shouted over her shoulder.

When she entered the front door of Ruth's cottage, all seemed quiet in the house. There was no sign of either her husband or her son. She was beginning to feel a sense of panic setting in when she heard the sound of his sonorous voice coming from the kitchen.

He was sitting where she had left him forty-five minutes earlier. She listened from the hallway as he read the last lines of *The Velveteen Rabbit*.

"... sat there a long time, too shy to move, if just then something hadn't tickled his nose, and before he thought what he was doing he lifted his hind toe to scratch it. And he found that he actually had hind legs! And he had brown fur, soft and shiny, his ears twitched by themselves, and his whiskers were so long that they brushed the grass. He gave one leap and the joy of using those hind legs was so great that he went springing about the turf on them.

"He was a Real Rabbit at last, at home with the other rabbits."

Louisa stepped into the kitchen as Martin said, "I guess that's the end of the story, James."

He pulled at the tea towel that was laying in a pile in front of him. His mobile fell with a clunk on to the wood table top.

Well, that explains why he didn't hear his phone vibrate, Louisa thought to herself.

He laid the towel across his sleeping son to keep him warm then sighed, shifting slightly to find a more antalgic position.

Louisa cleared her throat and he turned, his scowl deepening as she approached.

"I believe you forgot something," he said, nodding his head at the sleeping child on his lap.

"I know I did," she answered softly, kissing his cheek. "I guess you know where my head was at this morning."

"Mm. It's okay. I didn't think of it either until it was too late." His taut face relaxed as his wife rubbed her hands over his tired shoulders.

She glanced over at her husband's computer, the stylised, sketchy rendition of a leaping rabbit still up on the screen.

Martin caught her amused smile out of the corner of his eye and snapped the laptop shut. "What's going on with Poppy? This is entirely unacceptable."

"I don't know, Martin. She must have gotten held up by something."

"It's not like her." He shifted uncomfortably, trying to relieve the pins and needles sensation that was being caused by the dead weight resting in his arm. "Jeremy should be here in a few minutes. I'll send him out to look for her."

The faint sound of Louisa's ringtone could be heard coming from the living room where she had left her handbag.

"Maybe that's her now," she said as she ran through the hallway. Martin strained to hear his wife's words.

"Poppy! Where are you?

"Well, are you all right?"

He craned his neck, trying in vain to see into the living room.

"Well, the important thing is you're both okay. We'll see you in a few minutes, then."

"What's happened?" Martin asked anxiously when she re entered the kitchen.

"She's fine." Louisa reached down to reposition the towel over the baby. "It seems our childminder went home with your assistant last night, and they had some car trouble on the way back to Portwenn this morning. They couldn't call for help or call us because they were in a black spot."

Louisa noticed her husband flexing his fingers in an attempt to get the blood moving, and she leaned over to pick up the baby.

"They walked more than five miles before someone happened along and gave them a ride into Bodmin," she said as she laid the boy in the cot in the corner of the room. "They picked up a rental and are on their way now. Should be here in a few minutes."

Martin scowled. "What do you mean, she went home with him?"

"She went back with him to his flat in Truro last night. Poor Poppy and Jeremy. What a start to their day!"

"Mm, yes."

Louisa noticed the disapproving scowl on her husband's face. "Martin, they *are* both adults."

"Technically, yes. But they're young ... especially Poppy. She's hardly more than a *child*."

Putting her hand against the back of his head, she kissed him firmly. "It's very sweet that you're concerned, Martin, but they *are* adults. And Poppy has a father. It's *his* job to worry about these things."

"But I'm a doctor, Louisa. How would it look if something should hap—"

"Shhh, Martin. It's none of our business. And besides, given our own track record, we aren't really in a position to be giving advice."

He released a dissatisfied sigh. "Yes."

The present crisis dealt with, Louisa's mind went back to the scene that had played out in her office earlier.

"Martin."

He closed out of the children's story and snapped his laptop shut. "Hmm?"

"Could you stand up for a minute, please?"

He looked at his wife inquisitively but did as she asked.

Wrapping her arms around him, she began to tremble again as she replayed the conversation with the Bollards in her head, the image of Mr. Bollard's angry face still vivid. The fear and feeling of being dominated swept over her again.

"Martin, just hold me ... tight," she pleaded.

Once again, he did as he was asked. But he found himself getting impatient with what he felt to be an excessive amount of drama over car trouble and a late childminder. *Perhaps she's premenstrual?* he wondered silently.

"For goodness' sake, Louisa. They're just fine. They'll be walking in here at any moment, so try to calm yoursel—"

"Martin, just be quiet and hold me," she said as she began to cry into his shirt sleeve.

He tightened his grip and rubbed her back.

"I feel safe when you have your arms around me, you know," she said as her ragged breaths began to ease.

"Louisa, you really needn't worry. They'll be walking in that door at any moment."

She tipped her head back to look at him. His eyes bore a softness and expression of concern. "Martin, I'm upset about something that happened at the school this morning."

"Oh, you were late. Is that it?"

"*No*, Martin. I'm not this upset because I was late for work." Louisa tried to keep the annoyance from her voice, but she found her husband's complete cluelessness frustrating at times.

"I had a meeting with a mum and dad first thing. The children have been floundering this term, and I was hoping to work with the parents. Maybe provide their girls with a home environment that would be more conducive to learning. The father was belligerent, and he got very angry with me. I was *afraid*, Martin. That's why I'm upset."

Martin took her shoulders and pushed her back, looking her over carefully. "Are you all right? Did he touch you, Louisa?"

"I'm fine. I'm fine. It was a frightening situation, and it just hit me a minute ago, is all." She caressed his arm, trying to calm an obvious agitation in him.

He pulled out the chair beside him and pressed her down into it. Taking her chin in his hand, he tipped his head back and inspected her face with his scrutinising doctor's eyes. Then he lifted each arm, looking for any sign of injury.

Louisa gave him a sheepish smile. "I didn't mean to worry you. I just needed to be close to you."

He stood, lips pursed. "Who was this, Louisa? Who was the man?" he asked softly but firmly.

"Gene Bollard. According to their girls, their mum drinks a lot, and they're worried about her health. The poor woman seems scared to death of the man. Which is completely understandable after seeing his behaviour in my office."

"Ah." Martin nodded his head, knowingly.

"I told her that you could get her the help she needs. I hope you don't mind. Is she an alcoholic?" She held on to her husband's hand, stroking the back of it with her thumb.

He looked down at the floor and shook his head. "I can't discuss my patients."

"Of course, I shouldn't have asked." She tipped her head to make eye contact with him. "I need to get back to the school. James is asleep, and Poppy and Jeremy should be here any minute now. Will you be okay here alone with him for a bit?"

"Yes, you go ahead. But Louisa ... don't take any chances with this man. Take precautions ... maybe leave your office door open. And don't be at the school alone at the end of the day. At least until things have settled down a bit."

"I'll be fine. I'm sorry I worried you." She got to her feet and took his face in her hands. Then she kissed him before picking up her handbag and hurrying out the door.

Poppy and Jeremy entered the back of the house as Louisa left through the front.

"I'm really sorry for bein' late, Dr. Ellingham," the childminder said as she slipped her coat over a peg.

"Yes. Well, I'm glad that you're both all right. Jeremy, we should be leaving in a few minutes. Why don't you grab a bite to eat before we have to go?"

Jeremy looked at his boss apprehensively. Martin didn't need to say a word. The expression on his face communicated his feelings quite effectively.

"Do you need my help with anything before we leave?" the aide asked.

"I would have said if I did. Just get something to eat while I finish getting ready."

Martin left the kitchen and headed down the hall to the lavatory. Jeremy watched as he disappeared around the corner and then turned to Poppy.

"Do you think he's mad?" she asked, pulling her shoulders up nervously.

"Well, I don't think he's happy. But I'm pretty sure it's got nothing to do with you. It could be a long drive to Wadebridge," he said, breathing out a heavy sigh as he slathered peanut butter on his bread.

Chapter 19

They had passed the turning to St. Minver before either Martin or Jeremy uttered a word to the other. Martin stared out the passenger window, oblivious of the passing scenery. His thoughts flitted between his uneasiness over the most recent development in Jeremy and Poppy's relationship and his very real concern for his wife's safety at the school.

Jeremy cleared his throat nervously before venturing into potentially dangerous territory. "I, er ... I'm sorry that I didn't have Poppy to your house on time this morning, Martin. We would have been fine if it hadn't been for that bloody alternator belt."

Martin glanced over at the young man before returning his gaze to the passing countryside.

"It's my fault," the young man continued. "The check engine light had come on last week, and I should have gotten the car into the shop. And I shouldn't have been driving out in an isolated area. We took the back roads. I thought Poppy would find it romantic. So, Martin, please don't be angry with her."

Martin turned. "I'm not angry with Poppy. It does concern me that you took her home with you last night. You've known her how long, Jeremy? *Three weeks*? Poppy's young and not very worldly. She could be easily hurt in this relationship! You *do* understand that, don't you?"

"Martin, I'm being careful ... we're being careful. You don't need to worry," he said, pulling a pack of gum from his shirt pocket.

The doctor shook his head. "Do I need to insult your intelligence by reminding you that *being careful* doesn't provide you with any guarantees?

"How are you going to handle it if you decide you don't want to see her anymore? How are you going to feel if she decides the relationship isn't going anywhere, and she doesn't want to see *you* anymore?"

The diatribe continued to build in intensity. "Just what do you think you're going to do if you find out she's pregnant, for heaven's sake? And how do you think it'll feel when she springs it on you, and you suddenly have to get your head around the fact that *you* are responsible for the situation? *You've* gotten her pregnant! *You're* going to be a father!

"Are you going to be willing to step up and help her out? And there's every chance that you'll *want* to help her out ... to be involved, and she won't want to have anything to do with you! What do you think it'll feel like if she says, *it's fine, Martin; it's not your problem*? It's an *impossible* situation!

"Do you have any idea how painful it would be for you to *want* to be a part of things... *want* to help but not be wanted? Good God, Jeremy! Did you give any thought to all of this before you asked her back to your flat last night?"

The aide raised his eyebrows at him and then huffed out a breath. "Martin, I share a flat with my sister. Poppy slept in *her* room. Do I need to insult *your* intelligence by pointing out that for conception to occur, both parties involved need to be in close proximity to one another? I can't say other options didn't cross my mind, but neither of us is ready to take things to that level yet. We both got a very good night's sleep ... I'm sorry to say. *Nothing* like you're suggesting."

Martin sat quietly for a few moments. "I never actually suggested anything." he mumbled. "I was just expressing ... concern for you. And Poppy. That's all. Mm."

Jeremy glanced over at his friend, breaking into a grin. “Thanks, Martin. I appreciate that.”

Martin sat silent for several minutes, his elbow propped against the window and his head in his hand. He pulled in a deep breath. “Er, Jeremy ... I had a call from Chris Parsons this morning. It seems Caroline Bosman, the resident rumour monger and gossip aficionado, wants to meet with us at the radio station at three o’clock this afternoon. Are you available?”

“Yeah. Yeah, I can be there,” he said, anxious to extend an olive branch of sorts to his employer.

“Good. I have to warn you though; she’s going to try to turn this into some kind of seedy on-air melodrama.”

“I’ve got your back, mate,” he said as he patted his shoulder.

“Mm.”

Martin spent the next two hours working with Kieran, strengthening his arm in preparation for the use of crutches. Then with Max on balance, proprioception skills, and his ability to navigate stairs.

“Do you think I’ll be able to handle the steps at the surgery by the end of the week?” Martin asked as he lay on the table while Max worked to loosen his muscles and joints.

The therapist gave a final push against his patient’s foot, forcing his knee towards his chest. “Let’s see how you take to crutches on Friday. Your new brace should have arrived by then, so you can give it a test drive.” He gave Martin’s foot a pat and then grabbed on to his good arm, pulling him to a sitting position.

“Good luck with the radio gig tomorrow.”

“Thank you. If history is any predictor of the future, I’ll need it.” Martin slipped off the table and sat down in a nearby chair to pull his warm up pants and trainers back on.

“You need any help in here?” Jeremy asked as he stuck his head in the door.

"Nope, I've got it." Martin looked up and gave the young man a small smile. He regretted his superfluous lecture in the van earlier. The thought that he had let private feelings slip during his rant caused his stomach to churn.

Martin and Jeremy arrived at the radio station promptly at three o'clock, but Caroline left them sitting in her outer office until almost half three, a pre-contrived strategy to throw Martin off his game. She and every other villager were well aware of his intransigent attitude towards having his time wasted, and she was using it to her full advantage.

Martin had been grumbling under his breath for fifteen minutes when the door to the woman's office finally opened and she stepped out to slather Martin in honeyed commiseration.

"I just couldn't believe it when I heard the news, Doc. You *poor* thing! And how are you doing now? Better, I hope." She cocked her head and gave him a contrived smile.

"Obviously, I am! Now can we please get on with this?" he snapped.

"Of course." She extended her hand to Jeremy. "I'm Caroline Bosman. You must be the doc's new assistant!"

"Yeah, sorry. This is Jeremy Portman," Martin mumbled.

Jeremy held out his hand and gave the woman his most winning smile. "Dr. Ellingham's told me a *lot* about you," he said, delivering the line of faux blandishment so effectively as to elicit a flush over the woman's cheeks.

She gushed accordingly. "Oh, please. I'm just doing the best job I can for our little village."

Martin cast an incredulous glance in his assistant's direction, and it was returned with a devilish grin.

Caroline waved them into her office. "Please, have a seat. Doc, can you bend your legs? Can you sit down?"

Martin grimaced at her syrupy tone and the absurdity of her questions before retorting, "No, my wife stands me up in the corner at mealtime and ties a feedbag on my head. Of course, I can sit!" He blew a puff of air through his lips and shook his head. *Gawd!*

Caroline shrugged her shoulders at Jeremy and took a seat behind her desk. The aide stepped aside, showing feigned interest in the plaques on the wall while he choked back the laughter that was threatening to spill out. He inhaled deeply before returning to his seat.

"So, as I was telling Dr. Carson on the phone the other day—"

"Parsons," Martin said with a sneer.

"Whatever. I was telling him I'm just absolutely *thrilled* to have you come on my show, Doc! You can't believe how much curiosity there is surrounding your little mishap."

"I have a pretty good idea, Caroline."

"Well, it's good of you to come on and shed some light on all of this."

He leaned forward and looked directly at his adversary. "Just to be clear … I'm not coming on your ridic—"

Jeremy elbowed his boss's arm. Martin looked down to see the young man's finger wagging back and forth in warning.

Refocusing his attention on the woman on the opposite side of the desk, Martin attempted to choose his words more carefully.

Clearing his throat, he continued. "I'm coming on your show because it's important that everyone in this village has a clear understanding of how the surgery will operate for the next several months. We're opening it up earlier than anticipated, so certain precautions need to be taken if I'm to stay healthy enough to continue to treat my patients. I am *not*, however, going to be answering any questions that I find to be intrusive."

Caroline slumped down into her chair and huffed out a breath. "Well, Doctor, I don't *have* to allow you any air time, you know. All I'm asking is that you take a few calls … answer a few questions that have been on all our minds for the last two months."

She straightened herself back up and flashed him a Cheshire grin. "Now, Doc, let's go over how I intend for things to be handled tomorrow. The format is very straightforward. I'll ask a question, and you'll try to give a reasonably complete answer."

Martin threw his head back, "No, no, no, no, no. Jeremy and I have a very specific agenda. Certain points must be covered in the way we see fit in order to avoid any confusion. We can't have an uninformed, self-aggrandising radio personality directing this!"

"Well, maybe you should investigate other communications media that would be willing to conform to your rigorous standards!" Caroline snipped sardonically.

Jeremy had been watching the verbal sparring match, finding it somewhat humorous up to a point. But he could now see the wheels falling off their plan to get his patient's surgery up and running again, so he reluctantly waded into the mire.

"Why don't we show Caroline the agenda that we intend to follow, and hopefully we can come to some sort of an agreement as to what questions would be appropriate for her to ask. Then we could work them into the programme."

Neither Caroline nor Martin looked particularly happy with the plan, but Jeremy decided to forge ahead.

"For instance, it's of utmost importance that Dr. Ellingham's patients understand that because of the injuries he sustained in the accident, his body can't fight off infections very effectively. They *must* make an appointment to be seen. Morwenna will screen them when they call in to the surgery, and then they'll be screened again by me before Dr. Ellingham will see them."

"Explain that to me," said Caroline as she shook her head and furrowed her thick eyebrows.

"Jeremy already explained it as simply as possible. What part of ... you must make an appointment and be screened by my receptionist and assistant ... are you having trouble grasping?" Martin said bitingly.

"Excuse *me*! I am merely trying to establish why we should have to jump through these hoops to get in to see our local GP." Caroline stared Martin down, tight lipped and red-faced.

Jeremy wiped his palm across his face and took in a deep breath. "All right, that's a reasonable question, don't you think, Dr. Ellingham?"

Martin grunted indignantly. "Yes, I suppose I can answer that one ... *on the phone-in tomorrow*."

"Good, that's one thing sorted." Jeremy looked down through his notes. "If a patient is suspected of being contagious, then they'll be sent over to Wadebridge to see the doctors there. Dr. Ellingham will only be seeing patients who may have sustained an injury, be suffering from migraines, have a chronic disease such as a heart condition, thyroid problem, diabetes ... It'll be a few months yet before he'll be back to seeing patients as usual."

It was a solid hour later before Caroline and Martin had finally come to a grudging agreement on the format to be followed the next day.

"You know, Doc, I really just want for the people in our little village to understand what this has all been like for you. The pain and the *horror* of it all," Caroline said theatrically.

"Can we *please* adhere to the format we just agreed to, Caroline?" Martin said rubbing his forehead as he tried to ease the pounding behind his eyes.

Jeremy glanced over at him. "I think we need to wrap this up, Ms. Bosman. We do appreciate your time today, and we'll see you at ten o'clock tomorrow morning."

"Yes, but *please* ... call me Caroline," she said coquettishly as she laid her hand on the young man's arm.

"Oh gawd," Martin groaned as he rolled his eyes in his aide's direction.

"Well, you seemed to thoroughly enjoy that," Martin said as the two men walked through the car park.

Jeremy began to chuckle. "I did, actually. I found it quite ... entertaining really."

Martin glanced over at him and his scowl deepened. "Well, let's hope that you aren't so enthralled by Caroline's charm and quick wit tomorrow that you prove useless to me."

"Don't worry about Caroline. It was *your* charm and quick wit that I found distracting today, mate."

"Nonsense." Martin pushed his shirt sleeve back and looked at his watch. "Erm, do you mind stopping by the school on our way home. Louisa should be about ready to leave, and we could give her a ride."

"Sure, you're the boss," Jeremy replied before pulling his door shut.

Martin could see his wife hunched over her desk when he entered her outer office. "Louisa..." he said as he stood in the doorway.

The sound of a male voice sent her heart racing and she jumped noticeably in her seat, holding a hand to her chest. "Oh, Martin, you startled me!"

"I'm sorry. I didn't mean to. Can you come over here?" he asked, wanting to take her in his arms but finding his legs tired and failing him after the walk into the school.

She stood up and moved quickly to him. Pushing the walker aside, he embraced her tightly.

"Oh, Martin," she sighed. "This feels absolutely wonderful." She basked in her husband's warmth and solidity for a few moments before pulling back to look at him. "What are you doing here? Is everything okay? There's nothing wrong with James is there?"

"Nooo! Jeremy and I just finished our meeting with Caroline, and I thought we could give you a ride home."

He glanced around the room and out into the hall. "Louisa, I'm glad to see you had your door open, but there doesn't seem to be anyone around. You shouldn't be here by yourself."

"Well there *were* people around when I started in on this paperwork. I was trying to finish it up so I wouldn't have to take it home with me tonight. I wanted the time with you." She wrapped her arms around his neck and pulled his head down, pressing her lips to his.

"I'll just get my things together and we can go, hmm?"

"Yes." Martin breathed out, his gaze fixed on her as she walked away from him.

She pulled her papers together and slipped them into her bag, and then turning towards the door, she saw her husband staring at her dreamily.

"Okay, let's go," she said, patting his bum as she passed by him.

"Mm, yes."

Jeremy and Poppy left the Ellingham's together that afternoon. Martin and Louisa exchanged glances, but no more was said about the pair's late arrival that morning.

"Well, husband ... it's just you and me again."

James let out a string of excited baby conversation, and his mother stooped to pick him up from the floor. "I stand corrected. You, me, and James."

Martin stroked a hand over the boy's head before running his thumb gently across his wife's cheek. "Why don't you relax tonight and let me make supper."

"I don't think that would be advisable, Doctor," she said pointing to his still bandaged finger.

"He leaned down and kissed her gently. "I'll just heat up that soup that's left over from yesterday's lunch. Put James in his high chair. Then go in the living room and put your feet up for a while."

Louisa settled her son and retreated to the sofa. Martin handed James a piece of Melba toast and his fire engine before turning to dinner preparations. Louisa craned her neck, watching as he moved about the kitchen. Even hobbled by the hardware attached to his limbs and the use of the walker, there was still a poise about him that made her heart beat faster.

There was just something about Martin that she found intriguing … that made her want to know him on a deeper level. She thought that perhaps it was the enigmatic nature of the man. She had been so eager to uncover everything there was to know about him, but now she wondered if she should just let the mystery play out in its own time … let him reveal his hidden talents, memories, and fears when he was ready to reveal them.

Hmm, possibly, she thought to herself. *But Martin seems to want to expose that hidden side of himself. Something just won't allow it. Fear… or embarrassment maybe. It's as if he needs someone to open the combination lock on that emotional vault of his, so he can let some of these things go. I wonder if he knows how much I want to help him. Just how much I love him.*

The electricity had been building between Martin and Louisa all evening. It seemed as though every time her gaze shifted to her husband, she found him staring at her in that almost semi-conscious state he so often slipped into, oblivious to anything but her. The idea that she could have this effect on him stroked her feminine ego.

With James now in bed, they stood together at the kitchen sink … Martin washing a dish then rinsing it before giving it to his wife to dry it. She watched as he wiped the cloth against a plate, soap bubbles clinging to his bare arm. She found something quite sensual about that image.

She laid her palm against the back of his hand as he passed a plate to her, and their eyes met. Laying the dish down, she wrapped her arms around him as she pressed against him.

He took in a ragged gasp and bent his head down to nuzzle his face into her neck. Cool air moved against her skin as he inhaled deeply, taking in her scent. Leaning back against the edge of the countertop, he wrapped his good arm under her bum and lifted her, pushing against her firmly.

"Oh, Martin," she said breathlessly. "I think we should leave the rest of these dishes and move on to something more pleasurable, don't you?"

"Mm, I agree." He forced the words out through his tightening throat.

Stretching up, she pressed her mouth to his, the warmth of her tongue playing along the fullness of his lips. Then she slipped away down the hall, taking a lingering glance over her shoulder.

Martin watched as her hips undulated gently with each step. He closed his eyes and blew out a long breath before making his way to the bedroom.

Chapter 20

Martin and Jeremy arrived at the radio station on Thursday under grey skies and a cold, wind-driven rain. The two men slipped their macs from their shoulders and shook the water off.

"I hate to say it, Martin, but this weather doesn't bode well for our radio appearance today," Jeremy said as he wiped his face on his shirt sleeve.

Martin pulled his handkerchief from his pocket and ran it over his wet head. "For they sowed the wind, and they shall reap the whirlwind," he muttered.

The young man glanced up at him, his brow furrowed.

"It means that when you do something stupid you reap a monsoon of consequences." Martin glanced at his watch, then dried the face of it on the leg of his trousers.

"Thanks for the bit of inspiration, mate. You ready to face the impending storm, then?"

"I can't wait," Martin groaned.

Once again, the two men found themselves in Caroline Bosman's outer office. With only ten minutes to air-time the woman couldn't keep them waiting the way she had the previous day, and they used the little time they had to conduct a quick review of the issues that needed to be addressed over the course of the next hour.

Martin watched his aide out of the corner of his eye. He'd seen it all before on Coronation Street. The frequent wiping of the hands on the thighs, the drumming fingers, the knees bouncing up and down. Jeremy was suffering from anxiety.

"Are you all right?" Martin asked him worriedly.

The young man looked over and gave him a weak smile. "Just a bit nervous, I guess. Like I said, I'm not good in front of large groups."

Caroline's office door opened and she hurried out. "Good morning! Why don't you follow me, and we'll get things set up and ready to go."

She led them down a short corridor before turning into a small broadcast room with a wide desk sitting in the middle of the floor.

She instructed them to take a seat opposite her. The Radio Portwenn theme music was queued up and ready to go.

"Now, try not to think of all those people listening out there. Pretend it's just the three of us in the room," Caroline said.

Martin glanced around him, then back at her. "It *is* just the three of us in the room."

She narrowed her eyes at him in warning, and Martin gave her a naive stare.

The music began to play, and as it faded away, Caroline entered with, "Good morning, Portwenn! Caroline here with you once again!

"Our guest today on Portwenn Personality Playlist is our very own GP, Doc Martin. Looking a little the worse for wear, but I'm glad you managed to make it over today. And we get a bonus this week because you've brought your soon-to-be assistant with you this time."

"Yes, Caroline. This is Jeremy Portman. Anyone coming to my surgery in future weeks will be seen first by Jer—"

"Yes, we'll get to all of that in a bit. Now, Doc, we're all aware that you were involved in a terrible car accident, what ... eight weeks ago, now?"

Martin leaned forward into the microphone. "Almost nine."

"Well, we've all been very concerned about you, and *of course* that's meant that you've been the topic of conversation on many of our programmes over the course of the last two months."

Martin gave her a steely gaze. *"Naturally."*

"Well, as I'm sure you can imagine, there's been much speculation about what exactly occurred on that horrible night back in September. Perhaps you could tell us all about what happened."

"I believe we had agreed to cover the more important matters at hand first, Caroline. It's important that everyone in this village is clear about the—"

"Oh, we'll get to that, Doc. But first, let's see if we can answer all these burning questions, shall we? Why don't you tell your fellow villagers about what transpired that night? Put all the rumours to rest."

Martin clenched his jaws and stared the woman down. "As I was saying, I think it would be best, Caroline, if we started with the plans for the reopening of the surgery. It's very important that all of my patients have a clear understanding of how the practice will be operated in the months to come."

Caroline looked back at him, slit-eyed, as her upper lip twitched. "Whatever you say, Doc," she said, gushing with insincere civility. "Why don't you tell us about the changes we can all expect when we come in to see you." She reached for her water bottle, taking a swig and throwing the doctor a black look.

Martin straightened himself and laid his forearms on the desk in front of him. "First and foremost, everyone needs to understand that I will *only* see patients who have been screened twice. Once by my receptionist, Morwenna Newcross, when they call in to make an appointment, and again by my assistant, Jeremy Portman, when they arrive at the surgery."

Caroline folded her hands in front of her and leaned forward into her microphone. "And why is that, Doc? Are you trying to weed out the whingers and malingerers?" she asked, chuckling at her own sarcasm.

"Yes," Martin answered matter-of-factly. "As well as anyone who could be carrying in a communicable disease."

"And just why is that exactly?"

"Because I find them extremely annoying, and I don't like having my time wasted," Martin deadpanned.

Caroline sighed and gave him a benevolent smile. "I don't mean the whingers and malingerers. Why is it, Doc, that someone who has, say ... the flu or a cold can't be seen by you. Isn't a doctor, by definition, someone who heals people ... helps them to get well? Of what use are you to the people of Portwenn if you won't even let them in the door?"

"I'll be more than happy to see any patient who has an injury that needs to be attended to, anyone who may need treatment for a chronic illness such as a cardiac ailment, arthritis, diabetes, thyroid di—"

"Oh, thank goodness!" Caroline whined. "I was afraid I'd have to drive all the way over to Wadebridge for my check-up next month!"

"No, Caroline. You're one of the lucky few who I can actually be of use to," Martin said with a sneer. "However, because of injuries that I sustained in the accident, my immune system has been compromised. Which means that if I'm exposed to a communicable disease, it's likely that I'll become infected with it. So, in order—"

"I don't mean to pry, but I'm sure our listeners are very curious about these injuries. What happened to make your immune system compromised?"

Jeremy glanced over, waiting for his boss's expected vitriolic reaction to the intrusive nature of the question. He was surprised when the only annoyance he could detect was the working of his jaw muscles.

Martin sighed and then cleared his throat. "My spleen was ruptured in the accident. The sple—"

"Oh, yeah. That's what happened with the little Cronk kid a few years back, isn't it, Doc?"

"I'm not going to discuss my patient's personal medical history on live radio! For God's sake, Caroline!" He hissed out a breath.

"The spleen is an internal organ located under your ribcage in the upper left part of your abdomen, towards your back. It's part of the lymphatic system and defends the body against infection. Due to the extent of the damage done in my accident, a splenectomy was performed, meaning they surgically removed the organ. I also experienced something called hypovolaemic shock which has stressed my immune system further.

"My doctors in Truro will not allow me to open the practice back up unless a strict protocol for screening patients is in place first. In order for me to stay healthy and continue to treat all of you, I need to limit my exposure to pathogens. I realise it's an inconvenience for everyone, but I would appreciate your patience and cooperation."

"And tell us how you plan to do that, Doc. To limit your exposure to these illnesses," Caroline said nodding her head vigorously.

"Perhaps Mr. Portman could explain how the screening of patients will work." Martin turned to Jeremy, sliding the microphone in his direction.

The aide stared back at him, wide-eyed and frozen in place. He gave his head several small shakes as his lips pleaded a silent *no*.

Martin lifted the young man's arm from the desk and slid a sheet of paper over in front of him. He leaned over and whispered into his ear. "Just read it."

Jeremy swallowed hard, and then followed his employer's directions, reciting the typewritten words in front of him. "I'd like to introduce myself. My name is Jeremy Portman. I'm a registered nurse and have been working as a home health aide for the Ellingham's for the last month. Dr. Ellingham has asked me to come aboard as his assistant at the surgery."

The sheet of paper began to rustle as the aide held it in his hands. He tried to lay it back on the desk, but it clung to his moist fingers.

He licked his dry lips and Martin slid a glass of water towards him. Taking a sip, he set the glass back down with a clunk.

Caroline gave a huff and screwed up her face. "Doc, maybe you could just expl—"

Martin put his finger to his lips and shushed her. Then he tapped on the sheet of paper and gave his young friend a nod.

"I'm honoured to have this opportunity to serve all of you..." Jeremy hesitated as he read to himself the words that Martin had scrawled in red ink. *A derisive sneer would be appropriate here.* A grin spread across his face.

"... and I'll strive to provide you with the best medical care possible. As Dr. Ellingham mentioned, there will be a screening process in place when you call in to make an appointment. The receptionist will have a series of questions that she'll ask on the phone. When you arrive at the surgery, I'll have a few more questions for you. I'll take your temperature, check for swollen lymph nodes and any other indications of illness. My job will be to protect your doctor from exposure to contagions as well as to assist him with wound treatment."

Jeremy looked over at Martin, and the doctor raised his thumb in the air and gave him a nod of his head.

"All right! Let's open up the phone lines!" Caroline said as she adjusted her headset. "Give me a call at Portwenn ... sixty-one ... seven ... eight!"

The radio host jabbed her finger down on a button in front of her. "Go ahead caller. You're live with Caroline."

"Hello, Caroline. This is Beth Sawle. I was wondering if Dr. Ellingham would still be making house calls." The woman hesitated to take in a breath of air. "Or will we need to come ... to the surgery to see him?" The elderly woman's brittle voice trailed off.

"No, Miss Sawle. Mr. Portman can help me to get out to your place if you can't make it into the village. He'll go in and check you over before I enter the house." Martin pulled the sheet of paper away from Jeremy's hands and pulled his biro from his pocket before scribbling down a note to himself.

"I'm so glad to hear that, Doctor. And I'm glad to hear you sounding so well!" the woman replied.

"Thanks for calling in, Beth." Caroline poked at another button. "And who do we have on line three?"

"Hi, Caroline. It's Lucy Holmes. I'd just like the doc to clarify how his accident happened."

"Doc, can you tell us what happened that night back in September?" The woman's head nodded vigorously.

Martin sighed. He had hoped this question had already been asked and answered enough times that he wouldn't have to address it today. "A lorry driver fell asleep at the wheel of his vehicle and drifted into my lane."

"Yeah, but I heard there was more to it than that," Lucy responded insinuatingly.

"Oh, did you!"

"Thanks for calling in, Luce. Let's give someone else a chance to ask a question, shall we?" The host said, flipping a switch. "You're through to Caroline."

An unidentified male voice began. "Yeah, I just wanted to say I 'erd somethin', too. Some blokes were sayin' down at the pub one night that they 'erd you was comin' home from a party over in Truro. That you'd been tippin' back a few with some'a yer mates and were squiffy drivin' home. That's why ya didn't git outta the way of that lorry. That true, Doc?"

Martin's eyes flashed across at Caroline. "*For the record* ... I was not at a party in Truro. I was at an NHS meeting at the Royal Cornwall Hospital, trying to keep an air ambulance for a village full of ingrates and—"

"Go ahead caller, you're li—"

An officious voice at the other end of the line cut the host short, and Martin's head dropped into his hand.

"This is PC Joseph Penhale. I am calling in my capacity as an officer of the law," he intoned. "I'm gonna set the record straight for everyone ... right here and now!

"Dr. Ellingham was neither squiffy nor was he tippin' back that night. He was just drivin'. The lorry driver was the offending party at fault, and the official police investigation proved that fact. And if you want to see proof of said fact, you can go over to the police station in Wadebridge and see the official police record.

"The lorry driver fell asleep at the wheel, and Dr. Ellingham had no way of removing his automobile from the path of the aforementioned lorry, because it happened on the River Camel bridge. And I'm statin' that officially ... right now ... in my official capacity.

"And I'll also have you know that if it weren't for Dr. Ellingham, you wouldn't have yer air ambulance anymore. That's what that meetin' was about. So now it's official. And that's all I have to say."

There was a loud click on the line before Caroline spoke again. "All right, that question's been answered ... officially. I see we have another caller. And who do we have on line two?"

"This is Jimmy Millinger. I'm just wonderin' if you and Miss Glasson was plannin' on anymore kids."

Martin's nostrils flared as he spat into the microphone. "That is none of your business! It's a private matter between *Mrs. Ellingham* and myself!"

"It's just that I seen you at The Mote the other night, Doc. And I just don't know how you could make that happen with all that metal stickin' outta ya. You probably won't find it so easy the next go-round ya know."

"Mr. Millinger, that is absolu—"

"Ah, I see we have another caller. Go ahead caller, you're live with Caroline."

Martin sat, red-faced and fuming as Bert Large's distinctive, spattery voice broke the air waves. "Here, Doc. You don't worry about it none, you hear. Just say the word and I'll cook up another batch of my special soup for you."

Martin didn't have time to get a word in edgewise before Caroline opened another line, and Chippy Miller's bass voice boomed out.

"I have a question for the doc, but first I wanna ask Bert about his special soup. What are you cookin' up for the doc, Bert?"

Bert's jovial chuckle reverberated through Caroline's headset as she realised too late that she'd lost control of her own phone-in show.

"Oi, Chippy. You better warn that little lady of yours before you try any of my soup. It has magical properties, I'm tellin' ya. Magical properties. Oh, ho. Why poor Irene wouldn't know what hit 'er!"

"What kinda magical properties, Bert?"

"Gawwd," Martin said, rolling his eyes.

"Well, it's like this, Chippy ... let's just say I don't imagine the doc and Louiser got much sleep the night I brought the first pot over to em. If you get my drift."

Martin looked frantically between Caroline and Jeremy.

"I don't remember seein' this on yer menu, Bert," the fisherman persisted.

"Oh boy, that would be dangerous, Chippy. If I had this stuff on the menu the night of the Portwenn Player's Dance ... why there could be explosive consequences! Poor ol' Doc would be doin' nothing but deliverin' babies nine months later!"

"What was your question for the doc, Chippy ... before we move on to another caller," Caroline prodded.

"Yeah, I got this bump on my..."

"Oh, for goodness' sake! Call the surgery once we're open or go over to Wadebridge, Mr. Miller!" Martin said, becoming increasingly exasperated.

Caroline looked down at the console in front of her, now lit up like a Christmas tree, and realised she had a smash hit on her hands.

"Let's take another call. You're through to Caroline!"

"Hi, Caroline. It's Ethel Macready here. I just wanted to suggest to Bert that he *should* put his soup on the menu. Sound's to me like he's sittin' on a gold mine!"

"Oh, believe me, Ethel, I've thought about it many a time. But what happens when I'm gone? I got a responsibility here you see. If all the fine Cornish gentlemen get a taste, so to speak, of my special soup and then suddenly I'm gone... Well, to have the supply suddenly cut off ... that just wouldn't be good for no one, now would it. No. I must be the bigger man here and do what's in the best interests of the great Cornish public."

"Well, you made it for the doc. Why not all the other men in Portwenn? And their wives for that matter?"

"Could we get back to the matter at hand... ***PLEASE!***" Martin pleaded.

"Oh, of course, Doc. The doc's right, Ethel. This show's s'posed ta be about him, not the general male population of

Portwenn. So, let's try not to change the subject," Bert sputtered. "The way I see it, Ethel ... in the doc's case, my special soup was strictly medicinal. If I put it on the menu, don't you think it'd be like one of them procreational drugs? Like heroin or meth. No, no. Puttin' it on the menu just wouldn't be ethical. It's like that sayin' ... what the eye don't see, the heart don't *grieve* over."

Martin shook his head desperately at Caroline, making a slashing motion across his throat. She gave him a dismissive eye roll before going on to the next caller.

"And we have another call on line five. Go ahead caller!"

"Hi, Caroline. It's John, down at the pub."

"Hi, John. Do you have a question for the doc?"

"No, but I have a question for Bert. What are you plannin' to *do* about the doc. Are you going to keep him in soup for the rest of his life or are you fixin' to just let him ... *grieve*?"

"Oh, *you* know the doc. He'll do just fine without my soup." Bert chortled. "I mean, how long did it take him to get our sweet Louiser preg—"

Martin reached his arm out and slapped his hand down on the console, effectively putting an end to the humiliating conversation. "Dammit, Caroline! What the *bloody hell* do you think you're doing?"

Caroline leaned forward into her still-open mic. "Annnd ... let's take a break. When we come back, the doc will explain to us about how the doctors in Truro are fixing his fractured arm and legs. And give us some advice on how to avoid the spread of germs during our impending cold and flu season."

Flamenco music faded in and the radio host gave her guest a magisterial stare. "Well, you've outdone yourself this time, Doc. Three expletives in one appearance."

Martin closed his eyes and heaved a heavy sigh. "Oh, gawd."

It was obvious to Jeremy that his patient was beyond frustrated as they sat quietly in the van before heading home after the radio fiasco.

"I'm really sorry, Martin. I told you I'd have your back and ... sorry, I just froze."

"It's fine. I knew something like this was going to happen. I just didn't expect it to go in the direction it did." He glanced over at Jeremy. "*You* did just fine."

"Yeah, well ... thanks for putting it in writing for me." The aide watched him as he rubbed at his throbbing head. "Does Louisa take a lunch break about now? We could stop and pick her up ... make a quick trip to Wadebridge for sandwiches ... get you out of the village for a while, and she could probably use a break from the kids."

Martin's chin dropped to his chest as he now remembered the conversation he'd had with his wife that morning. "Aww, that's just bloody brilliant! The teachers were going to have the students listen to the show," he said, releasing a long groan when he realised that he'd once again *disappointed the boys and girls*. He sank back into his seat and ceded his last shred of dignity to the village of Portwenn.

Chapter 21

Martin walked through the corridors of Portwenn Primary, his feet slowing as he approached his wife's office. Pippa Woodley brushed by him, looking at him as she always did. As if she were the ever-watchful headmaster anticipating his next indiscretion.

He stopped, just short of Louisa's office door, and took in a deep breath. Then, swallowing hard, he tried to ease the tightness in his throat, but it proved to be an ineffective action. He reached up to loosen the tie that was the usual cause of constriction, only to be reminded of his atypical attire when his fingertips touched his exposed skin.

He felt a sudden vulnerability. As a boarder at St. Benedict's, to be caught without his tie neatly and properly fastened around his neck was a punishable offense. It had only happened once, and Martin reflexively caressed his palms as he remembered the painful sting of the cane as it made contact with his hands. On that occasion, as was usually the case during the course of his childhood, he knew that he wasn't guilty of any impropriety.

He had been put into a biology class with boys three years older than himself, and he had incurred the wrath of one of the boys by pointing out his flawed methodology while conducting an experiment. The teacher overheard Martin explaining the error, and the student and his erroneous experiment were then used as an object lesson for the rest of the class.

The older boy had lain in wait for Martin to emerge from the room, shoving him and smacking his head into the hard, tiled corridor wall. He had then grasped his tie and pulled it tight around his neck. Martin had frantically tugged at the strip of fabric, finally ridding himself of the compulsory accoutrement before fleeing down the hall. As he rounded the corner he ran directly into the headmaster coming from the other direction.

Not only was he punished for being in violation of the school dress code, but he received several more whacks with the headmaster's cane for running in the halls. He hadn't dared to explain himself as it would have meant grassing up the older boy and certain retribution. So, he took his punishment without so much as a word.

Louisa had promised him that she would support him no matter what he muttered over the air waves that morning, but neither of them could have predicted what had transpired in the last hour and a half. "That bloody Bert ... and Caroline," he muttered.

He waited outside her open office door, relieved that she was complying with his wishes. She was involved in a conversation on the phone, doing far more listening than talking, but she gestured for to him to come in.

He took a seat on the vinyl covered sofa in the outer office to wait for her. He watched warily as she approached.

She sighed and dropped down next to him. He looked for all the world like a little boy who had just broken his mother's favourite vase. "Well, that was ugly ... hmm?" she said as she stared in front of her.

Martin's thumb worked away at his palm.

She rubbed at her temples. "I've already had two calls from Stu Mackenzie. He's quite upset with me for having allowed the students to listen in on the programme. I'm sure to be fielding calls from angry parents tomorrow, too."

"I'm sorry," he said, his shoulders sagging. "But it wasn't my fault, Louisa. I tried. I really tried. I didn't want to disappoint you."

She turned her head to look at him. "I know that. You didn't think I was going to be angry with you, did you?"

Martin picked at a small split in the vinyl on the sofa. "Well, no. It's just ... well maybe I was a bit worried."

Louisa put her hand on his knee. "Oh, Martin. I've had such unfair expectations of you, haven't I. I'm as bad as your awful parents!"

"Louisa!" The frown lines on his forehead deepened, and he gave her a small shake of his head. "I'm sorry, Louisa. I don't follow."

"Carole and I talked about this last weekend. She pointed some things out to me ... things that were hard for me to hear because I know there's a lot of truth to it. *You* can't win. I mean, I demand way too much from you when it comes to the people in this village. You're a man of logic ... of reason. And this village is the antithesis of logic and reason. Caroline and her stupid phone-in today is a prime example!"

His wife was watching for his reaction to her words in much the same way that she'd watched for his reaction to James Henry the day he was born.

He dipped his chin and peered up at her cautiously. "So, you're not angry then—not disappointed?"

"No. I'm not angry, Martin. I think you accomplished what you needed to, and you didn't throttle Caroline either." She leaned over and placed a lingering kiss on his lips. "There are a few villager's that *I* could throttle, however! I'm sure we haven't heard the end of it yet."

Martin screwed up his face and grimaced at the thought. "Stupid Bert ... and his bloody soup! I can only imagine the number of completely inappropriate questions that I'll get from patients now, let alone the cackling we'll get from that band of female miscreants!"

Reaching up, Louisa brushed her fingers back through her husband's hair before smoothing it into place again with her palm. "I'm not disappointed either," she said softly. "Quite the opposite. I'm proud of you. What you said at the end was understandable."

Martin sighed and let his eyes drift shut for a few moments. "Mm, I guess I haven't asked you. Would you have time to make a quick trip to Wadebridge for a sandwich with us? Just to get out of the village for a bit?"

"I think I better give it a miss, Martin," she said, nodding towards the papers strewn across the top of her desk. "You and Jeremy go ahead without me."

"Nooo, I'll have lunch with you at home," he said, gazing at her before stroking her cheek with his thumb.

"I think I better have a working lunch, I'm afraid. I'll get Allison in the cafeteria to make up a salad for me. You go on ahead with Jeremy."

"Mm, yes."

He got up and moved towards the door, and then turned. "You *will* leave before everyone else is gone today, won't you?"

"Yes, Martin. I will. It's nice to have someone who worries about me." She gave him a smile, and he left the office caring a bit less about the opinions of his fellow villagers.

Martin and Jeremy got their lunch at the sandwich shop they frequented on physical therapy days and then headed back towards Portwenn.

"Do you have your backpack with you, Jeremy?" Martin asked.

The aide glanced over at him, giving him a quick visual inspection. "Yeah, why? Is there a problem?"

"No. No problem."

When they reached the east side of St. Endellion, Martin asked Jeremy to make a left turn.

"I'd like to stop in to see Beth Sawle, the elderly woman who called in this morning. She sounded stridorous over the phone. With her history of aspergilloma and her frequent bouts with pneumonia, I don't want to leave this until the surgery opens."

"What's Dr. Parsons going to say about this?"

Martin waggled his finger aggressively as they rapidly approached the turning. "Right here! Right here!"

Jeremy slowed the van quickly and pulled off the tarmac on to a gravel road. "I don't know about this, Martin. I think we should clear it with Parsons and Christianson first. You're already pushing this, you know."

"Yes, I'm aware of that. Let me deal with Chris and Ed. You just ... drive."

As was typical of the Sawle home, the place appeared deserted when they arrived. Martin jotted down a list of signs and symptoms that he wanted collected by his assistant and then sent him to the door.

In the years since the infamous aspergillosis outbreak, the older of the two Sawle sisters had experienced a stroke and was now in a care facility in Padstow. Beth Sawle had taken a boarder who happened to have a nursing degree. In exchange for free room and board, and a monthly stipend, the boarder assisted Beth with her daily care needs. It was an arrangement that had worked out well for both women.

Jeremy returned to the van, the boarder at his side. "Hi, Doc. Heard ya on the radio today. Here to check up on Beth, are ya?"

"Yes, I am. I noticed some stridor when Miss Sawle called in to the show this morning. I'd like my assistant to check her over before I come into the house, though," he said.

"Sure, Doc. Whatever you say."

Jeremy disappeared through the door with the nurse, returning a short time later. "Well, she's febrile ... temperature is one hundred point two. Some swelling of the lymph nodes, and I could hear bilateral rales. Her nurse says she had a cold a couple of weeks ago. Seemed to shake it, but the last couple of days she's been coughing a lot and her temperature spiked today."

Martin reached his hand out and took the notes that his assistant had collected, scanning them over. He nodded his head then opened the door to get out of the van. "Okay, let's go."

Beth was sitting in a recliner in the lounge, and she gave the doctor a weak smile when he entered the room.

"Hello, doctor. It's very nice of you to come all the way out here."

Martin gave his head a shake. "Not a problem, Miss Sawle. We were actually on our way back from Wadebridge, so it was a good time to stop."

Jeremy grabbed a chair from the kitchen, placed it next to the patient, and then took the doctor's arm, supporting him as he dropped into the seat.

The old woman eyed him worriedly. "Are you sure you're up to this, Doctor?"

"Be quiet, please, Miss Sawle," Martin said softly as he closed his eyes and took in a deep breath.

Jeremy tried to fill the awkward silence with casual conversation. "How long have you lived in this house, Miss Sawle?"

Beth tugged at the front of her blouse, straightening it self-consciously. "Eighty-two years!" she said with pride in her voice. "I was born in this house and have never lived anywhere else."

"All right, Miss Sawle. I'm going to listen to your chest," Martin said as he flipped the tips of his assistant's stethoscope into his ears. His brow furrowed as he moved the instrument around on her chest and back. "Could you cough, please?"

The elderly woman did her best to do as the doctor had instructed, but she had difficulty getting enough air to produce the desired effect.

"I'm sorry, Doctor," she wheezed.

"It's all right. That's why I'm here. I suspect you're aware that you have pneumonia, but I'm concerned about a heart murmur that I'm picking up." Martin turned to face the nurse. "Can you get her over to Truro for a cardiac ultrasound?"

The woman stood wringing her hands. "I don't drive."

"You'll need to take a taxi, then. I'll call and make the appointment, then let you know when they want you over there."

He wrapped the stethoscope around his hand and gave it back to his assistant. "Try not to worry about this. I think you may have a mild aortic stenosis. If that's the case, it bears watching, but it's nothing to be overly concerned about. I just want to make sure that you have a cardiologist keeping an eye on it."

The old woman reached a bony hand out and placed it over her doctor's solid paw. "You're a nice young man, Dr. Ellingham."

Martin glanced over at her and their eyes met, Beth's sparkling as she gave him a timid smile. He replied with a grunt before getting to his feet.

The elderly woman watched him, concern registering on her face. "Does that hurt, Doctor?" she asked as she gestured to the hardware on Martin's limbs.

He sighed softly. "*You're* the patient, Miss Sawle."

The assistant collected his bag and waited while his boss moved across the room. "Jeremy, if I have Mrs. Tishell get a prescription ready could you drop it off here on your way back to Truro this afternoon?"

"Sure. Yeah, I can do that."

"I'll come out next week and check up on you. But I want to hear from you if your fever goes any higher or the symptoms worsen."

It had been a long and stressful day, and by the time Louisa had taken the baby up to bed that night Martin was exhausted.

She found him in the bathroom tending to the tedious task of cleaning his fixator pins. Dark circles had formed under his eyes. He had his foot propped up on the edge of the bathtub, and she sat down next to him.

"Here, let me finish up," she said as she held out her hand for the tray of supplies.

"It's fine. I know this bothers you."

"Martin..." She tugged the tray of cleaning solution and cotton buds from his hand. "It's going to be a tough year, isn't it?"

"It'll be a *long* year. Yes." He massaged his aching temples and closed his eyes, trying to tune out the uncomfortable sensation as the swabs rubbed at his sensitive skin. "I saw a patient today. Beth Sawle."

Louisa's head popped up from her work. "Oh? What did Chris have to say about that?"

Martin shook his head. "Not much," he answered evasively.

He shifted uncomfortably as his wife fixed her gaze on him. "You didn't ask him, did you?"

"He would've been fine with it, I'm sure. I didn't want to bother him. It was just a short house call."

"Oh, *Mar-tin.*"

He waggled his head at her. "It wasn't planned. We were coming back from Wadebridge and were going right by her lane, so I thought we might as well stop in."

"Hmm, I see." Louisa gave him an admonishing glare, but he saw her face soften and a slight smile spread across it as she returned to the task at hand.

"Okay, now you're squeaky clean again," she said as she returned the tray to the small table next to him.

Louisa went upstairs to tend to her nightly ablutions before returning to the downstairs bedroom. Martin was already tucked in, lying drowsily under the bedclothes.

She crawled in next to him, pulling her feet up to his warm body.

"Geesh, Louisa! Warn me before you do that!" he yelped.

"Sorry. You're just kind of irresistible."

She gave him an impish grin, and he scowled back at her. "Yes, well … that has a rather powerful effect on my central nervous system and cardiovascular system. If you were suitably concerned about my—"

She interrupted the impending medical discourse with a finger to his lips. "I *said* I'm sorry. And I'll try to warn you next time."

"Mm, yes."

His scowl eased as she caressed his cheek. "You know, I'm afraid that I helped to create a very difficult atmosphere for you."

"Mm. It's okay, they'll warm up eventually."

An amused grin slid across her face. "I'm not talking about feet anymore, Martin."

"Well, what are you talking about then?"

She propped herself up on her elbow and kissed him on the forehead. "I'm referring to when you first came to Portwenn. I certainly could have done more to help you assimilate."

He tried to roll himself to his side, yanking at the bedclothes that were hanging up on his fixators.

"I suspect that if I'd supported and encouraged you when you first came to the village instead of always bangin' on about everything I thought you were doing wrong and how you weren't the right doctor for this village, things could have been very different for you."

Air hissed from his nose as he tried, unsuccessfully, to free himself from the blankets. "Mm. But you didn't really like me back then."

Louisa sat herself up, tucking her cold feet under her. "That's the thing, Martin. I liked you *very* much. You didn't seem interested in me, so I kept looking for all these reasons to *dis*-like you."

"Louisa, the day we met, I ran headlong into a bloody door because I was so taken with you. Of course, I was interested in you. I nearly concussed myself because of you!"

"That's very romantic, Martin." She bent down and placed a languid kiss on his lips.

"Can we go to sleep now?" he asked irritably.

"Yes, Martin. We can go to sleep. And my feet are warm now, by the way."

"Yes."

Chapter 22

Friday brought with it a full schedule of activities. After Martin's physical therapy appointment, they would drive to Truro where they would first make a stop at the Lexus dealership.

Even though he didn't particularly like to drive, Martin was getting anxious to be back behind the wheel of his own car, with the freedom and independence to go when and where he wanted.

He had been forced to tolerate a lot in the last week and had done it with a surprising amount of self-restraint. But his patience was wearing thin, and Louisa could see it in his general edginess and irritability that morning.

She and Carole had made plans to meet for a late lunch, something that seemed to have put her husband out of sorts about the trip into the city.

He would have preferred to leave the afternoon open-ended so they wouldn't be so pushed for time before his appointment with Dr. Newell later. He suspected the therapist would want to conduct another exhumation of long-buried memories from his childhood. Not something he relished after a stressful week.

"Could you please move it along, Louisa? We're going to be late," he said, pulling at his sleeve and holding his arm up in front of him to check the time, yet again.

"I'm trying, Mar-tin! Your son seems to have designs to disrupt our plans!" she said as she struggled to wrestle a very wriggly James into yet another set of clean clothes.

The child had first managed to get hold of the open jar of nappy cream and make a mess of it. The second set of clothes had been soiled at breakfast when he dropped a piece of banana on to his lap and smeared it into the new pair of trousers Louisa had dressed him in.

Martin blew a hiss of air from his nose.

The atmosphere in the van was thick with tension as they drove to Wadebridge. Louisa tried to keep quiet and give her husband the mental space that she knew he was needing, but once again, the younger Ellingham had other ideas.

The boy kicked and screamed for the first five minutes of the trip, unhappy to be restrained so early in the morning. He finally settled when Martin handed him a children's book before slipping the accompanying disc into the slot on the dashboard. This was a story that James particularly enjoyed sharing with his father, due in large part to the fact that it was one that *Martin* enjoyed. He appreciated the cleverness and imaginativeness of the tale, regardless of the illogicality involved in the narrative.

One evening, after thinking it over for sometime, Harold decided to go for a walk, the female raconteur's voice singsonged. James's face lit up, and he released a happy chortle. Louisa watched her husband out of the corner of her eye and was relieved to see him settle back into his seat.

"Everything okay today?" she asked.

He turned a well-scowled face to her. "Yes, fine." Resting his elbow on the window ledge, he propped his head in his hand.

She sat awkwardly on the other side of the vehicle trying to decide whether she should press him any further. She opted to leave him be for the moment and hoped his mood would improve after physical therapy.

Louisa waited with James in the seating area by the reception desk while Martin met with Kieran and Max. The new brace had arrived and Kieran checked it for fit before they took him to a large room to work on gait training—the proper use of the crutches that he would be transitioning to.

The brace did a good job of supporting Martin's shoulder and distributed his weight evenly from his torso around to his under and upper arm. He'd been quite nervous about the stress that the joint would be taking. As he had told his wife the night of their disastrous honeymoon, a dislocated shoulder *is* agonising, and the thought of a recurrence was causing him a good deal of anxiety.

"You're doing great, Dr. Ellingham. I see you lean forward a bit at times, but for the most part your posture is good and your gait looks good as well," Max said. "Let's go work on the stairs now."

They returned to the large main room where platforms, ranging in height from a few inches up to ten inches, were arrayed along one wall. Over the course of the next hour, Martin worked his way up to the tallest platform, making repeated steps up and down. They then went to a series of three steps of differing heights.

"Well, you seemed to handle that quite well. Let's give you a bit more of a challenge." Max waved a hand at Kieran who was setting up equipment on the other side of the room.

The two therapists led Martin down the corridor before opening a door leading into a stairwell.

"We'll be right beside you in case you lose your balance, Dr. Ellingham. If you get tired, stop and catch your breath. Are you ready?"

Martin looked up at the fifteen steps in front of him and took a deep breath. Because of the stiffness in his right knee and the still weakened muscles in his thigh, the therapists had him lead with his left leg going up the stairs, bringing his right leg up from behind.

He'd made it halfway to the top step when his muscles began to flag. "I need to stop for a minute," he said. Air rushed in and out of his lungs as he shook the fatigue from his arms.

Kieran and Max were in constant contact with him, assisting him with balance without giving him any physical support.

He glanced over at Kieran and nodded his head before continuing his ascent.

“Great job! You’ve worked hard, Dr. Ellingham, and it’s really showing today,” Max said. “Take a little breather, then we’ll try going the other way.”

This had been harder than Martin had anticipated, but the surgery steps had a lower rise and there were fewer of them. If he could handle this, he should be able to handle the steps at the surgery.

Once his breathing had slowed and the burn in his muscles had eased, he gave a nod to Max. “Okay, I’m ready.”

“This first time going down the steps, we’ll hang on to you,” Kieran said. “This will definitely require more finesse than going up.”

Martin turned himself around on the crutches to face the stairs. The sight in front of him made his heart race. He shook his head. “Finesse isn’t a quality people normally ascribe to me.”

“Well, prove them wrong then. That right leg goes first this time,” the therapist said. “Make sure you take a few moments to think things through before you start down a flight of stairs. It’s very easy to have that hardwired muscle memory kick in and start off with the wrong foot if you’re not careful. You’re sure to take a header if you do that, so think—it—through.”

Martin tried to adjust his grip on the crutches, his hands shaking noticeably as he did so. He focused his thoughts on how his body was moving rather than letting his eyes drift to the bottom of the staircase.

Descending the steps proved to be less taxing on his muscles but most certainly more stressful, and he breathed a sigh of relief when his foot touched the floor at the bottom.

"Excellent job, Dr. Ellingham. How did that feel for you?" Max asked.

"It was one of the most terrifying things I've done in my life," he said, gripping the crutches tightly in an attempt to steady his hands.

"Do you have a handrail in your stairway at home, Doctor?" Kieran asked as he stooped to tie a loosened lace on his patient's shoe.

"On one side. Yes, we do."

"I'd recommend you get a rail on the other side as well. That would actually be safer for you than trying to navigate the steps on crutches. But you're going to encounter stairs all over, so this is a skill you need to learn regardless."

Martin practiced for a solid half hour before Max called a halt to the session. "You're wearing out. Let's go and work on your range of motion, then we'll cut you loose for the day."

"What do you think? Can I handle the stairs at the surgery?" Martin asked.

"I don't see why not. I'm in agreement with Kieran though. Get another handrail put up, and make sure they're both secure. Until then, have someone rest their hand on you to help with balance whenever you're on the stairs." Max gave Martin a pat on the back. "Let's go."

Louisa waited, trying to keep James busy as her husband's session dragged on. The boy toddled back and forth across the room, clinging tightly to her thumbs.

"Your back must be killing you, dear. Why don't you let me take him for a bit? You can go look in on your husband," one of the receptionists behind the counter said.

Louisa hesitated before reluctantly handing over her treasured, tow-headed little boy. "Are you sure? He can be a handful."

"Positive. I take care of my grandbabies all the time. You go now," she said, giving a jerk of her head.

Louisa stepped into the main therapy area and looked around. “He’s in the room on the end, Mrs. Ellingham,” Max said as he approached. “Go ahead, there should be an extra chair in there.”

“Thank you, Max.” She walked down the hall and stood in the doorway, watching as Kieran performed the now familiar stretching exercises with her husband’s limbs.

Martin was facing away from her, but the tensing of his body and the soft, stifled groans betrayed his pain. She blinked back tears as she experienced her own brand of pain.

“Okay. Roll on to your back, and we’ll work on that arm, Dr. Ellingham. Martin grimaced as Kieran forced his elbow to bend past the point of comfort. Louisa stayed back out of sight until the therapist pulled out his pot of cocoa butter and began the soothing massage that marked the conclusion to the session.

“Hello,” she said as she laid a hand on her husband’s head.

He tried to pull himself up, but Kieran pushed him back down. “I’m not done with you yet.”

“What’s wrong, Louisa? Why aren’t you with James?”

“Nothing’s wrong. The receptionist just thought I needed a break from our little bundle of energy. Thought I’d come and see how you’re getting along.”

“I’m ... good. Once we get a handrail on the other side of the stairs at the surgery we can move back home.” He gazed up at her with a sparkle in his eyes.

“Martin, that’s wonderful!” She impulsively leaned over and kissed him twice, once on each cheek, causing him to pull back quickly before casting a self-conscious glance at his therapist.

Kieran smiled. “Don’t mind me. It’s nice to see, Dr. Ellingham. Happy patients. Happy wives. You two just made my day.”

Martin grunted and reverted to his usual staid demeanour. "Perhaps you could ask Al to put the handrail up for us," he said.

Louisa pulled her mobile from her pocket. "I'll go do that right now. Then I'll stop back in and give you a hand, hmm?"

"Yes, that'd be good."

Having collected their son from the receptionist, the Ellingham family walked out of the physical therapy centre a half hour later. It was almost half ten when they crossed the River Camel bridge and just after eleven o'clock when they pulled into the Lexus dealership on the west side of the city.

A middle-aged salesman, dressed in a smart bespoke suit, approached them before they had made it halfway to the showroom door. Introductions were made and Martin handed the man a sheet of paper with the model number of the vehicle he was interested in typed out in bold face at the top of the page. A list of specifications followed, each preceded by a bullet.

Richard Smyth had dealt with this type of customer before, and he knew he was going to have a tough time trying to sell him on any pricier options. Martin Ellingham knew what he wanted and wasn't going to be messed about with. The salesman would have to handle him delicately if he didn't want to overplay his hand.

"I do have that model," he said after reviewing the inventory on his tablet. *And,* fortunately for you, that vehicle comes with the executive-class seating package as well!"

Martin shook his head and eyed the man suspiciously. "Is that something I'm supposed to be happy to hear?"

"Vehicles purchased with this package tend to have a higher resale value, Dr. Ellingham. Rear seat massage. Blu-ray and DVD player. The little one would—"

"No. Mr—" Martin glanced down at the shiny gold placard on the man's chest. "Mr. Smyth, I gave you a list of the options that my wife and I are interested in. Do you see either a Blu-ray player or rear seat massage on that list?"

"It *is* a beautiful vehicle, sir. All the creature comforts. If you'll follow me, we can go and take a dekko at it." The salesman pivoted on his foot to head off to the other end of the show lot. He knew from experience that his odds of making a sale increased greatly once the customer had laid eyes on a car.

A rapidly intensifying ache had begun in Martin's legs and the strenuous therapy session had left him exhausted. He was not in any frame of mind for the salesman's dog and pony show.

"No! I have no interest whatsoever in that vehicle. I believe I've been quite clear about what I want, and I have absolutely no intention of playing any kind of shell game with you today."

Martin was growing more indignant by the minute. He tried to wipe the perspiration that had begun to trickle down his temples on to his shirt sleeve, but the crutches prevented him from lifting his arm.

Louisa watched her husband nervously, hoping that his impatience wouldn't intensify into an all-out fulmination.

James reached his hand out and grabbed at his father's shirt, and Martin's focus shifted to his son. This had an immediate calming effect on him. He lowered his voice and clenched his jaw as he again addressed the salesman. "As you can see, I'm a bit hobbled at the moment. *Can* you or can you *not* show me a vehicle with the options that I've asked for?"

Mr. Smyth realised he was in danger of losing a sale. "I'm sorry if I've offended you in any way, Dr. Ellingham. I was only concerned for your comfort ... given your current condition. How 'bout we go inside and discuss this where you can get off your feet. I can get you both a cup of espresso if you like."

Martin curled his lip at the man. There were few things that annoyed him more than salesmen who used specious solicitudes to sell a product.

"That sounds like a brilliant idea," Louisa said, turning to her husband. "Can you make it inside, Martin?"

"Of course I can!" he snapped.

Once inside the showroom, Martin collapsed into a chair, resting with his eyes closed while the salesman went to collect the promised beverage.

The man returned a short time later, setting a tray with three cups of the aromatic brew on the table in front of them.

"Mm, this looks tempting," Louisa said as she reached for one of the chocolate Hobnobs sitting on a plate.

Martin eyed her disapprovingly. "Best not, Louisa. It's been a while since you've eaten anything, and we have a late lunch planned. The high sugar content in the biscuit will cause a blood glucose spike now, but your glucose levels will crash before we have lunch. This can result in sweating, shaking hands, irritability and—"

Louisa shot him a warning glance. "If I find myself irritable, Mar-tin, it *won't* be because of this Hobnob," she said under her breath, snapping a bite off the biscuit.

"Mm." He was learning that there were certain subjects his wife seemed to be especially sensitive about. And for reasons he could not fathom, her dietary intake was one of them. He decided to let the Hobnob issue drop.

"Now, this is a list of the vehicles that I have available at the moment," the salesman said. "I can, of course, help you to build your own package, and we can get a vehicle on order if you'd prefer."

Martin snatched the list from his hand and scanned over it. "What about your dealership in Plymouth? Do they have what I want in their inventory?"

"I can check on that for you, sir." Mr. Smyth glanced over at Louisa, raising his eyebrows. He had detected a vulnerability in his customer when his wife had displayed her annoyance with him. Perhaps, the salesman thought, if he appeared to be sympathetic to her unfortunate pairing with such an obstinate man, he could turn her frustration to his advantage. He gave Louisa a pat on the shoulder as he walked by.

The gesture was not missed by Martin, and he felt his hackles rising. He looked over at her and their eyes met.

"I'm sorry, Louisa," he said quietly in the tone that never failed to soften her ire.

She reached for his hand. "I'm sorry, too. Are you doing okay ... feeling all right?"

Martin looked over as he saw Mr. Smyth approaching and pulled his hand away. "I'm fine. Here ... have another biscuit," he said as he slid the plate towards her.

Chapter 23

Mr. Smyth had confirmed that the Lexus dealership in Plymouth did indeed have a vehicle meeting Martin's required specifications. Louisa sat with James on her lap, watching as the salesman tried to provoke her husband into the customary bargaining process involved when buying a car.

But Martin refused to negotiate and made himself very clear about what model Lexus he wanted as well as how much he was willing to pay for it.

Mr. Smyth, however, had been equally persistent in his efforts to wheedle his customer into a more extravagant options package. The salesman's prevarications had gone on for the better part of an hour before Martin's aggravation with the man boiled over into a verbal outburst.

"Oh, for God's sake! This car is costing me upwards of eighty thousand pounds, and you want to know if I'd like to pay an additional sixty for a rear bumper applique with your company logo on it?" he bellowed.

Louisa placed a hand on his arm. "Martin, calm—down!" she hissed.

He brushed her away before continuing on. "You should be paying *me* you unprincipled, greedy little—n-nit!"

"Martin!" She gave him an admonishing stare before turning a contrite gaze towards the salesman.

Martin returned it with a fiery glance before quickly adding imperiously, "Now, get back on that phone and work out how you're going to get that car up here to Truro this afternoon, or we'll take our business elsewhere!"

Louisa tipped her head at Mr. Smyth. "I'm really sorry about this. Martin's had a difficult day and he's—"

"Don't apologise for me, Louisa!" He struggled to his feet and hobbled off towards the lavatories.

James watched his father, wide-eyed, until he disappeared around the corner, and then he began to cry.

Louisa held him close and bounced him gently. She looked over at the salesman. "Sorry about that; I'll have a talk with him."

"My only concern, Mrs. Ellingham, is that you and your husband are happy with your new vehicle. And I have yet to hear a mum say they regretted the investment they made in the executive package."

He leaned his elbows on the table and steepled his fingers, staring at her sympathetically. "Many husbands just don't understand how difficult it is to be a mum. They have so many demands placed on them, nowadays. I feel that the least a husband can do is show his appreciation by making his wife's job easier when given the opportunity. You can't put a price on that."

Louisa looked at the man, suspiciously, then gave him an uneasy smile. "I'll go and talk with him. Again, I'm sorry."

Mr. Smyth went into his office, and Louisa could see him pull his mobile from his pocket. She stood up with James and walked him around the showroom, humming a tune in his ear to calm him. Then she went in search of her husband.

She tapped on the men's room door. Not hearing an answer she opened it cautiously. The room appeared to be empty. But as she craned her neck around the corner, she saw Martin leaning up against the far wall with his hand over his eyes.

Detecting her presence, he quickly straightened himself.

"Louisa! You shouldn't be in here! Wait outside for goodness' sake!"

She walked across the lavatory and wrapped an arm around his waist, hugging up against him. "There's no one else in here at the moment. It's fine." His heart pounded against her and fine tremors rippled through his body periodically.

James tried to pull himself into his arms by grabbing on to the front of his shirt. Feeling the boy's touch, Martin glanced down. A wonky grin spread across James's face when his father made eye contact with him.

Pulling his hand up, he brushed the backs of his fingers across the boy's cheek. His eyes shifted and they met his wife's.

"I'm sorry, Louisa ... again." He sighed and let his head drop back against the wall.

"I know something's wrong, Martin. If you want to talk, I promise to just listen and not try to solve the problem for you."

"I *don't* want to have this conversation in the men's toilet, Louisa. Please ... can we do this somewhere else?" he pleaded, pushing against her as he tried to move towards the door.

Louisa looked around her, taking note of the pair of urinals against the wall. "I s'pose you're right."

"We'd better go see what that scheming salesman is up to," he said as he took a step forward.

"I don't think you can say he's scheming, Martin."

"Well, what would you call it then?"

"I don't know. Maybe he's just trying to put food on the table." She brushed her hand over the top of her son's head, trying to tame a wisp of hair that seemed determined to pop up.

"Rrright. He wears bespoke suits to work every day and drives a Lexus home every night. I doubt very much that the man is struggling to get by." Martin opened his mouth again to speak, but thought better of it and quickly clamped his jaws shut.

"What?" she asked, cocking her head at him.

He closed his eyes and huffed out a puff of air. "Best not to say it. Let's get on with this, shall we?"

"No, Martin. I'm not leaving this room until you tell me what you were going to say."

He could almost see his wife's heels digging into the floor tiles below her feet. He gave a nervous glance at the door before letting his restrained words tumble from his mouth.

"Good God, Louisa! Can't you see what he's up to? He's playing you against me. What do you think that hand on your shoulder was all about earlier?"

She shook her head and knitted her brow. "It was just a reassuring pat, Martin. Things were getting tense between us, and he was just showing me some kindness and understanding. I don't think it's fair for you to assume he's scheming."

"I don't think I'm making an assumption! I think it's pretty obvious that he's using you to weaken my position in trying to get a fair deal here. And to great effect I might add!" He gave a firm nod of his head to emphasise his point.

He noticed his son's eyes begin to fill with tears in response to his angry words, and he softened his tone. "The man could clearly see that I don't have your support, that's all I'm trying to say."

He limped to the door and then, realising he couldn't manage it on his own, he turned to his wife. "Would you help me here, please?" he said tersely. "*And come out of this lavatory!*" he added in a strident whisper.

Louisa said no more as her husband's words were churning in her head. She tried to see things from his perspective, and the probable motive for the salesman's behaviour became more apparent.

For someone who found social interaction so terribly problematic, her husband had a very keen sense when it came to recognising designing behaviours in people. He'd never really had an ally in his life, but he'd figured out how to manage on his own. Always being on the lookout for people who might try to take advantage—those with ulterior motives—instantly suspicious and on guard when anyone even showed him kindness.

This was self-protective behaviour that he had honed to near perfection. *He must be feeling as though he's been fighting an offensive battle with this salesman while simultaneously protecting his rear flank—fighting a defensive battle with me,* Louisa thought.

Mr. Smyth was waiting for them at the table when they returned. Martin held out his hand, gesturing for his wife to take a seat first. Louisa took a moment to move her chair a bit closer to his before sitting down. She turned and gave him a confident smile.

"Well, I had a little chin wag with the manager in Plymouth," Mr. Smyth began. "The vehicle that you're interested in hasn't been detailed as of yet, and they just can't see how they could possibly have it ready for you this afternoon.

"They do, however, have the same vehicle with the executive-class seating package that's ready to go right now. It would normally add an extra fifteen hundred pounds to the cost of the vehicle you have here on paper. But we want you to leave happy today, so we'd be willing to compromise ... let you have it for only an extra twelve hundred. That's a very generous offer, Dr. Ellingham. And someone could drive it up here for you as well," Mr. Smyth said with a self-satisfied smile.

The salesman turned his head to address Louisa. "What do *you* think, Mrs. Ellingham? I bet that DVD player would be a godsend with that little one there."

Louisa glanced over at her husband before giving the man a penetrating stare. "I think, Mr. Smyth, that my husband and I are on the same page here."

He turned to Martin. "It's a fine deal, Doctor."

Martin glared at him. “Mr. Smyth, no matter how we conclude our business dealings today, I will *not* be leaving here happy. Now, if you can’t have the car I’ve specified ready and here on your lot this afternoon, then we’ll drive down to Plymouth ourselves and pick it up. I’ll happily make the cheque out to the dealership down there. But I’ve allowed you to waste far too much of my time already. If you’re incapable of making this happen, we’ll be on our way.”

Martin made a move to get up and Louisa rose from her chair. She put her hand under his uninjured arm and helped him to his feet.

Mr. Smyth breathed out a heavy sigh. “I’ll tell you what, let me have another go at it with the boys down in Plymouth ... see what we can get done.”

Martin glanced at his watch. “You have five minutes.”

The Ellinghams left the dealership fifteen minutes later, papers signed and an agreement made for the car to be ready for them before the dealership closed that evening.

It was now almost one o’clock, the agreed upon meeting time with the Parsons. Louisa helped Martin with the van door and then strapped James Henry into his car seat.

“Okay. I’m ready to listen,” she said after pulling the driver’s side door shut behind her.

Martin tipped his head to the side and gave her a blank stare. “To what?”

“To you! Remember in the lavatory? You said you’d tell me what was bothering you.”

He shook his head dismissively. “It’s nothing. Ed suggested I try and taper back on the morphine a bit before I start seeing patients. That’s caused some minor issues.”

“Why didn’t you mention this before now?”

“Because it hadn’t really been a problem until last night. Not even a problem really. Just some uncomfortable symptoms as my body adjusts to the decrease in the medication.” He pulled his arm up and looked down at his watch. "We really need to be going. The Parsons are probably waiting."

"Yes, and I'm sure they won't mind waiting a bit longer. What do you mean by uncomfortable symptoms?"

Martin huffed out a breath. "I just feel a bit tense ... agitated. I get a bit shaky feeling at times. And I get some tremors. It's really quite minor, so I don't want you to worry. I told Ed I'd walk over and see him after I get done with my counselling session. I thought you could have some time with Dr. Newell while I'm over at the hospital."

"Why didn't you tell me you were cutting back on the morphine? I feel like you're shutting me out when you keep things from me."

"Louisa, I really didn't try to keep this from you. My mind's been on other things, and when we've had time to talk, we've gotten involved in conversations about other issues. I'd forgotten to bring it up. I hadn't given it much thought until I woke up around two o'clock this morning and didn't feel right."

"You should have told me *then* Martin!"

"You were asleep, Louisa. I wasn't going to wake you to tell you that I was feeling agitated. And there hasn't been a good time today to discuss it."

"Well, next time, wake me up ... please," she said, reaching over to brush her fingers through his hair.

Grumbling under his breath, Martin swung his head around towards the passenger side window.

Louisa drummed her fingers impatiently on the steering wheel. "You need to speak up, Martin. I didn't hear that."

"I'd feel ridiculous waking *you* from a sound sleep to tell you that *I'm* agitated," he said, the words pattering from his mouth. "It doesn't make sense."

"Maybe not, but I do want to know." She picked up his hand and pressed it to her cheek. "I worry about you because I love you. You know that, don't you?"

He turned to look at her. "Mm, I do," he said, swallowing. "Thank you for that."

"There's no need to thank me, Martin. I just can't seem to help myself."

They leaned towards one another and exchanged a tender kiss.

Chapter 24

As expected, the Parsons were already at the restaurant when Martin and Louisa arrived. Chris stood up and waved a hand to get their attention. He smiled broadly when he saw that Martin had made yet another major step forward in his recovery. "Nicely done, mate!"

"Mm, yes," Martin said self-consciously as he balanced on the crutches wedged under his arms.

Carole got up from her chair, and she and Louisa exchanged hugs, kisses, and what Martin had decided must be an obligatory transaction of compliments that women seem compelled to make on the other's attire. He squirmed uncomfortably and glanced away, finding the women's prescribed greeting to be embarrassingly effusive, especially when it was conducted in a public place.

"Martin, you look more and more like your old self," Carole said. Her accompanying pat on the cheek earned her a scowl.

Louisa rolled her eyes. "That should be taken as a compliment, Martin. It's customary to say thank you," she prodded.

Carole cringed at her friend's admonishment, knowing how hurtful Christopher and Margaret Ellingham's constant belittling remarks had been to their son. "A thank you is *not* necessary, Martin. I'm just very happy to see you looking stronger."

"So, tell me how the big radio show went," Chris said as he patted a short riff out on the table top.

Martin groaned. "Let's just say that Jeremy and I were able to squeeze the essential details in amongst the imbecilic and completely inappropriate calls that came in. I believe we satisfied the stipulation."

"Good. Glad to hear it. Didn't prove to be the balls-up you thought it'd be after all then?"

Martin glanced over at Louisa and screwed up his face. "I didn't say that. I'm just saying that we fulfilled the requirement."

Chris tipped his chair back and crossed his arms in front of him. "All right, let's hear it. What happened?"

"Ohhh, can we just..." Martin gave his menu a toss on to the table.

"I'd like to know if I should be battening down the hatches, Mart. What happened?"

"Let's just say that the reopening of the surgery didn't end up being the primary focus of the programme," Louisa said as she dug through the nappy bag for James's purple dinosaur.

"Okaay." Chris leaned forward and picked up the pitcher of water. "Well, do you feel like you're ready to be seeing patients again?"

Martin slowly ran his finger around the rim of his glass. "I do. Strictly speaking, I've actually seen my first patient."

"Oh, care to elaborate?"

"It was one of my regular patients, an elderly woman. She happened to call in to the show yesterday morning, and I detected a stridor as she was talking. Jeremy and I had run over to Wadebridge for lunch and we happened to go by her house on the way back to Portwenn."

Chris speared a cocktail shrimp from the tray of starters in the middle of the table. "How did you handle it, send Jeremy in first?"

Martin tried to stretch his right leg out to relieve a cramp that had developed. "Mm. I wrote down a list of signs and symptoms for him to gather, then I went through them before I went into the house to examine her."

"And ... what was the diagnosis?"

"I felt quite confident it was a pneumococcal pneumonia. She has a history of aspergilloma and has had several bouts with pneumonia since. She's responded quickly to antibiotics in the past, so I started her on a course of moxifloxicin. I believe I caught it early, so I anticipate a full recov—"

A waiter arrived, and Martin tabled the conversation until after their orders had been placed.

Chris watched as the young man collected the menus and moved off. "So, you were saying, Mart?" He turned in his chair and threw his arm over the back.

"Mm, just that I anticipate a full recovery. Jeremy picked up the woman's prescription on his way out of town and dropped it off for her. Her house is quite isolated and she doesn't drive so she relies on a live-in nurse. Seems to be a workable solution for both women, but I don't think either of them is very comfortable making the trip into the village."

Chris rubbed his palm vigorously across the top of his bald head, a mannerism that Martin had decided was a tensional outlet. It seemed to have developed in recent years, which now, as he watched his friend from across the table, made him wonder if the stress of his job was too much for him.

"Could you catch this pneumonia, Martin?" Louisa asked.

"It's highly unlikely given that it's not a particularly contagious infection, though it is communicable to some extent. I'll have to weigh different factors when patients need to be seen though, Louisa. In this particular patient's case, I felt the risk was relatively low, and the woman needed treatment."

He gave his napkin a vigorous shake and draped it over his lap. "And I've had the Prevnar ... er, the pneumonia jab, as well as the latest influenza jab. These are all things that I took into consideration yesterday. When the practice opens back up, there *will* be times when I'll have to make a judgement call. This was one of those times."

The waiter arrived with their meals and placed them on the table.

"Your sea bass looks wonderful, Martin," Louisa said as she chased a tomato around in her salad, jabbing at it with her fork.

She watched as her husband picked at his food, rearranging it on his plate but not actually ingesting anything. Chris had not failed to notice this change in his friend's appetite either.

"You feeling okay?" he asked.

"Yes ... why?" Martin bristled.

"Just looks like you're conducting a spirited game of croquet on your plate. Are you planning to eat any of that?"

"Did someone appoint you housemaster?" he snapped back.

Putting his hands up in front of him, Chris said, "You're right, you're right. Sorry, mate."

Martin cleared his throat, regretting his churlishness. "Ed's started to taper my morphine. It's just temporary symptoms."

"Nausea?"

Chris cut into his steak and Martin turned his head away. "Mm. I'm seeing Ed later this afternoon. He wants to get some pictures of the fractures, and we'll also discuss the morphine problems."

"*Problems*... are there other problems?"

Louisa fidgeted as her husband's knuckles whitened around his fork. "Chris, has the funding for the air ambulance come through yet?" she asked, attempting to shift the conversation in a different direction.

"No, not as of yet. We have to work our way through all the bureaucratic hoops first, I'm afraid." He jabbed his fork at his friend. "What other problems, Mart?"

A stream of air hissed from Martin's nose. "Oh, for heaven's sake! Tremors. Anxiety. Agitation. Now if the interrogation's over I'll excuse myself. And since you all probably want to know where I'm going..." He struggled to his feet and walked away from the table. "I need to pee!" he barked.

Louisa pushed her chair back and stood up.

"Maybe you should let him be for a few minutes, Louisa. He might need a little break from humanity," Carole suggested.

Louisa reluctantly pulled her chair back up to the table.

James whimpered and began to struggle to free himself from the constraints of the high chair as his father disappeared from sight.

"I'll get him; you finish your salad," Carole said.

"Thank you, Carole." Louisa turned to Chris. "Do I need to worry about Martin?" she asked.

"What ... the pneumonia, you mean?"

"Yeah. How much of a risk is it to him?"

He scratched at his jaw. "Well, it's pretty much like he told you. There's some risk, but the Prevnar jab greatly reduces his chances of developing sepsis if he *should* contract pneumonia.

"Hippocratic oath and Martin's commitment to his patients ... I'm not surprised he made the decision he did. I can't come down too hard on him because I probably would have come to the same conclusion. He's doing what we asked him to. Evaluating his risk and making a judgement call. Your standard run of the mill influenza, norovirus, and rhinovirus cases are much more contagious and will be more straightforward. I doubt that he'll hesitate to send them over to Wadebridge."

"And the morphine problems? Is that anything to worry about?" Louisa asked, pushing her half-eaten salad to the centre of the table.

James Henry began to squirm in Carole's arms, and he reached out to get to Chris. He took the boy and sailed him through the air a few times before standing him up on his lap.

"The morphine is something to watch, but I wouldn't say you need to worry about it. Ed'll help him to figure out what kind of tapering schedule to use. Some people experience no problems at all when they try to cut back. Some are like Mart and have to endure a period of some rather uncomfortable symptoms."

Chris craned his neck to look for his friend. "I think Martin's had it up to his eyeballs with people trying to take care of him ... look out for him. I'm sure that's why he just threw a wobbler."

Louisa stared off in the direction of the lavatories and rubbed her fingertips over her temples.

"How 'bout I go check up on him?" Chris said.

"That'd be good, thank you." Louisa reached her hand out and brushed it across her son's fuzzy head before pulling him to her lap.

"So, what happened with the radio programme?" Carole asked as soon as her husband was out of earshot.

"Oh, gawwd. I think Martin saw it as more of a catastrophe than I did. It *was* pretty embarrassing, even for me. And *I'm* used to how things work around Portwenn. But I think Martin found it positively humiliating."

She glanced around at the nearby tables. Seeing them empty she continued on, bringing her friend up to speed on the details of Bert's, now famous, soup. "I think there was one question that related to the opening of the surgery before it all came apart at the seams.

"One of the villagers saw Martin and me when we'd gone out to eat the other night, and he had to call in and ask about how Martin could ever ... you know ... with the fixators." Louisa gestured vaguely with her hands.

"Oh dear, I think I know where this is going—Martin went ballistic."

"Actually, no! He kept his cool ... told Jimmy it was none of his business ... that it was a private matter." Louisa shifted James back to the high chair and gave the boy his Sippy cup and a handful of dry cereal.

"Well done, for Martin! You must be mellowing the man, Louisa." Carole reached for the pot of coffee and refilled her cup.

"I must admit, I was very surprised at how composed he kept himself. But then Bert Large had to call in and offer to bring over another pot of his soup. So, of course, everyone started calling in with questions about its *magical properties*, to quote Bert. And Caroline, the host, did absolutely nothing to put a stop to it all!

"Bert made a comment about how quickly Martin was able to ... you know ... get me pregnant with James Henry. That was the final straw." Louisa gave an exasperated huff. "Martin took matters into his own hands and hit the switch thingy ... whatever you call it ... and cut off all the phone lines. Then, thinking he'd turned off the mics as well, he uttered a few choice words for Caroline over live Radio Portwenn."

"That village is not really the *ideal* environment for a guy with Martin's constitution, is it?" Carole said sympathetically.

Louisa shook her head. "There are a lot of *good* things about the village too, you know."

"Oh, I realise that. I like Portwenn. It's a wonderful little village." Carole peered up from her coffee cup before continuing warily. "I do wonder sometimes if you really appreciate what Martin's given up ... what he tolerates so that he can be with you."

Louisa fought off her knee-jerk reaction to lash out defensively and took in a slow breath. "It's not all one-sided, Carole. There are things about Martin that I've had to learn to tolerate."

"It's not a competition, Louisa. I'm just saying that when Martin gets upset and frustrated by the people ... the way things are in the village, maybe you should let it be a reminder to you of just how much he loves you and James. How desperately he wants you to be a part of his life." She reached for the pitcher of cream and stirred some into her coffee.

The two women sat quietly for some moments before Louisa spoke again. "I tried to talk to Martin about why he gave up the piano. He got angry when I tried to get him to tell me why he quit."

"Chris and I got the same response when we asked him about it years ago. I'm pretty sure it has something to do with Edith Montgomery. Oh, that woman is evil incarnate!" Carole spat out through clenched teeth.

"You're preaching to the choir there. But regardless of what Martin's reason was for giving it up, it just makes me sad that he's lost something that once brought him enjoyment."

"Oops! Louisa..." Carole said wagging a finger at the baby who was now spitting a mixture of drool and macerated cereal into his hand before wiping it on his front.

Louisa reached for her napkin before grabbing James's wrist, just preventing the child from smearing the next handful into his hair. "All right young man. No more of that." The boy giggled and batted playfully at his mother's face.

Carole waited until the current emergency was under control and then said, "Maybe you could get him to discuss it with the psychiatrist he's been seeing."

Louisa shook her head. "I've been giving it some thought. I think Martin's being pushed in so many directions right now that I should just let the matter drop. For the time being anyway."

"That's probably wise." Carole craned her neck. "Where have those men gone to?"

Louisa tried to suppress a grin. "Well, mine couldn't have gone very far."

Chris had found Martin sitting on a bench just outside the restaurant doors. "Mind if I join you?" he asked.

Martin gave him a shrug of his shoulders and slid over to make room for him.

"Sorry, mate. Didn't mean to make you feel like you were getting the third degree." Leaning forward, he rested his elbows on his knees.

"Mm. I know." Martin let his head drop back to rest against the restaurant wall. "I've taken care of myself all my life, Chris. It's been a big adjustment ... with Louisa. I was beginning to get used to it, though. But now..." he rocked his head back and forth as his eyes drifted shut. "You'd think I was incapable of wiping my own nose, let alone be trusted to make an objective decision about which patients I should see."

"I *do* trust you, Mart. I hope I haven't given you the impression that I don't. I just know that you take your duty of care very seriously, and there'll be times when you're going to feel the patient's need for medical care outweighs a possible risk to your own health. It makes me nervous is all."

"I see."

"Ah, this feels good." Chris sighed as he let the sun's rays fall warmly on his face. "You know, Martin, nobody means it that way. That we think you're incapable of taking care of yourself. We just genuinely care about you, believe it or not. Louisa, Ruth, Carole, me ... we all really care about you. I know that's a foreign concept to you, but that's the way it is. We're going to worry. Just tell us when we need to back off a bit."

Martin opened his eyes and shifted his dubious gaze sideways to his friend. "And how do you suppose Louisa's going to react if I tell her to back off a bit? Chris, how long have you been married? What do you suppose Carole would have to say if you told *her* to back off?"

"Okay. Okay. Then maybe say something like ... I don't know ... like, *Cupcake, I appreciate that you're trying to be helpful, but right now I just need a little personal space.*"

Chris turned when he heard his friend give a derisive snort.

"Cupcake? Can you really imagine me using the word *cupcake* when referring to anything but a sugar laden self-indulgence or a certain local police constable? And *personal space!*"

"Fine. Point made and acknowledged. How about, *"Louisa, I realise you're concerned, but I need you to trust me to tell you if there's something wrong or if I need your help."*

"Maybe."

"Look, I'm just saying that we might need a reminder now and then."

"Mm."

Martin sat pensively for a few moments before turning his attention back to his friend. "Cupcake? Chris ... seriously?"

Chapter 25

The Ellinghams returned the rented wheelchair to the medical supply store and then took the van back to the car hire office. The Parsons picked them up and drove them to the medical centre for their respective appointments, keeping James Henry with them. They would pick Martin and Louisa up again later to take them to the car dealership.

Louisa waited in the seating area just outside the office doors while Martin went in for his session with Dr. Newell. The therapist smiled broadly at him when he saw that more gains had been made in his recovery.

"That looks like progress," he said, gesturing to the crutches Martin clutched under his arms.

"Mm, yes. I can move faster than I could with the walker. They're cumbersome, though."

The therapist pulled the door shut behind him, gesturing for Martin to take a seat.

"How have things been otherwise?" he asked as he dropped into his chair.

Martin took in a long breath before answering. "I'm improving overall, I would say. Not as quickly as I'd like, of course. But I'm seeing steady progress."

Rolling his chair up to his desk, the psychiatrist opened up the file in front of him, scanning it over for a few seconds. "If I remember correctly, I gave you an assignment to do ... to make a list of the emotions you felt when you were bullied or received unfair punishments as a child. How's that coming along?"

Martin pulled a folded-up piece of paper from his shirt pocket and handed it to him. “I’m not at all sure if that’s what you had in mind,” he said, waving a finger at the result of his efforts.

Dr. Newell spread the sheet of paper out on the desktop. “Well, how ‘bout if I just read it aloud, and then we’ll discuss it.”

“That’s fine.”

The therapist donned a pair of reading glasses and then pushed himself back into his chair, settling in for the long narrative.

“This has been the most difficult exercise you have asked me to complete, by far. I’m not comfortable inflicting reflections of my miserable childhood existence on anyone. I’ve always found the tales vaunted by people of their youthful indiscretions and feckless exploits to be extremely annoying. Somewhat akin to the nouveau riche boasting of exorbitant expenditures on piddling desires. Whether it’s time wasted or money wasted, neither behaviour is of any benefit to them, or anyone else for that matter.

“Let’s talk about that first paragraph,” the therapist said as he looked across the desk at his patient. “I find it interesting that you equate talking about your abusive childhood with people telling stories about the less than admirable things they did in their youth. Can you explain what you mean by that?”

“I mean, they wouldn’t appreciate hearing tales of my unhappy childhood even if I did want to talk about it ... *which* I don’t ... so it’s a moot point.”

“Do you see a difference, though, Martin ... between the stories that other people tell and the stories that you would have to tell, say over a pint at the pub?”

Martin scratched at an eyebrow. “I’m not a big beer drinker, so I don’t frequent the pub.”

“Humour me then and imagine for a moment that you do.”

"Well, obviously, the tenor of the stories I could tell would be incongruous with the typical pub atmosphere. I doubt very much that the sharing of my unhappy childhood would go down well amongst the inebriated revellers there to swill beer."

"But the retelling of their youthful indiscretions would be acceptable ... even enjoyable?"

"Well, *I* wouldn't enjoy it."

"Let's just think about those inebriated revellers for the moment, then. Why do you think they enjoy relating these tales from their youth?"

"Because they're mindless barflies who have nothing more productive to do with their time? I don't know! I suppose they, for some reason which I can't fathom, have fond memories of the things they did."

"Do you have fond memories of the things you did, Martin?"

"What things I did?"

"The stories of your youth."

"I didn't *do* anything!"

"Precisely. The people in the pub would be talking about things *they* did. What you would be relating to them would be things that others did to *you*."

His brow drawing down, Martin puzzled over the psychiatrist's words for several moments. "Does it make a difference?"

"The people in the pub are relating stories of things they did of their own free will ... things they were responsible for. Who was responsible for the elements in the stories *you* would have to tell?"

Martin's gaze settled on the floor. "Mm."

Dr. Newell's biro tapped against his lips as he watched him for a moment before returning to the reading of the narrative.

"However, everything that you've asked me to do thus far has proven to be useful in some way, so I'll do my best to complete this

assignment. Although, I find that aside from a few happy memories from my childhood, the remainder of that time period seems to blend into a nondescript amalgamation of negative experiences.

"The happy memories, mostly of times spent with my aunt Joan and uncle Phil, and with my grandfather as well, were my refuge during the darkest times. It saddens me that some of those memories are now tainted by recent recollections. I think in particular of my grandfather's death, of course.

"When I look through my adult eyes ... doctor's eyes ... at the events of that afternoon in my father's study, I can understand the failure of that seven-year-old boy to act in a logical and responsible manner. I can even empathise with him, I suppose.

"However, there's guilt that washes over me in waves at times, triggering the familiar feelings of nausea and panic that have held sway over my life for the last six years.

*"I **do** want to let go of that sense of guilt and shame. I just can't do it. It's as if letting go of it means letting go of my grandfather. The security that I felt with him, happy memories that were a refuge. My father's hand never struck me in Grandfather's presence."*

The therapist rocked back in his chair, tapping his biro against his lips and furrowing his brow. "I find that to be quite perceptive, Martin. I wonder if there are ways of maintaining a connection with your grandfather other than through hanging on to that guilt and shame. Perhaps you could think about that between now and when we meet again."

He picked the file up from the desktop and entered a note before tossing it back on to the desk. "Okay, let's move on, shall we?

"You asked me to think about the emotions I felt when I was unfairly punished. This was difficult because I never thought of the punishments I received as anything other than what I believed to be conventional at the time.

"It was only after my son was born that I began to realise the harsh punishments from my father, and my confinements in a locked cupboard, were unreasonable. When I look at my son it seems abusive. But at the time, I felt that it was justifiable retribution for whatever annoyance or inconvenience I may have caused them. Whether I was guilty of an indiscretion or not seemed to be of little consequence. Did it matter? I had made them unhappy in some way, so I felt guilty. And though, of course, I didn't enjoy them, I felt deserving of the punishments."

Dr. Newell peered up over his reading glasses. "This relates to what we were talking about before, doesn't it—about who's responsible."

He cleared his throat and read on.

"Guilt, that's an emotion, isn't it? I think that's one I actually understand. Whether I was guilty of any wrong-doing or not, I was painfully aware of the physical manifestations of that emotion. Nausea, tachycardia, palmar sweating. Yes, I do think I understand guilt.

"Why do you suppose it is that you associate these visceral reactions with guilt?" the psychiatrist asked as he came around to take a seat on the desktop.

Martin gave him a blank stare. "I'm sorry. I don't understand why you're asking me this. That's like asking why I would associate the growling sounds coming from my stomach right now with the fact that I haven't eaten anything since breakfast. Isn't there an obvious correlation?"

"No, Martin, there's not. Guilt does not normally trigger those particular reactions. We more commonly associate those reactions with fear. Do you think it's possible that you could be linking the fear and sense of panic you felt that day in your father's study with the guilt that you felt ... still feel, for your inaction in that situation?"

"Oh, now that's just psychoanalytical claptrap!" Martin struggled to his feet and limped over to the window. He took in a deep breath and blew it out.

"Perhaps it is. I'd prefer to call it a supposition, though. As you know, memories are formed when specific neurons fire together. The more those neurons fire together, the more they wire together, thereby strengthening the memory. But when a memory is formed during a highly emotional experience, such as a traumatic event, the memory can be formed after that single experience.

"When you witnessed your grandfather's death you experienced an intense fear ... of what was happening in that room and of the consequences of leaving that room to get help. I'm not sure that you, as a seven-year-old in the midst of that terrifying situation, would have considered that your inaction could result in your grandfather's death. But because of—"

Martin's head swung back and forth. "*No*. No, I remember distinctly being aware that I should get my parents."

"I don't doubt you, Martin. That's how you remember it, but memories can be easily manipulated by our later experiences. Your parents' handling of the situation and its immediate aftermath certainly would have left you with the impression that you should have done something and that your failure to act resulted in your grandfather's death. As a sensitive child ... which we know you were ... you would have undoubtedly been left with a strong sense of guilt. When the memories of that day were wired together in your brain, the guilt and fear that you felt would have almost certainly been linked."

The creases deepened in Martin's brow as he cocked his head.

The therapist picked the sheet of paper up from the desk. *"Emotions: Fear, is that an emotion? The knot that would develop in my stomach. The impulse to run ... to try to get away when I heard the clinking of my father's belt buckle and the snapping sound it made as he yanked it from his belt loops. The inability to move. Not being able to do anything about it but to watch as he stepped forward. The involuntary jerk of my body as the belt raced towards me.*

"Why do you ask if fear is an emotion, Martin?"

Martin's fingers twitched around the crutch handles as he kept his gaze glued to scenery outside the window. "It seemed ... or seems ... like more of a physical sensation to me. Not a mental process, per se."

"I see. Well, fear is most certainly an emotion. Bear in mind that emotions trigger a physiological response. You're actually learning to understand ... or to recognise and identify your emotions ... when you name the physical sensations that you're experiencing. But fear is definitely an emotion, and it can produce a strong physical response. The fight/flight/freeze responses we've discussed in previous sessions."

The fixator on Martin's arm clicked against his crutch as he worked his way around to face the therapist. "I've realised recently that I do tend to react to fear by getting angry."

"We've touched on this before, I know, but people often deal with fear by getting angry. It's that fight response. When you were seven, you responded to the fear you felt in your father's study that day by freezing.

"Learning to recognise the actual emotion of fear that your anger is masking is a huge achievement ... a big step in the process we're working through together. Remember, though, that anger can mask other emotions. When you find yourself feeling angry, try to look deeper ... see if you can identify an underlying emotion."

The sheet of paper rattled in the psychiatrist's hands. "*Relief. I'm not sure if relief is considered an emotion, but if it isn't, it should be added to the nomenclature. Relief is the reduction of an unpleasant sensation, and aren't emotions sensations? Maybe it's not an emotion. But the relief that I experienced after a punishment had been administered felt like an emotion to me.*

"That's an astute observation, Martin ... relief being sensed as an emotion. It *is* considered, by some in the claptrap community, to be a secondary emotion ... joy being the primary emotion.

"Let's say that relief is *not* an emotion in and of itself but rather that certain emotions result in a sense of relief. Or that relief brings about certain emotions. What emotions would you have experienced after a punishment?"

Dr. Newell walked back around to the other side of his desk and took a seat, his hands gripping the armrests as he swivelled back and forth.

Martin stared absently for some time before returning to his chair. "I can't think of any emotions that I felt afterwards. It was more an absence of emotion; I'd feel temporarily absolved."

"Absolved of what?"

"What do you mean?"

"I'm wondering what you felt absolved of."

Martin blinked as he struggled with the question. He shook his head. "I don't know."

The psychiatrist pulled his chair forward to rest his elbows on the desk, steepling his fingers. "Try a little harder, Martin. Absolved of what?"

Martin's fingers tapped against the armrests of his chair before anger flashed across his face. He slammed his fist down on to his knee, grimacing as it sent pain through his injured leg. *"N-nothing!"* he spat. "Nothing! I did nothing wrong! Is that what you're wanting to hear? That I did nothing wrong? That my parents took their anger at one another out on me?"

He fought back tears as he tried to calm himself, taking in several deep breaths and pressing trembling fingers to his eyes.

The therapist sat quietly for a few moments before asking, "If you could step into the shoes of your child-self, what emotion would you feel, Martin? What emotion would you *expect* a child to feel after such unfair treatment?"

"I didn't *feel* anything."

"I understand that you remember an absence of emotion after these incidents. But what emotion ... emotions would you expect a seven-year-old to feel?"

Rubbing his palm across his eyes, Martin sighed heavily. "I don't know."

"All right, we'll come back to this another time."

Dr. Newell looked back down at his patient's narrative. "*This is a very frustrating exercise. What emotions* ***should*** *I have felt? There was nothing that I could do to change my circumstances so what point would there be in feeling emotion?*

"I remember one summer at my aunt Joan's, I was watching the television with her and Uncle Phil. The Americans had landed on the moon and we were witnessing the historic first steps. I wanted, at that moment, to be an astronaut. To bounce around on the lunar surface, far away from the troubles that came with home and boarding school.

"I told my aunt and uncle about my sudden inspiration, explaining that I wanted to know what it would feel like for my body to be so light that I could hover in the air with every jump. To float around outside the Command Service Module, weightless. I would be far away from my parents and the bullies at school if I were in space.

"Then my uncle pointed out that the astronauts might be weightless, but they were tethered to the ship and confined to space suits, completely dependent on their friends inside the capsule to keep them safe. That the tether connecting them to the ship was like an umbilical cord and the ship like the mother, there to provide them with what they needed to survive ... to keep them

safe. The dream became a delusion, and I thought better of the whole idea.

"So, did those astronauts feel as I did? Completely under the superintendence of someone else, be it housemaster, headmaster, peers, parents. I guess one could say, helpless. I'm not sure if that's an emotion or more a condition, but either way, it really didn't matter. There was nothing to be done about my situation."

The doctor laid the sheet of paper down slowly on his desk. "Your words convey not only a feeling of helplessness, Martin, but also a feeling of *hopelessness*. Would you say that's an accurate interpretation?"

Martin pressed his thumb back into his palm and lowered his head. "Yes, I would say that's accurate."

Glancing down at his watch, the psychiatrist said, "Well, I guess we'd better wrap it up there if I'm going to have time to chat with Louisa today." His chair squeaked as he leaned forward and stood up.

"Mm, yes." Martin got to his feet as quickly as he could.

"Erm, Martin." The therapist put his hand on his arm. "Between now and our next session, I'd like for you to think about that absence of emotion that you felt after punishments. See if something more comes to you. Perhaps an emotion you're not remembering at the moment."

The doctor pulled open the door. "You did an excellent job on this assignment. I know this one had to sting a good bit."

"Mm, yes. It did."

Chapter 26

Louisa looked up when she heard the door to the therapist's office open. Martin looked spent and disheartened. She smiled at him but feared her face may have betrayed the uneasiness she felt.

"Louisa ... would you like to come in now?" Dr. Newell asked, stepping aside to let her by.

She reached out for her husband's hand, but he brushed on by her. "I'll meet you in the lobby at the hospital, then?" she said.

"Yes."

The psychiatrist hurried ahead of his patient. "Let me get the door for you, Martin. I'll see you next week, but don't hesitate to call if you'd like to talk before then. Understood?"

"Yes, thank you." Martin moved out into the crisp fall air. Once he'd rounded the corner of the building, he leaned back against the wall, closing his eyes and willing his body to relax. His gaze shifted to his next destination, the hospital across the street, and the strain of the day fell over him like a heavy weight on his shoulders. His legs shaking, he forced himself forward to a bench along the sidewalk. He took a seat, waiting a few minutes before getting to his feet to complete his journey.

The door to the surgeon's office was open, and he waved Martin in. He hurried over to lend him support before helping him into a chair. "Long way up here, eh?" Ed said, taking a quick visual inventory, noting the pallor and sheen of moisture on his patient's skin.

"Mm. I walked over from Barrett Newell's office." He winced as pain shot through his left leg.

Ed tipped his head to the side and furrowed his brow. "How are you doing with the tapering schedule we worked out?"

"I started having some symptoms ... erm, difficulties last night. Anxiety and agitation mostly. But nausea today as well," he said, rubbing at a cramp in his thigh.

"Have you been able to keep food down today?"

"I'm sorry, I need to move." Martin stood up and shook his right leg, attempting to find some relief.

Ed knelt down next to him and palpated his calf and thigh. "That's a fierce spasm you have going. Let's see if you can walk it off," the surgeon said as he guided him across the room.

"Any better now?"

Martin nodded his head and returned to his chair.

"How about tremors? Your hands are shaking now. Is it a withdrawal symptom or just muscle fatigue?"

"I suspect withdrawal. It started today. It's tolerable, though."

Ed walked around and sat down behind his desk, pulling his patient's records up on his computer. "I'm thinking we should up your dose a bit and start the taper more slowly in another week or so."

"No, I want to keep the dose where it's at for now. I don't want to have to start all over with this."

The surgeon hesitated. "Well, I'll let you decide. But if we're going to leave things as they stand, I must insist that you notify me of any worsening symptoms or if anything new crops up. Got it?"

Martin screwed up his face and huffed out a breath. "Fine."

"Good enough." Ed picked up his phone and punched a button. "Can you have someone bring up a wheelchair? I have a patient that I want taken down to radiology," he said into the receiver.

Wagging a finger back and forth, Martin said, "I can manage just fine. He scowled as he watched Ed hang up the phone.

"That's completely unnecessary. I'm perfectly capable of walking down there myself."

"You looked like you were ready to collapse when you came in through the door a few minutes ago. I can see you've already overdone it. You're done walking for the day, my friend. Enough said?"

Martin gave him a begrudging nod.

Across the street, Louisa tried to stay focused on the conversation in Dr. Newell's office, but her thoughts and her gaze kept drifting towards the hospital.

"Louisa, did you hear my question?" the therapist asked.

"I'm sorry. I guess I'm a little worried about Martin."

"I'd like to talk about Martin yet today, but first I want to finish our discussion about your strong reaction to your husband's mishap with the knife. Have the two of you talked about the night of the accident at all?"

Louisa fidgeted with her purse strap. "Not really. Well, just with you ... at the hospital. But we haven't talked just the two of us, if that's what you mean."

"That is what I mean. Has the subject just not come up, or do you think you've been avoiding it?"

"Hmm, I think it's a little of both probably. We *have* been very busy and Martin hasn't, of course, been feeling at his best. And I..." Louisa looked down at her lap, biting her bottom lip. "I'm afraid of how it might affect Martin to have to relive that night. And he already talked about it with you, so is there really any point in discussing it further?"

"There may not be. But you don't need to be afraid to discuss it either. And yes, talking about it could cause some emotions to surface, especially for Martin. But avoiding the issue won't make it better."

The doctor rolled himself back up to his desk and jotted something down on a piece of paper. "You don't have to replay the entire experience in one evening, but do try to be open with one another if a memory crops up or you have questions."

Louisa gave a nervous laugh and shook her head. "Martin may have questions, but I doubt he'll ask them."

"Yes, he may very well not. But if he feels he's helping you by talking about these things, he may be more apt to open up about his own questions. He must certainly have some voids in his memory.

"Martin's always going to be a reluctant communicator, but he's more comfortable with it now than he was a few months ago.

"Now, about your reaction to your husband's recent injury. Those very graphic images from the night of the accident are still fresh in your memory. Was it seeing him experiencing pain that seemed to trigger your reaction?"

Louisa swallowed. "It was the blood running on to the cutting board. When I saw Martin in the trauma centre, there was so much blood. They had his arm elevated, and a woman was trying to slow the bleeding, but it was running down into a puddle on the floor."

She batted at the tears on her cheeks. "Martin was terrified. I could see it in his eyes. He's always so level-headed and in control in situations like that, but he was absolutely helpless that night ... and he knew it."

Dr. Newell scratched additional words on to the piece of paper in front of him and then returned his attention to his patient. "Seeing your husband frightened and helpless was a new experience for you?"

A gentle smile spread across Louisa's face as she recalled Martin's reaction to James's unexpected appearance in that little pub in the middle of nowhere. "I've seen him lose his cool in a medical situation, when it's involved James or me. He's always known exactly what to do. He just gets a bit ... hmm, overly zealous when it comes to the two of us. But no, never helpless."

"Would you say that one of the attributes that first drew you to Martin was his level-headedness, his ability to take control in a tenuous situation?"

"That's definitely a characteristic that I found ... *find* attractive. That and his strength, physical and emotional ... his confidence," Louisa said, her ponytail bobbing. "I feel safe when I'm with Martin."

"But when you were with your parents, you didn't feel safe?"

"Gawd, no. I mean, I never feared my parents or felt unsafe physically or even emotionally the way Martin did, but both of my parents were prone to flights of fancy. My mother with her wanderlust and roaming eyes. My father with his crazy get-rich-quick schemes."

"It must have been horribly difficult to see your husband in so much pain that night."

"It was terrible. When it comes to medicine, Martin's always so sure of himself. I just know everything's going to be okay because there's a confidence in his eyes. But that night, he looked so afraid. He said he didn't want to leave us. It terrified me. He was afraid *he* was going to leave. And the thought of being left again..." Louisa put her hands over her face and pulled in a deep breath.

Dr. Newell nodded. "That security you felt ... that he wouldn't leave you. It was shaken that night?"

"Yeah. And I didn't know if I could do it."

"Do what, Louisa?"

"Stay. Be there for him when he can't be my—my rock. Part of me just wanted to get away from the situation. To leave it all behind. But this time I didn't run when I knew he was crumbling. I tried to be strong for him this time."

"Is that why you've run before? Because you knew your rock was crumbling?"

Her eyes shot up at the man before she turned her gaze to the floor. She had let slip information that she had, until now, kept secreted away.

"It's been hard to admit, but yes, I think that had something to do with it." She folded her arms across her chest and then looked up at him. "Terrible, isn't it?"

"Well, it's not a healthy way to deal with relationship difficulties. However, given your own family history, I can understand why you might have a proclivity for flight."

The man's chair creaked as he rocked back and forth. "But you stayed this time. A person can't get much more helpless ... more vulnerable than Martin was after his accident. You stayed by his side, though, and you fought through a very tough time together. Do you think you're a stronger person for it?"

Louisa sat up a little straighter in her chair. "I do. Definitely. I have more self-respect than when I went running off to London a couple of years ago ... shut him out of things when I was pregnant with James. Or when I got on that plane to run off to Spain last summer."

She leaned forward, poking her finger in the air. "And do you know who made me see how unfair my running away was to Martin? His bloody mother! What a *godawful* woman!

"When Martin found out she had come to ask for money, not to let him know about his father dying, he told her to leave. We ran into each other at the airport. It was her telling me *well done* that did it. That Martin was never going to change and I deserved a better life. I had to be taught about dealing with relationship difficulties by the world's poorest excuse for a wife and mother."

Brushing her hair from her face with a forceful swipe, she huffed. "But our now-infamous Sports Day row was just the straw that broke the camel's back. It was really all the rest of it, I think, that I just couldn't deal with anymore."

"Can you explain what you mean by *the rest of it*?"

"His odd behaviour. His lack of social skills." Louisa quieted and blinked back tears. "Seeing him struggling.

"But I realised before I got on that plane that I didn't want to leave him." She peered up at the therapist. "I never told Martin, but I had decided to spend a few days with my mother, then come back. Stay just long enough to make him worry he might have lost us for good."

Her purse strap twisted in her hands. "And ... I used our son to hurt him. I knew how painful it would be for him if I took James away."

The psychiatrist nodded his head. "Like when his parents refused to let him see his aunt."

"Yes. They punished Martin to hurt Joan. I would have been doing the same thing really. It would have been a hurtful thing to do to both Martin and James."

The doctor's fingers tapped a light beat on the armrests of his chair. "And you feel guilty for this because you now realise that you were motivated by anger rather than a desire to help your husband and heal your marriage?"

Louisa's fingers stroked her throat in a self-soothing manner as her gaze shifted to the window. "Yes. I suppose you could say I was angry. I mean, that's understandable ... isn't it?"

"I'm not here to pass judgement," the psychiatrist said.

He tapped his biro against his hand and rocked back and forth in his chair. "Do you think it's possible that the fear you felt, when watching your husband struggling, may have manifested itself as anger?"

She tipped her head to the side. "I guess I hadn't given it any thought." She stared, absently, for a moment before shaking her head. "No. I was angry."

"And your reaction the day Martin had the mishap in the kitchen. Perhaps you could take me through the emotions you experienced."

"Well, I think at first I was angry. But that had more to do with the word that slipped out of his mouth than anything else," she said, giving the therapist a half-smile.

"Then I looked over at him ... at the blood... and the adrenaline kicked in. I was just focused on doing what needed to be done."

"That's good. You kept your cool and worked through the situation, then?" the psychiatrist said.

"Well, obviously not or I wouldn't be sitting here talking about it, would I?" she snapped. "Just thinking about it now makes me feel..."

Her hands worked tightly around her purse strap. "When things calmed down and Ruth had taken control of the situation, this flood of memories and sensations from that night in the trauma centre hit me. Things I'd been trying to forget.

"I tried to focus on something else ... cleaning up the blood and taking care of the melon Martin had been cutting up when he sliced into his finger. He started banging on about how we shouldn't eat it ... about it being biological waste, and I kinda went a little spare."

Pulling his chair up to his desk, Dr. Newell steepled his fingers, tapping them against his lips. "I want to make sure I'm understanding this, Louisa. Why don't I go through your account with you, step by step? Please correct me if I have anything wrong.

"As soon as you saw that Martin had injured himself, you went into rescue mode. And it sounds like you handled things well up to that point."

"Yes, I think that's true."

"But once that initial surge of adrenaline had passed, the sight of the blood running on to the cutting board brought back all those sights, sounds and smells of the trauma centre. It brought back the fear you felt with the very real possibility that your husband might leave you. Do I have things right up to this point?"

"Yes. That's an accurate description."

"And it was at that point that anger took over. I'm wondering if it's possible that you used anger to quash the fear you were reliving."

Louisa's ponytail swung gently side to side as her brow creased.

"We all have coping mechanisms that we use to deal with stresses in our lives, Louisa. Anger gives us a sense of power and control as opposed to the vulnerability we often feel with fear. As you think back on your life, do you think it's possible you've used anger as a mechanism of self-protection? A way of controlling your fears?"

"I guess I'd never thought about it, really."

The therapist drew in a deep breath. "I'd like to revisit your most recent flight event. I'm curious as to what you were hoping to achieve in making Martin worry he may have lost his wife and son for good. Were you trying to force him to seek help?"

She pulled her arms around her sides and looked down at her lap. "I'm not sure that my intentions were so admirable. I wanted him to try harder. To be more sociable ... more romantic. More *normal.*

"I knew there was a problem, but he'd been doing better for a while ... for a few months before and after our wedding. So, I felt like he just needed to give it a bit of effort. I just wanted him to *try* a little.

"Yes, get help if that's what it would take, but to be perfectly honest, I didn't want to deal with it anymore. I was tired. I was tired of trying to get him to talk. Tired of making excuses to people for his boorish behaviour. Tired of the lack of affection. I needed a break from him."

The therapist cocked his head. "You do understand now that your husband couldn't just apply himself and make all his troubles go away? That it wasn't something a simple attitude adjustment could fix?"

"Yes, I do understand that ... now. I feel guilty. I feel guilty for not telling him about all of this. I let him believe that I could think of nothing else to do. That I didn't think he loved me. I've *always* known Martin loves me.

"I let him believe that he'd failed as a husband and father. I let him think that's why I left. I had almost convinced *myself* that was the case.

"But he's practically turned himself inside out trying to be the man I want him to be ... to make changes so that I can be happy with him.

"I do want to see him make an effort to be less rude. I still have to remind him of basic manners. And I *would* like to see him take more of an interest in people. At least *try* to fit in."

The psychiatrist sighed heavily, folding his hands in front of him. Louisa waited for what seemed like several agonising minutes before he looked up at her.

"Martin's trying, but he's never going to relate to people the way that you or I do. He can make some changes, and I think we've seen some of that already.

"But he will always have to work at the social skills that come so naturally to you and me. Try to remember that and to see his efforts as a demonstration of the love he feels for you and James. Acknowledge those small achievements even if his attempts to socialise may seem clumsy.

"Don't praise him for his attempts but do let him know you appreciate his efforts. And be reasonable in what you ask of him."

Dr. Newell got up from behind his desk and pulled a chair up next to her. "You and James are Martin's motivators. But be careful to encourage and not admonish.

"He was never given the opportunity to develop the usual social skills. But he's not a child, and it will only serve to humiliate him if you try to act the parent at this point in his life. Treat him respectfully when you make suggestions. And above all, do it in the privacy of your own home, not in the presence of others."

Louisa's face warmed at the thought of her chastisement at the restaurant earlier in the day. "I have a very hard time remembering that.

"I spend most of my days with children, constantly reminding them of their manners. It's become a habit that I've slipped into with Martin as well. The words are out of my mouth before I realise it."

"I can see how that could happen. You might try wearing a rubber band around your wrist. Give it a snap when you catch yourself saying something you shouldn't."

Louisa grimaced, picturing Mrs. Tishell and the band she wore as part of her cognitive behavioural therapy. The mere mention of her husband's name sending the woman's fingers pulling at the device.

The psychiatrist noted his patient's less-than-enthusiastic response to his suggestion. "If you don't like the rubber band idea, give yourself a pinch. It'll have a similar effect without detracting from your ensemble," he said, giving her a grin.

Then, leaning forward, he looked Louisa in the eye. "Martin will never *fit in*, as you say. He'll always stand out from the crowd. But you and James ... and Ruth ... you can give him a place where he *does* fit in."

He got up and walked towards the door. "Ed Christianson mentioned that Martin's on a tapering schedule with the morphine, so this wouldn't be the best time to have any discussions regarding tender issues. He's not likely to handle it well.

"But once things have settled down, I would recommend you talk to him about our conversation today ... about your reasons for leaving. Remind him that you're both learning and that you didn't have the benefit of knowing his history when you made your past decisions."

He walked Louisa out into the waiting area. The sun was now setting early in the evening and it was nearly dark.

"Wait just a minute and I'll accompany you over to the hospital," he said as he hurried back to his office to grab his jacket.

"This really isn't necessary. It's well lit," Louisa said as she buttoned her coat.

"Well, my intentions aren't completely chivalrous. I'm hoping to find out how Mr. Christianson plans to handle your husband's medications." The psychiatrist pulled the office door shut behind him, and it rattled as he checked to be sure that it was locked.

Martin was sitting at the far end of a sofa in the corner of the otherwise empty lobby when Louisa and Dr. Newell came through the door. He picked up his crutches and got to his feet when he saw them approaching.

"Is something wrong?" he asked, the man's presence raising a red flag.

"No need to worry, Martin," the psychiatrist said. "I just thought I'd come over ... see how things went with Ed. Was he comfortable with how you're doing with the morphine tapering?"

"I'm doing fine. The symptoms are manageable at this point, so we'll keep on course, and I'll let Ed know if things go south." His wife looked at him askance when he reached up to wipe a trickle of sweat from his temple. "But for now, it's nothing I can't handle."

Dr. Newell cleared his throat. "Louisa, could Martin and I have a few moments?"

"Sure. I'll just go call Chris and Carole ... let them know we're done here, hmm?" she said, giving her husband a smile.

"Yes." He watched her as she moved away from him, his chest swelling.

"I just wanted to mention that you should be extra vigilant for any signs that you could be backsliding with the depression," Dr. Newell said. "A dosage change in pain meds can play with neurochemicals, so be sure you call me if you notice any problems.

"And I'd recommend you discuss this with your wife, so she can be watching for any changes as well. An issue could creep up on you without your noticing."

"Mm, yes. I'll do that. Thank you."

It was almost nine o'clock by the time the Ellingham's arrived back at Ruth's cottage that night. Both Martin and James slept on the drive home from the Lexus dealership. Louisa carried the baby in and laid him down in his cot before going back out to park the car. When she returned to the house, she found Martin asleep on the sofa.

Leaning over, she placed a kiss on his forehead and brushed her fingers through his hair, rousing him.

"Mm, sorry. I guess I dozed off," he said as he gazed up at her.

"Yeah, I guess you did." He pushed himself up, and she sat down next to him. "Been a long day, hmm?"

"Yes. A stressful day." He rubbed his fingertips against his forehead, trying to ease the tension.

"Then let's go to bed. You look positively shattered."

"Mm, thank you."

An amused smile flitted across her lips before she turned for the stairs. "I'll go up and use the bathroom. Be right back."

She stood in the bedroom doorway a few minutes later, watching her husband as he lay on his back, an arm flung up over his eyes. The fine tremors that she had noticed earlier in the day were visible in his fingers. Going into the bathroom, she retrieved a jar that she had placed in the cabinet several days earlier.

Martin pulled his arm down and began to slide over when he heard her movement by the bed.

"Just stay there, but turn over on your tummy for me," she said.

He eyed her warily but did as she asked.

She unscrewed the cap from the jar and scooped out a dollop of cocoa butter. "I picked this up at Mrs. Tishell's the other day. I've been wanting to give it a try."

"What do you have there?" he said as he tried to pull his elbow under him.

Concealing the jar behind her back, she pushed him down on the bed. "Just relax," she said as she massaged the cream into his shoulders.

He tried again to peer back at her.

"I *said* … relax," she whispered in his ear.

"Louisa, what is that?" He craned his neck, attempting to see in the jar. "It could stain the—"

"Shush! Just lay down and quit worrying about the sheets." She giggled as she worked her way down his back to his waist before moving back north and down each arm, pausing to nuzzle her face into his neck.

The ripples of movement continued in his fingers as they slid through her hands. Slowly he allowed himself to give in to her ministrations, and his muscles loosened.

"That's better," she cooed as she moved down his back again. He startled as her hands slipped under the band of his boxers.

"Louisa! What are you doing?"

Stopping, she huffed out a breath. "I'm *trying* to get you to relax a bit. Roll over," she said, giving him a firm nudge.

He worked his way around the fixators and on to his back.

Tipping her head down, she gave him a reproachful look. "I'm going to feel like a failure if I let you go to sleep tonight all tense and edgy, you know."

"Mm, I see."

Climbing up on the bed, she straddled him, caressing her palms across his chest. As her hands reached his scars, they brushed lightly over them.

Leaning over, she trailed kisses along the wound on his belly and on up to his neck, causing his body to strain against hers as he released a soft, involuntary growl.

She sat back up and pulled her nightdress over her head, the soft satin sliding past his palms before she let the garment slip to the floor. Then she worked his boxers down his legs, stopping to stroke her lips along the length of the scar on his thigh.

"Louisa." Her name spilled unconsciously from his lips. Reaching down, he pulled her to him, wrapping his arm around her tightly as they lay face to face.

His contented sigh brought a smile to her face. This was a special moment in their lovemaking. That moment when he seemed to feel truly loved, truly happy. When he allowed himself to be cherished.

He held her for some time, his breathing gradually becoming more rapid as his contentment deepened, and a moan caught in his throat as he pressed against her.

The tension built between them before coming together in a mutual release.

Louisa breathed out softly, staring back at him. He watched her for a time, the merest glimmer of a smile on his face, before he collapsed on to his back with a sigh.

"Thank you, Martin. It was *lovely*."

"You're welcome." His eyes sparkled. "I couldn't have you going to sleep tonight feeling like a failure ... could I?"

"No, Martin. You would never allow that to happen."

He lifted his head and kissed her goodnight.

Chapter 27

Louisa was awakened in the night by her husband's movements in the bed. "Martin, wake up, you're dreaming," she said softly as she reached out to shake him from his sleep.

"I *am* awake!" he barked as he roughly pushed her hand away.

She switched on the light by the bed and he groaned, slapping a hand to his eyes.

"You're soaking wet!" she said, reaching for his forehead.

The movement caused him to flinch, and he batted at her arm. Rolling on to his side, he grabbed for his crutches. "I need the lavatory," he said, groaning as his feet hit the floor. "Oh, God," Louisa heard him mumble.

She hurried around to give him support, but her efforts were again rejected, more violently this time as he pushed her away forcefully. Louisa stumbled back, now frightened by her husband's behaviour and his darting eyes.

"Martin, you need to calm down. It was just a nightmare. It's over now. Just sit back down before you fall."

"I didn't—have a bloody nightmare! I need—I need the lavatory!" He tried to straighten himself up enough to wedge the crutches in under his arms, but the action caused an intensification of the stomach cramps he was experiencing, doubling him over in agony. "Oh, God—Louisa, it—" He groaned. "It hurts. Call—Ed." He struggled to get the words out through his gasps for air. His crutches clattered to the floor as his hands grabbed at his belly.

Louisa picked up her mobile and dialled the surgeon's number as Martin moved slowly towards the bathroom, laying his forearms on the mattress as he worked his way around the bed.

"Come on! Come on!" Louisa whispered stridently.

A sleepy male voice answered on the other end of the line. "Christianson."

"Ed, it's Louisa Ellingham. Martin told me to call you. Something's wrong."

Several seconds of silence passed on the other end of the line before she heard the surgeon clear his gravelly voice. "Tell me what's going on. Is it withdrawal or is he sick?"

Louisa clutched the phone as she watched her husband nervously. "I don't know!"

"Well, is he feverish?"

"He won't let me touch him, so I don't—know. He's drenched with sweat, though. He's trying to get to the bathroom but he's doubled over, holding his stomach. I don't know what to do, Ed! I'm afraid he's going to fall!"

"Okay, calm down, Louisa. What's Martin's aunt's number? I'll ring her first, then I'll call Jeremy Portman ... get him over there. It sounds like some intense withdrawal symptoms. See if he'll let you help him to the lavatory. Try to keep him there until Ruth or Portman get there. He's probably nauseous or it's intestinal distress. What's that number?"

Louisa gave him Ruth's contact information and rang off.

"Martin, Ed said I should help you to the bathroom. I'm going to give you my arm, okay?" She reached out apprehensively.

He nodded and grabbed on to her, clinging to her tightly as she inched him towards the lavatory. She gritted her teeth as his fingers dug into her arm, and he let out a long groan, clutching his belly.

"Come on, Martin. You can make it. We'll do this together, hmm?" she said, nodding her head and giving him a nervous smile. He looked up at her briefly. The distress he was feeling was obvious in his clenched jaw and deeply furrowed brow.

Louisa breathed a heavy sigh of relief once she had her husband sitting down on the toilet. She was wiping his face with a wet flannel when she heard the back door open. “We’re in the bathroom, Ruth!” she called out.

A wave of humiliation passed over Martin’s face when he saw the elderly woman appear in the doorway. “Gawwd,” he moaned.

“Oh, for goodness’ sake, Martin. It’s not as if I haven’t seen a patient on the toilet before. And you’re in no condition right now to be worrying about losing your dignity to an old lady.”

She turned to her nephew’s wife. “Louisa, could you bring me a chair, please?”

“Yeah, I’ll be right back.” She hurried towards the hall.

“Get me that little stool that I keep next to the washing machine!” Ruth called out after her.

When Louisa returned, Ruth seated herself in front of her nephew and pulled an IV set from the bag she had parked next to her. She tugged on his arm, laying it on top of his thigh before deftly sliding the needle into the back of his hand.

“Louisa, tear off some of this tape for me, please.”

She gave the younger woman a crooked smile and secured the catheter in place.

Taking an IV bottle from the bag, she snapped the tubing into the catheter before passing the bottle to Louisa.

“There we go.” Ruth patted Martin’s arm and he grimaced and flinched again. Turning to Louisa, she asked, “Could you fetch a glass of water?”

“Yeah.” With trembling hands, Louisa pushed the IV bottle towards the older woman before hurrying from the room.

She returned shortly with a glass, and Ruth took a small vial from her bag. “Here you go, Martin,” she said, pressing a small tablet into his palm and passing him the glass of water. "Swallow that down."

He shook his head. "I won't be able to keep it down."

Ruth left the room momentarily and returned with an empty waste bin. "Use this if it comes back up. But you have to try."

Martin leaned forward, moaning as another wave of stomach cramps hit. He looked up at the two women with fire in his eyes. "Just—sod off!" he sputtered. "It doesn't help having you two gawp—ing at me!"

"I don't think you should be left alone, Martin," Louisa said as she reached out to rub her hand across his back.

He grabbed her wrist and yanked her arm back. "Don't do that! Just—don't touch me!"

Ruth urged Louisa towards the door. "Wait for me in the kitchen," she said. Louisa hurried off and Ruth turned back to her nephew. "I'll give you a few minutes to calm yourself down, Martin, then I'll come back to check on you. But you must try to get that clonidine down. Is—that—understood?"

He glared up at her. "Yes! Now, get out!"

Ruth left the room, leaving the door ajar.

Louisa was sitting at the table when the elderly woman entered the kitchen. "Is Martin all right?" she asked.

"He's going to have a rough few days, but morphine withdrawal isn't dangerous. It *is* a painful and very unpleasant experience, however," Ruth said as she flipped the switch on the tea kettle and took two cups from the cupboard, setting them on the table.

"I've given him clonidine. If he can get it down and keep it down long enough for it to get into his system, it might ease the anxiety, stomach cramps, and nausea a bit."

Louisa looked anxiously towards the hall.

"How are you doing?" The elderly woman dropped a teabag into each cup and filled them with boiling water before taking a seat.

"I'll be fine. It's just..." Louisa waved her hand through the air. "Nothing."

Ruth peered up at her. "Out with it. What's bothering you?"

"Aside from the fact that my husband's in the midst of acute withdrawal?" she snapped. She took in a deep breath. "I'm sorry. You're here to help and I'm taking it out on you."

"It's quite all right, dear. I've been treated *much* worse at Broadmoor."

Louisa twisted her wedding band back and forth. "This medication will help, then?"

"It doesn't ease the symptoms for everyone. And Martin's going to be rather miserable for the next several days, regardless."

"What do you mean ... miserable?"

"He'll probably feel as though he has a very bad case of influenza. Body aches, nausea, vomiting, severe abdominal cramps ... and anxiety and restlessness on top of it. Like I said, *quite* unpleasant."

Ruth watched her nephew's wife over the top of her teacup. Her hands covered her eyes and she sniffled occasionally. "Louisa, I know it's hard to see after all that Martin's been through, but I assure you, this *will* pass."

Louisa wiped the tears from her cheeks as she rubbed her wrist absent-mindedly. "Martin's never hurt me before ... *never*."

Ruth reached across the table. "Let me have a look." She palpated Louisa's arm tenderly, finding nothing more than a spot of superficial bruising to the skin. She gave her a reassuring pat.

"Martin's not himself right now. Every sensation is magnified, everything hurts, and he's very anxious. His not wanting to be touched right now isn't a rejection of you, it's simply a defence mechanism... a reflex. It hurts to be touched. And given his history, I would imagine his brain is sending very strong flight or fight messages. He needs space at the moment."

"I'm glad you were able to come so quickly, Ruth." Louisa said as she rested her hand on the woman's frail one.

"*I'm* glad my nephew keeps a well stocked medicine cabinet in his surgery. I do hope the clonidine will relieve his symptoms a bit." She ran her finger around the rim of her cup.

"Penny for them, Ruth?" Louisa said.

"It's nothing really. I just hope ... I hope that at some point Martin can come to terms with his childhood ... forgive Margaret and Christopher."

Louisa looked at her, taken aback. "I never would have thought I'd hear you say something like that, Ruth. After all that those two monsters put that little boy through?"

The old woman looked up at her with a typically impassive expression. "For *his* sake, dear. Not his parents' sake. I hope he can let go of his understandable anger and resentment."

She glanced at her watch. "Well, I'd better go and check on my nephew." Getting to her feet, she headed down the hall.

"How are you doing now, Martin? Any better?" she asked, peering in the partially opened door.

Martin sat as she had left him, his arms folded across his knees, his head resting on them. "Maybe a bit. Bring me my crutches, I want to go back to bed," he said groggily.

Jeremy came up behind her. "Hey, Martin. What's up, mate?"

He tried in vain to bring the young man's face into focus. "I want to go back to bed."

"I gave him a dose of clonidine. The torpidity would suggest he was able to get it down." Ruth eyed the aide, taking note of the disparity in build between the two men. "I'm not sure that you can manage my nephew."

Jeremy guided her out the door. "I'll take it from here. We'll be fine."

He returned to the lavatory and took a seat on Ruth's stool. "I'm going to check your pulse, Martin," he said before taking hold of his wrist. "Hmm, your heart's going like a Thoroughbred at Epsom Downs."

"Help me up. I wanna go back to bed." Martin struggled to get to his feet.

"Just sit tight. I'll get you cleaned up a bit and into dry clothes." Jeremy took a facecloth from the stack on the shelf and went to the sink. He took a quick step back when his patient had another go at getting to his feet.

"Martin, you have to stay put or you're going to end up on the floor and in a world of pain. Do you understand?" Jeremy waited for a response as Martin's head bobbed up and down a few times before dropping back down to his lap.

"Louisa!" he called out through the open door. He waited a few moments as he heard rapid footsteps approaching from the hallway.

"Yes? What's wrong?" Louisa asked.

Jeremy smiled up at her from his perch on the stool. "Just wondering if you could put clean sheets on the bed. I'll clean your husband up and get some dry clothes on him."

"Yeah ... yeah, I'll do it right away." She breathed out a heavy sigh and hesitated a moment before putting her arms around Jeremy's shoulders. "I'm glad you're here."

"I'm glad I can be of help," he said. "It'll be fine; don't worry."

The aide detached the IV bottle from the catheter in Martin's hand and helped him into a clean vest and boxers. Then he fastened a gait belt around his waist before pushing himself up under his patient's good arm. "Okay, let's see if we can manage to do this without ending up in a pile on the floor."

Martin was struggling to keep his eyes open let alone his feet under him, but with a great effort from his aide, he found himself lying back in bed and much more comfortable. The intense abdominal cramps had eased into a constant ache with only periodic twinges of more severe pain. The strong sedating effect of the medication allowed him to drift off to sleep.

It was after four o'clock in the morning before things had calmed down, and Jeremy sent Louisa upstairs to get some sleep. Fortunately, baby James had not been disturbed by the commotion in the house and slept until almost half eight. Prompted by a call from Jeremy, Poppy had arrived to help out with the little boy.

When Louisa entered the kitchen late Saturday morning, James was in his high chair having a snack of cereal, and Jeremy and Poppy were at the table, each with a cup of coffee in hand.

"Oh, what a night!" Louisa said as she reached up in the cupboard for a cup.

"I just checked on Martin. He's still dead to the world," Jeremy said as he pulled a chocolate digestive from a package in the middle of the table. "Let's hope he sleeps through the worst of this. How did you sleep, Louisa?"

"Okay," she said, setting her cup on the table and taking a seat. "It's hard when I'm worried about Martin." Eyeing the biscuits, she asked, "Who's guilty of that treasonous offense?"

"That would be Ruth," Jeremy answered. "She felt the need to apologise for getting me out of bed in the middle of the night. Don't know how she knew they were my favourite."

"The woman has a sixth sense about these things." She reached for the package. "Do you mind?"

Jeremy gave it a nudge. "Help yourself. Just don't tell Martin I was complicit."

James whirled around when he heard a knock on the door. His Sippy cup fell with a thunk on to the floor. "Uh, oh!" he said as he leaned over to peer past his high chair tray.

Louisa got up from the table and rescued the errant cup, giving it to the boy before going to the door. "Al! Morwenna! Come on in."

"We brought you some lunch. Thought you could use it. Lots of vegetables ... for the doc, you know," Morwenna said as she set a casserole dish on the counter.

"Oh, how kind of you! Mmm! Chicken pie?" Louisa asked as she leaned over to breathe in the savoury aroma emanating from the pastry covered entree.

"Yep, one of the doc's favourites, according to Ruth. We heard he wasn't feelin' so great. Thought maybe a nice hot meal would cheer him up." She wagged a finger at the dish. "You might wanna take the crust off for him though. I kinda don't think he'd approve."

"Yeah, I'll do that. But how did you hear Martin was under the weather?" Louisa never ceased to be amazed by the speed and efficiency of the village grapevine.

"Ruth mentioned it. She brought Buddy back out to the farm. Found him sleepin' outside on the back porch when she went ta leave here earlier this mornin'," Morwenna said.

"So how is the doc, then? Any better?" Al asked, scratching at his jaw.

"Why don't you come in and sit down and we can talk a bit. Cup of tea?"

"Yeah, I'd like that," Morwenna said as she ruffled a hand across the baby's head. "Hi there, James. I think yer bigger every time I see you."

Louisa set the basket of tea bags in front of the receptionist and then poured hot water into her cup. "Martin had a bad night. His doctor's cutting back on his morphine, and he's having some rather nasty withdrawal symptoms. He's sleeping right now, thank goodness."

Al reached into his coat pocket and pulled out an envelope, handing it to Louisa. "We're havin' a bit of a do at the farm. Jus' so's people can see how things turned out ... maybe get some business ... we hope ... who knows," he said, giving his shoulders a shrug.

"It sounds lovely, Al. We'd like to be there. When is it?"

"Two weeks from today ... two o'clock." He jabbed a finger at the invitation.

Louisa pulled a card from the envelope, smiling at the picture on the cover. An artist's rendering of Joan overlaying a drawing of the house.

"Lots'a food and cider, games for the kids. Morwenna's in charge a that, though," Al said, giving the young woman a nudge with his elbow.

"Yeah ... thanks for that." she said, returning the nudge and wrinkling her nose at him. "It was *his* idea, and now he doesn't wanna have nothing ta do with it."

"I could help out," Louisa offered.

"That'd be great! I'm pretty rubbish when it comes to that kinda thing."

Jeremy began to get up from his chair. "Excuse me, I'm just going to go check on Martin."

Morwenna glanced over at Poppy. "You an' Jeremy would be welcome too, you know. I just didn't know you'd be here, or I would've brought an invitation."

"Erm, sorry to interrupt," Jeremy said as he stood in the kitchen doorway. "Could I see you for a minute, Louisa?"

Fearing the worst, she got up quickly from her chair and followed after him. "Has something happened?"

"Not exactly. I'm just not sure about how I should handle a situation in here," he said, gesturing towards the bedroom doorway.

Louisa peered nervously around the doorjamb, then slapped her hand over her mouth to stifle a giggle. "He must have come back ... slipped in with Al and Morwenna!" she whispered.

Martin was lying on his side, sound asleep. Next to him, curled up tightly under his chin, was Buddy, Auntie Joan's little white and brown terrier. The little animal still lived at the farm, but showed a clear preference for Martin's company. The feeling was *not* mutual.

She tiptoed into the room, intending to remove the little dog before her husband woke to find it there, but her husband's fingers were embedded in the the animal's fur.

Jeremy sidled up next to her. "I didn't know what to do," he whispered. "I get the impression Martin's not overly fond of dogs."

"That's putting it mildly." Louisa took note of her husband's more relaxed affect. The tension in his face seemed to have lifted, and his breathing had slowed.

Remembering his recollections of the comfort he'd found with the stray during his early childhood years, she directed the aide towards the door. "I'll probably live to regret this, but I think we should let sleeping dogs lie, Jeremy."

Chapter 28

Louisa looked in on her husband shortly after noon and found him just beginning to stir. She watched him surreptitiously, anticipating a violent verbal eruption when he discovered the "filthy animal" lying beside him. *Probably inoculating the bedding with all manner of bacteria, fungal spores, and parasites*, she thought.

He wiped a broad palm across his face and rolled on to his back, dislodging the terrier from his nest, which in turn startled his sleeping partner. He pushed himself into an upright position and stared down at him for a few seconds before rubbing at his eyes and looking around the room, trying to get his bearings. As the sun peeked out from behind a cloud and the rays coming in the window shone on his face, he brought his hands to his head, groaning before falling back on to his pillow.

Buddy took the opportunity to scramble up on to his chest, and the small creature swiped its tongue across his cheek.

"Oh ... gawd! Get off!" Martin said, giving him a feeble shove. The little dog was undeterred and reclaimed his position on the bed. Louisa watched as her husband gave the dog a sneer and a grunt before flinging an arm up over his eyes in apathetic surrender. She slipped away and returned to the kitchen.

Jeremy and Poppy were finishing their lunch, and James was sitting on the floor playing with the quieter toys and board books his mother had allowed him.

"He's awake in there. I didn't talk with him though," Louisa said as she grabbed for a kitchen roll and wiped baby drool from the floor. "Jeremy, you're clued-in about all of this. Do you mind?"

He pushed his chair back and got up from the table. "I'll see if I can get him to eat something."

Making his way down the hall, he tapped lightly on the bedroom door. "Hey, Martin. Feeling any better?" he asked as he entered the room.

Martin put his hands to his ears as the aide's voice seemed to bounce around in his cranium. "Do you have to talk so damn loud?" he barked.

"Sorry, mate; is this better?" he whispered.

"Mm. Can you get me some tissues?"

"Yeah, hang on." He went to the bathroom and returned, setting the box in his patient's lap. "Got the tears and snot going now, huh?" Jeremy asked as he helped him to sit up.

Martin reached for a tissue and wiped the moisture from his eyes before blowing his nose. "Ohh, gawwd." The pressure increase inside his skull caused his pulse to throb loudly in his head.

"You're due for another dose of clonidine. Think you can get it down?"

"I might be able to get it down, but I'm not sure it'll stay there."

The aide slapped a blood pressure cuff around his patient's arm and squeezed the inflation bulb. Air hissed as he released the valve.

The harsh ripping sound as the cuff was pulled from his arm chafed at Martin's brain, causing him to flinch and squeeze his eyes shut.

He waited as Jeremy laid the instrument on the dresser and pulled a notebook from his ever-present backpack, recording the numbers.

"Well? Are you going to tell me, or do I have to get the bloody cuff and do it myself?" he snapped.

The aide stared expressionless at him for a moment. "Get the clonidine down and see if you can eat a bit of dry toast. Then I'll give you the numbers," he said, handing him a glass of water and a small pink tablet.

Martin mumbled unintelligibly then popped the pill in his mouth and took a sip from the glass. His face blanched, and he closed his eyes, trying to fight his body's urge to expel the medication. The aide reached for the bin beside the bed, but Martin swallowed and blew out a breath before waving him off. "It's all right," he said.

"Good. Well done. I'll go make some toast and be back in a bit."

"Jeremy, I er…" Martin sighed. "I need to pee. Would you mind helping me to the bathroom?"

The aide hesitated. "I'm going to bring you a urinal. Your blood pressure's pretty low, and I don't want you to take a header when you stand up."

There was no argument from Martin. He closed his eyes and nodded his head in resignation.

"How is he?" Louisa asked anxiously when Jeremy entered the kitchen.

The aide looked down at his girlfriend who sat cross-legged on the floor next to James Henry. "Poppy, could you give us a few minutes?"

She scrambled to her feet before picking up the baby along with a few of his toys. "Yeah, we'll be in the living room."

The two young people exchanged meaningful glances in passing before the aide returned his attention to his patient's wife.

Louisa went to the refrigerator and took out a bottle of milk, getting a clean glass from the draining rack by the sink.

"There you go, Jeremy," she said as she set the glass on the table and filled it. He took a seat across from her and reached for a digestive.

"So?" she asked.

"Martin's going to be fine, you know. But the next few days will be pretty miserable. He's starting in with the tearing and runny nose now ... the headache, nausea, sweating, and general crankiness will probably continue for another day or two as well." He brushed the biscuit crumbs from the table and into his hand before depositing them in the sink.

Louisa eyes followed him back to his chair. "Martin prepared me for some of this, but I had no idea he'd feel this sick. I wish he'd been completely honest with me. It's a bit of a shock."

"I don't think he was trying to hide anything. A lot of people have much milder symptoms than what your husband's experiencing. Or for a lucky few, none at all. Martin's taking an SSRI for his depression. They make this kind of a reaction to the tapering protocol more likely."

Louisa reached for another Hobnob, giving the aide a demure smile. "Hard to resist." She gazed absently across the room. "So, after the next few days ... he'll be back to normal again?"

"I'm not sure about normal, but he should be feeling much better. He'll be tired though. The sedating effect of the clonidine can be slow to clear the system. And I should mention ... another side effect of the drug is a drop in blood pressure. Your husband probably uses it prophylactically with some of his hypertensive patients.

"Anyway, Martin's blood pressure is pretty low as a result, which means he's prone to orthostatic hypotension, or a sharp drop in pressure if he stands up. That can result in a syncopal episode ... fainting. So, I'm not allowing him to get out of bed until we get through this intense withdrawal period."

"Oh." Concerns about her ability to take care of a temporarily bed-ridden husband immediately flitted through her head.

“I thought I’d spend a couple of nights here ... if that’s okay with you. I can sleep on the sofa.”

Louisa released an audible sigh. “Thank you, Jeremy. Last night was frightening. I’d be so nervous here with Martin by myself.”

“You’re welcome.”

Louisa bit at her lip as her fingers clenched around her coffee cup.

“He really will be fine,” the aide said. His chair legs screeched against the slate floor as he got up to put his dishes in the dishwasher.

“It’s not a bad day out there ... a little windy. Maybe you and Poppy could take James for a walk ... get some fresh air and take a break from all of this. I can stay with Martin, maybe do a bit of clean up around here.”

“It *would* help to get out of the house for a bit. You sure you don’t mind?”

“No, I’m fine. I have some work to do on my paper,” he said, waving her off. “You go try to relax.”

Poppy, Louisa, and James headed out the door with plans to stop at the pottery shop before going to the pastry shop.

Jeremy looked in on Martin, and after finding him asleep, he busied himself tidying up in the bathroom and kitchen. By the time he finished with his cleaning he had two full bags of trash. He headed out the front door to take them to the bins on the side of the house.

Martin woke and propped himself up against the head of the bed. His head pounded with the positional change, but after lying horizontally for much of the last twelve hours, he felt the need to move.

What started as an annoying jangle quickly grew louder until it sounded as if church bells were pealing overhead. The image of Joe Penhale appeared in the doorway. He blinked his eyes several times as the blurry figure came closer.

"Hi ya, Do-*c*. Heard you weren't feelin' the best, so I thought I'd stop by to see if you'd like a bit of company."

"I think people typically want to be left alone when they're not well, Penhale."

"Well, I noticed yer front door was hangin' open, so I thought I'd better check things out. Might be a good idea to get in the habit of checkin' the latch. Old Mrs. Honold always had trouble with it not catchin', and the wind would blow it open. Could attract an unsavoury element, you know."

"An unsavoury element ... in Portwenn?"

"This village can be deceptively quiet, Doc. That's why, as the community's first line of defence, I can't let my guard down ... become complacen-*t*. As a matter of fact, when Edna lived here, she had a badger get in one night. Helped himself to a hand-baked treacle tart before trackin' down the tube of toothpaste in the bathroom. Least he had a regular dental hygiene routine." The constable chuckled. "Gotta give 'im that. Eh, Doc?"

"God!" Martin muttered before whipping his head to the side. He grimaced as the movement set the room spinning.

Joe gave his belt an upward yank, and another series of harsh tintinnabulations pierced his ears. "Penhale! *Please* ... be quiet. I have a headache."

Joe's eyes narrowed and he peered closely at Martin's face, his brow furrowing. "Doc ... are you *hung-over?*"

"*No*, of course not, you idiot!" Somewhere in Martin's muddled mind rose a feeling of regret for his choice of words, and he tried to soften his tone. "It's a symptom of withdrawal from the morphine, Penhale."

"Ah. *I* try to stay away from drugs. Don't want to end up addicted to 'em ya know. What with me bein' an officer of the law and all," he said, straightening himself up and giving another hoist to his tool belt.

Martin cringed as the sound intensified the pounding in his head.

"It might be frowned upon ... considering my position as the village's chief law enforcement officer," the constable continued. "And really, Doc, it might be a good idea if you took a bit more care with what you put into *your* body. I mean, think of those kiddies over at the school. If word gets out that our local hero's an ... *addic-t*, your bad example could put *them* on the fast track to usin'."

Martin rubbed the side of his head with the heel of his hand. "I'm *NOT* an addict! My body's just having to adjust to a decreased opiate level."

He laid his throbbing head back and closed his eyes. He imagined the policeman exploding into a puff of smoke, a gentle breeze wafting him away. Then he drifted back to sleep.

Joe tipped his head and quirked his mouth. "I *think* I know what an addict is, Doc. I'm *not* stupid," the constable said, rolling his eyes. He leaned forward, peering inquisitively at the doctor's unresponsive face. "Doc? Doc? Hmph." He gave his shoulders a shrug and left the room.

Jeremy was making himself a sandwich while he waited for the bread to finish in the toaster when he heard the front door open and close again. He stepped through the hall and into the living room when the expected sounds of female chatter didn't materialise. Surprised to find it quiet, he returned to the kitchen and put the toast on a tray and grabbed a glass of water.

"Hey, can you wake up and eat something, mate?" Jeremy said softly.

"Hmm?" Martin forced his bleary eyes open and tried to pull himself upright, the movement sending the room spinning. He let his head drop back to the pillow.

"Get your bearings *before* you try to sit up," the aide advised. He set the tray down on the dresser and moved Buddy to the foot of the bed.

"Can you get rid of that? It smells." Martin wrinkled up his nose and gave the animal a look of disgust.

Jeremy shook his head at him before picking the little dog up and setting him outside the door. "Better now?"

Martin gave him a scowl. "It still smells in here."

"Can't do anything about that," the aide said as he hooked his arm under his patient's good arm and pulled him slowly to a sitting position. "How's that?"

"Mm, better." Martin looked around the room, finding his surroundings confusing.

The young man set the tray down on the bed. "I brought you some toast and a glass of water. You need to try to get something down."

The smell of browned bread hit Martin's nose, causing an immediate upsurge of queasiness. He turned his head away and let out a low groan.

"I'll put the bin right next to you and leave the tray here. See if you can eat a few bites," Jeremy said before leaving the room.

Martin waited until the aide had disappeared around the door before pushing the toast as far away from him as his arm would reach. He laid back again and closed his eyes.

Just as Jeremy reached the kitchen, he heard a tapping on the door. He could see Al Large through the window.

"Hey, Jeremy, is the doc awake?" he asked as he stepped into the kitchen.

"Yeah, I just left him with orders to eat something. Can I do something for you?"

"I got somethin' I wanna show 'im ... ask 'im about. Is it all right if I just..." The young Large jabbed his thumb towards the hallway.

"Yeah, I suppose that'd be all right. But don't stay more than a couple of minutes; he's feeling pretty crummy. And don't wake him if he's asleep." Jeremy picked up a dishcloth and wiped the toast crumbs from the counter as the young man headed down the hall.

Al knocked softly on the door. Not getting a response, he opened it and stepped into the room. Martin lay with his eyes closed. He pulled a small metal object from his pocket and laid it on the dresser, the soft clink it made causing the doctor to stir.

"Sorry, Doc. Didn't mean to disturb ya. I just wanted to ask you's if this was a piece from that old clock of Ruth's. Found it on the floor ... couldn't think what else it might be from."

Martin rubbed at his eyes and then held out his hand. "Let me see it."

Al picked up the part and gave it to him.

"Yeah, it's a pendulum nut," Martin said, squinting at the small object. "Where did you say you found it?"

"It was back behind the clock. I was movin' it out from the wall so's Morwenna could clean back there. Ruth's got us scrubbin' the place from top ta bottom before the big open house. We got lots ta do to get ready. Been washin' windows, paintin', gettin' everything shipshape and Bristol fashion. Now I'm stiff as a gate ... can hardly move."

Martin handed the nut back to him and let his head drop back to the pillow.

"Took Dad's van in for an oil change today," Al said. "Should've had 'em oil my joints while I was there, eh, Doc?"

"Mm, yes. I'm sorry, Al. I'm really tired."

"Oh yeah, right. I'll jus' be goin' then. Hope you get ta feelin' better." He set the clock part back on the dresser and moved towards the door. "I'll keep my eyes open for any more funny little parts layin' around."

"Good." Martin gave the younger man an anaemic wave. "Oh, Al, could you, um ... take this tray back to the kitchen?" he asked, giving it a final shove.

"Sure, Doc. You rest and get ta feelin' better now."

As Al pulled the door open, the little terrier slipped through, jumping back up on to the bed and reclaiming his position next to his recalcitrant master.

"He sure does like you. Want me ta take 'im back to the farm with me?"

Martin glanced at the little ball of brown and white fur, and Buddy peered up at him with his black shoe button eyes.

"No. The miscreant seems to be a necessary evil," he said, curling his lip at the dog and heaving a resigned sigh.

Al hesitated, then pulled the door shut behind him.

The women had returned from their outing and were in the kitchen with Jeremy when Al came through. "Seems the doc didn't want this anymore," the young man said as he set the tray on the counter.

Louisa glanced up from the marking she was working on at the table. "Did he eat something?"

"Not a bite," Jeremy said, holding up the untouched slice of toast. "I'll go check in on him ... see if there's something that sounds remotely appealing to him."

"I don't think he's eaten a thing since breakfast yesterday, Jeremy. He just poked around at his dinner and didn't want anything for supper last night," Louisa said, biting on the eraser end of her pencil.

"Well if he doesn't get something in his stomach by the end of the day, I'll call Mr. Christianson ... see if he wants me to start him on an IV nutritional supplement." He headed down the hallway towards the bedroom.

Martin opened his eyes when the aide placed a stethoscope to his chest.

"How are you doing? Any better?" Jeremy asked as he reached for the blood pressure cuff.

Martin scowled at him. "No. And you still haven't given me my numbers from earlier," he grumbled.

"That's right. And *you* still haven't eaten anything." The young man wrapped the cuff around his patient's arm. "Is there anything that sounds remotely palatable? Some poached fish maybe?"

Martin shook his head slowly and swallowed back the flood of saliva that filled his mouth at the mere mention of it.

"Let me see how hard you can squeeze," the aide said, taking his hand.

His patient's fingers limply encircled his own.

"Kinda pathetic, mate." Pulling his hand back, he removed the cuff. He jotted the numbers into the book on the dresser and then glanced over at Martin who was staring at him threateningly.

"Don't mess with me this time. What's my BP?"

"Pretty low, sixty-three over forty," the aide said. "You feeling dizzy?"

Martin squinted his eyes, trying to bring his face into focus. "I don't know ... it's hard to think."

"I'm going to ring up Ed Christianson, see what he thinks. You try to get some rest."

"Yeah."

Jeremy went into the living room to call and confer with the consultant before returning to the kitchen. "Ed's calling in a couple of prescriptions to the chemist. I'll go and pick them up after a bit."

Louisa gave the young man a once over. "You look knackered. I think you and Poppy should go get some dinner. I'll stay here with Martin."

"You sure?" he asked.

"Positive. I'll get James bathed and ready for bed while you're gone." She ran a flannel under the tap and proceeded to wipe the spaghetti sauce from her son's face.

She had just turned on the faucet to run water into the tub for the baby's bath when Bert Large knocked on the back door.

Not getting an answer, he let himself into the kitchen, setting a sizable stew pot on the counter.

He wandered down the hall, spotting Martin lying on his bed. The sound of Bert's light tapping on the door frame got his attention and he opened his eyes.

"Oh good, Doc, you're awake!" Bert's jovial voice echoed through the air. Martin cringed as the sound hit his eardrums. "Oh, gawd," he groaned. "What do *you* want, Bert?"

"Just a minute, Doc. Stay there, I'll be right back," he said with an edge of excitement to his voice. Martin slapped a hand over his eyes.

The portly restaurateur waddled off, returning shortly, sporting a broad smile and toting the stew pot. "Gotta surprise for ya. Heard you weren't feelin' so hot, so I brewed up a double batch'a my soup."

He lowered the pot down so that Martin was hit with the full impact of the savoury aroma. His face blanched, and he reached for the bin on the dresser next to him, dry-heaving into it.

The chubby man recoiled and pulled in his chin. "A simple no thank you would have done!" he said.

Martin swallowed hard, steeled himself, then looked over at him. He felt a pang of sympathy when he saw the wounded expression on the jowly face.

"It's *not* your soup. I'm having some intense nausea and smells trigger ... a reaction," he said through clenched teeth. "*Please* ... take that out to the kitchen."

"Right you are, Doc. I'll go do that."

Martin watched the man's broad back disappear around the corner. He had just closed his eyes when Bert's voice again broke the silence as he called out from the kitchen. "I gotta say, I admire the courage of your afflictions, Doc!"

He reappeared shortly in the doorway "I get the collywobbles just lookin' at that metal stickin' outta ya. Then, there you are today, lookin' rough as a badger. But you don't let it get you down none. You know, *I* could use a bit more of that sort'a courage, don't you think, Doc?"

Martin rolled away from him and pulled the pillow over his head.

"Oh, say. Here's an idea. Do you got somethin' you can give me? Maybe you could write me a prescription. Do they put that courage in a pill?" Bert took hold of a corner of the pillow and pulled it up. "What'd you think?"

The doctor yanked it away and wrapped it back down over his head. "Go away, Bert!"

The man stepped back, scowling and sulky-mouthed. "Right. I'll just naff off then," he grumbled as he shuffled out the door.

Martin was roused a short while later by his wife's caresses. "Can you wake up? It's time for your medicine."

He pulled the pillow from his head and rolled on to his back.

Louisa leaned over and kissed him on the forehead. "How are you doing?"

"I'm tired. It's been impossible to get any sleep with the villagers queuing up to torment me," he grumbled.

She cocked her head at him. "The villagers?"

"*Yes!* The villagers. Why did you have to let them in here? It's been miserable!"

"Oh, Martin," she said sympathetically. "Ruth's right, you really *aren't* yourself right now."

He looked back at her, perplexed. "I think I'm very *much* myself, actually. Penhale had a perfectly predictable effect on me. He's dumb as a wagon horse and has half as much sense! I think the man's head must be full of straw."

"Joe Penhale was here?"

"Mm!" Martin rubbed his palm across his forehead. "He lectured me about the dangers of hard drugs ... called me an *addict* and suggested my recent fall from grace will lead the children of this fine village into a drug induced oblivion!"

"Hmm." Louisa pulled a chair up next to the bed, resting her forearms on the mattress.

"Can you hand me a tissue? They're behind you," Martin said, pointing towards the dresser.

Louisa pulled one from the box and dabbed at her husband's cheeks before pressing it into his hand.

"And Al stopped by. He'd found a little part from Ruth's clock. It was laying on the floor behind it." He pulled his head back and blinked his eyes, trying to focus on her face.

"That was nice of him ... to drop it off for you," Louisa said, brushing her fingers through his hair.

"Yes. Seems he was in the village to take Bert's van in for an oil change. He said he should have had them lube his joints while he was there. I think Ruth's working him too hard."

Louisa rested her chin on her hands and furrowed her brow. "Hmm."

"And then that stupid Bert came by! Prattled on about the *courage of my afflictions* and suggested I could write him a prescription for a bit of courage of his own. The man has no gumption whatsoever. Heaven forbid he show a bit of fortitude of his own accord."

"Ah, I see," Louisa said, sure of her sudden revelation. "You must have been watching movies with the sound off again, hmm?"

Martin shook his head. "I'm sorry, I don't follow."

She leaned forward and placed her hands on his face, stroking her thumbs across his cheeks.

"The Wizard of Oz. I think you've had a very colourful dream, Martin."

She stood up and began to work her way towards the hall. "I'll let Jeremy know that you and ... *Toto* ... are awake," she said wagging a finger at the little terrier on the bed.

Martin tipped his muddled head and scowled at his wife as she walked out the door. “But it *wasn’t* a dream. Louisa? Louisa! Who’s the bloody Wizard of Oz?”

Chapter 29

Louisa returned to the kitchen, a late dinner now on her mind. Her husband's aide had picked up some monkfish on his way back from eating out with Poppy and was poaching it in a pan on the hob.

"Oh, Jeremy, that's kind of you. I hope Martin can get some of it down."

"It's worth a try," he said. He lifted the lid on the frying pan and poked at the fillet before pulling the pan off the heat.

"I know he likes Bert's soup, but it's probably too rich for his stomach at the moment."

Louisa leaned back against the countertop and cocked her head at him. "Bert's soup?"

"Yeah. I think that's what it is; it was sitting on the counter. I didn't expect anyone would be eating it tonight so I put it away," he said, jabbing his fork in the direction of the refrigerator.

"What?" Louisa hurried over to the appliance, yanked the door open, and lifted the lid on the stew pot. "Crikey, he *didn't* dream it!" she said, slapping a hand over her eyes.

"Didn't dream what?"

"Martin said he couldn't sleep this afternoon because there'd been a parade of people in and out of his room. I thought he must have dreamed it. I mean, if you weren't here, I was here. Wouldn't one of us have noticed people com—"

"That would explain it! I was sure I heard someone come in the front door. I thought it was you and Poppy, but when I found the living room empty I decided it was my imagination." Jeremy threw his head back. "*And* that would explain why the door was closed when I came back from taking the trash to the bins."

"It was probably Bert. He must have dropped off his soup then stopped in to see Martin." Louisa speculated.

"No, I didn't see any sign of the pot on the counter until after I got back from dinner. Bert had to have come later. Must have been someone else."

Louisa snapped her fingers. "Al … Martin said Al stopped by."

"No, no. I let Al in. He wanted to talk to Martin. I sent him on back … told him to make it quick." Jeremy rubbed his chin thoughtfully, "When you have eliminated the impossible, whatever remains, *however improbable*, must be the truth."

She looked at him askance.

"Sherlock Holmes. "

"Oh, I see. Well, that leaves Joe Penhale then," she said, wagging her pointer finger in the air. "And Bert must have come by while I was bathing James."

Jeremy nodded. "The lowest and vilest alleys in London do not present a more dreadful setting for repose than does the affable but overly solicitous Cornish village of Portwenn," he said with mock gravity.

"Sherlock Holmes again?"

Jeremy shrugged his shoulders. "*Very* loosely paraphrased. Nice sleuthing, Mrs. Ellingham!"

"Elementary, my dear Watson," Louisa said with a grin.

Jeremy reached for a glass and filled it with water. "He never actually said that you know … elementary, my dear Watson. But still … nice sleuthing. Sir Arthur would be pleased." The aide took a sip from his glass and set it down on the counter. "I'd better go and check on our patient."

He slid the fish on to a plate and placed it on a tray. Then, grabbing a fork and the bag of supplies he'd picked up from Mrs. Tishell's, he walked down the hall.

"Hey, mate. You awake?" he asked softly. Martin opened his eyes slowly and nodded.

"Good. I have something for you."

He raised the head of the bed and set the tray over Martin's lap, stimulating his visual and olfactory senses as well as his gag reflex. He turned his head away and swallowed several times as saliva filled his mouth.

Jeremy pulled the tray away and set it on a chair on the other side of the room. "Let's try something. I'll put a piece of fish on the fork and bring it over. Don't look at it; just put it in your mouth."

Martin let his head drop back and he closed his eyes. "No, I don't think so."

"How 'bout you try one bite. If you can't keep it down, I'll leave you alone."

Martin waved his hand. "Okay, let's give it a go."

"Keep your eyes closed, and I'll put it in your mouth ... open up."

Martin did as he was told, and the aide fed him the bite of fish. He mentally went through the list of elements in the periodic table, trying to distract his brain from the fact that he was forcing food into his wildly churning stomach. *Hydrogen, helium, lithium.* He swallowed. *Beryllium, boron, carbon, nitrogen*. He took in a deep breath and let it out.

Jeremy waited. When he felt confident Martin had conquered the nausea for the moment, he retrieved the tray and set it in front of him. If looks could kill, the aide would have been dead several times over.

"I'll leave you with that for a bit, then come back and get your meds taken care of." The young man left the room, pulling the door shut behind him.

Martin released a feeble groan, and Buddy responded with a soft whine.

His eyes focused in on the little canine. "Dog," he whispered. The terrier twitched its ears. "Dog ... come here!" he said a little louder, giving the mattress a lacklustre pat. Buddy got to his feet and stood watching him uncertainly. "Come *on* you stupid animal!" he snapped. "Come here and make yourself useful."

The little Jack Russell mix took two leaps forward and put his front paws on Martin's chest, his stub of a tail vibrating side to side. "Oh, gawd ... not like *that*! Here, eat this." He gave the plate a few taps with his finger, and the terrier pounced on the monkfish, taking it in his jaws and giving it a shake. Bits of fish now littered the bed as well as the floor below.

"Oh, jolly good! *Now* look what you've done! *Clean that up!*" Martin barked as he snapped his fingers at the dog.

The latch on the bedroom door clicked, and Louisa stepped in from the hall. "How's it going with your dinner?" she asked, the little terrier getting her attention as he lapped frantically at one titbit after another. Her eyes scanned around the room, taking note of the white particles spread around haphazardly.

"What happened here, Martin?" Louisa waited as her husband grasped clumsily for the words to explain the minor calamity in front of her.

"It's not my fault! Well, it *is* my fault ... but it's not *just* my fault," he sputtered. He poked his finger in the dog's direction. "*He* did it."

"Oh, dear. That's a shame. Jeremy went out of his way to buy that fish for you and took the trouble to cook it the way you like it." She brushed her fingertips across her husband's forehead. "Can I get you anything else? A boiled egg ... toast? Or I could make you some porridge or rice or—"

"Louisa, stop!" Martin swallowed hard. "I really can't eat anything. I—I—I gave the dog my fish. The little hellion made a mess of it."

"Yes, I can see that." She crouched down and began to clean up the pieces from the floor, smiling at the thought of her husband having a simpatico relationship with an animal.

Binning the bits, she turned back to him. "Martin, I'm sorry that I jumped to a conclusion. Jeremy and I figured out that your afternoon visitors were *not* a figment of your imagination." She leaned over and pressed her lips to his head.

"It was all completely in the realm of possibility in *this* village, you know."

"Yes. I do know that, and I'm sorry if I further muddled that brain of yours." Her fingers fondled the rim of his ear.

He flinched and batted it away. "Don't do that! It's … irritating."

She pulled her hand back quickly and he sighed. "I'm sorry, it's just..."

"You don't need to apologise. I forgot."

"Mm." He pulled in his chin. "Erm, we're quite obviously not going to be able to move back to the surgery this weekend. I hope you're not too disappointed."

"I *am* looking forward to being back home with you and James, but this will give them time to get the work done."

"Work?"

"The railing in the stairway."

"Ah, yes. I'm afraid Al won't have time to do that, but I can manage with my crutches until he can get to it."

Louisa tipped her head down and peered up at him. "I … have someone lined up to do the work … a man from Wadebridge. Hope you don't mind."

Martin fought his knee-jerk reaction to launch into a lecture about the importance of thoroughly vetting a prospective contractor before hiring them. "Good. Yeah, that's good."

"I asked him to do another job as well." Louisa worked her lower lip in her teeth and eyed him warily. "You're going to need a shower. There's just no way around it, Martin. You'll never get yourself in and out of a bathtub, and we've talked about doing it for a while now so—"

"Louisa, a job like that needs to be done by someone who's certified to do the work. Did you check? Is the man licensed? Is he properly bonded? You can't just ring someone up and—"

"Martin, slow down," she said softly as she stroked his arm. "He comes highly recommended by Chris Parsons."

He grimaced and pulled his arm back before looking at her contritely. "Yes, good then."

She scowled at him. "And just so you know ... and *remember* in future ... I *did* check on his credentials. All licences, certifications *and* proof of proper insurance accounted for," she added emphatically. "I had him send me copies if you'd like to see them."

Martin stared down at his lap and picked a bit of monkfish from the plush blanket covering his legs. "I don't think that will be necessary."

Louisa pulled a clean tissue from the box and dabbed gently at the tears on her husband's cheeks. "That must be irritating."

"No. It's ... nice actually," he said as his eyes locked on hers.

She knitted her brows and stared back at him for a few seconds before a small smile graced her face. "I *meant* the tears, not the ... you know," she said, holding up the wadded piece of tissue.

"Mm, I see."

She surveyed his face, the pallor to his skin and the dark circles under his eyes. "Will it bother you if I tousle your hair a bit?"

He gave her what she thought to be a rather childish, but strangely charming, frown. "Just don't touch ... my ears."

"I'll do my best, but they *are* your most attractive feature."

"Don't make fun," he said.

She cupped his cheeks in her hands. "You're in no condition to have an emotional conversation at the moment, so I will just say this ... I was *not* making fun. I was completely serious. You may not be comfortable with your appearance, but I find you extremely attractive ... ears included."

"This has nothing to do with my comfort level! It's just..." Martin shook his head and turned away. "You're right, I'm not in the mood for this conversation, so just ... drop it. Here ... you can take this with you," he said, depositing the bit of meat he had picked from the blanket into her hand.

She looked down at it and gave him a half-smile. "I'll go let Jeremy know about the sad end to his carefully prepared dish. Ed wants him to start you on some IV nutrition or whatever it's called, and I think he picked up something to raise your blood pressure a bit. If it works, maybe he'll let you get up."

She glanced down at Buddy as he traversed the perimeter of the bed, looking for any remaining bits of fish. "I think I better let him out for a while. He's been in here all day ... must be about to burst." She leaned over and kissed the top of her husband's head, then bent down to collect the little terrier.

When she reached the door, she turned back. "Oh, by the way, we're keeping the doors locked. So, you shouldn't have any Munchkins or scary looking monkeys dropping by.

Chapter 30

By Monday morning Martin's appetite had returned, and he was more than making up for the weekend's lost calories with a hearty breakfast and the consumption of his protein-heavy shakes and snacks.

Jeremy had insisted that he wait until Tuesday for his next physical therapy session. Though the nausea and intestinal distress had eased considerably, the headaches and tremors continued, along with occasional outbursts due to the anxiety and agitation that still plagued him.

Instead of the usual trip to Wadebridge, the two men spent Monday morning at the surgery, inventorying the drugs and medical supplies in the practice and making a list of what needed to be ordered from Mrs. Tishell. If all went according to plan, the surgery would open the following week.

Shortly before noon, Ruth stuck her head in the door of the consulting room. "When you two are ready to take a break from making out your shopping list, I'll have some lunch ready at my cottage."

Martin looked up from his desk and gave her a single nod of his head. "Yes. We're almost done here. Thank you, Ruth."

"You and your aunt seem to have a very close relationship," Jeremy said as he finished stacking the boxes of gauze pads and alcohol swabs.

Martin swivelled around in his chair and leaned back, gripping the armrests. "Why in the world would you say that?"

"Sorry, mate. None of my business. Erm, you might want to add medium-sized surgical gloves to your list. All I see is small and extra-large."

"Why would you say that?" Martin asked sharply.

The aide shrugged his shoulders. "Because I'm going to need gloves, and I use medium-sized?"

Martin screwed up his face. "Not the gloves! What you said about my aunt."

Jeremy walked over and sat down on the top of the desk. "Look, I'm sorry if I've opened an old wound or something. It's just that she seems to be rather maternal in her behav—"

"Maternal! Ruth?" Martin turned and began to gather papers together. He stood the stack on end and tapped it more sharply than necessary on the desktop until the sheets were aligned with one another. Then he glanced up at his aide. "Look, maternal relationships haven't worked out brilliantly for me in the past. I'd prefer to think of my relationship with my aunt as one of friendship and nothing more."

Jeremy leaned over, resting his forearms on his knees. "I think we've both been a bit short-changed in the familial bond department, although I suspect I came out a far cry better than you did. But I experienced enough dysfunction growing up to be able to empathise if you ever feel like discussing it."

"Mm." Martin stared absently for a few moments before laying his stack of papers down and getting up from his seat. "Are we done here?"

"Yeah, I think so."

He walked towards the door, and the aide followed after him.

"You know, I'm about as comfortable in the driver's seat of your new car as a long-tailed cat in a room full of rocking chairs," Jeremy said as he pulled the door of the Lexus shut.

"It's only a few blocks. I think you can manage to get us there without deploying the airbags," Martin said, giving him a sideways glance.

"You want to stop at the chemist now or after lunch?" Jeremy asked, slowing as he approached the intersection of Roscarrock Hill and Church Hill.

"Let's do it later. I'm hungry, and I can't deal with Mrs. Tishell on an empty stomach."

Jeremy had heard comments from the villagers about the chemist and her eccentricities. He had also heard murmurings about an unconventional romantic relationship between the woman and his boss. He was anxious to meet this mysterious vamp. "You make her sound quite intriguing," the young man said as he turned on to Dolphin Street.

"That was most certainly not my intention!"

"Well, regardless of your intentions, my curiosity is piqued now. Sounds like an adventure in the offing," the aide said as he shifted the car into park.

Martin rolled his eyes at the young man. "Yeah ... right. Let's just go and eat lunch, shall we?" He grabbed on to a crutch with his left hand and pulled himself from the car.

Jeremy came around and pushed the car door shut behind him before following him up the hill to the steps.

He watched carefully as his patient slowly scaled the short stairway to the porch, then reached around him and pushed the door open. Martin stopped and glanced back over his shoulder.

"It would be in your best interests to not mention either Mrs. Tishell or the fact that we'll be stopping in at her shop this afternoon to Louisa. She could be a bit touchy about it."

"Hmm, this just gets curiouser and curiouser," Jeremy said with faux gravity.

"What?" Martin furrowed his brow at the young man.

"Oh, it's a line from Alice In Wonderland."

"Gawd, not a reference to that piece of literary tosh again," Martin grumbled.

"You're just not in a playful mood at all today, are you?" the aide said, shaking his head.

"When you have something vaguely humorous to say I'll let that fun-loving side of my personality shine. Until then, can we just go eat lunch, please?"

"Sure, sure. Sorry, Martin." Jeremy gave his mildly annoyed friend a sly grin. "But ... now *you're* sounding quite intriguing, you know."

"Oh, go wash your hands, you procacious little twerp."

The aide might have been offended by the remark if he hadn't caught the glint in his friend's eyes.

Ruth was putting bowls and plates on the table when the two men entered the kitchen. Martin went immediately to his son, who was sitting in his highchair picking through an assortment of peas, carrots and bits of chicken that had been placed on the tray.

Reaching out, he cupped the boy's head in his hand, caressing it gently before brushing the backs of his fingers across his cheek. "How are you, James?"

The little boy looked up at him, his blue eyes clear and bright, and gave him a smile. One corner of Martin's mouth rose slightly, and his eyes softened as he ran his thumb gently along the baby's lower lip, clearing away the drool before wiping his hand on the towel laying on the table. "Eat your lunch now, James," he gently admonished.

The baby's eyes followed him as he walked to the refrigerator. A light metallic tapping sound could be heard as a fixator on his arm made contact with the crutch. He reached into the appliance and pulled out one of his shakes, dropping it into the bum bag that he had donned when he'd gotten dressed that morning. He was able to get around more quickly and easily on the crutches, but he was still left with no free hand with which to carry things.

Martin's left leg was still quite painful when weight bearing, so he tended to favour it. However, the femoral fracture, in addition to the tibial and fibular fractures in the right leg, had led to stiffness in his knee and hip.

This caused him to put more weight on the right leg when standing but to take a longer stride with his left leg when walking, at times dragging the toes of his right foot on the ground, which could throw him off balance. The strength in his right leg was returning, however, and Martin could see a bit of improvement as the weeks went by.

Jeremy had already taken a seat at the table next to Poppy when Martin came to sit down. He glanced over at the pair, shifting his gaze uncomfortably when he noticed the evocative way they were looking at one another.

The door opened and Louisa hurried into the kitchen. "Hello, everyone," she said as she hung her coat over the rack on the wall.

"Louisa, I didn't know you were coming home for lunch," Martin said as he quickly struggled to his feet and pulled a chair out for her.

"Just thought I'd surprise you." She walked over and took her husband's hand, giving it a tug. "May I see you for a moment, Martin?"

He followed her apprehensively. The words *may I see you for a moment* were typically followed by a sharp rebuke for his most recent peccadillo, usually social in nature.

"Louisa, I don't know how I could possibly have done anything wrong this time. I've hardly been out of the—"

She put a finger to his lips, "Shhh, you *didn't* do anything wrong. I've just missed being close to you, and now today you're feeling better, but I've had to be at the school all morning, sitting at my bloody desk thinking about how it feels when I wake up next to you ... how you smell when you get out of the shower.

"I thought about that look you get on your face when you watch me and how you leave no doubt in my mind as to how much you love me. I came home so that I could see you and ... so that I could do this." She took his face in her hands and placed a long, lingering and decidedly passionate kiss on his lips before pulling back.

He swallowed back the lump in his throat. "I see. If I'd known this I would have sent that coterie in the other room to The Crab for lunch."

"We'll just have to look forward to tonight then, hmm?"

"Mm, yes." He blinked slowly as he watched her move away. She had put him off his stride. He waited a moment to collect his thoughts before following after her.

As he slid his chair up to the table Ruth slipped a bowl in front of him. Immediately recognizing it as Bert's soup, with the *magical properties*, he glanced over at his wife.

"I called Ruth this morning and asked her to heat it up for lunch ... thought we should get it eaten." She flashed him an innocent smile before adding, "Wouldn't want to let it go to waste, would we?"

Her warm hand came to rest on his knee. "Well, *I* had a perfectly tiresome morning, how 'bout the rest of you?" she asked.

Jeremy gave his mouth a wipe with his napkin and took a sip of milk from his glass. "Your husband and I were taking inventory and making a list of what supplies need to be ordered."

"In other words, our tedious complements your tiresome quite nicely," Martin added acerbically before scooping another spoonful of Bert's soup into his mouth.

Louisa's hand gravitated suddenly, and Martin started as her fingers began to explore inquisitively under the table. Inhaling sharply, he aspirated some of the liquid. He reached quickly for his water, trying to stave off the coughing fit he could feel coming.

Jeremy watched, his brow furrowed, as Martin guzzled the entire glass and blinked the tears from his eyes. "Maybe a sandwich would go down easier, mate. Want me to put one together for you?"

He put his hand up in the air. "No, I'm fine." He picked up the water pitcher and refilled his glass before taking another swig and swallowing hard. "It just went down the wrong way," he choked out.

Louisa gave him an apologetic smile and mouthed the word, *sorry*.

Clearing his throat, he looked across at the childminder. "What did you and James do this morning, Poppy?"

The girl's head shot up. She was not accustomed to being addressed so directly by the doctor and certainly not with such a mundane question. She peered up at him with a bowed head. "We, erm we went for a walk, then came home and built towers with his wooden blocks. And we er, we read some stories."

"Mm, interesting." Martin reached for his glass again.

The room was silent for several moments before Ruth said, "Well, no one seems at all curious about the circadian comings and goings of an old lady, but I'll tell you anyway."

"Oh yes, Ruth! We'd like to hear about your day so far!" Louisa said, nodding her head as she dabbed at her mouth with her napkin.

"Don't grovel, dear. It's not becoming."

The napkin hung, suspended in the air, as Louisa was hit by the directness of the elderly woman's words.

Ruth continued. "It seems our little soiree in two weeks will be attended by a member of the press ... The Telegraph to be exact."

"What in heaven's name for?" Martin blurted out.

Louisa gave him a jab with her elbow. "Ruth, that's so exciting! How did that come about?"

"I had a patient at Broadmoor a number of years ago. A paranoid schizophrenic who was convinced that someone working for Royal Mail was stealing his post and burying it in the backyards in the area. They finally had the poor man committed when he inadvertently dug up a communications cable, cutting off phone service to the entire neighbourhood and nearly electrocuting himself."

She pushed her dishes forward and folded her hands on the table. "But I digress. This particular patient was the father of an up and coming reporter at the Telegraph. The man later went on to become an editor for one of the bureaus. I rang him up, told him about our venture, and he's sending someone down to cover the event as part of a series the paper is doing in their travel and entertainment section."

"That's so exciting, Ruth! No wonder you want everything in perfect order. This *is* exciting, isn't it, Martin." Louisa said, giving her husband a vigorous nod of her head.

She may have been wearing a smile, but her eyes told a different story, and Martin nodded in agreement as he rubbed the pain left in his side where his wife's elbow had previously connected with his tender ribs. "Yes ... yes, it's interesting news."

"Please let us know, Ruth, if there's anything we can do to help you prepare," Louisa said.

The elderly woman stood and began to clear away the dishes. "I believe Al and I have things in hand, and you two have enough to keep you occupied at the moment," she said as she wagged a finger at her nephew.

Ruth glanced at the clock on the wall. "You'd better watch the time dear. You should be getting back to the school."

Louisa gave her a peevish look. She adored the woman as a general rule but found her occasional forays into authoritarianism to be off-putting.

"Yes, I *do* have a lot to get done this afternoon." She forced herself to loiter in her chair in silent intransigence slightly longer than she would have preferred.

Martin slid his chair back from the table as his wife got to her feet. "I'll walk you to the door."

"Oh, thank you, Martin."

He pulled in his chin and got to his feet.

"This is a pleasant surprise ... you seeing me out." Louisa stroked her fingertips over his forearm as they stood on the front porch.

"Yes. I, er ... I'm sorry I didn't do it more ... before now. I should have."

Louisa couldn't help but smile back at his sweetly contrite expression. "A very wise man told me once that we should leave things in the past and move on, but remember the lessons learned. And that applies to me as much as it does to you."

"Let me guess, Bert Large?" Martin said, curling his lip.

"Hmm?" Louisa cocked her head at him.

"The *wise* man."

Louisa placed her hands on her husband's chest and tipped her head back. "No, it *wasn't* Bert. It was our very dear friend, Chris Parsons. And we could both learn a thing or two from that couple."

"Yeah, a thing or two. If I remember correctly, that's the limit of Chris's knowledge about women."

Louisa gave his chest a firm slap. He winced and sucked in a breath of air.

"Oh, Martin, I'm so sorry!" She leaned forward and pressed her lips to his ribs.

"Mm. It's okay. I think that was deserved. I will most certainly reflect on Dr. Parsons' words of wisdom."

She pulled him down and gave him a proper kiss. "Good. And I'll make up for that slap later."

"Mm, yes."

Chapter 31

By the time they had finished lunch, Martin's fatigue was obvious. Jeremy insisted he have a short lie-down before they ventured out to the chemist. That short lie down turned into a two-hour nap, but Martin woke feeling much better able to deal with Mrs. Tishell.

"We're going to walk down there, Jeremy," Martin said when he saw his aide pick the car keys up from the basket on the counter. "I want to get the ogling and asinine questions out of the way before we open the surgery."

"And you think walking down to Mrs. Tishell's will accomplish that?"

"It'll be a good start. Word travels fast in this village. If just one person sees us before we get to to the chemist, chances are good that every gossipmonger within a five-mile radius will have been advised of our whereabouts before we even leave her shop."

"You think you're that popular, do you?" the aide asked as he pulled the door open and waited for him to step through.

Martin turned around and gave him a scowl. "Are you going to be like this all day?"

"Sorry, mate." Jeremy watched carefully as Martin navigated down the ramp in the back of the house. "Now don't get cocky and go too fast on the hill, Martin. You're likely to end up flat on your face."

"Don't worry, I'm not feeling that confident yet. Your optimism and sensitivity are touching though," he answered irritably.

As they approached the bottom of Middle Street, Martin saw Lucy Holmes exit the pottery shop, and he slowed his pace. "Perfect," he muttered under his breath.

"Doc! Doc Martin!" the woman called out. Her footsteps crescendoed as they pattered on the pavement. "Doc, how are ya doin'? I haven't seen you in a crow's age!"

"Mrs. Holmes. Have you noticed any improvement in your symptoms since I started you on the propylthiouracil?"

"Sure 'nough have. You was right, Doc. It *was* my thyroid that was causin' all the trouble. Found out last week we got another baby on the way. Hard to figure who's happier, me or Billy. It's such a relief for him ta know he weren't the one causin' the problem, you know. And me ... I'm just happy to squeeze one more baby in before I get too old ta do a proper job of it."

"Good. Make sure you don't miss your first antenatal check-up. Your doctor will want to get you scheduled for a scan. The PTU has the potential to cause developmental problems in the foetus, but this can be treated quite successfully if problems are caught early."

"What do you mean? You're not gonna be my doctor?"

Martin shifted his weight from his left leg and stretched it out, trying to relieve a cramp that had begun in his calf. "You have Grave's disease. Your pregnancy will be considered high risk, so it would be best if you were under the care of an obstetrical specialist."

Whether it was fear, worry or concern on the woman's face, he couldn't be sure, but Martin did know that his words had made her uncomfortable in some way. He spoke quickly, trying to calm her. "That's not as bad as it sounds. It just means that you'll need to be monitored more closely than a patient without any complicating health issues. I'd prefer you were followed by an obstetrician in Truro. I'll make a call this week and set something up for you."

Lucy's face fell. "No, Doc! You may be a cranky bugger, but I trust you. You stand by yer standin', and you do your best by your patients. I want *you* to be my doctor."

"Please call in to the surgery on Friday, Mrs..." Jeremy said when he noticed his patient resting more heavily on his crutches and beads of perspiration on his forehead.

Martin waved a hand at the woman. "Jeremy, this is Mrs. Holmes. Mrs. Holmes, this is my assistant, Jeremy Portman."

The aide extended his hand. "I'm pleased to meet you, ma'am. As I was saying, please call into the surgery on Friday. You can make an appointment to see Dr. Ellingham next week." Jeremy turned to Martin. "You've been on your feet long enough. We need to go sit down somewhere."

"Mm, yes. Mrs. Holmes, we can discuss this further when you come in to see me, but I *do* think it would be in your best interests to see a specialist," Martin said as he moved forward. "Jeremy, let's make a stop at the pub before we go to Mrs. Tishell's."

The two men moved away and Lucy called out. "But, Doc, I don't want to have to drive all the way over to Truro!"

Jeremy took hold of his patient's arm and kept him moving along. "The pub? You want to go for a drink?"

"I noticed the tide's in. The pub should be full of fishermen ... a good crowd."

The aide pointed in the direction of the bench outside The Slipway. "This way ... now. You need to take a break."

As they moved towards the restaurant, Martin's pace slowed quickly. Jeremy took his crutches in one hand and his good arm in the other and lowered him on to the seat before sitting down beside him.

"Okay, what's up? Why the sudden need to be sociable?" Jeremy asked.

Martin tipped his head back and wagged his nose in the air. "It's neither sudden nor a desire to be sociable."

"So, what ...you're thirsty then?"

Martin sat silent, his jaw set and his brow furrowed. There was a flurry of activity as a group of schoolchildren ran down the hill. When the squeals and laughter faded away Martin glanced towards his aide.

"I'm feeling a bit ... I'm getting more and more uncomfortable about having a parade of people coming into the surgery next week ... people staring at me ... asking questions about things I don't want to talk about. I'd prefer to get this over with."

"Martin, I'm sorry. I knew you didn't want the questions and ogling wasting your time, but I didn't realise it was eating at you this way. I had the impression you didn't really care what people thought of you, what they said about you. I thought you'd just tell 'em to bugger off and move on to the next patient."

Martin said nothing. He leaned forward and rested his elbows on his knees, worrying his thumb into his palm.

The aide tapped his fingers together. "I don't know about this, Martin. It could be risky. Do you really think getting it over with in a pub packed with drunken fishermen is the best way to go about it?"

"You *are* prone to exaggeration, aren't you," Martin said, rolling his eyes at the young man. "It's the middle of the afternoon. They shouldn't be too bladdered yet."

Jeremy threw up his hands. "Okay, if this is what you want to do. You gonna buy me a pint, then?" He got up from the bench and handed the crutches to Martin.

"I can. But you do realise that alcohol has an appalling effect on the liver and central nervous system, don't you?" Martin said as they walked towards the pub.

"I'll take my chances."

A hush fell over the room as Martin ducked through the low doorway. He focused his gaze on the bar and moved slowly forward, trying to avoid catching his crutches on the irregularities in the old wood floor or on the feet of the patrons who moved back to give him room to pass.

"What'll you have, Jeremy?" Martin asked as he pulled out his wallet.

"A pint of Extra Smooth. Thanks, mate."

Martin handed John, the pub landlord, a five pound note and then went to look for a place to sit. He could feel eyes on him as he moved along.

"Good ta see ya out 'n about again, Doc," Chippy Miller said as he passed a table surrounded by fishermen.

Martin glanced at Chippy, expecting his gaze to be glued to the cumbersome metalwork affixed to his limbs, but the fisherman didn't seem to take notice.

Eddie Rix gave him a thumbs-up and a nod of his head. "Doin' great there, Doc."

He pulled in his chin. "Mm, yes."

It had been more than a half hour since Martin and Jeremy left Ruth's cottage. Most of that time Martin had spent on his feet, and an intense ache was beginning to radiate through his fractured limbs.

Grimacing as a particularly sharp jolt shot through his left leg, and feeling a desperate need to get the weight off his limbs, he hurried towards a booth.

He glanced over as he passed a table on his left, turning away quickly when he made eye contact with the two leering men seated there. As he took the next step, the forward momentum of his left crutch was stopped abruptly by the foot of one of the men, sending him hurtling towards the floor. Jeremy watched helplessly from behind. He pushed the leering men and their table aside, dropping to his knees alongside his patient.

Martin's face contorted in pain, and he struggled to pull in a breath of air. He had landed hard on his right side with his fractured arm pinned under his own weight. Jeremy rolled him on to his back. "Martin, try to take shallow breaths."

Martin lay, eyes closed, trying to focus his thoughts away from his screaming nerve endings. "Breath in ... breath out," he repeated to himself.

"Doing better now?" Jeremy asked when he noticed his patient's respirations had returned to normal.

Martin opened his eyes and tried to sit up, the action sending a jolt of pain through the right side of his chest that forced him back to the floor.

"Where does it hurt?" the aide asked.

He clenched his jaws, holding back a groan. "It's the—thoracotomy wound. I— landed on the fixator—in my arm." He reached up with his left hand and palpated his side. "It's okay."

"What about the leg and arm?" Jeremy asked as he inspected the fixators in his patient's calf and thigh carefully before gingerly palpating his forearm.

"Jeremy, it's fine! Just help me up."

"'ere, Doc. Let me 'elp ya thar," said Peder Teague, one of the fishermen who had been sitting at the table with Chippy Miller. Martin glared at him for a moment before recognising him as the younger of the two fishermen who had found Ruth's former patient unconscious on the beach a number of months earlier.

Chippy moved to Martin's other side, and with instructions from Jeremy, the two burly men hoisted the doctor into a chair.

"Oi, someone get the doc a glass of water!" Chippy yelled over the hubbub of voices. "You better slow it down a bit, Doc. Hate ta see ya back in hospital again," he said, leaning over with his hands on his knees to stare into Martin's face.

"It wasn't Dr. Ellingham's fault," Jeremy said, taking a step towards the two men who now sat snickering nearby. "He was intentionally tripped."

Martin followed his aide's gaze, the growing rage on the young man's face becoming a concern. He put his hand on his arm. "It's over now. Best to just leave it."

The aide pulled his arm away and moved aggressively towards the two men. "You rat-arsed, pusillanimous, morons! That was a right bollocks thing to do! Are you completely bladdered or do you have sweet Fanny Adams for brains?"

Martin grabbed on to his crutches and pulled himself to a standing position. "Jeremy! We're going! Now!"

He could see the possibility of a brawl breaking out growing by the second. Just as the aide turned, the man who had tripped Martin jumped up, sending his chair clattering like tenpins in a bowling alley.

He grabbed the aide by the front of his jacket and shoved him to the floor, quickly landing a solid punch to his face. Jeremy tried to roll away, but the man's companion quickly joined in the fracas, and he found himself helpless.

What followed was over in seconds. Peder Teague, his father, Awen, and Chippy Miller grabbed the two aggressors and pulled them off the young man, hauling them outside the building. Eddie Rix hurried over and helped Jeremy to his feet.

He was seated in a chair across from his boss, and Martin was palpating his face for any sign of serious injury when a strident, nasal voice resonated through the room.

"All right, break it up! Break it up now! Fun's over, boys!" Joe Penhale called out imperiously.

He pushed through the small crowd of onlookers. "Well ... it's a sad day for Portwenn when our most upstanding citizen has stooped to the level of instigator in such a shameful act of drunken and disorderly conduct," the constable said as he stood eyeing Martin, shaking his head.

"I'm not drunk, you idiot! And I had nothing to do with this!" Martin sputtered, now thoroughly frustrated with the calamitous turn the outing had taken. "Help me get Jeremy up to the surgery, Penhale."

Joe came around from behind and looked the young man up and down. "I see, now. *You're* the trouble-making malcontent." The constable hooked his thumbs over his toolbelt and narrowed his eyes at the aide. "Well then…*Jeremy*…we'll let the doc get you patched up, but then you're comin' down to the station with me where we can get this all sorted … officially."

"Penhale! For goodness' sake, just help him to your vehicle and drive us up to the surgery!" Martin grimaced as he wedged his crutches under his arms and moved towards the door.

They made their way to the constable's Land Rover, parked on the slipway. Martin groaned as he forced his painful and stiffened legs into the vehicle.

Jeremy lowered the towel-wrapped bag of ice that John had handed them as they left the pub. "Well, you didn't get any asinine questions out of the way, but you sure got a lot of the ogling taken care of," he said with a forced smile as they turned on to Roscarrock Hill.

Martin looked back at him with a scowl and concern in his eyes. "Be quiet and keep the ice on that face," he said, pushing the aide's hand back up.

Joe walked into the surgery with the two men and waited in the reception room for Martin to finish tending to Jeremy's wounds. Having heard the commotion, Ruth came out to see what was going on.

"I'm not privy to all the fac-*ts* as of yet, but it sounds like a classic case of the alcohol-testosterone effect," Joe explained.

Ruth cocked her head and stared back at him, expressionless, for several moments. "You *do* understand what the alcohol-testosterone effect *is* … don't you?"

The constable rolled his eyes at her. "Of course, I do. I wasn't born yesterday. I believe our young medical assis-*tant* in there had a bit more than he could handle, resulting in an alcohol-induced testosterone rage. He went off on one of the other patrons in the establishment. He'll have to suffer the consequences of his unlawful actions, I'm afraid."

Ruth sighed and took a seat next to him. "Penhale, in large quantities, alcohol can *lower* testosterone levels in men, but it will most certainly not raise testosterone levels, nor will it lead to a testosterone rage."

The constable rose from his chair and began to pace slowly across the room. "That means I still have a crime to solve, then."

The consulting room door opened, and Martin followed his patient through to the reception room.

"Martin, what in the world happened?" Ruth asked as she scanned over both men.

"Some moron down at the pub tripped me, and Jeremy here felt the need to defend my honour. This is the result." He pulled the ice pack away from the young man's face, revealing a deep purple bruise to his cheek, a swollen eye and a bloodied lip.

"Oh for goodness' sake," Ruth gasped.

"So, that's your story, is it? The law doesn't look kindly on vigilante behaviour, I'm afraid," Joe said.

Martin furrowed his brow. "If you want to arrest someone, you're going to have to talk to Chippy Miller, Penhale. Or one of the other fishermen that were in the pub ... get the names of the two men who did this. Jeremy didn't even get a punch thrown. But for now, can you give us a ride back to Ruth's?"

The deflated policeman nodded his head. "Sure, Doc. Now, I don't want either of you to worry. I'll handle this matter expediently and in full accordance with the law."

Martin sighed. "I'm sure you will."

After they returned to Ruth's, Jeremy checked Martin over for any signs or symptoms that could be cause for concern. He was just finishing with his examination when Louisa arrived home from work.

"Are you sure he's all right ... you're all right?" she asked as she bounced James on her hip while her eyes darted between the two men.

"I'm fine. Just not real pretty to look at right now," Jeremy said as he laid several cold packs on his patient's right leg and arm as well as along his ribcage. "And your husband seems to be okay as well. He'll probably have a nasty bruise and more stiffness and pain for the next day or so, but I'm pretty confident no serious damage was done. I'll follow up with Mr. Christianson, though, just to be on the safe side."

He moved towards the door. "I guess we'll have to finish our other business tomorrow, mate. I'll see you in the morning, eh?"

"Yep." Martin raised his head up. "Erm, Jeremy ... thank you, for..." he said, giving the younger man a nod.

"Your welcome. Sorry I made such a hash of it." The aide began to pull the door closed behind him before stopping and sticking his head back into the room. "You *do* realise it wasn't just me who was on your side in the pub, don't you?"

"Yeah. Goodnight, Jeremy."

Louisa came downstairs after putting the baby to bed that evening and dropped down on the sofa next to her husband. "Quite a day, hmm?"

"Mm, yes." Martin reached his arm behind her and pulled her up against him, kissing the top of her head.

She felt his chest rise and fall slowly with a silent sigh.

"How do you feel knowing that when push comes to shove, you have the support of the villagers?" Louisa asked.

"It might be easier to believe if pushing and shoving didn't have to be involved before they showed it. It's ... hard to not be suspicious, Louisa. To wonder about an ulterior motive."

She fingered the buttons on his shirt, working them loose. "Do you think with time you'll be able to trust their motives? Believe that you *do* have their support?"

"Perhaps. It would help if fewer disparaging remarks were being thrown my way."

"Yeah, well..." She tugged at his shirttails and then undid the last of the buttons before casting the garment aside.

He ran his palm across her head, allowing her ponytail to slip through his loose fist, and his fingers brushed her cheek before dropping down to fondle her breasts. The soft fibres of her cashmere jumper further softened her feminine curves, whetting his tactile thirst.

Louisa got up from the sofa and eyed him coyly. "Let's go to bed, Martin. Hmm?"

"Yes."

As they lay side by side in bed later, Louisa smiled at him, causing the light to dance in his eyes.

"I do love you, Louisa," he said, stroking her cheek with the backs of his fingers.

"I love you, too." She tipped her head down and peered up at him. "And I'm sorry for slapping you earlier."

"Mm, it's okay. It was worth it." A worrisome thought crossed Martin's mind. *Gawd! Could this be the sort of scenario that led the Rixes' down the path to their aberrant bedroom behaviour?*

He groaned internally before pushing the thought aside and pulling his wife to him.

Chapter 32

Monday's excursion to the pub had diverted Martin from his original objective to pay a visit to Mrs. Tishell. He was determined to accomplish the task first thing Tuesday morning. Jeremy had arrived at Ruth's cottage early, joining him for breakfast before their day got underway.

Martin sat at the kitchen table, his list of errands and tasks to be completed lying next to his plate of bangers, eggs and toast. He scribbled another item on to the sheet of paper. "I don't know, Jeremy. Things are piling up here. I feel like I'm spinning my wheels," he said, rubbing a hand over the back of his neck.

His growing dissatisfaction with the speed of his recovery as well as the mounting tensions stemming from the looming reopening of the surgery were resulting in an irritability that seemed to grow exponentially with each passing day.

"One thing at a time, Martin. You're going to drive yourself crazy if you keep trying to operate like you did before your accident," the aide said as he painted a thick layer of orange marmalade on his toast.

"You have a dreadfully poor diet, you know," Martin said, scrutinising his aide's fat and sugar-laden plate with an expression of disgust. He pushed his eggs around with his fork, peering up at him. "Are you icing that face the way I told you to?" he asked sharply, jabbing the utensil at the young man.

Jeremy gave him a roll of his eyes. "Yes, I've been following your instructions to the letter. Twenty minutes every two hours."

The aide picked up his newspaper and gave it a firm shake before folding it back on itself. The two men sat silent for a minute or two, the disquiet thick in the air.

"You should have just let the matter drop you know," Martin said, giving his sausage a petulant poke.

Jeremy glanced up at him as he picked up the salt shaker and proceeded to liberally season his eggs.

"Good God! You're not preserving those you know!" Martin spluttered.

Jeremy gave his fork a toss on to the table. Then taking his plate to the waste bin, he dumped the remnants of his breakfast into it.

"I'll be in the living room when you're ready to go to Mrs. Tishell's," he grumbled, stomping off towards the living room.

"Well, that wasn't necessary," Martin mumbled as he watched him disappear down the hall. He stared absently before returning to his list.

Louisa walked into the kitchen with James Henry perched on her hip, and she tousled her husband's hair as she passed by. "You look like you just lost your best friend," she said, settling the baby into the high chair.

Martin lifted his head and gave her a scowl. "Thanks, Louisa. That's really helpful!" He pulled himself from his chair and limped off towards the bedroom.

When Poppy arrived, promptly at eight o'clock as usual, Louisa passed off care of the baby to her before going in search of her husband. She found him sitting on the bed cleaning his fixator pins.

"Hmm, your favourite activity," she said as she sat down next to him.

"No, it's not!" he snipped before returning his attention to the task at hand.

"I wasn't serious, Martin," she said, taking the band from her ponytail and readjusting it. "I'll have to be leaving for school in a few minutes, but if there's something you'd like to talk about I'd like to listen."

Martin paused from his detailed work, the cotton bud hanging from his fingers. He sighed then went back to wiping at the metal that penetrated his leg.

"It might help to share what's bothering you," she urged.

"Louisa, my body hurts. I'm trying ... rather unsuccessfully, mind you ... to prepare for patients next week. My assistant had the bloody heck beaten out of him because of me. On top of that, due to morphine withdrawal, I can't stop my hands from shaking and I'm as edgy as a—a *tax evader* in a HMRC auditor's office! Do you *really* think I want to talk about this in the few minutes you have before leaving for the school?"

Louisa leaned over, trying to make eye contact with him, but his gaze refused to meet hers. She slipped from the bed and wrapped her arms around him. "Okay, we'll talk later. But for now, will you let me hold you? If not for you, then for me?"

Martin stared at her for a moment before giving his cleaning supplies a shove to the side. He put his arms around her, reluctantly at first, but his body gradually yielded to her. "I'm sorry," he said softly. "I shouldn't take my frustrations out on you."

She held him at arm's length. "Martin, unloading your troubles on someone who cares about you is not the same as taking out your frustrations on them. You didn't push me away or shut down when I asked you if you wanted to talk just now. Do you realise how happy you make me when you talk to me ... about anything?"

Martin's shoulders sagged. "I *do*. I do realise that. I'm just not very good at it. I wish I were better at it."

"Well, we *will* talk more about this later. I know it's easier said than done, but try not to worry about all this stuff that seems to be piling up on you. Make a list of the things that need to be done, and I'll help you wherever possible. Her hand caressed his cheek. “You don’t have to do things alone anymore, Martin. I know it’ll take time for you to get used to the idea, but let people help you carry the load ... okay?”

“Mm.” He pulled in his chin and reached for another cotton bud.

“I’ll see you for lunch then?” she asked, putting her hands on his shoulders.

“Erm, no. Jeremy called Ed last night. He wants to see me today. Just to make sure nothing’s shifted out of place.”

A hint of concern passed over her face, but she gave him a smile and kissed his forehead. “I’ll see you after school then.”

“Yes.”

Martin shaved and dressed before going out to the living room to talk with his assistant. There had been many times in his life that he had regretted his choice of words, but in addition to the remorse that he felt for his behaviour with Jeremy earlier, he feared that he may have alienated the young man. He dreaded having to face him, and the ever-present anxiety that he had been experiencing lately wasn’t making it any easier.

The aide was sitting on the sofa, papers spread out on the coffee table in front of him. “Jeremy ... I, er ... I’d like to talk to you for a minute ... before we go to Mrs. Tishell’s.”

Jeremy gave the notebook he’d been writing in a toss on to the table and looked up at him. “I’m all ears.”

Martin backed up and sat down on the arm of the sofa, his back to him. “I owe you an apology.”

The aide waited before huffing out a breath. “Well, if that was the apology, it was pretty rubbish, mate. You could at least look at me.”

Martin swung his legs around, trying not to snag his fixators on the sofa. “Look, if you want to ingest all the saturated fat and refined sugars that soda and crisps contain and pickle your neural pathways with alcohol, that's your lookout. It's none of my business, and I'm sorry I butted in."

"It's all right, Martin. I know you just get on people about this stuff because you care about their health. But it might come off better if you put a more positive spin on it."

"A positive spin? Leading a reasonably healthy lifestyle is intrinsically positive, and a healthy diet is an inherent component of a healthy lifestyle. Why in God's name would I need to *spin* it?"

"Okay, okay. That may have been a poor choice of words. I just mean that people are more apt to listen to you if you tell them what they *should* do, not what they *shouldn't* do ... just like kids. When James gets a little older, you'll have better luck getting him to listen to you if you tell him to stay on the sidewalk than you will if you tell him to stay out of the street."

Martin quirked his mouth and shrugged his shoulders. "I guess I can see some logic in that." He ran his hand up and down a crutch. "Jeremy, there's something else I wanted to talk to you about. Yesterday at the pub ... I really wish you'd stayed out of it. You wouldn't have gotten hurt if you'd just kept quiet and let it go."

"Oh, no. There's absolutely no way I could have let that go, Martin. People can't be allowed to get by with that kind of behaviour."

"You should have let Joe Penhale handle it, then. You didn't need to get involved."

Jeremy got to his feet and stared down at him. "I bloody well *did* need to get involved! You're my patient ... my boss. And more importantly, I thought we were friends. Would *you* stand back and let someone do that to a friend?"

"I don't ... really have friends."

He screwed up his face. "*Yes* ... you do!" Air hissed from the aide's nose and he scratched roughly at his head. "Okay, then imagine it's a patient. Would you just stand there if someone did what that jackass did yesterday?"

Martin shook his head. "Of course not, but..." He heaved a heavy sigh. "That's not what we're talking about here. I ... I appreciate what you did, but I wish you hadn't gotten hurt because of me. I'm sorry that happened."

Jeremy stared back at his boss for several moments. "What do you mean, that's not what we're talking about here? That's exactly what we're talking about!"

Martin reached up, pressing his fingers to the bridge of his nose. "Ohhh, never mind. Just ... in future, I'd appreciate it if you didn't try to defend me. I do have an unerring knack for pissing people off, and I don't want you to suffer the consequences for it."

Jeremy began to shove his papers forcefully into a binder. "I'm sorry, Martin. I don't understand this. You seem to get what it means to *be* a friend but you don't seem to get what it means to *have* a friend. And it's pretty hard for a bloke to be your friend if you won't allow them to do what friends do for one another."

He slipped his binder into his satchel and stood up. "Ready to go see Mrs. Tishell then?"

Martin sat for a moment and then patted his shirt pocket, double checking that he had the list of supplies that needed to be ordered. "Yes, I guess I am."

The bell on the door jangled as they stepped into the chemist shop a few minutes later, and the woman's singsongy voice called out from upstairs. "I'll be right with you!"

Jeremy explored the collection of lotions and perfumes on the rack by the front window. He walked over to his boss and held a bottle up to his nose. "What do you think of this one?" he asked.

Pulling his head back quickly, Martin screwed up his face. "I don't think it's you."

"Very funny. What about for Poppy?" the aide said, setting it back on the shelf.

He peered up from his supply list. "Trust me, you don't want to rely on me for advice on either perfume or women in general."

Footsteps could be heard approaching on the stairs, and Mrs. Tishell emerged from behind the wainscot partition. She stopped in her tracks when she saw Martin standing on the opposite side of the counter.

"Dr. Ellingham!" she said breathlessly, her fingers gravitating automatically to the top button on her cardigan.

Martin glanced up, the woman's mere presence causing him to take an involuntary step backwards. "Mrs. Tishell. I need ... er, we need to order some supplies," he said quickly.

"How *are* you, doctor?" she asked sympathetically. "I just couldn't believe it when I heard about your accident!"

"I'm improving," he answered tersely. "Mrs. Tishell, this is Mr. Portman. He'll be assisting me at the surgery when we begin to see patients next week. You'll be seeing a lot of him until I'm physically able to handle things on my own again."

The woman leaned to the side and peered around him to get a better look at the young man. "Oh, *dear*! I heard about the dust up down at the pub yesterday," she said, eyeing Jeremy's bruised face. "It's a shame people have to behave in such an uncivilised manner." She clicked her tongue before her love-struck eyes settled on Martin.

The aide stepped over to the counter and held out his hand to her. "I'm pleased to meet you. You can call me Jeremy, though."

Martin glanced over at him quickly, giving his head an almost imperceptible shake as he furrowed his brow at him.

She looked him up and down, then cocked her head at him. "You've been in to pick up Dr. Ellingham's prescriptions, haven't you?"

"Yes, I was in last weekend."

"Well, I'm happy to meet you ... Jeremy," she said. Her gaze flitted back to Martin as she toyed nervously with the buttons on her jumper. She leaned towards him slightly, and he slid his list of needed supplies across the glass countertop.

"Mrs. Tishell, if you could just get these supplies together for me, I'd appreciate it," Martin said, shifting his weight to his right leg.

The woman knitted her brow. Then, placing her hand on his arm, she leaned towards him, lowering her voice. "Are you in pain? It looks to me like you're in pain."

He pulled his arm back. "Mrs. Tishell, just get busy and get my supplies together!"

She straightened herself and turned to go up the stairs. "I'll have this ready for you toot sweet, Dr. Ellingham," she said, throwing a coquettish smile over her shoulder.

Jeremy watched the woman disappear behind the wall, then looked at his boss. "*That's* Mrs. Tishell?" he hissed.

"Yes, of course it is. Why would I have introduced her as such if she wasn't?"

"I was just expecting someone a bit ... younger. She doesn't really seem like your type."

"My *type?* What in the world is that supposed to mean?" Martin said, the colour rising in his face.

Jeremy returned the perfume bottle that he'd been holding in his hand to the shelf by the window. "I didn't mean anything in particular. It's just ... well, I've heard mention of a romantic relationship of some sort between the two of you."

"What?" Martin squawked. "That's absolutely preposterous!"

"Well, I don't mean a *current* relationship, of course! Although, she obviously still harbours feelings for you. And I could see how in a little village like this ... not too many women to choose from and all."

Martin's eyes fixed on the aide and anger began to smoulder in them.

Jeremy tried desperately to dig himself out of the hole he knew he'd gotten himself into. "I mean, it'd be perfectly understandable. She does have a certain je ne sais quoi that might appeal to certain men. I suppose. If there were no other options. Be nothing wrong with it is all I'm saying. I didn't mean to suggest there'd be anything wrong with it if you *were* to—"

"Shut—up—Jeremy." Martin said, his words soft but pointed.

The aide looked down at his shoes. "Yup." He turned away, taking a sudden and inapt interest in the feminine supplies on the shelf behind him.

The bell on the door jangled and Marianne Walker stepped through. "Dr. Ellingham! Look at you out and about finally!"

"Mm, yes. Hello, Mrs. Walker."

"Oh, it's just Marianne ... *please.*" She pulled off her gloves and folded them in half before placing them in her purse.

Mrs. Tishell clomped back down the stairs. "I thought I heard someone come in the door. How are you, Marianne?"

"Oh, about the same as everyone else, I suppose." Reaching up, she loosened the top button on her coat. "I just need to pick up some paracetamol. My son and daughter-in-law are coming for a visit this weekend. My migraines always flare up when they're here."

The chemist reached up on the shelf behind her. "The one hundred count bottle again?"

"Yes ... please."

"And how *is* Donald these days? The last I heard he was living in Bristol." Mrs. Tishell set the bottle of pills down on the counter and punched several buttons on the cash register.

"Yes, he still is. Married a lovely girl who owns a clothing shop up there."

The chemist leaned her forearms on the glass countertop and folded her hands. "Still an accountant, is he?"

Martin breathed out a heavy sigh. "Mrs. Tishell!"

"Oh, yes doctor. I'm sorry. That'll be three pounds fifty, Marianne."

Mrs. Walker pulled a purse from her handbag and dug through it, pulling out a ten pound note. "There you are," she said, handing it to the chemist.

The bell on the cash register rang out, and the drawer popped open. Coins clinked in their respective receptacles as Mrs. Tishell dug around for the correct coinage.

"What about grandchildren? Any on the way yet?" she asked as she handed Mrs. Walker her change.

Martin threw his head back. "Mrs. Tishell! My supplies!"

"Oh, of course, Doctor. How could I be so insensitive. I *am* sorry. I mean, there you are standing on those poor painful legs, and here I am, *yakking* away!" she said with a flourish of her hand. "I am *so* sorry! I'll get to it straight away."

"Thank you!" Martin shifted the crutch under his right arm, trying to reach over with his left hand to massage the new bruise on his side.

The chemist disappeared back up the stairs, and Mrs. Walker exited the shop, the cowbell swinging behind her.

Jeremy sidled up next to his boss. "Sorry if I broached a sensitive subject earlier. One of those messy break-ups I assume?"

Martin looked incredulously at his aide and then pulled his shoulders back, peering down at him imperiously. "I am only going to explain this to you once, Jeremy, so listen closely.

"There has never *been*, nor will there ever *be* ... a relationship between Mrs. Tishell and me. She had at one time formed a fixation on me. That, in combination with a drug induced psychosis, led to her kidnapping our son. The woman's received treatment, and the whole sordid affair's in the past now. I would greatly appreciate it if that's where you'd leave it."

Jeremy raised his eyebrows. "Wow, sounds like something you'd see on the telly!" He scratched at the side of his head and furrowed his brow. "I won't bring it up again after this, but I have to tell you, mate … it may be in the past for *you*, but *that* woman's still got a thing for you."

Martin didn't have a chance to react before the approach of the chemist's footsteps could be heard again. "Here you are, Doctor," she singsonged. "I'm sorry to have kept you waiting."

He looked over at her, noticing her fingers fondling the now open buttons on her cardigan. His head snapped towards his assistant who gave him a knowing look and a barely perceptible nod in the direction of her wandering hand.

Flustered, Martin snatched the box off the counter and shoved it at his aide before hurrying as quickly as he could towards the door. "Put it on my account, Mrs. Tishell!" he yelled back over his shoulder.

"So nice to meet you, Jeremy! And goodbye, Dr. Ellinghaaam!" The cowbell jangled one more time.

Chapter 33

Martin sat watching the landscape pass by the passenger side window as they drove to Wadebridge later that morning. His thoughts turned to the conversation he'd had with his assistant earlier in the day. Jeremy had said he didn't seem to get what it means to have a friend. He tossed the idea around in his head.

What does he mean by that? Do you have to learn to have a friend? You either have friend's or you don't, and I don't have friends because..." Martin sighed and leaned his head back against the headrest.

He sat with his eyes closed. *Okay, so what do you have to get when you have a friend? Where am I mucking this up? He implied that it's hard to be my friend because I won't let him do what friends do for one another. So, letting him defend me ... that's a requirement for having him as a friend?*

If I don't know what it means to have a friend, do I know what it means to have a partner ... a wife? Being a good husband means caring for my wife physically ... and to provide for her. I do reasonably well at that. But it also means caring for her emotionally. I'm bloody rubbish there. What does it mean to have a wife?" Martin furrowed his brow and massaged his temples. His head was pounding as he tried to make sense of his aide's words.

Jeremy glanced over at him. "You okay?"

He gave him a dismissive shake of his head. "Just thinking."

"Must be some pretty serious thinking, judging by that scowl on your face." Jeremy glanced down at his patient's hands as they clutched at his knees.

Martin whirled around. "Why did you say I don't get what it means to have a friend? What the hell is that supposed to mean?"

The aide looked over at him. "Well, first of all, it was meant as an observation, *not* a criticism. And I just meant that you don't seem to understand what having a friend is about."

"Oh, that makes it less ambiguous," Martin grumbled as he shifted back and rested his elbow on the window ledge.

Jeremy drummed his fingers on the steering wheel. "Okay, let's just say that you seem very reluctant to let me put myself out there for you. You don't seem to trust me either, and I'm not real sure you even *want* to trust me."

Martin's jaw dropped open as he blinked at him. "For goodness' sake, Jeremy! I picked you to defend me from any pathogen infested villagers who might try to breach the door to my consulting room, didn't I? I'm allowing you access to my patients' medical records, and I trust that you'll protect the confidences contained in them. I've placed complete trust in you regarding my own health care. What more do you expect?"

"You're talking about a professional relationship, and I'm talking about a friendship. Are you going to force me to use the word?"

"*What* word?"

"Awww, mate. Don't make me say this!" the aide pleaded. He sighed heavily, hesitating. "*Feelings*! You don't trust me with your feelings!"

Jeremy smacked his hand against the steering wheel. "Thanks a lot, Martin. You've made me embarrass us both."

Martin turned his head to the passing scenery. Both men sat speechless for several minutes before the silence was broken by the doctor's words.

"Jeremy, there are only three other people in my life who I've been more open with than I've been with you. And one of those is my therapist; I'm not sure he counts. I hope you'll be able to see that as meaningful when you consider how little time we've known each other."

He glanced at the aide surreptitiously as the young man turned to look at him. The eye contact was fleeting, but thoughts were tacitly exchanged and the air was cleared.

An hour later, Martin was wrapping up his physical therapy session. This was to be the last until the fixators were removed. The exercises that he had been doing with Kieran and Max would be continued at home, a few with Jeremy's assistance.

"You've made great progress, Martin. It's been amazing to see the results that can be achieved with the determination and effort you've shown," Kieran said as he helped Martin to wipe the swimming pool water from his legs.

"Mm, I have a very compelling objective." Martin handed him his towel then pulled his warm up pants on over his boxers.

The therapist walked to a nearby chair and picked up his patient's vest, tossing it to him. "Let me guess; you have a big trip planned?"

Martin pushed his arm into the sleeve before backing it out again, trying to untangle a thread from a pin near his elbow. "Much more consequential than a trip ... my son. He's begun to walk, and I need to be able to keep up with him. There are things I'd like to do with him. Things I'd wished for when I was—" He cleared his throat and pulled the vest over his head.

"Well, thank you, Kieran. I appreciate what you've done to help me," Martin said as he extended his left hand.

"You're more than welcome. We'll see you back here in a few months. You should see some real changes once that hardware comes off."

Jeremy was waiting in the seating area and got to his feet when his boss stepped through the door. "All finished?"

"Yes. No more trips to Wadebridge for a while."

The aide had picked up sandwiches while Martin was in physiotherapy, and they ate their lunch on the drive to Truro. A stop needed to be made at radiology before going up to meet with Ed in his office, and they were on a tight schedule.

By the time he finished with his CT scans, Martin was running ten minutes late. Apologising to his surgeon, he took a seat on the opposite side of his desk.

"So how do the pictures look today?" he asked apprehensively. He had been experiencing considerably more pain in his arm since he took the fall, and he'd been harbouring concerns. Fidgeting nervously with his wedding band, he waited for Ed to review the images.

"Would you say you came down harder on the arm or the leg?" the surgeon asked as he squinted his eyes and leaned towards his computer monitor.

"Probably harder on the leg," Martin replied. The intensity of the man's scrutiny caused his stomach to churn.

He breathed out a hiss of air through his nose and scowled deeply as the surgeon seemed to be taking an inordinate amount of time to come to a conclusion. "Well? Are you going to tell me what you're thinking, or should I come around there and decide for myself?" he snapped.

Ed held up a hand, quieting him. He leaned back in his chair, steepling his fingers. "I see some mild sub-periosteal haematomas around the two most proximal pins in the ulnar fixator. The femoral and tib/fib fractures appear to be fine. But I do think it's time to discuss removing a few pins. Shall we try to get that done later this week so it doesn't interfere with your appointment schedule next week?"

Martin shook his head. "I'm sorry, what about the *haematomas*? Can we discuss that a little more? Is it going to set me back at all?"

The surgeon pulled his chair up to his desk. "It may slow the callus formation down a bit, but I think ultimately we'll stay on schedule. Just be especially careful with that arm for a few weeks. It's going to be extra tender. Now, about the pin removal..."

It was almost three o'clock by the time Martin and Jeremy arrived back in Portwenn. Martin pulled up his arm and glanced at his watch. "Jeremy, would you mind dropping me at the school?" he said.

"Yeah. You want to give Louisa a ride home, I take it."

"No. I want to walk with her. You can drive the car home."

"Very funny, Martin," the aide said with a chuckle. "If you're trying to wind me up it's not going to work, mate."

Martin swivelled his head around. "Jeremy, you know bloody well that I don't *try* to wind people up. It—it just comes naturally."

He squirmed in his seat. "I think the idea of another procedure on Friday may cause Louisa a bit of stress. She seems more relaxed when we take walks together."

"I don't know, Martin. What are you going to do if you get halfway home and can't make it any farther? That's a pretty long hill, you know."

"Yes, I'm quite familiar with it! Now are you going to drop me off or not?"

The aide hesitated and then emitted a low growl. "All right. But you *have* to call me if you get tired. I'll come and pick you up." He shook his head. "*Jeez*, I hope you prove to be easier to deal with as a practitioner than you are as a patient." He turned off Trewetha Lane to head for the school.

"Don't get them up *too* high."

Jeremy turned a puzzled face towards him. "What?"

"Your hopes ... don't get them up too high."

"That ship has sailed, Martin. You're practically a mythological figure around here, so my expectations are *sky* high. I can't wait for next week," he said with a puckish grin. He shifted the new Lexus into park and got out of the vehicle.

"What do you mean, a mythological figure?" Martin snorted as the aide handed him his crutches, swinging the door shut behind him.

The young man walked back around to the driver's side. "You know, your ability to diagnose the most obscure illnesses. The tales of your heroics ... lives saved and all that. Your ability to leap tall buildings in a single bound."

He slipped in behind the steering wheel and rolled the passenger side window down. "And your lovable irascibility is legendary. In fact, I have it on good authority that you even made the bin man cry. So yes, I have my hopes set quite high. Don't let me down, mate!" he hollered as he pulled away.

Martin screwed up his face as he watched the Lexus drive down the hill. "Utter rubbish! We don't *have* any tall buildings in Portwenn," he muttered as he turned to walk into the school.

The year twos and threes were outside the school, participating in some sort of a game that Martin couldn't make heads or tails of. But he worked his way carefully across the tarmac, wary of stray balls hurtling his way as well as the children that were sure to be following after them.

He had just reached for the door handle when he felt something bump his left crutch. He heard a voice behind him. "I can help you, Dr. Ellig-am!" He whirled his head around with a frown on his face, ready to admonish the child for not watching where he was going.

"Evan!" he said, his face immediately softening when the wide-eyed boy took a step back. "Erm, I'm sorry, Evan. You startled me." He forced a small smile.

The boy grinned shyly in return and put all his weight into pulling the heavy school door open. Martin stepped through and Evan followed after.

When the two reached the bench in the hallway, Martin stopped and took a seat. The child stood, nervously watching, his eyes drifting to the doctor's right arm. Noticing the fearful look on the boy's face, Martin shifted. He pulled his arm back against his side before trying to distract him.

"Would you like to have a seat?" he asked, giving a nod to the empty space to his left. The little Hanley boy tentatively climbed up on to the bench, his feet dangling in the air.

"How are you keeping, Evan? Did the arm heal up okay?" the doctor asked as he reached out to take hold of the boy's wrist.

Evan jumped, pulling his arm back reflexively before his body relaxed and he allowed Martin to examine him.

"Still a bit sore probably, hmm?" he said as he laid the arm back on the child's lap.

"It hurts a little ... sometimes."

"It's likely to be tender for a while. It actually takes months to even years for the remodelling to be complete. It's quite an interesting process, really. There are cells produced by the periosteum ... er, the membrane covering your bones. Those cells form cartilage and then a callus, which eventually hardens into bone."

The child stared up at him with a puzzled face.

"That's the simplified version," Martin said.

Squinting his right eye, Evan asked. "If my bone isn't complete yet, does that mean it could come to part again?"

The doctor bit at his cheek as he struggled to come up with a simpler explanation. "The bone in your arm that was broken has repair—er, it's fixed itself now. Your body has grown new bone to, erm ... it's like your body's glued the broken bone back together. It's strong now, but over the next several months to a year that glue will turn back into bone and it will be like new again. But until it *is* like new again, it may be a bit tender."

"So, it won't come to part again if something hurts it?"

The look in the child's eyes made Martin squirm. He knew exactly what was going through his head ... why he had asked the question.

"That ... glue that's holding your bone together isn't quite as strong as the bone itself, so it *is* a weak spot in your arm ... if that's what you were wondering."

The little boy's shoulders sagged, and he looked down at his feet as they swung back and forth nervously.

Martin glanced around him then asked softly, "Evan, how is your father doing? Is he well now, or does he still drink?"

Evan's feet swung faster, and he took in a deep breath before looking up at Martin. "He does after I go to bed. I can tell 'cause he knocks things over then."

"And what about your mother ... does she drink?"

"*Uh-uh!* She doesn't like it. That's how come she leaves."

Martin leaned his head back against the wall, closed his eyes for a few moments, and then looked down at the child. "Evan, I was going to walk Mrs. Ellingham home from school today. I get rather tired, though. Could you come along and give me a hand? Then we can give you a ride home."

The little boy's face brightened, and he jumped down from the bench. "Sure, I'm *good* at helping!"

The two walked down the hall to Louisa's office, and Martin tapped lightly on the door. He could see her huddled over the paperwork on her desk. She looked up, and seeing him, she hurried over.

"Well, this is a nice surprise!" she said as she stretched up to kiss him.

Martin pulled back and cleared his throat, nodding down at the boy. "I have company today."

"I see that!" she said. She crouched down so that she was at eye level with the child. "It was very nice of you to help my husband get to my office, Evan. I think I can take care of him now though. You can go back out with the rest of the children."

Martin cleared his throat again, and Louisa stood up, cocking her head at him.

"I thought I'd walk you home today, and Evan offered to help me out. I told him we'd give him a ride home ... hope you don't mind."

"Oh?" She furrowed her brow and looked back down at the boy. "Evan, could you have a seat here in Miss Woodley's office while I chat with Dr. Ellingham for a minute?"

"Mm, hmm." The child scrambled up on to the vinyl sofa.

"What's going on, Martin?" she asked as soon as her office door had closed behind them.

"I need to talk with Children's Services about the situation in the Hanley home. According to Evan, his father's still drinking. It sounds as though he limits it to the times when the children are in bed, but it seems Mrs. Hanley leaves when her husband's intoxicated. He's defenceless, Louisa. Anything could happen when he's alone with that belligerent sot."

"Oh, poor Evan." She glanced at her watch. "Well, the final bell is in a few minutes. We can leave then. I'll get Pippa to stay until four."

Martin moved slowly as they headed down Fore Street a few minutes later, thinking through each step before moving a leg forward. They had waited until the initial rush of children had left the school, but there were still sporadic groups of rough-housing boys and chattering girls that would brush by them. As they approached the Platt, the herd of female hecklers, omnipresent in the village, swooped past. They bandied around disparaging remarks about the fishermen heading to the pub at the end of the day but quieted when they saw the doctor making his way towards them. They passed him by in silence.

The hill leading to Ruth's cottage wasn't very long, but it was steeper than the hill on Fore Street, and Louisa was feeling some apprehension as they approached. Her husband's pace had slowed, and his fatigue was becoming apparent. "Martin, you look tired. Maybe we should sit down and rest a while," she said, gesturing towards the bench outside the Slipway.

He glanced down at the small boy by his side. "I think we need to get some things taken care of and get Evan home before his mother wonders what's become of him, don't you?"

"*I'll* help you, Dr. Ellig-am," the Evan said, giving Martin a gap-toothed grin. He took two skipping steps to catch up before wrapping his fingers around his wrist. Although this meant he now had to watch that he wasn't tripped up by his small charge, the gesture gave the doctor the mental boost he needed to make it to Ruth's.

Chapter 34

Louisa had discreetly apprised Poppy and Jeremy of the situation with their small guest and then busied Evan on the kitchen floor, playing with James Henry. "Poppy, can you watch over these two while I go see how Martin's doing?"

"Sure, Mrs. Ellingham." The childminder turned to the seven-year-old. "Evan, maybe you could see how high you can stack the blocks before James knocks them down."

Louisa gave her a nod and hurried down the hall. She could hear her husband's stern voice as she approached the bedroom. He had put in a call to Children's Services and was still on his mobile when she walked into the room.

He stood with his back to her, the phone glued to his ear. "Well you can be bloody sure I'm not taking the boy back out there until this has been thoroughly checked out!"

Louisa eased the door shut behind her, watching nervously as her husband shifted his weight from one leg to the other.

"I could advise you on what you can do with your proper channels if you like. I'm this family's doctor, and I know for damn sure that there's a serious problem in that house! It's not a secure environment for these children! I have a duty of care, and the boy stays with me until you can assure me that it's safe for him to go back home!"

His fist clenched and unclenched, a sign Louisa had come to know as an indicator of building anger. She walked over and placed a hand on his back, the gesture eliciting a startled gasp from him. He whirled his head around and stared at her, wild-eyed, and she backed away.

Martin closed his eyes and inhaled deeply before continuing with his end of the conversation. "Look, I would rather not have to defend my actions in front of a review committee, so I'd appreciate any assistance you can give me. I don't want to fall foul of the law, but I will *not* send that boy back into a dangerous situation. Do I make—myself—clear?"

He grimaced and lifted his left leg from the floor as he listened to the person on the other end of the line. He uttered a sharp *"thank you"* before ringing off.

"Louisa, would you take this please," he said breathlessly, passing off his mobile with trembling hands before limping to the bed, collapsing on to it.

"Martin, what is it? What hurts?"

"My left leg. Just give me a minute," he said hoarsely.

Louisa went to the kitchen and retrieved several cold packs from the stash in the freezer. "Jeremy, could I see you a minute please?" she said with feigned aplomb, tousling Evan's hair before hurrying back to the bedroom.

"Is it getting any better now that you're off your feet?" she asked as she tucked the packs in around the painful limb.

Martin licked his dry lips and shook his head.

"What's happened?" the aide asked when he saw his patient squirming in obvious agony.

"Nothing's—happened!" Martin spluttered. "And if you—say I told you so, Jeremy." He gave the aide a warning stare before another jolt coursed through his lower leg.

"You want something extra for the pain?" Jeremy pulled open the Velcro fasteners on his patient's trousers, scrutinising his wounds.

"No!" Martin grimaced and grabbed for his leg. "Awwwr! All right—yes!"

"You definitely have more oedema in this leg and more seepage around the pins than I've seen in a while. Hang on, mate. I'll be right back."

The young man hurried out of the room and returned shortly with his backpack. He pulled out a heavy plastic box and opened it up, revealing a small array of vials and syringes with needles.

Martin raised himself up, trying to get a look at what the young man was doing. "Noth—ing sedating."

"Yep. I was thinking of Toradol, but I need to clear it with Mr. Christianson first." He pulled his mobile from his pocket and stepped into the hallway.

Louisa went to the bathroom and returned with a wet flannel. She wiped the perspiration from her husband's face before leaning over and placing a kiss on his forehead.

"Okay, we're good to go on the Toradol," Jeremy said as he re-entered the room. "Louisa, could you help your husband get his trousers pulled down. I need access to his left thigh." He pulled a vial from his box of supplies and drew the medication into a syringe before injecting it into the muscle on the front of Martin's leg.

Louisa shuddered and turned her head away quickly. "Oh, I hate needles." She watched, waiting for her husband's clenched jaw to relax. "It doesn't seem to be helping, Jeremy."

"It takes about a half hour to kick in."

Martin tried to focus his thoughts on what to do about his young charge in the kitchen. "Erm—Louisa, could you call Mrs. Hanley. Tell her Evan helped you out with a project or somethi—" He squeezed his eyes shut and tried to swallow back a moan. "Mmrrr."

"Oh, Martin. I wish there was something I could do to help."

"Just—just go make that call. Tell her anything to buy me a bit of time to think—to think this through. *Please.*"

Louisa lingered, not wanting to leave her husband's side.

"Now!" Martin snapped.

"Yeah. Sorry." She got up and went into the living room to ring the boy's mother.

When Mrs. Hanley answered, she explained that Evan had helped her with something after school, causing him to miss the bus. The woman made no bones about her displeasure at having to come to collect her son, but after being assured that the child would be provided with a ride home, Mrs Hanley seemed more cordial, thanking the head teacher before ringing off.

Louisa was drawn to the kitchen by the sound of small giggles. She stood in the doorway, unnoticed by the children. James's blocks had been pushed aside, and the two boys were lying prone on the floor, their heads buried under her son's blanket. The scene was in stark contrast to the reality that the adults were dealing with in the other room, and she smiled at the brief moment of happiness that the little Hanley boy was enjoying.

By the time she returned to the bedroom, the Toradol had begun to work its magic, and Martin was more comfortable. He sat up on the edge of the bed when he saw her.

"How are you doing?" she asked.

"Better." Martin said as he rubbed his hand over his thigh.

"That Toradol burns, doesn't it," Jeremy said as he lifted his patient's hand and placed a warmed gel-pack over the injection site.

"Mm. Better than the alternative, though. Did you get through to the boy's mother, Louisa?"

"I did. Mrs. Hanley's expecting me to bring Evan home before dinner. Hope that's okay." She moved to her husband's side and put a hand on his cheek. "You look exhausted, Martin."

Pain is tiring, and Martin wanted nothing more at the moment than to lie back and close his eyes to the world, but he had a child in his house who needed an adult willing to intervene on his behalf.

Louisa pressed her lips to his head. "I don't suppose it'd be possible for you to just let Joe Penhale handle this?" She pulled back and looked into his eyes. "I'm worried about you."

"I'm tired, yes. And I overdid it on the walk home from the school, but I'm fine. And no ... I can't let Penhale handle this. He's nobbled by the jurisdictional limits of his job. But I have an idea. Can you bring the boy in to see me?"

Jeremy pulled the zipper closed on his backpack and glanced over. "I can get him," he said.

"No. I need to talk to *you*. Louisa, please get Evan for me." Martin gave a quick nod towards the door, and Louisa moved off down the hall.

"What's up?" Jeremy asked as he picked up the gel-pack and massaged the lump on his patient's thigh.

"I don't know what to do here, Jeremy. Do you have any experience with this sort of situation?"

"What, with the boy?"

"Of course, with the boy! Did you work with any abuse or neglect cases at the hospital?"

"A few. But just on the medical end of things. I did pick up on *some* of the legal aspects, though."

Martin furrowed his brow and pursed his lips. "I can't leave the boy to fend for himself. What's my best course of action here?"

"Blimey, Martin. You're in a tough spot. Children's Services won't intervene?" Jeremy pulled back the leg of his trousers and began to wipe at the clear drainage seeping from around the pins.

"Unless there's sufficient reason to believe Evan's in imminent danger they have to work through the *proper channels* before removing him from the home. All I have to go on is past history and what the boy told me today—that his father's inebriated after the children go to bed and the mother leaves them alone with him.

"Children's Services considers that cause for concern, not proof of imminent danger. The most they can do is to initiate a home visit to check up on things. Most assuredly scheduled during the daytime hours, not in the overnight hours when Mr. Hanley does his imbibing." Martin rubbed at his eyes. "I don't know what to do here, Jeremy. What's best for this boy?"

The young man sighed and shook his head. He could see that the situation was weighing heavily on his boss, but he was also very aware of the realities. "Martin, you're not going to like what I'm about to say, but ... you *have* to take him home. You'll be of no use to the kid if his parents file an injunction order against you."

Martin sat silent for a few moments before nodding his head. "Could you drive me over to Wadebridge tomorrow? I want to stop in at the Foneservice store."

The aide's brows pulled together. "Yeah, I can do that."

There was a rustling in the hall, and Louisa entered the room with Evan in tow. The little boy climbed up on to the bed and sat down to the right of the doctor. Martin moved his arm protectively to his lap, and Evan's eyes followed.

"Does that keep your bones from falling to part again?" he asked, reaching out tentatively and running a finger lightly along the metal framework.

"Mm, hmm. Like the cast on your arm did."

He took hold of Martin's hand and lifted his arm up, inspecting the apparatus carefully, touching where a pin penetrated his flesh. "Did they stick that on with glue?"

"No, a surgeon reduced the ... er, he put the broken bones back into place and then put those metal pins into them. Then he had to adjust this metal bar to hold the pins in place," Martin said, pointing to the frame on the side of his arm.

Evan looked up at him quizzically.

"He, erm ... he made it the size it needed to be to fit my arm," Martin said, beginning to squirm uncomfortably at the child's questions.

"Huh! The doctor said a pastor from Paris made mine." He jumped to the floor and eyed the fixators on the doctor's legs. Squatting down on his haunches, he peered into the slits the tailor had fashioned in his trousers. "Wow! Those ones look just like the other ones, 'cept those ones are bigger! How come those ones are bigger, Dr. Ellig-am?"

Martin sighed heavily. "Evan, I asked Mrs. Ellingham to bring you in here so that I could talk to you. Do you know how to use a mobile phone?"

The child poked a finger into an opening in the fabric, asking again, "How *come* those ones are bigger, Dr. Ellig-am?"

Louisa decided it was time she intervened. "Dr. Ellingham will answer your question, Evan. Then you need to listen to what he has to say, all right?" She took him by the hand and pulled him to his feet. "Dr. Ellingham, I believe Evan was wondering how *come* those ones are bigger." She gave her husband an impish grin.

Martin scowled back at her. "I would presume, Mrs. Ellingham, that you meant to say, *why* are *those* bigger."

Evan leaned his elbows on the mattress, resting his chin in his hands. "Yeah, why come are those ones bigger?"

Martin hissed out a breath. "Those are bigger because the bones are bigger," he said quickly. "Now, I need to talk to you about something very important. So, pay attention."

The little boy straightened up and folded his hands behind his back, donning a serious expression.

"Do you know how to use a mobile phone?"

"Hmm. No. But my mum has one, so *she* knows how to use one."

Martin groaned softly and rubbed at his eyes. "I tell you what, I'm going to bring a phone to the school tomorrow. This will be a secret between you and me." Martin glanced up at his wife. "I guess we'll have to let Mrs. Ellingham in on the secret as well. I'll let you borrow the phone from me, but only if you promise to take very good care of it. Take it home and put it somewhere safe in your bedroom ... where no one will find it."

"'cept for me, right?" the little boy said as he swung his arms back and forth behind his back.

"That's right. Do you know how to call for help if you ever feel as though you're in danger?"

Evan furrowed his brow and shifted his eyes to the ceiling. "You mean like if there's a robber ... or I have a heart attack?"

"Yes, those would be two possibilities. Although, given your age and health history it would be highly unlikely that you would suffer any sort of cardiac event."

The boy stared back blankly for a moment before screwing up his face. "So just for robbers, then?"

Louisa once again decided it necessary to act as facilitator in the verbal exchange. "Evan, are there times when you feel frightened at home ... or unsafe?"

The boy climbed back up on the bed and leaned against Martin.

Louisa knelt down in front of him, restating her question. She watched as a small hand worked its way slowly towards her husband, coming to rest on his forearm.

"It was scary when that happened," the child said.

"It was scary when what happened?" Louisa asked softly.

"When my arm broke. I don't like it when he looks like that."

"Are you talking about your father?"

He nodded. "It's scary when he has his angry eyes."

"Evan, I want you to call me the next time you feel afraid of your father," Martin said. "It doesn't matter what time of the day it is. You can call in the middle of the night if you feel afraid. I'll stop by the school tomorrow and give you the mobile. I can show you how to use it then."

Evan gave him a broad grin. "You're gonna come see me tomorrow?"

"Yes, I will. But right now, we need to get you home to your family. Your mum will be waiting on you for supper." Martin reached for his crutches and pulled himself to his feet.

The boy's face fell before brightening suddenly. "I could just stay here tonight. Then you wouldn't even have to drive me home!"

Louisa reached out her hand. "Come on, Evan. Your mum's waiting."

It was beginning to get dark by the time the Ellinghams turned on to the gravel drive leading to the Hanley farm. The rocks crunched under the tyres, an occasional clink being created as a stone hit the undercarriage of the vehicle.

The outdoor light burning on the side of the house did little to make the dwelling appear more welcoming. A single tree stood in the yard, it's leafless branches hanging like a hag's gnarled fingers over the front door.

Louisa shifted the gearbox into park, and Martin pushed the passenger side door open. "I'll walk you to the house, Evan," he said, waiting for the boy to get out of the car.

The child emerged reluctantly and threw his weight against the door, slamming it shut forcefully. His feet scuffed at the ground as he followed behind the doctor. When they reached the porch, the child pulled at his sleeve. "Dr. Ellig-am, I have something to tell you."

Martin sighed and then leaned down. Small clouds of vapor puffed from the boy's mouth as his breaths became more rapid and the moisture from his lungs condensed in the chill night air. "I don't like it here!" he whispered stridently.

Martin swallowed back the lump in his throat. He heard his Auntie Joan's voice in his head and paraphrased her words—

words that had brought him comfort when he was a child. "I know. But remember, when you think of me, I'll be thinking of you, Evan."

He straightened himself up and knocked on the door.

Chapter 35

They were halfway back to Portwenn and Martin hadn't spoken a word. Louisa glanced over at him. "You were wonderful with Evan today," she said softly.

"No, I wasn't."

"Yes, you were!"

"Yeah," he grumbled, rubbing his hand roughly across the back of his neck. He directed his attention to the moon peeking out above the trees, hoping his wife would let the subject drop. It had been a very tiring, discouraging and, at times, painful day, and he was finding her positive perspective on a matter that was causing him a great deal of concern to be quite chafing.

"You really were, Martin! He was so curious about your fixators and so full of questions, but you handled it beautifully. I was actually quite impressed with your ability to connect with that little boy."

Martin turned an angry face towards her. "Well, unfortunately for Evan my ability to connect is not going to get him out of that house!"

"Yes. I'm very sorry about that." She placed a hand on his knee. "Sorry for Evan *and* for you. But you're doing everything you can, Martin."

"That won't be any consolation to him when his father's coming after him in a drunken rage, though, will it?" He returned his attention to the moonlit scenery outside the window, and his wife focused on the twists and turns of the hedge-hugged roadway.

She breathed out a silent sigh, sitting quietly for a few minutes before asking, "Martin, what was it like for you when you were growing up?"

He rolled his eyes. "Why do you want to start flogging *that* dead horse again?"

"Well, I'm just wondering if this whole thing with Evan ... I mean, how does it make you feel? I would think it could be dredging up some very painful memories ... feelings. So, I thought it might be helpful for you to talk about it. It'd be helpful for me, too. To understand you ... and Evan as well."

It was readily visible by her husband's stiff carriage and set scowl that the lock on his emotional vault had just been set, and Louisa let the subject drop. She reached over and took his hand in hers.

"I had my scans today and consulted with Ed," he said. "Everything checked out all right. Just a bit of bruising to the bone around a couple of the pins."

"Well, that's good news ... isn't it?"

"Yes. Yes, it is. Ed also wants to remove a few of the pins. It's scheduled for Friday morning."

"Why are they taking pins out? There's not a problem, is there?"

Martin could hear the tightening of his wife's voice and knew the news was having the anticipated effect on her.

"No, it's a *good* sign actually. The bones have enough intrinsic structural integrity to be less dependent on the fixators. Reducing the support will allow them to strengthen further, but it needs to be done gradually, so Ed only plans to remove about one fourth of the pins now. He'll remove more at a later date."

"That's a positive step then ... right?" Louisa nodded her head enthusiastically before a disturbing thought crossed her mind. "Martin, you said it's been *scheduled* for Friday morning. They don't have to do this surgically, do they?"

"It's just an out-patient procedure. Jeremy can take me over to Truro."

"No, Martin. I'm going with you."

"Ohhh, Louisa. I don't want to have a disagreement about this," He said, rubbing his temples. "Really, it's a very simple procedure. It'll be done under conscious sedation and will probably take no more than fifteen minutes at best to do the actual pin removal. In fact, I could ask Ed to do it without sedation if you'd be more comfortable with that."

"Martin Ellingham, don't you *dare*!" Louisa grimaced and gave a theatrical shudder. "Promise me you won't do that, Martin."

He tipped his head back and wagged his nose in the air. "I'm merely saying, Louisa, that it *is* an option ... if you're concerned about sedation."

The couple sat quietly for several minutes before Martin picked up the conversation where it had left off. "It really isn't necessary for you to take time away from work just to spend the better part of a day waiting around for me to—"

"Martin, I *will* be going along. Now, if you were serious about wanting to avoid a row, then you should just ... shut up about it."

"Mm ... yes," he said, dipping his head.

A cold fog was beginning to drift into the village from the sea, becoming progressively denser as they descended New Road.

Jeremy had stayed at Ruth's, helping Poppy to prepare dinner. The table was set and spaghetti marinara was ready to be served when Martin and Louisa arrived home.

"Aren't you and Jeremy joining us?" Louisa asked, noticing the single pair of plates in front of them.

Poppy blushed and clutched her hands together in front of her. "Jeremy and I are going out, so you two can have a quiet dinner."

"This is such a treat, Poppy. How thoughtful." Louisa said, giving the girl a hug.

"I'm going to wash," Martin mumbled, averting his eyes from the display of affection as he moved past them.

Jeremy laid down the knife he was using to chop carrots for the salad and followed him down the hall.

"Did you get Evan back home all right?" Poppy asked.

Louisa slipped her coat over the rack on the wall then leaned over and scooped James Henry up from the midst of his collection of toys on the floor, nuzzling her nose into his neck. "Well, we got him home. I think Martin has some real concerns about the little boy's safety, though. It's a really tough situation for Martin considering his own history of abu—" She looked up at the childminder, aware that she had let her husband's closely guarded secret slip.

She lowered the baby into his high chair and pulled a bib over his head. "I would really, *really* appreciate it, Poppy, if you could pretend I never said that."

The girl stared at her, wide-eyed. "Erm, yes. Of course." Turning quickly, she busied herself filling a pitcher with water before setting it down in the middle of the table. She found it difficult to imagine the gruff and commanding doctor as a child, let alone a vulnerable and abused child.

Martin finished in the lavatory and walked through the living room on his way to the kitchen. Jeremy laid his magazine down and got up from the sofa. "How's the pain, Martin? Feeling any better?"

He hesitated, trying to choose his words carefully. "Yes, it's ... better. The Toradol seems to have yielded a reasonably acceptable result."

The aide eyed him suspiciously. "Not sure I know how to interpret that, mate. Are you saying the pain's just tolerable, or are you comfortable now? I want you to be able to get a good night's sleep."

"I don't know why you're having difficulty with my answer. I believe I said the result was acceptable! Now just bugger off! I've had about all the tender loving care I can take for one day."

He moved off towards the kitchen, and Jeremy followed. "I'm taking Poppy to The Crab for dinner, but I'll check in before I head back to Truro. Give some thought to whether or not you want another dose of Toradol," he said as he and the childminder went out the door.

Aside from the occasional burst of chatter from James, Martin and Louisa ate their dinner in silence. Louisa, not wanting to belittle her husband's burdens with false reassurances, and Martin, unable to shake the image of Evan's haunted face when he turned to leave him in an uncertain situation.

Louisa placed her silverware quietly on her plate and took her dishes to the sink. She took in a small gasp when she turned around to see him standing by the high chair with James in his arms, his back to her.

"Martin, you need to be *very* careful," she said softly, coming up from behind and putting her hands on his shoulders to steady him. "Why don't you let me take James while you sit down. Then you can hold him on your lap."

She slipped around in front of him and reached out for the child, but he had him clutched tightly to his chest. The boy, now sleepy with his bedtime quickly approaching, had grasped his father's shirt in his fists and had his left thumb firmly implanted in his mouth.

She stroked her husband's cheek. "I think you should give James to me. He's getting heavy, and I don't think the added weight is good for either your arm or your legs right now. Do you think Ed would approve of this?"

Martin blinked his eyes several times and then turned to look at her. "I'm sorry?"

"James, Martin. Give James to me. I know you'd feel terrible if you fell with him and hurt him." Louisa could see the confusion on her husband's face as he quickly surveyed his surroundings, his eyes settling on his son. Embarrassed and disquieted by his mental lapse, he handed the boy brusquely to his wife and limped down the hall.

"Martin? Martin, are you all right?" Louisa called after him. She glanced down at her son's tomato sauce covered face and reached for the flannel by the sink. "What are we going to do with your daddy, James Henry? Hmm?"

Once the supper dishes had been cleared away and the baby was in bed, she went in search of her husband. Not finding him in the cottage she slipped on a coat and stepped out into the cold night. Martin was sitting on the porch bench in his typically erect fashion.

She took in a deep breath of cold salt air as a gust of wind blew through between the houses and her coat flapped open. Pulling it closed, she wrapped her arms around herself. "Mind if I join you?" she asked.

Martin looked up and gave her an anaemic wave.

"Martin, you're freezing! You need a coat," she said when she took hold of his hand. She started to get to her feet but he held tight, pulling her back down beside him.

"I'm fine, just stay here." Wrapping his arm around her shoulders, he slid closer to her. "Did James go down all right?"

"Mm hmm. He didn't even make it halfway through *Goodnight Moon*. I think Evan tired him out today."

Neither of them said anymore for several minutes. Mr. Moysey, Ruth's neighbour, trudged past them up the hill, mumbling an obligatory greeting. "Evening."

"Hello, Mr. Moysey. How are you?" Louisa asked.

"Doing the best I can with what I have, I suppose. You planning to come back to work anytime soon, Doctor, or do I have to keep running over to that quack in Wadebridge? It's very inconvenient you know," the old man carped.

Louisa bristled. "Mr. Moysey! My husband nearly died in a car accident three months ago, and I think he's reopening the practice far too soon the way it—"

Martin placed a hand on her knee to quiet her. "Mr. Moysey, call the surgery on Friday and make an appointment for next week. I can see you then."

The old man gave the couple a sharp nod. "Good ... 'bout time," he muttered.

She shook her head as the crotchety neighbour moved on towards his cottage. "Unbelievable! What a self-centred, miserable old coot! I have half a mind to—"

"Ohh, it doesn't matter. Just let it go." Martin tipped his head back against the front of the house.

Another gust of wind blew through the little street, sending shivers through Louisa.

"We should go inside; you're cold," he said. He pulled himself to his feet, and they retreated to the warmth of the cottage.

Jeremy stopped back shortly before nine o'clock, and after convincing him that another dose of Toradal would be in his best interests, he gave Martin the injection.

"Jeez, that hurts!" He squirmed, rubbing at the painful spot in his thigh.

"Yeah, so I've heard," the aide said as he placed a hot pack on his leg. "Keep that there for fifteen minutes or so and rub that knot periodically." He eyed him for a moment. "You gonna be okay, now?"

"I'm fine. I'll see you in the morning. And don't forget to keep icing that face."

Jeremy gave him a crooked grin. "Don't worry. Poppy keeps reminding me. I don't think she likes kissing a mug that looks like this."

"Mm, yes," Martin said, clearing his throat and giving a tug on his ear.

Louisa saw the aide to the door and then returned to the living room to join her husband on the sofa.

He leaned forward, placing his elbows on his knees and resting his head in his hands. "I'm tired. Are you ready for bed?"

"I am. I'll be back in a minute."

She headed upstairs, and her husband headed off towards the bedroom. Returning a short time later, she found him already sound asleep. She slid in next to him and turned out the light.

Chapter 36

Martin's mumblings woke Louisa a few hours later. Wrapping her arm around him she caressed his chest. "Martin, you're dreaming," she said softly.

Martin heard her voice calling, but he couldn't tear himself from the scene playing out before him. A small boy struggled to free himself from the clutches of a man, bent over with his fingers wrapped firmly around his neck. He couldn't see the man's face, but the child's eyes darted wildly, looking pleadingly from a woman sitting on the study desk back to the face of the authoritarian figure who had him in his clutches. Fear and humiliation registered on her face as she wiped tears from her cheeks. She pulled her black dress down from its current position around her waist before straightening the overlaying ruffled white pinafore.

"Do you have any sense whatsoever?" the man said as the boy struggled to pry the fingers from his neck. "How dare you come barging in here unannounced! From now on, you better make damned sure you knock before entering!" he continued, accentuating his words with a vigorous shake. "You owe me an apology, boy!"

The child fought to pull in enough air to get the words out. "I'm—sor—ry, sir." The man's back straightened, and he released his grip, allowing the boy to drop to the floor.

Martin heard the familiar clinking of a belt buckle and mentally implored the child to get to his feet and flee the room. But he lay helpless, pulling his arms up in front of him to protect his face. Reaching out quickly, Martin grabbed at the belt as it hurtled towards its victim. He felt the painful sting as the leather slapped his arm before he stopped its movement, grasping it tightly in his hand.

He grabbed on to the man's arm and pulled forcefully, turning him around.

"Martin, wake up! You're dreaming, wake up!" Louisa grimaced as her husband's breath quickened and his grip on her wrist tightened.

"Stop!" he cried out before his eyes shot open. He looked wildly about the room as wakefulness slowly returned. His muscles began to relax, and he became aware of his fingers wrapped around his wife's arm. He pushed himself to a sitting position, and Louisa sat up next to him, caressing her wrist.

"Turn on the light," he said as he gave his head a shake, trying to clear the last vestiges of the dream.

She reached over and flipped the switch on the table lamp, shielding her eyes from the sudden glare.

Martin cleared his throat and rubbed a hand over his face before taking hold of her arm. "Here, let me see." His chest tightened when he saw the red marks that had been left on her wrist, the sure precursors to eventual bruises. He closed his eyes and took in a long, ragged breath. "I'll go get some ice," he mumbled, rolling off the bed while reaching for his crutches.

"Martin, let me get it. It's easier for me and you—"

"Louisa, just—stay there!" he snapped.

He returned shortly and crawled back in alongside her.

"Martin, it really is fine," she said as he gently wrapped the cold pack around her arm. "It doesn't even hurt any—"

"Shh, shh, shh, shh, shh." He moved his right arm carefully behind her, embracing her and burying his face in her hair. "I'm sorry."

"It really *is* all right, Martin. Please don't feel bad about it. You weren't even aware of what was going on." She tipped her head back, placing a kiss on his cheek. "You doing better now?"

"Yes. It was just a dream."

A tremor went through him, and Louisa pressed her hand to his chest. "If you want to talk, I'd like to listen."

He hesitated a moment. "Mm." Cupping her jaw in his hand, he pressed his lips to hers. What began as a gentle, apologetic gesture deepened into something more passionate, and he pushed her on to her back, tugging frenetically at the ribbon closure on her nightdress.

He paused a moment to remove his boxers, and Louisa pulled his vest over his head, casting the garment aside. His hands roamed freely under her nightdress, her soft skin and the gentle curves of her breasts and hips igniting something in him that he'd not felt for his wife before—a pure libidinous desire.

She looked up at him before averting her gaze, unaccustomed to the anger and lust that she saw in his eyes.

The indecipherable emotions that had been building in him were articulated in his uncontrolled movements. He fumbled clumsily with her nightdress, his dexterity still hindered by the damage to his arm.

Sensing his growing irritation as well as his growing need, she placed her palm over the back of his hand. "Let me help, Martin," she said softly as she untangled the ribbon. Pulling the front of the garment open, she slipped it over her head and pushed it aside.

She was perplexed by her husband's behaviour. His lovemaking seemed neither romantic nor tender, but rather an act born of anguish. Perhaps a desperation to release some of the emotional pressure that had built up in him to a point no longer bearable.

It was as if he was in his own world. His actions seemed aggressive as he heaved his body against hers. It was apparent to Louisa that she was not a part of the lovemaking but merely a vessel in which to satisfy a need.

He groaned softly and shuddered as his movements slowed. Opening his eyes, he looked down at her, the anger and carnality that she had seen before softened into an expression of confusion. Then into despair.

He squeezed his eyes shut tightly and took in a ragged breath. "Oh, God, Louisa. I'm sorry!" He shifted himself to the side and rolled on to his back, flinging his arm up over his face. He wanted desperately to flee the room, to seek solitude somewhere quiet and dark where he could get control of his emotions, but he felt trapped in the bed by his physical limitations and his current state of undress.

Louisa rolled over to face him and reached up to caress his cheek. He brushed her hand away and automatically reverted to a coping mechanism he had taught himself as a child when needing to contain his feelings—mentally calculating the number of years, months, days, minutes, and when necessary, an approximation of the seconds that had elapsed since the moment of his birth. This required that he focus entirely on numbers as he multiplied each unit of time, leaving no room for emotional expression that could result in anger or ridicule being directed his way.

He had just begun to work out the number of minutes that had elapsed since twenty-eight November, 1961, when his wife's voice interrupted the silence in the room.

"Martin ... please talk to me. Tell me what's upset you." She stroked her fingers lightly up and down his arm.

His wife's tender gesture broke his concentration. "Louisa, shut up!" he barked, feeling the control he had regained quickly evaporating.

She sat herself up. "No. No, Martin. I *won't* shut up! You just made love to me and now you can't even look me in the eye when you talk to me? I don't know what's going on in that head of yours, and I assume the worst when I don't know what you're thinking. Is that what you want—to start down that ugly path again?"

He lay unmoving. "I can't look at you right now."

Reaching over, she turned off the lamp. "Okay, the light's off. Can you talk to me now ... please?"

She could see his arm move away from his face. "I feel sick, Louisa ... what I just did. I'm so sorry."

"I don't understand, Martin. What do you mean, you're sorry? You're sorry you made love to me?"

He pressed the heel of his hand to his forehead. "No! I'm sorry because there was nothing *loving* about it! I wasn't even thinking of you!"

She laid her head on his shoulder and stroked her fingers back and forth across his chest. "What were you thinking about then?"

"I'm not sure I was thinking about anything. I was—just trying to—" He pulled in a breath through clenched teeth. "I don't know. Maybe I was trying to get some relief from everything. The worries, people wanting to help, the hovering. And today with the boy—" He rolled to his side and wrapped his arms around her.

His manner and his body trembling against her was reminiscent of the Martin she saw the night he first proposed to her. Standing in the entryway of her cottage, pleading with her to marry him, like a drowning man pleading for a lifeline. He had clung to her so tightly and for so long that night that it had been unsettling. She now understood what he was feeling and why he behaved the way he did. Martin had been overwhelmed by emotions that he was ill equipped to deal with then as he was now, and she was his lifeline.

"I'm so sorry, Louisa. It won't happen again." He pulled her in more tightly. "Did I hurt you?" he asked.

"Not in the least!" she said. She tried to move back enough to see his face, but he held her firmly in his grasp. "I'm not sure I understand why this is bothering you. Sex doesn't always have to be tender or romantic, you know."

He took in a deep breath before releasing a heavy sigh.

"Martin, *please* talk to me about this."

Martin rubbed a palm across his face, hesitating. "The dream I had tonight … it was about something that happened when I was a child. I'd gone into my father's study, unannounced. I hadn't given the incident much thought until tonight, but…"

She reached up and put her hand on his cheek … against the tightly clenched muscles in his jaw. "What happened, Martin?"

"The pieces came together in my dream. The maid was in the room … sitting on my father's desk. Her dress was pushed up around her waist, and she wasn't wearing knickers. I wondered why she was crying … wondered why my father's belt was open and his trousers unzipped. But I didn't really give it much thought. I remember how angry he had been with me, but I'd not given the specifics any thought before … or put the pieces together until tonight."

He took in a gasp of air. "I realise now why she was crying … and why my father was so adamant that I never come in his study without knocking first."

"What an awful thing to see. And so confusing for a little boy."

"It didn't register with me. I think my father's anger occupied my attention." He squeezed his eyes shut and took in a deep breath. "Louisa, I'm sorry for the way I was … with you just now. That was so much like my father."

"Oh, Martin, your father was an awful man. What happened tonight was *nothing* like what your father did. You needed to relieve some stress, and I was more than happy to accommodate you. You didn't *force* me into anything." She brushed her hand across his head. "It was … different tonight, but not in a bad way. Just different."

She traced around his ear with a fingertip. "You remember that officious little oaf in the pub the day James was born?"

"Mm, yes."

"He was right in a way. You do seem to have a different set of rules for yourself than you do for everyone else."

"I *do not*!" He pulled his arm out from under her and rolled on to his back.

She smiled as she stroked her thumb across his lips, just making out the pout that was on his face. "Yes ... you do. If a patient came to you and said he felt like he'd assaulted his wife because he'd used sex to relieve stress, what would you tell him, hmm?"

"I hardly think the two situations are comparable, Louisa," he grumbled

"I think they are, Martin. And you'd probably think he was being a moron. And I'm sure you'd tell him so."

Martin pushed himself up and replied defensively, "That is an *outrageous* assumption! You don't know what goes on behind my closed consulting room door, Louisa. I *am* capable of behaving in a professional manner, and I *can* be compassionate. It would be a perfectly legitimate concern for a male patient to have, and I'd do my best to alleviate his concerns."

He sank back down on to his pillow, his heart racing. He closed his eyes and tried to calm himself as he lay quietly for some moments. "Are you suggesting that allowing this to bother me is moronic?" he asked.

"I think you're the last person in this world that I could accuse of being moronic," Louisa said as she shifted herself over, cuddling up against him.

He sighed heavily and pulled his arms across his chest. "You should go back to sleep. You'll be tired tomorrow," he said indignantly.

Even in the darkened room, Louisa could sense her husband's shift into his self-protective mode, and she replayed their conversation in her head. "Martin?" she sighed. "I'm sorry. I dismissed your feelings ... your concerns, didn't I?"

She waited for a response and had begun to think that he'd fallen back to sleep when she felt him move. "Louisa ... take James and leave if I start behaving like my father."

She laid her head on his chest and pulled his arm up around her, listening to the rapid and heavy pulsations of his heart. "Martin, you're a good man. You will *never* be capable of doing what—"

"I don't want to discuss this anymore! Just promise me that you'll take James and leave if I ever mistreat either of you!"

She sat up and reached her hand out, turning the switch on the lamp beside the bed.

Martin slapped a hand over his eyes. "Louisa! For goodness' sake, warn me before you do that!"

She squinted back at his screwed-up face. "Sorry 'bout that. But if I'm going to say this I want to be bloody sure that you see me when I say it. I don't ever want to have to say something like this to you again."

She cleared her throat and then took her husband's head in her hands. "Martin Ellingham, I'm no idiot. In my infinite wisdom, I married a kind, gentle and loving man who may have a sharp edge to his tongue at times but is otherwise harmless. And he, quite obviously, loves his wife and son more than anything else in the world. I love you dearly, Martin. But if you ever do anything to intentionally harm either James or me, I *will* take your son and run away to hide in some far corner of the earth." She tipped her head down and furrowed her brow at him. "That what you wanted to hear?"

He turned his head away from her penetrating gaze. "Yes, but I'm not sure you took me seriously."

"I did take you seriously, Martin. I just can't believe for one second that you would ever hurt James or me. But if it gives you a sense of peace to know that we won't stick around if you should suddenly turn into the monster that your father was, then it was worth saying it."

She laid back down and draped an arm over his chest. "I'm sorry that you have another sordid memory to add to the collection in that head of yours," she said as she leaned forward to place a kiss on his forehead. "Think you can sleep now?"

"If you turn that light back off again ... yes, I think I can."

Reaching over, she flipped the switch one last time before reclaiming her position in next to the warmth of her husband.

"That's a ridiculous expression you know. The Earth, by definition, is a sphere. And a sphere has no—"

"Martin ... you're overthinking it. Just say goodnight and go to sleep."

"Mm, goodnight."

Chapter 37

Louisa tried to stay focused on the paperwork on her desk, but she was continually distracted by her concerns for both Evan Hanley and her husband.

Martin was taking a risk providing the boy with a mobile. If his parents were to discover the phone, they could take legal action against him. How the authorities would view the situation was uncertain. The last thing Martin needed at the moment were legal issues in addition to his physical and emotional challenges.

She had worked through her lunch hour in return for the extra time that Pippa had put in when she left early the day before. Getting up from her desk, she stretched her arms. It was a seasonably cool day, but the sun was shining and calling to her. She gave a single glance back at the piles of papers on her desktop then proceeded through the hallway and out the school doors.

The year twos and threes were out on the playground, and as she walked across the tarmac Evan Hanley raced to her side. "Mrs. Ellig-am, when is Dr. Ellig-am going to come to see me?"

Louisa leaned over and spoke softly to him. "Remember, Evan, this is something special between you, me, and Dr. Ellingham. If we're going to keep it a secret, then you need to be *very* careful that no one hears you talking about it."

"I know, I won't say *anything* about *that*!" the boy said, donning a serious expression and shaking his head. "I just wanna know when Dr. Ellig-am is coming."

"I'm not sure, Evan. But when he arrives, I'll come and collect you from your classroom." She straightened back up and tousled the boy's hair. "You're a very special young man, Evan."

"Is that 'cause I'm so good at maths?"

"You *are* good at maths! But you're also special because you have a heart that lets you see past Dr. Ellingham's rough outside to the kindness in him."

"That's a silly thing to say, Mrs. Ellig-am! We can't see with our hearts!" The boy giggled before skipping off across the playground.

Louisa watched him for a few seconds before turning to head down the hill towards the Platt. A parade of fishing boats worked its way through the harbour walls. Gulls circled in a disorganised flock overhead, screeching excitedly in anticipation of the certain easy meal to be had as the boats were unloaded.

The sun, now very low in the sky, cast a long shadow of her silhouette as she hurried over to The Slipway to grab a cup of hot tea to take back to the school. The restaurant would be closing for the winter season soon, as would the other places of business on the Platt. The inevitable seasonal storms would push the sea well into the harbour, flooding a number of the old buildings that were lined up around it. The surgery was positioned high enough on the hill to escape the surges, but it was frequently buffeted by the gales and pelting rains that accompanied winter weather.

But today was a day to be enjoyed. The sun shone brightly, and the air was clear but for a thin line of clouds hovering over the horizon. Louisa started back up the hill, reflecting on the conversation that she'd had with Martin the night before.

It's impossible for a person to prevent the personalities and conduct of their parents from being displayed, at least to some extent, in their own behaviour. Be it nature or nurture, a footprint is left on each child born, and Louisa knew this fact weighed heavily on her husband.

Martin had been fending off the demons from his past, but she had been chasing her own demons away as well. Her propensity to run from a relationship, rather than face a problem head-on, was a gift no doubt bestowed on her by Terry and Eleanor Glasson. But her demons were there in the open, quite obvious when she took the time to contemplate her own behaviour. Martin had the daunting task of ferreting out demons he didn't even know existed, often releasing excruciatingly painful memories that had been packed away and securely locked up in his emotional vault.

Yes, she had her own battles to fight, but her parents had made it clear that they loved her, even if it was a rather self-serving sort of love. And she had been surrounded by caring villagers who stepped in when her parents failed her.

Martin, on the other hand, had been given few tools ... few weapons with which he could battle his demons. His single-minded nature, including his finely-honed focus on all things medical, was the sword that he had used throughout his life to beat back any external or internal emotional threats that came his way. Now he was being asked to relinquish that weapon and face his demons with untested ones.

Louisa clenched her bottom lip in her teeth. Martin wouldn't be able to do this on his own, but up to now, on his own was all he had known.

Stopping outside the school gate, she turned to gaze over at the surgery as she had done so many times since she met Martin. Watching him as he stood on his terrace, perfect posture, coffee cup in hand, surveying the little village. He had been entrusted with the health care of the community, a responsibility which he took very seriously ... too seriously, she had often complained. But, as Joe Penhale had so eloquently put it in his "best man's" speech at their wedding reception,

Martin was the greatest thing to happen to Portwenn since the new parking area at the beach. Louisa turned towards the now empty schoolyard.

The first order of business for Jeremy and Martin that morning had been a stop at the surgery to check on the contractor's progress with the handrails in the stairway and the shower in the bathroom.

Martin was still feeling on edge after the events the night before, and his mood darkened further when he found the progress made to be less than satisfactory.

Jeremy followed after him, keeping a hand on him as he worked his way back downstairs before continuing on to the kitchen in search of the man who had been hired to do the work. They found him hunched over a magazine that was lying on the table, enjoying a leisurely cup of tea.

"You *do* realise that this work needs to be completed no later than the end of the day on Friday, don't you?" Martin asked as he stood in the doorway, drumming his fingers against his crutch handles.

The contractor, Lawrence Grady, looked up in surprise, and using the back of his hand, quickly wiped the biscuit crumbs from his grizzled whiskers. "Right you are there, Doc. Just have to get myself on the outside of this," he said, holding up his half empty teacup.

"Well, get on the outside of it faster, then. And get back to work!" he barked before limping back under the stairs. "Good gawd! I could pass a kidney stone in the time it's taken that idiot to do this job!" he grumbled to his aide.

Jeremy squinted his eyes at him. "You okay, mate? You seem a bit testy."

"Oh, *do* I?" he snapped.

"Yeah, you do. How's the pain today?"

Martin mumbled unintelligibly then gave a nod towards the door. "We'd better get over to Wadebridge."

He stepped out on to the terrace and took in a deep breath, balancing his weight on his crutches. Several fishing vessels, working their way through the harbour walls, caught his attention. Chippy Miller leaned over the gunwale of the lead boat and secured a cable to the winch. He straightened up with a grimace, reaching around to rub his back.

The aide stepped through the door and stood next to his patient, taking note of his furrowed brow.

"Call Chippy Miller on Monday, Jeremy. Tell him I want to see him in the surgery by the end of the week," Martin said before moving down the short, slate covered slope leading from the terrace to the street.

Jeremy hurried to catch up with him, watching closely in case he should trip or lose his balance.

The two men rode to Wadebridge in silence, broken only when Jeremy spoke to ask for directions to the business that Martin wanted to visit.

It was high tide, and by the time they crossed the River Camel bridge the sea water had pushed into the estuary. Several Oystercatchers worked their way through the shallow brackish waters, their gaudy bright orange bills and pink legs in stark contrast to their black and white plumage.

The birds' natural attire reminded Martin of Pauline, his erstwhile receptionist. Or as she preferred to be called—practice manager.

As they reached the far side of the span, Martin's eyes fixed on the scrapes in the concrete guardrail and the silver glint of paint that still remained from that night almost twelve weeks ago. He swallowed, trying to relieve the tightness in his throat.

The shopping centre was just past the bridge. Jeremy turned into the car park and stopped the car next to the electronics store.

At Martin's request, the aide remained in the Lexus while he went to do his shopping. He got back into the vehicle a short time later, a bag in hand.

"Back to Portwenn, then?" Jeremy asked as he shifted the car into reverse and backed out of the parking space.

Martin glanced across the street before looking at his watch. "Er, no. Why don't you pull into that shop over there? I have one more thing to pick up before we head back."

Jeremy glanced across the street, and then turned away to hide the smile on his face. But his effort was too little, too late.

"Is it that hard to believe that I might want to buy my wife flowers?" Martin said indignantly as he glowered at the young man.

"Sorry, Martin. I'm just a little surprised is all. It's really quite charming, actually."

Martin's face reddened, and he whipped his head to the side. "Well, *there's* the great mystery, isn't it? I've been found wanting in the art of romantic persuasion, but when I try to buy a woman flowers I become a source of amusement. What the bloody hell am I supposed to do, Jeremy?"

The aide pulled the Lexus into the carpark. "You suck it up and buy the stupid flowers, mate. It's the male curse. We have to make fools of ourselves to keep women happy, I'm afraid."

Martin sighed heavily and pushed the car door open. "I'll be right back," he grumbled.

A chime rang softly as he pushed through the shop door, and the earthy smell of freshly watered potted plants, mixed with the sweet and slightly spicy smell of roses, lilies and carnations, met his nose. His thoughts flashed back to one of the most significant nights of his life.

The minutes had dragged that day. He felt sure that his date that evening would be the turning point in his nebulous relationship with the primary school teacher he had long admired from the opposite side of the harbour. It seemed as if he'd managed to put her off him at every opportunity. Usually with his unerring ability to say something to raise her ire. He had been determined to not allow it to happen again.

That night though, he had topped all of his previous faux pas with the ultimate insult to a woman like Louisa. The mere mention of hormones seemed to set her off, a peculiar sensitivity that he continued to find enigmatic. He had since learned that any discussion regarding the female reproductive system was best avoided, but he was still clueless as to why she was so touchy about the subject.

I can understand how she might possibly have misconstrued my remark about her perfume, Martin mused as he sniffed at a large bouquet of roses decorating the checkout counter. *Although, in all honesty, it did carry a subtle hint of urine.*

But in hindsight, perhaps I should have explained that a urine-like nuance is a quality shared by all finer perfumes. Maybe she wouldn't have taken my comment so negatively. Martin decided it was a subject he should take up with Dr. Newell.

Footsteps could be heard approaching from a back room, and a short, rather squat but comely, middle-aged woman emerged behind the counter. "Oh, dear. You look completely lost, love!" she said as she gave her customer's physical condition a quick visual appraisal, taking note of his eyes, which darted from one container of flower stems to the next. "What is it that you're lookin' for?"

Martin shifted uncomfortably on his crutches as the clerk continued to eye him up and down. "I'm not sure yet. I want to buy some flowers," he grumbled.

She gave him an amused smile. "I see. Why don't you tell me a bit about your lady friend, and perhaps the two of us can put our heads together and come up with something that would make her happy."

Martin gave her a blank stare. "Mm … no," he said flatly. "And what makes you think it's for my *lady friend?*" He gave her a scowl and returned his focus to the array in front of him.

The clerk shrugged her shoulders and breezed off to tend to the potted plants in her shop.

Another customer entered the store and the shopkeeper hurried back to the counter, carrying with her a fragrance that Martin found almost as intoxicating as his wife's scent.

He walked to the display under a sign reading *tropicals*. There was just one species blooming, and he leaned over to investigate more closely. Martin had found what he wanted, but now—how to get it to the car?

Feeling a nudge to his shoulder, he whirled his head around.

"Hey, mate," Jeremy said, joining in the examination of the greenery. "Decided I better come in and give you a hand if you want to get the flowers to Louisa in one piece. The clerk making them up?" he asked, giving a nod in the shopkeeper's direction.

"Ah, no. Can you carry this for me?" He gave a half-hearted jab at a drab green pot. It held a plant bearing glossy green leaves, and it was peppered with large, white, heavily scented blossoms.

Jeremy glanced over at his friend. "No flowers, then?"

"It has flowers!" he replied defensively. "And you didn't answer my question."

"Yeah, yeah, yeah. I've got it. Sorry, mate. But … you sure this is what you want?"

Martin glared at him and then turned to head for the checkout.

The shopkeeper watched as he limped up to the counter, Jeremy following close behind. "You decided against flowers then, did you?" she asked.

"It *has* flowers! Just tell me what I owe you … please!" Martin balanced on his crutches and tried to reach around to his back pocket for his wallet. However, some days his limbs were stiffer than others, and this was a particularly bad day. Jeremy reached out and dug around briefly for it before handing it to him.

"That'll be twenty pounds, fifty, please," the clerk said, giving Martin a knowing smile. "I'm sorry about earlier. I made an assumption ... 'bout the lady friend." The woman's grin continued to spread between her rounded cheeks. "I'm glad to see you have a special someone to help you, though ... condition you're in and all."

He laid a twenty pound note and a five pound note on the counter, glancing up at the clerk with a puzzled expression on his face.

The cash register drawer popped open, and the shopkeeper fished around for the necessary coins. "What *did* happen to you ... may I ask?" she said as she dropped the change into his hand.

"No, you may not!" He shoved it into his front pocket, the coins jingling.

The two men worked their way out of the shop and back into the cool, sunlit air. The aide pulled the passenger side car door open and waited as his patient lowered himself into the seat.

"What was *that* all about?" Martin asked.

Jeremy dropped the purchased plant into his lap. "I believe she thinks we're a couple ... *Cupcake*," he said, giving him a puckish grin.

Chapter 38

"You do know I was just trying to wind you up back there ... the cupcake thing and all, don't you?" Jeremy asked as the doctor's continued silence made him increasingly uncomfortable. Martin could be a difficult character to read, and Jeremy was beginning to worry he may have taken his good-natured teasing too far.

"It's fine. That didn't upset me. Although, you *can* get a bit annoying," Martin said, giving his aide a sideways glance.

Jeremy's jaw clenched as he stared at the road in front of him. Several painfully quiet minutes passed before words burst from his mouth. "How can you say *I* annoy *you*? I've tried to keep my opinions to myself when you've lambasted some poor sod for not performing up to your rigid and, might I say, *unreasonable* standards. I've bent over backwards to try to be your friend! *And* I've bent over backwards to give you the best care possible, for God's sake! How can you say *I'm* annoying?"

"Maybe it's all that bending over backwards," Martin said dryly. He gave him another glance before turning his head towards the passenger side window. "You look like a complete arse when you do that. It's *extremely* annoying."

The young man's knuckles whitened as he gripped tightly to the steering wheel, his face flushing red in anger. "I can *not* believe you just said that! Do you know how bloody difficult you can be?"

"I *do*. I'm *quite* aware of how difficult I can be," Martin said, the slightest glimpse of a smile peeking out from one corner of his mouth. "Do *you* know that I'm just trying to wind you up?"

Jeremy shot him an incredulous look before breathing out a heavy sigh, his body slumping into his seat. “Don’t do that! My blood pressure must’ve shot up twenty points just now.”

“Mm, yes,” Martin mumbled. He sat, trying to ignore his now uneasy stomach. His past attempts at the light-hearted ribbing that seemed to come so naturally to everyone else had, on almost every occasion, gotten him into trouble, and he feared this attempt may have had the usual negative effect.

The oppressive silence returned and stayed with them until they reached St. Endellion.

“I was wondering, Jeremy ... about your father,” Martin said. Do you ever worry about the effect his behaviour towards your mother might have on you? Whether you’ll abuse alcohol ... or possibly...” He huffed. “Well, that it could affect how you treat your partner ... or wife?”

The aide kept his eyes on the road, tapping his fingertips against the steering wheel. “The thought has crossed my mind, I suppose. But I’m not real worried about it. I never really saw Dad when he was at his worst. In fact, I didn’t know until I was a teenager that the bruises I’d see on Mum occasionally were the result of his benders. She always had some story. She stood up into a cupboard door, she tripped and fell. You know.”

He nudged the turn signal arm before veering left on to New Road, the narrow lane leading into the village. “My mum drilled it into me pretty good that I had bloody well watch my alcohol consumption, *if* I drink at all.

“And she’s been a good mum ... always been there for me. The good things I picked up from her outweighed the bad things I was exposed to with Dad, I think. I never doubted her love for me, and I think that had more of an influence on me than my father’s less desirable characteristics did.”

“Mm, I see.”

The large Labrador retriever that acted as sentry at Trewetha Farm ran alongside the Lexus as they neared the village, its image growing quickly smaller and the animal's yapping growing softer as Martin watched it in the wing mirror. "Jeremy, I'd like to stop at the school before we go home. You can wait outside for me if you like. If you have an errand to run that'd be fine too. I don't know how long I'll be."

"Sure," he said. "I think I'll run down to the chemist ... pick up some of that perfume you got wise with me about the other day. I think Poppy'll like it."

They wound their way past the empty carpark on the hill. The ice cream truck, that was a permanent fixture there during the warmer months, was now absent. The few potential customers that remained in the village would almost certainly opt for a cup of tea, with which to warm both belly and hands, rather than to turn to the cold confection.

The work on the old St. Peter's church continued, and a sprinkling of broken slate roofing tiles rained down on to the ground below.

Martin grumbled under his breath as an overall-clad young man jumped playfully out of the path of the falling debris, seeming to find his close call with the heavy, sharp fragments amusing. "Idiot. Just a matter of time before he'll be walking into my consulting room, expecting me to stitch up that vacuous head of his."

They rounded the curve on to Fore Street before turning into the schoolyard. The aide shifted the Lexus into park and got out to help his patient with the door.

Martin handed the gardenia off to him before pulling himself from the vehicle. Taking few steps towards the school gate, he turned around. "By the way, my standards are neither rigid nor are they the least bit unreasonable." He limped away, leaving Jeremy shaking his head.

Martin worked his way through the hall as the occasional student passed him by, eyeing him warily before their eyes were drawn to his fractured limbs.

He had tried, when he first arrived in the village, to ease the children's worries with attempts to distract them with jokes, but he quickly discovered he lacked the finesse needed to pull them off. Rather than easing their worries, he had frightened them.

Aside from Peter Cronk, the young boy whose life he had saved by performing a crude, but successful, manual ligation of his splenic artery while hurtling down the A-39 in an ambulance, he was generally feared or loathed by the village children.

Louisa's door was open, and Pippa Woodley sat at her desk in the outer office. She glanced up when he entered the room. "Well hello, Dr. Ellingham! Out and about, are ya?"

Martin was aware that the woman's feelings towards him were less than positive and that she had only served to add fuel to the fire as his and Louisa's marriage was going up in smoke.

"Miss Woodley," he said, giving her a nod as he went by.

Louisa got up from her desk when she heard his voice and closed the door behind him. "How are you?" she asked as her arms slipped around his waist.

He tipped his head down to kiss her before answering. "I'm fine."

"Did your trip to Wadebridge go okay? Get what you needed?"

"Yes, I believe this should be adequate." He pulled the small mobile device from his pocket. "They put both my number and PC Penhale's number into it before I left the store. Also, the nine-nine-nine emergency number. Do you have some of your nail varnish with you by chance?"

Louisa gave him a questioning look before taking her brown leather bag from her bottom desk drawer. She rummaged through it and presented him with four different bottles. "There are several shades here. Is there a particular ensemble you're trying to coordinate?" she asked, giving him an impish grin.

He pulled his chin back as his brows drew down. "I just want to colour code the buttons the boy will need to use ... make it as easy as possible for him."

She set the assortment of bottles on her desk and Martin selected three of them—white, pink, and a bright red that he had always found to be too harsh a colour for his rather delicate wife. "These'll do."

"I'll go down to the classroom and fetch Evan. You better wait here. You tend to attract the children's attention, you know," she said, brushing her fingers across his cheek before moving towards the door.

"Mm, yes. It might help if you could give them some idea about what to expect if they come in to see me. Perhaps limit the number of cheeky questions that are bound to be asked ... minimize the gawping."

Louisa stopped, her hand resting on the doorknob. "They're just curious about it all, *Martin*. Just briefly explain what's happened, and show them what the fixators look like," she said. "I'll just run and collect Evan." She gave him a smile before slipping into the hallway.

The students were involved in an art project when Louisa stuck her head in the door of the year two classroom. "Miss Soames, I need to borrow Evan Hanley for just a bit," she said as the young teacher approached.

Trisha glanced over at the little boy. "Of course. Is there a problem?" she asked nervously.

"Not at all. I'd asked him to help me with a little project, and he was kind enough to say yes."

Evan noticed Louisa, and pulling his feet out from under him, he quickly dropped from his chair.

She wiggled a finger at him and he raced over. "Is he here?" he asked excitedly.

The head teacher put a finger to her lips and shushed him. “We don’t want to disturb your classmates, so you need to use a small voice.”

Evan bounced excitedly on his toes. “Is he here?” he whispered.

“Yes, he is. He’s waiting in my office. Let’s go and find him, shall we?”

She bit her lower lip as she took the child’s hand. He had attracted the attention of his classmates, and she had serious doubts that he would be able to handle their inevitable questions.

As they walked through the corridor, she tried to formulate a reasonable and truthful excuse for the child’s visit to her office. By the time they reached her door she had a plan, but she suspected it was a plan Martin would find quite unpalatable.

Pippa had left for lunch but, just to be on the safe side, Louisa closed the door to the hallway as well as to her office. “Hi, Dr. Ellig-am!” Evan said as he bounced into the room.

He tipped his head and tugged at his ear. “Mm, yes. Evan, I brought you a mobile. But I need to make sure you know how to use it.”

Louisa pulled a second chair over next to her husband’s, and the boy climbed up.

“The most important thing for you to remember, Evan, is that you need to put the phone someplace where no one will find it. Do you have a special hiding place in your room? Under your bed or in a corner in your closet?” Martin asked.

Evan stroked his hand up and down the fixator on his arm. “That feels cold. How come that feels cold, Dr. Ellig-am?”

He rolled his eyes as air hissed from his nose. “Evan, pay attention. Do you have a place you could put this mobile where no one else can find it?”

"I gots a really good hiding place," the boy said, giving his head a vigorous nod. "You wanna know where it is?" The child scrambled to his knees and gave a tug on his shirt sleeve.

"No, that won't be necessary," Martin said, pulling his arm away. "I need to show you how—"

"I'll tell you where it is." The seven-year-old cupped his hands and held them to the doctor's ear. "It's in a hole in the wall in my room. You gotta get under the bed to find the hole. It's where I keep all my special stuff," he whispered. "But you have to promise not to tell anybody, 'cause just you and me know about it ... kay?"

Martin pulled his ear away from the boy's steamy breath and gave him a scowl. "That sounds acceptable. Now let me show you what to do if you need my help."

"But you have to *promise* first!" Evan whined.

He screwed up his face and snapped back, "Oh good grief. I'm not going to tell anyone where your hiding place is."

The child's face fell, and Martin immediately regretted his sharp words. "I won't tell anyone, Evan. Now let me show you how to operate this phone."

The boy's chin dropped to his chest. "But you didn't promise, Dr. Ellig-am," he said softly.

Martin let out a low growl. "I promise to not tell anyone where your hiding place is."

Louisa smiled at the power the boy seemed to wield over her gruff husband and at the pleased expression on Evan's face when he relented, saying the words he was hoping to hear.

Martin closed his eyes for a moment and let out a heavy sigh. "You need to pay *very* close attention to what I have to tell you now. And don't interrupt."

The seven-year-old got to his knees. Leaning his forearm on to Martin's shoulder, he peered at him closely and gave him a nod. "'Kay, I'm listening," he said, pushing his face to within inches of the doctor's, his gaze operose.

Martin swivelled his head quickly to look at his wife. "Is he being cheeky with me?"

She took a step forward, lifting the boy up and setting him, bum-down, on the chair. "I think you can listen closely enough from down here, Evan." She gave her husband an apologetic grin. "I think he's a very concrete thinker ... like someone else I know."

"Mm, I see." Martin held the phone up in front of the child. "This will be your mobile to use. But you must only use it in an emergency situation. I want you to have a way of reaching either PC Penhale or myself if you ever feel afraid of your father."

He handed the device to the boy, and Evan ran a small finger over the buttons before cocking his head at him. "How come these ones are different colours?"

"That's to help you remember which buttons to push. The white one is my number, the pink one is PC Penhale's number, and the red one is the general emergency number."

"The emergency number's nine-nine-nine. Did you know that, Dr. Ellig-am? We could paint it red on your phone, too, so *you* remember it."

Martin caressed his temples with his fingertips. "That won't be necessary. I want you to try calling me, Evan. Do you remember which button is my number?"

"Mm, hmm. That's 'cause I closed my attention on you when you told me. It's the white one." The child held the mobile up to his nose and gave it a sniff. "It smells like tyres!"

Her husband's growing vexation obvious, Louisa crouched down in front of the boy. "Evan, hold the white button down. Let's see what happens."

A small finger pressed the button, and seconds later the doctor's mobile began to ring.

"It works! You did it!" the child said as he gazed up at Martin. "You're really good at mobiles, Dr. Ellig-am. You should fix *them* a'stead of people!"

"Ah, yes. Fourteen years of medical training should most certainly qualify me to paint buttons on mobile phones."

"Yeah. You'd be really, *really* good!" The boy got to his knees and returned his arm to Martin's shoulder. "You want me to try the pink one and the red one now?"

"No, I think you have the general idea. The important thing to remember, Evan, is that you should only call if you're frightened. And don't talk about the mobile to any of your friends. This is just between you, me and Mrs. Ellingham," Martin said, pulling his head back from the boy's uncomfortable proximity.

Evan rolled his eyes to the side before replying hesitantly. "Okay, but that was *two* things to remember."

Martin opened his mouth to reply, but Louisa intercepted his words with her own. "Evan, please wait here for just a minute while I have a word with Dr. Ellingham." She gave a nod towards the door. "Martin ... a moment?"

He peeled the boy's arm away from his shoulder and pulled himself to his feet.

"What did I do?" Martin asked warily as they stepped into the outer office.

"Nothing, nothing! You're doing fine, Martin. I just think that Evan may need a little assistance with keeping this quiet. I ... have an idea. But try not to get upset about it."

He looked at his wife, askance. "What's the idea?"

"I thought you could come to the school tomorrow and ... and Evan could use you for ... well, for show and tell," Louisa said, her head tipped down as she peered up at him.

"Show and tell! Oh, Louisa. You can't expect me to humiliate myself in front of a classroom full of seven-year-olds!"

She grimaced. "I was kind of thinking we could have an assembly. You could show all of the—"

Martin shook his head. "*No!* Absolutely not! I'm not going to allow myself to be put on display like—like someone's lab rat in a research presentation! No!" He looked back at her. The confident defiance that he felt quickly slipping away as her eyes pleaded with him. "No! No. Oh, gawd. *Please,* Louisa."

"Martin, just hear me out. Your coming to the school tomorrow would be perfect cover for Evan. No one will think anything of his sudden friendship with you if it looks like you've been working on a presentation together. And Evan would be the obvious choice to help you ... his broken arm and all. Hmm?"

Martin's shoulders slumped. *"Oh, Louisa,"* he said with a soft stridency.

She caressed his arm and reached up to place a kiss on his cheek. "I'll handle everything. All you have to do is sit there, and let the children ... gawp."

"Oh, *gawwd.*"

Chapter 39

The dishcloth ran lazy circles around a dinner plate as Louisa stared absently out the kitchen window that evening. Martin's voice drifted in from the living room where she had situated him on the sofa with James Henry, along with several children's books and instructions for the stories to be read to completion, with no substitution of medical journal articles. He had grumbled, as he always did, and laid the books aside.

She put the last dish into the draining rack and dried her hands before hanging the towel over the handle of the cooker door. Then she walked quietly down the hall where she watched unseen.

Martin shoved the first book across the coffee table before the pair started in on a game of Martin's more reserved version of patty-cake, his hand held out flat and motionless as James slapped his palm against it. The child seemed to delight in the smacking sound it created, releasing a string of chortles and *da-ees*. He gave his father a crooked smile, and Martin's cheeks nudged up.

"It seems your mother has one more book she wants us to read, James," he said, reaching for the last board book in the stack. He glanced at the cover. "Oh, for goodness' sake."

He tossed it back on to the sofa but picked it up again when his son began to complain. "You really want me to read this?" Grimacing, he shifted the child's weight away from the still tender wound in his thigh.

James reached up and batted at his father's face, and Martin pulled back, clearing his throat as if preparing to give a presentation at a medical conference. "*Where did Hennie lay her egg?*"

He flipped back the flap covering the nest box in the stylised henhouse decorating the page, and the baby let out a squeal.

"That bird would never have been able to pass something that large without some sort of medical intervention, James." Martin turned to the biography on the back cover and threw his head back. "Naturally. An American author. I understand medical accuracy isn't of prime importance over there." He watched his son for a moment and then tapped his finger against his nose.

"*Mr. McNeely can't find the bunny. Can you?*"

James lifted the next flap, shaped like a cabbage leaf, to reveal a cowering plush-covered rabbit. The little boy's fingers worked their way into the chocolate-coloured fur.

Louisa stepped into the living room and took a seat next to them. "Oh, that's one of your favourites, isn't it, James!" she said. She smiled up at her husband. "And it's extra special because his Daddy's reading it."

"Mm. This is a bit graphic for a children's book, don't you think?" Martin said, wagging a finger at the brightly coloured picture of a farmer, poised to do in the little vegetable thief with his garden hoe the moment his whereabouts are revealed.

"I don't think James is old enough to appreciate the implication, Martin."

"Yes, but isn't that your argument against James watching surgical videos or enjoying the occasional journal article with me?"

Louisa gave an uneasy laugh. "Well, that's different, Martin."

"Is it?"

James flopped himself off his father's lap and on to his mother's. He pulled his blanket over his head and waited for the appropriate response from Martin.

"Ah. I'm supposed to look for you, is that it?" Martin gave a tug on the soft flannel, triggering a gale of laughter from the boy.

He glanced at his wife, pulling in his chin when he noticed the amused smile on her face. "That's a rather pointless game, don't you think?"

"Children his age love to play peek-a-boo, Martin."

The baby seemed unfazed by his father's lack of enthusiasm for the game, rolling on to his stomach and grabbing on to his shirt before pulling himself to his feet. "*Da-ee.*" James pulled at his stern-looking father's nose.

Martin glanced down as his wife leaned her head against his shoulder. His face softened and he pulled her close.

"Evan adores you ... you know that, don't you?" she said, tipping her head back.

He stared absently across the room for several moments before shaking his head. "It's only going to make it harder for him, Louisa. I'm not sure I'm doing the right thing."

She sat up. "What do you mean? Martin, you *have* to help that little boy! Of course, you're doing the right thing!"

"I'm not referring to trying to help him out of an abusive situation." He rubbed his palm across his forehead. "I know Evan ... likes me. That's going to make it harder for him. It's not good for a child like Evan to have someone they feel secure with; someone they know cares about them..."

His fingertips pressed against the bridge of his nose. "What if his parents take legal action against me. What if they move away and the boy's left on his own with it all?"

Louisa looked at her husband's pained face and leaned forward, placing a kiss on his chest. "When Joan was taken away from you ... that's what you're thinking about, isn't it?"

"Mm." Martin swallowed back the lump that was working its way up his throat. "That was a lonely time in my life. Very nearly the loneliest. I just wonder if it wouldn't have been easier if I'd never had the good ... if it just made the bad worse."

"I understand what you're saying. But maybe it's the time you had with Joan that allowed you to become the man you are today. What might your life be like if you hadn't had Joan for the time you did?"

Her fingers tapped tentatively against his arm. "Even if your relationship with Evan can't continue, for one reason or another, the poor little boy will know that someone cares about him."

"No. No, he *won't* know that! For a while, he'll excuse away my failure to help him. But eventually, he'll have to conclude that I wasn't worth the trouble! That I'm on my own!"

Louisa settled back and wrapped her arms around his chest. "Martin, you just said, *I* wasn't worth the trouble. *I'm* on my own."

His body stiffened. "No ... I didn't."

She patted her hand against his cheek and reached up to kiss him. "Yes, Martin, you did. Hard to understand what *not* being on your own is all about, hmm?"

"Mm. We should put James to bed," he said, looking down at his young son, now growing sleepy in his lap.

Louisa sighed. Martin had yet again managed to avoid discussing a tender issue. "Well, I guess *we* means me, doesn't it?" she said, getting up from the sofa and lifting James into her arms.

She walked towards the stairs, stopping part way up. "What did you mean, very *nearly* the loneliest?"

He hesitated. "I don't think you need to ask, do you?"

"Ah, I see ... me in London. I'm sorry, Martin," she said before continuing up the steps.

Martin was in the bedroom, tending to the daily maintenance of his wounds, when his wife returned.

"Sound asleep and off to the land of nod," Louisa said. She stood in the doorway watching him. "Can I do that tonight ... please?" she asked, walking over to pick up the tray of cotton buds and antiseptic wash from the bed.

Martin watched her as she wiped at the crusts of drainage that had oozed from around the pin sites. "Louisa ... it's may I, not can I," he said softly.

She paused from her work and peered up at him. "Mar-tin."

He pulled in his chin. "Mm, yes." Lying back on the bed, he slipped a hand under his head as he watched her.

She had changed into pyjama bottoms and a soft cotton top, printed with small purple flowers. The fabric clung to her curves, and he fought the urge to reach out and caress them.

Several minutes elapsed before she patted his leg and pronounced the job finished. She walked off towards the lavatory with the tray, and Martin lay listening to the sound of drawers opening and closing.

"I got something for you today," he called out to her.

A wisp of a smile crossed his face when she immediately appeared in the doorway.

"Oh?"

Louisa delighted in receiving gifts. Something Martin knew he'd failed at with every opportunity. He hoped this one would prove more to her liking.

"I, er ... I'd like to be able to give it to you myself, but I'm afraid you'll have to get it. I had Jeremy put it on the floor in the cupboard."

Louisa's natural impulse was to immediately express her pleasure if someone was kind enough to present her with a gift. But given his previous expressions of love, gifts no more romantic than a bag of yams, she decided to reserve judgement until she had laid eyes on it.

She opened the door, and a wonderful fragrance wafted from the space. Looking down, she saw the pot of greenery standing in the middle of the floor.

"Martin!" she gasped. "You bought me flowers!" She turned and hurried to the bed to embrace him.

Pulling back, she gave him a smile that left no doubt he had finally hit the mark.

He released the breath he'd been holding in. "Are you going to leave it there in the dark?" he asked, giving her a small smile.

"Oh! No, of course not." She carried the plant back to the bedside and set it on the table. "Martin, I absolutely love it."

Pulling the blankets back, she crawled into the bed. They lay, facing each other, Louisa propped up on an elbow.

Martin brushed a wisp of hair from her face and tucked it behind her ear before letting his thumb slide gently across her lips. "I want to apologise ... for last night. I wish I could explain ... justify my actions. But I can't understand it myself. I don't know what I was thinking. I *wasn't* think—"

She pressed her fingers to his mouth. "Martin, stop worrying about it. You were half awake, and you'd just had an awful dream. And with everything else, I suspect it was a perfect storm of emotions. I'm very happy I could be there to hold you until it passed."

He eyed her warily. "I, er ... suspect you remember that concert we went to ... the one that friend of yours performed in—Polly."

"*Holly*! And yes, I remember."

"I was thinking about our kiss that evening ... how I bollocksed it up. I didn't mean what I said in the way you thought that I meant it. I was just trying to say that all of the best perfumes have a slight ur—"

She stopped him mid-sentence, slapping her hand over his mouth. "Martin, don't go there," she said, warning him with tight lips, narrowed eyes, and a fixed glare.

"Mm, yes."

Her face softened, and the glare was replaced by a smile. "That's better." Leaning over, she left a lingering, and most definitely passionate, kiss on his lips.

His gaze flitted between her and the fragrant plant on the bedside table.

"What?" she asked, tipping her head down and peering up at him.

He pulled in a breath through his teeth, holding it for a moment before beginning to speak. "Louisa ... I just wanted to say that I looked at a lot of flowers ... looked for something as—as beautiful as you. But I couldn't find any.

"I noticed a scent in the air, and it reminded me of you ... of your scent. I've never smelled anything as intoxicatingly wonderful as you, but the gardenia has a certain mysterious quality ... like you. That's what I wanted to say that night. That your scent was irresistible. I was quite ... nervous. I didn't intend to hurt your feelings and I'm sorry."

She stared down at him, shaking her head. "Are you trying to sweep me off my feet, Martin Ellingham?"

His cheeks nudged up and his eyes glimmered in the light coming from the table lamp. "I don't believe that's necessary, do you? You're already in my bed."

"Hmm, point taken." She tugged his vest over his head. "I like to feel your skin, you know."

"Yes, I'm aware of that. There's actually a very logical explanation for it. Oxytocin is released in response to the stimulation of nerve endings in—"

She pressed her fingers to his lips, once again silencing him. "Shhh. Now's not the time, Martin. You'll *spoil* it."

His eyes fixed on her, and he seemed oblivious to anything else. This was a mannerism which Louisa found quite seductive, and any thoughts of an early bedtime were pushed aside.

"Shall we see if we can find something more stimulating for you than our son's board books?" she teased, trailing her fingertips lightly from his chest to his belly. She toyed briefly below the elastic waistband of his boxers before sitting back up to peel her pyjama top over her head and to slip out of her bottoms.

Martin hurried his final preparations before pulling her tightly to him.

His lovemaking was in stark contrast to the frantic pace of the night before. He was slow, tender and completely attentive to her needs.

As they lay some time later, he cupped her chin in his hand, slowly stroking his thumb across her flushed cheek. Rolling forward, he nuzzled his nose into her neck, breathing in her scent. "So lovely," he whispered.

"Thank you, Martin. And thank you for my gardenia."

They fell asleep in the warm afterglow of their lovemaking, leaving behind for the moment the niggling unease about the changes ahead.

Also by Kris Morris

Battling Demons

Battling Demons

Fractured

Fragile

Headway

Insights

A Cornwall Christmas

About the Author

Kris Morris was born and raised in a small Iowa town. She spent her childhood barely tolerating school, hand rearing orphaned animals, and squirrel taming. At Iowa State University she studied elementary education. But after discovering a loathing for traditional pedagogy and a love for a certain tall, handsome, Upstate New Yorker, she abandoned the academic life to marry, raise two sons, and become an unconventional piano teacher. When she's not writing, Kris builds boats and marimbas with her husband, who she has captivated for thirty years with her delightful personality, quick wit, and culinary masterpieces. They now reside in Iowa and have replaced their sons with ducks.

Read more at www.ktmorris.com.

Made in United States
North Haven, CT
30 January 2022